GW00371325

OUT OF MECKLENBURG

OUT OF MECKLENBURG

THE UNWILLING SPY

JAMES REMMER

Copyright © 2017 James Remmer

The moral right of the author has been asserted.

Apart from any fair dealing for the purposes of research or private study,
or criticism or review, as permitted under the Copyright, Designs and Patents
Act 1988, this publication may only be reproduced, stored or transmitted, in
any form or by any means, with the prior permission in writing of the
publishers, or in the case of reprographic reproduction in accordance with
the terms of licences issued by the Copyright Licensing Agency. Enquiries
concerning reproduction outside those terms should be sent to the publishers.

This is a work of fiction. Names, characters, businesses, places, events
and incidents are either the products of the author's imagination
or used in a fictitious manner. Any resemblance to actual persons,
living or dead, or actual events is purely coincidental.

Matador
9 Priory Business Park,
Wistow Road, Kibworth Beauchamp,
Leicestershire. LE8 0RX
Tel: 0116 279 2299
Email: books@troubador.co.uk
Web: www.troubador.co.uk/matador
Twitter: @matadorbooks

ISBN 978 1788037 495

British Library Cataloguing in Publication Data.
A catalogue record for this book is available from the British Library.

Printed and bound by CPI Group (UK) Ltd, Croydon, CR0 4YY
Typeset in 11pt Aldine401 BT by Troubador Publishing Ltd, Leicester, UK

Matador is an imprint of Troubador Publishing Ltd

MIX
Paper from
responsible sources
FSC
www.fsc.org
FSC® C013604

Dedicated to the memory of my wonderful and adorable wife, Joan
Thank you, sweetheart. This book is for you, all of it.
Without you, none of it would have been possible.

AUTHOR'S FOREWORD

During WWII, Germany's insatiable appetite for political and military intelligence was fed principally by two, rival, organisations: the military Abwehr, headed by the enigmatic Admiral Wilhelm Canaris, and the foreign intelligence arm of the Sicherheitsdienst, or SD as it was known.

A Nazi-conceived organization, the SD formed an integral part of Germany's mainstay security apparatus, the Reich Security Main Administration (RSHA), to which the Gestapo was also responsible. Under the authority of SS supremo Heinrich Himmler, it was led by the fanatical and ruthless Reinhard Heydrich.

As chief of his foreign intelligence branch, Heydrich appointed an aspiring and startlingly young SS officer who would eventually rise to even greater heights in the Nazi pecking order. His name was Walter Schellenberg. Heydrich remained head of the RSHA until his assassination in June 1942, and was eventually succeeded by the equally ruthless Ernst Kaltenbrunner.

In the clandestine world of German espionage, the Abwehr and the SD should have been enough, but in 1941, as Hitler prepared to invade Russia, along came the quasi spy branch of the German Foreign Office, brainchild and hobbyhorse of the egotistical Joachim von Ribbentrop, Hitler's Foreign Minister.

This hotchpotch of espionage agencies spawned a culture of contempt, distrust and envy: the SD had no time for the Abwehr and the Abwehr held no respect for the SD, while both were equally dismissive of von Ribbentrop's fledgling Foreign Office spy branch.

AUTHOR'S NOTE

The end of WWII brought significant changes to the political map of Europe. National boundaries were redrawn and many villages, towns, cities and streets therein were renamed: for example, Krummhübel, which was once part of Germany, is now in Poland and known as Karpacz. For the sake of historical accuracy, I have used the designations pertinent to the period in which the book is set.

1

Monday 23rd June 1941

German Foreign Office, Berlin

It was terse, wholly unexpected and positively unnerving:

LEAVE CANCELLED. REMAIN IN YOUR OFFICE.
By Order, Doctor Alfred Wehmen, Assistant Under-Secretary of State.

Carl von Menen read the memo again and again, each time the author's signature sending a shudder of fear surging down his spine. *Wehmen, the spirit of Machiavelli. Why the hell hasn't Clarita phoned me?*

Convinced that the lid had been lifted on his clandestine life, von Menen paced impatiently back and forth the entire length of his office, wanting desperately to call a number at Wittenberge, but thinking better of it. *If Wehmen has the merest hint of my covert activities, he'll have alerted the switchboard and ordered all my outside calls logged.*

He sat down, took a deep breath, picked up his phone and dialled an internal extension. There was no reply.

Over the next three hours, he tried the same number repeatedly. No reply.

An hour later, his phone knelled into life. He reached

hesitantly across his desk, lifted the handset and brought it slowly to his ear, as if he were half-expecting to be shot in the back of the head.

'Von Menen,' he said cautiously.

'Carl, it's me.'

Von Menen sprang to his feet. 'Thank God! Where've you been? I've been phoning you for hours.'

'Shopping; he gave me a few hours off.'

'But I've been ordered to stay in my office and you knew I'd planned to leave early today. Why didn't you phone me?'

'Er… yes, sorry about that… but he wants to see you, immediately, with all your files.'

'All my…! Why?'

'No idea, but he was very insistent.'

Von Menen replaced the receiver and stared at the ceiling. *He knows… Wehmen knows.*

Clarita Brecht was standing before her desk, back to the door, prim and secretarial in a tight-fitting white blouse and black sheath skirt, stocking seams plumb line straight.

Von Menen hastened through the door and hurried towards her, dropping a huge bundle of files on her desk. Cautious of Clarita's feisty temperament, he didn't care much for her high-pitched voice, either, but the rest was perfect: a stunningly attractive face; radiant, cerulean-blue eyes; shoulder-length tawny brown hair and legs the length of the Kiel Canal.

'What the hell's going on?' he whispered, an eye on Wehmen's door.

Clarita gracefully sat at her desk, placed her hand on a dark blue folder lying next to the phone and eased it towards him.

'*That's* what's going on,' she said. 'Your personal file.' She read aloud the inscription set bang in the middle of the cover. '*Carl Franz von Menen, born 31.1.1913. Current Section: Foreign Information Department IIb, Iberia.* In and out of my office all last week, it was. The Minister asked for it last Wednesday—'

'*The* Minister?'

'Yes, von Ribbentrop.' She cocked her head in the direction of Wehmen's door. 'And *he* asked for it the next day… Called for it again on Friday.'

Von Menen could scarcely believe his ears. 'But why didn't you tell me?'

Clarita sprang to her feet, jabbed her hands on her hips, a potent look on her face. 'Because Wehmen warned me that if I breathed a word of it to *anyone*, he'd have me transferred to Goebbels' Propaganda Ministry within twenty-four hours. He wasn't joking, either. Imagine it; me, in the same building as that limping, licentious gnome. God, I can't stand the man, you know I can't.'

'But something's afoot, Clarita, and you're sure to know what it is.'

Clarita leaned over her desk, the buttons on her blouse tugging at the eyelets. 'I *don't*,' she insisted. 'Even if I did, I couldn't possibly tell you. You know that.'

'Not even after Saturday?'

'That's not fair, Carl.' Fidgeting nervously with the cameo brooch pinned just above her bosom, she met his bewildered look. 'All I know is that two men came to see him last Friday afternoon. They came again this morning and the moment they'd gone' – another nod in the direction of Wehmen's door – 'he told me to type out the memo. But I've no idea if their visit had anything to do with you. I really don't.'

'Two men? Where from?'

'No idea.'

'Names?'

'I don't remember.'

Von Menen looked guardedly into her large blue eyes, beyond the memory of Saturday night: a tiny apartment on Ritterstrasse, soft lights, a bottle of Veuve Clicquot and Artie Shaw's "When They Begin the Beguine".

'It's not like you to be so guarded, Clarita. Usually, you know *everything* that's going on in my department. So…'

'Well, this time I don't, so you'll just have to wait.'

And wait he did, all the while wondering what the misfit Wehmen was up to. *He'll be sitting there, a crumpled mess in his honorary Obersturmbannführer uniform, an insidious look on his face, a foul-smelling Turkish cigarette in his mouth. 'The Gestapo would like to have a word with you, von Menen… Something about a meeting at Wittenberge… Sounds very serious… Best you tell me everything…'*

The truth was, von Menen held no time for the Nazis, especially those of the sinister "Black Order", and Wehmen was one of them: a xenophobe, a believer in State dominance over the people, a man with a razor-sharp knife who could arrange the fitting, cutting and stitching of a field grey Wehrmacht uniform in less time than it took to hum the opening bars of "Lili Marlene".

A note of alarm was ringing loudly inside von Menen's head, and it *was* ringing loudly. Non-membership of the Nazi party was one thing; hiding a vehement dislike for Hitler and all he stood for, something else. He knew the risks, but his views were deeply entrenched in a covert fraternity of diverse political thinkers, people drawn together by the idea of a Nazi-free Germany.

Such was the philosophy of the Kreisau Circle and such was the belief of its leader, Count Helmuth-James von Moltke, whose image of a post-Hitler Germany was that of a free, democratic country with honourable values. Von Menen admired von Moltke's imaginative thinking, respected his unshakeable Christian values and saw his vision of life after the Nazis as highly creditable, but he did not agree with his passive, non-violent means of achieving it.

Von Menen wanted change and he wanted it fast. In his judgement, life in Germany would not change until Hitler had gone and since ousting him by political means was beyond anyone's wildest dreams, the only alternative was to kill him. A dangerous business, the penalties harsh and real: vice-like manacles, a complimentary stay at Gestapo headquarters on Prinz Albrecht Strasse and the painful procedure of what the Secret State Police referred to as "concentrated dialogue", followed by a one-way ticket to Flossenbürg Concentration Camp. Or, more conclusively, the gallows at Berlin's Plötzensee Prison.

The intercom on Clarita's desk sparked a dull tone, a red light blinking. She flicked down the switch, von Menen's ear set to the speaker.

'Yes, Doctor Wehmen?'

'Is he here?'

'Yes, sir.'

'Did he bring his files?'

'All of them, sir.'

'Good, lock them in your safe – I'll deal with them tomorrow. And bring me his personal folder.'

Clarita switched off the intercom and reached for the folder, an impassive look on her face. 'I shouldn't tell you this,' she said quietly, 'and you know I shouldn't, but when Wehmen told me to type out the memo, he *did* say something. He said…' She paused, Goebbels' office still on her mind.

Von Menen leaned halfway across her desk. '*What* did he say?'

'He said, "I think his time here is over".'

'I think his time here is… *over*?'

'His exact words.'

File tucked under her arm, Clarita made to depart, but halfway to Wehmen's door, she stopped, turned and walked back to him.

'There's something else you should know, too,' she said, her eyes exuding defiant finality. 'I won't be here when you come out, and please don't try phoning me at home this evening.' Clarita shook her head slowly, her face bereft of expression. 'You fit the old formula nicely, Carl. I like you very much, but we both know we're going nowhere with each other. Besides, Otto is back from Prague this evening. If ever he found out…' She stepped closer; kissed him softly on the side of his neck. 'Sorry,' she whispered, 'but it's over, end of story.'

At that, she padded hurriedly to Wehmen's office, knocked on the door and stepped inside. Von Menen waited in silence, a sense of unease casting a deep shadow over his usual composure.

A moment later, Clarita's pretty face appeared around the doorframe. 'Herr von Menen,' she called, 'Doctor Wehmen will see you now.'

The room looked like a Nazi shrine: a huge gilt-framed portrait of Hitler above the fireplace, hand on hip; furled swastika flags flanking the chimney breast. Even the handles of the glistening fireplace companion set were topped with encircled swastikas.

On the wall at the rear of Wehmen's desk, a more personal touch: large signed photographs of the disciples from hell; Göring, Himmler, Goebbels, Speer, Bormann and the man who would not be outshone, Joachim von Ribbentrop – *"Best wishes and kind regards, Heil Hitler!"* All that remained of Hess, who'd bailed out of his Messerschmitt over the lowlands of Scotland a few weeks earlier, was a brass picture hook and a square of faded flock wallpaper.

A man in his late fifties, overweight, with thin grey hair and a pale, chubby face, looked up from behind his desk, a fold of loose flesh hanging beneath his chin. Von Menen's eyes settled on the navy-blue suit, peppered with ash and dandruff. *No uniform, no 'Heil Hitler'. Thank God.* Wehmen picked up his pince-nez, rubbed the lenses with a large white handkerchief, and then planted them on the bridge of his nose, his sagging, joyless eyes peering at the folder before him.

'Sit down,' he said, in a grating voice.

Von Menen did as instructed, the green leather chair creaking beneath his eighty kilos, the stench of Turkish cigarettes filling his nostrils.

Wehmen folded his chubby hands and rested them on his barrel-like chest. 'Had a visit from two Gestapo officers this morning,' he said dryly.

Von Menen swallowed hard, a chill zipping down his spine.

'Asked me a lot of searching questions about a matter which requires my immediate attention. I'd like to think it doesn't concern you, von Menen, but if it does, you might be leaving this building for a place' – Wehmen looked fleetingly at the two open windows above Wilhelmstrasse – 'where there are *no* windows and the only food is thin cabbage soup.'

'Questions about what, Doctor Wehmen?'

'Trustworthiness… conscientiousness.'

Von Menen's heart froze. He could almost hear the sound of the cell door clanging shut behind him. 'Conscientious…ness, sir?' he ventured.

'Yes. A classified Foreign Office file was discovered on a train at Lehrter Station, just over a week ago – Sunday 15th, to be precise. It was found by a passenger who'd arrived from Wismar on the same train, saw it lying on a seat in a first class compartment and handed it to the police. It contained an unsigned draft report concerning the political relationship between Spain and America...'

Eyes wide open, von Menen leaned forward.

'There's no record of the file being withdrawn from registry,' continued Wehmen, 'but I *will* find out who took it. It's only a matter of time. The fact is, you have a certain responsibility for the Iberian Peninsula, Wismar is no great distance from your family's estate and I suspect you travel first class.'

'But, sir, not once have I left this building with any sensitive material. What's more...' – von Menen delved hurriedly into his jacket pocket, pulled out his diary, thinking aloud as he flicked through the pages – '11th, 12th... Yes, I have it here, sir... Friday 13th June... I *drove* to Potsdam, stayed at a friend's house for the entire weekend and returned to Berlin on Monday morning. My friend will vouch for that.'

'Good... just as well,' said Wehmen, 'because I've been looking at your personal record and it makes for impressive reading. Frankly, I didn't think you'd be so damn irresponsible to leave this building with a highly sensitive document. All the same, I had to ask you.'

Full of renewed confidence, von Menen checked his watch. 'With respect, sir,' he said, 'my leave? I don't suppose I—'

Wehmen snapped into life. 'Your leave! Haven't you grasped what's going on in this country? A new chapter in the Führer's crusade has just begun and all you can think about is your leave!'

I know about the "new chapter", you buffoon. Who doesn't? It's been reported by every radio network from Tokyo to Texas.

And it had, the news still ringing in von Menen's ears: Hitler had committed his fearsome war machine to his craziest scheme yet – the colonisation of the east. Since the early hours of Sunday, the Third Reich had been at war with the country many Germans conceived as the *real* enemy – Russia! From the Black Sea to the Baltic, a German army of unprecedented size was on the march, its sole aim to extend the ideology of a man who craved to be champion of Europe, Adolf Hitler. Next stop, The World.

Wehmen lit up a cigarette, dabbed a finger to his tongue, rubbed it against his thumb and began leafing through the file, turning each page with measured rhythm. He stopped, looked up and fixed von Menen with a long, curious gaze, his nicotine-stained fingers drumming on his silver cigarette box.

'Remind me,' he said, 'what *were* the circumstances of you being born in Spain?'

Von Menen's distant Mediterranean origins were not glaringly obvious, yet his dark brown, almost black, wavy hair seemed starkly at odds with his greenish-blue eyes.

'My parents were in Catalonia at the time, sir, visiting my grandmother – my grandmother being Spanish, you see. They were about to return to Germany when—'

'Ah, yes, your grandfather, married one of the...' Wehmen paused, scratched his thinning grey hair, flecks of dandruff fluttering to his shoulders.

'Devoto de Martinez family, sir.'

'That's right. Caused a right old stir at the time, I believe; your grandmother's decision to renounce the Catholic faith, I mean.'

'I believe it did, sir, yes.'

'The reason why you went to Madrid University, your ancestry?'

'One of them, sir.'

'Personally, never knew your grandfather, but history shows him to have been a fine diplomat, a textbook example of mediation and superbly mannered…' Wehmen paused again, a wheezing sound seeping through his lips. He coughed loudly and a fine mist of saliva sprayed out across the top of his desk. 'Attributes ideally suited to the Bismarck era,' he added, wiping his mouth with the back of his hand, 'but not so these days. We've no time for that starched, sedate nonsense anymore.'

Von Menen averted his eyes. *No time for refinement, either.*

Wehmen referred back to the file. 'Army service… you spent some time on the staff of General von Witzleben, now Field Marshal von Witzleben, *and* served an attachment with the Signals Corps?'

'Yes, sir… I returned to General von Witzleben's staff in December 1937 and stayed there until June 1938. That's when I joined the Foreign Office.'

Wehmen turned to the next page. 'Languages… you have an excellent command of French, English, Italian and Portuguese, and your Spanish is faultless.'

'I've been speaking, reading and writing Spanish since I was a child, sir.'

'Mm… I suppose so. A bit of a boxer, too, I see. Is that how you got the nose?'

'Yes, sir, but I haven't boxed since I left the army.'

'Other sports?'

'Fencing, sailing… riding.'

Wehmen coughed again, reached for a glass of water and took a quick sip. 'Any immediate plans?' he asked.

'Plans, sir?'

'Marriage?'

Another bizarre question. Von Menen's scepticism moved further into the ascendancy. 'No, sir, marriage isn't on my agenda at the moment.'

Pushing the file aside, Wehmen leaned over his desk, a penetrating look in his eyes. 'Von Menen,' he said, after a lengthy pause, 'what do you know about...' Another deafening silence.

'About what, sir?'

Wehmen replied in a whisper, as if the room was full of eavesdroppers. 'About... Information Department *Three*.'

Von Menen's face was full of puzzlement. 'Nothing, sir. I'd no idea there was such a department.'

'That's because it's new, formed only a couple of months ago, by the Minister himself. Its function is to collate intelligence for the Foreign Office.' Wehmen picked up another cigarette, slipped it between his lips. 'And you, von Menen, are its latest recruit,' he added, speaking with the cigarette still in his mouth.

Von Menen pushed back in his chair, face crammed with confusion.

'On the directions of the Foreign Minister,' continued Wehmen, 'you are being posted to...' He reached for his lighter, lit the cigarette, smoke swirling about his face.

'Posted to where, sir?'

'Buenos Aires, of course,' replied Wehmen, as if Buenos Aires was just two stops down the line from Potsdamer Platz Station.

Von Menen stared at the floor in bewilderment. *This is a dream. I've just made love to Clarita Brecht, freed myself from the luxurious entanglement of her legs and fallen into a deep sleep. In a moment, she'll prod me in the back.* But she didn't.

'Ar-gen-tin-a?' he replied. 'To... collate in-tell-i-gence? But I know *nothing* about intelligence, sir.'

'You don't need to! You're not going there as some seedy, grubby little spy! You're going there as an accredited envoy of the Third Reich, an envoy with a special remit.' Wehmen's head was almost halfway across his desk. 'You're going there because you're considered to have the brains, the intellect and the insight to obtain the kind of information

Herr von Ribbentrop wants. The Minister's expectations of you are very high,' he emphasised, peering over the top of his pince-nez. 'He wants a special pair of eyes and ears in Argentina and he's chosen yours. It would be most unwise of you to disappoint him.'

Wehmen settled back heavily and glanced at his notepad. 'At eight o'clock tomorrow morning you're meeting your new section chief, Herr Werner, and he will brief you more fully.' He slipped a half-flimsy across his desk. 'That's where you'll find him.'

Von Menen's face was a twisted picture of pain. 'But, sir—'

'But nothing! Orders, von Menen, orders.' Wehmen drew heavily on his Murad Turkish cigarette, a centimetre of rolled tobacco turning to ash, his steely gaze casting a stern warning. 'And remember, when you leave this office you are not to discuss this matter with anyone other than Herr Werner.' He flicked his hand dismissively in the direction of the door. 'That is all. You may go.'

★

Tuesday 24th June 1941

A small overnight case lay idly on top of the desk, a maroon folder beside it. An island of order in an office that otherwise looked like a junk shop.

Werner, a man in his late fifties, short, solid in stature, with untidy grey hair, a round sallow face and a pair of tortoiseshell spectacles poised on the tip of his nose, looked as though he had spent the last few nights in his office.

'Before we start,' said Werner, 'I gather you're not happy with your posting. Well, if it helps, I know how you feel. Last week, I had a comfortable office in Dahlem. I started at nine and finished at six. Now, my wife thinks I've left home. Anyway, take a seat.'

Von Menen looked around the room, the floor littered with half-empty boxes, files, reference books and a camping bed that might well have been used by Otto von Bismarck himself. 'Frankly, I don't feel like anything at the moment, sir,' he replied. 'I'm still reeling from the shock of being told that my immediate future lies on the far side of the South Atlantic.'

'Well, at least I've met *you*,' replied Werner, 'which is more than I can say for the person I'm meant to report to.'

'Who's that, sir?'

'I'm told his name is Andor Hencke, from the Political Department, younger than me, but in terms of seniority, well... on Wilhelmstrasse, things have a habit of changing overnight...' Werner peered over the top of his spectacles, a wry smile drifting across his face. 'Something *you've* just learned to your obvious displeasure.'

Von Menen was trying to fathom the protocol, his aversion for Wehmen uppermost on his mind. 'I assume, then,' he said, 'that Herr Hencke reports to Under-Secretary of State...?'

'Doctor Wehmen?' interrupted Werner, shaking his head. 'No, Herr Hencke will report directly to the Foreign Minister, meaning that all that stands between you and Herr von Ribbentrop is me and Herr Hencke. Anyway, whatever you feel about your new-found status with the Foreign Office, you're stuck with it, so...'

A good start; sounds like a man I can trust. Frank, calm; no party badge in his lapel, no portrait of the insane Adolf.

Werner made towards a huge safe in the corner of his office, withdrew a thick green file, laid it on top of his desk and sat down.

'Your assignment is very unorthodox. Officially, you're

being posted as an accredited Second Secretary. Unofficially, you're going there as, well, a kind of pseudo intelligence officer, I suppose, operating solely on behalf of the Foreign Office...' He peered over the top of his spectacles, a cautionary look on his face. 'It's a challenging remit, I'm afraid.'

'Challenging?'

'In the sense that you'll find others at the Embassy with similar remits; that is, to obtain intelligence. I'm referring, of course, to the Abwehr and the SD. You will know from your time in the army that the Abwehr is a military organisation with certain refined ethics... bit of a gentlemen's club, if you like, run by—'

'Admiral Wilhelm Canaris,' interrupted von Menen, 'wily, enigmatic and unassuming... so I've heard.'

'Frankly, I've never had any dealings with the man, so I can't comment on his personality. But I can tell you that the SD is nothing like the Abwehr. It is by no means a backwater for aristocrats, squires and grandees. Know much about the SD, do you?'

'A bit... It's part of the RSHA, the Reich Security Administration, run by Reinhard Heydrich, Himmler's right-hand man. Through the RSHA, Heydrich controls just about every aspect of Germany's security police apparatus, including the Gestapo.'

'Correct, but the SD is Heydrich's cherished invention. His agents in Buenos Aires – researchers, as they might well be described – will, assuredly, be intrigued by your arrival. So, for the record you are a Second Secretary, and you know nothing about Information Department Three. Understood?'

'Perfectly, sir.'

'A further point on the SD,' continued Werner, referring to his notes. 'Heydrich has just appointed a young SS Major as acting chief of the SD's foreign intelligence branch. His name is Walter Schellenberg and I gather he's a bit of a go-getter… useful if you remembered his name, I think.'

'Seems I'm fast becoming a rank outsider in a three-horse race,' said von Menen. 'I mean, me competing with the Abwehr and the SD is, to put it bluntly—'

'A bit odd?'

'In that I've had no training for this kind of work, yes.'

'From what I've seen of your record, I doubt that you'll be a rank outsider. As for training, you don't need any. This assignment is not about dingy, smoke-filled bars in Buenos Aires, invisible ink, dead letter boxes, disguises, false heels and knocking rhythmically six times on Carmen's door. It's about being a special envoy with a special remit, someone with good perceptive skills, someone who has the acumen to get the information the Foreign Office wants. You have those qualities. It's why you were selected.'

'I presume the Ambassador knows why I'm going there, sir?'

'Yes, but only the Ambassador and the Chargé d'Affaires. Others will have their suspicions, of course, but you'll have to deal with that in your own cautious way. Initially, focus your attention on what you're likely to find *outside* the Embassy, and by that I mean the Argentine Army Intelligence Service and the Policia de la Capital. If they suspect you're surplus to our genuine requirements, they'll take a keen interest in you, tap your phone, intercept your mail and follow you around. So, whenever you're away from the Embassy, use public call boxes and do not encourage people to write to you, or visit you, at your private address.'

A knock sounded on the door. A skimp of a girl tripped in bearing two cups of coffee. Werner waited for her to leave and when the door clicked shut he reached for the maroon folder, fished out a grainy photograph of a man in military

15

uniform and laid it on the table. 'He's a career soldier,' he said, 'a lieutenant colonel in the Argentine army, believes in State intervention over the economy and admires the philosophy of Germany. Personally, though, I'd say he's more inclined to the ideology of Mussolini. He was in Europe recently, as a military observer. Our main interest in him is his involvement with an organisation called the GOU, short for *United Officers Group,* a secret brotherhood of pro-Axis military officers. We want you to make a covert study of the GOU, assess its strengths and weaknesses and evaluate its prospects. In other words, find out all you can about it.'

Von Menen picked up the photograph. 'Mid-forties?'

'Yes, born 1895. His name is Juan Domingo Perón. We believe he's directing the Argentine army's mountain troop unit at Mendoza.' Werner removed his glasses, rubbed his eyes and heaved an arduous sigh. 'You'll be aware of Argentina's neutral stance, insofar as the war in Europe is concerned, but that is not to say that she has no empathy for the German cause. Within the Argentine military there are many people who are on our side. But the same cannot be said for the man in the street, whose support lies almost entirely with the British: for every pro-German in Argentina, you'll find at least five Anglophiles. You need to remember that.'

Another two hours flew by, Werner speaking at length about Argentina's volatile history – her roller-coaster economy, ambitious military expansionism, disdain for Brazil and Chile, and her continuing war of words with the United States.

'You've a lot to learn, Carl. The National Library in Buenos Aires will be a good start, but don't forget the newspapers; read as many as you can.' Werner delved into the folder and fished out a booklet headed *TOP SECRET*

– *AKROBAT*. 'All your reports will be encoded by special ciphers, unique to you and me. Make them precise. No extraneous rubbish. And remember the security code. Non-urgent reports will be sent through normal Embassy channels, but anything critical or ultra-sensitive will be sent via this' – straining over his desk, Werner released the two catches on the small – 'suitcase.'

Werner turned it round so that the handle faced von Menen, his half-empty cup of coffee spilling onto the carpet in the process. Ignoring the mess, he hinged up the lid, revealing a second, smaller suitcase, seemingly as innocuous as the first, but when its lid was raised…

'A transceiver,' said von Menen.

'The latest.'

It was a small, compact arrangement, complete with a set of headphones, a silent Morse key, a flexible antenna and a spare set of valves.

'I know all about your Signals Corps history,' said Werner, 'so I won't bore you with all the technicalities. Suffice it to say, the call sign for the Information Department Three home station is ZBZ9. Your own call sign is MEC9 and your personal code is *AKROBAT*. Bear in mind, also, that in the first instance your signals will be picked up by a relay station in Madrid. From there, they'll be transmitted directly to Berlin.' Closing the two lids, Werner slapped his hand on top of the case. 'A warning,' he added. 'It's not to be used for sending signals directly from the Embassy, or from your private residence in Buenos Aires, so you'll have to find yourself a "safe" house as soon as possible. Rent or buy, it doesn't matter. Just make sure that nobody knows about it, not even the Ambassador.' He slipped a second envelope across his desk. 'They're yours. Antenna layouts, security codes, ciphers, transmission times and frequencies. Memorise the security codes, transmission times and frequencies, and make sure to burn the paperwork before you leave the building. The ciphers are one-time pads.'

Von Menen plucked out one of the small booklets and fanned through the pages. 'Meaning, I have one copy and—'

'I have the other,' confirmed Werner. 'Use them in strict numerical sequence and be sure to burn each sheet immediately after transmission. As with the transceiver, keep them safe. Understood?'

'Perfectly, sir.'

Werner stroked his jaw. 'Your address, it's off Unter den Linden, isn't it?'

'Yes, sir.'

'Call me in a couple of days and I'll arrange for someone to deliver the transceiver and a spare set of crystals.'

Werner walked back to his safe, hauled out a fat manila envelope and dropped it on top of his desk. It landed with a deep thud. 'There's a lot of money in there,' he said; 'enough to quench the appetite of anyone who's got the information we're looking for. Inside, you'll find details of a personal bank account with the Banco de la Nación, in Buenos Aires. You have a safe at home?'

'Yes, sir.'

'Good. Make sure to keep everything in it until you leave... Oh, nearly forgot, the photograph you were asked to supply two weeks ago? My apologies for the guile, but it had nothing to do with the process of updating your personal file.' Werner delved into his drawer, pulled out a pristine diplomatic passport and pushed it across his desk. 'With that, you'll have full diplomatic privilege... No need for scrutiny by border authorities.'

Von Menen ran his fingers across the hard, dark blue cover, tracing the gold-embossed emblem of the Third Reich and the inscription *Deutsches Reich Diplomatenpass*.

'Any questions?' asked Werner.

'Yes. How long am I likely to be away?'

'Can't possibly answer that,' was the astonishingly frank reply. 'What I can tell you is that the Minister has taken a personal interest in your assignment, a *very* personal interest. Don't mention that I told you, but you were chosen from a shortlist of five. It was Herr von Ribbentrop himself who had the final say. He thinks you are, to quote, "expressly qualified for the role". There's no point in me making a secret of it; a great deal is expected of you.'

'And my next briefing?'

'There is no *next* briefing,' Werner apologised. 'You're flying to Stuttgart next Sunday, staying overnight at the Hotel Graf Zeppelin and continuing to Portugal the next day. You sail from Lisbon on 3rd July, a first class cabin on *Cabo de Hornos*. There's a full Wagons-Lits itinerary inside the envelope.'

Von Menen gasped at the urgency of it all. 'But—'

Shaking his head, Werner hauled himself up from his chair. 'No point in raising any objections with me,' he said. 'As of today, you're finished at Wilhelmstrasse, so I suggest you make the best of the next few days and visit your family. Remember, memorise the transmission times, frequencies and security code, and burn every scrap of paperwork before you leave the building. As for you and I,' he concluded, offering his hand, 'the next time we meet will be over the ether. Good hunting.'

Von Menen's mind was a whirlpool of doubt. In less than six weeks he would be in Buenos Aires, lost in a world of ciphers, transmission times, radios, an organisation called the GOU and a man named Juan Domingo Perón; a diplomat one minute, a spy the next; aiding those he despised and cut adrift from those he admired. He walked back to his office, trying to distil his misfortune, but knowing that he was hopelessly stuck, trapped between von Ribbentrop and the two giants of German espionage.

He knew something about the workings of the Abwehr and he had a measure of the questionable dealings of the Nazi-inspired SD, but like two north poles in the same box, the Abwehr and the SD didn't mix: Heydrich mistrusted Canaris, Canaris was watchful of Heydrich, and neither had any time for the insufferable and arrogant Joachim von Ribbentrop. His mind filled with the notion of a half-baked scheme contrived by von Ribbentrop in a vain attempt to seize the espionage initiative from the Abwehr and the SD, to win the favour of his beloved Adolf Hitler.

Von Menen unlocked and pushed open his office door. There was an unaddressed envelope lying on the floor, a brief message inside:

The next meeting of the Edelweiss Alpine Flower Society has been brought forward to this evening – same time, same venue.

Kind regards,

Ludwig Hamelin, Honorary Secretary

"Ludwig Hamelin" was the alias of Rudolph von Bauer, a former army colleague who'd transferred to the Abwehr shortly after von Menen had joined the Foreign Office.

Von Bauer wouldn't know the difference between a dandelion and a rare orchid, but he certainly knew the difference between non-violent resistance to Nazi rule and outright military rebellion. In that sense he was an important link to a man seen by many as a symbol of hope for a new, democratic Germany – Field Marshal Erwin von Witzleben. But von Bauer's affinity with von Witzleben went much deeper than a mutual hatred for Hitler. Like von Menen, he, too, had served on the staff of the illustrious field marshal!

Von Menen walked over to the window, pressed his head against the glass and felt the heat of the day on his forehead. *Something's afoot. Von Bauer said he couldn't make the meeting at Wittenberge because he had to go to Breslau. So why is he still in Berlin?*

He telephoned his friend, Gustav Helldorf, over at the Foreign Office Press Branch, cleared his desk, then trawled through the items Werner had given him, the contents of the manila envelope sending him into a cold sweat – thick wads of US dollar bills, Swiss francs, bundles of Argentine pesos and a green velvet pouch containing over fifty Swiss gold pieces.

Von Menen packed everything into his valise, sat down and began the arduous task of memorising call signs, frequencies and transmission times.

By early evening, a pile of charred papers lay smouldering in the fire grate.

2

Von Menen rode the U-Bahn from Kaiserhof to Klosterstrasse, arriving at the Letzten Instanz Tavern a little after eight-fifty.

He ordered two beers, found a quiet table and waited, certain that the punctilious von Bauer would arrive precisely at nine. He did; an impressive figure in a charcoal three-piece suit, gold watch chain looped across his waistcoat.

'Good to see you, Rudolph, though I'm surprised you're still in Berlin. I thought you'd be—'

'In Breslau?' whispered von Bauer. 'Should have been, but when I heard about your posting—'

'You thought you'd come and see me?'

Von Bauer peered over his shoulder, eyes darting around the room. 'That's about the way of it, yes.'

'How did you find out?'

'Got it from a little canary. Also, got a cryptic call from Gustav, said you'd mentioned… making a run for it?'

'Said in haste,' von Menen replied flatly, 'but it would suit my conscience.'

'Perhaps, but it wouldn't suit the rest of us.'

'It's *my* conscience, Rudolph.'

'Yes, but our cause is a collective endeavour…'

Von Menen glanced around the room, icy defiance in his eyes.

'I know how you feel,' continued von Bauer, 'but

staying in Germany won't change a thing. We want rid of them, yes, but now isn't the time. Hitler might be insane, but he's at the height of his power *and* he's popular. Moving against him now would be suicidal. We'd fail. Besides, he's already left for his new HQ in the east. Too distant for what you had in mind.' He reached for von Menen's wrist and squeezed it lightly. 'We have to be patient, Carl. I realise how disappointed you are, but disappointment heals much better than a severed head.'

'You're trying to tell me something?'

Von Bauer cast another furtive look around the room. 'Remember what you told me, just before you left the regiment? That your intention was never to join the Foreign Office, the thought of working for the Nazis too much to contemplate?'

'That's the way I felt, yes. It's the way I *still* feel.'

'But your grandfather persuaded you otherwise, his advice being, "Those idiots must be watched... closely".'

'He was right.'

'I'm glad you still see it that way, because your posting to Argentina will give you – and us – the opportunity to do some *real* watching. It suits our purpose. When the time comes – and it will – we'll need someone in South America, someone we can trust, someone like you.'

'That's all very well, Rudolph, but they're sending me there as a damn spy, for heaven's sake.'

'I know *why* they're sending you there, but why isn't important, why is just another von Ribbentrop vanity trip. Just act out the part.'

'Act out the part!'

'If we're going to defeat them, Carl, we must know what they're thinking, even in Argentina. But you'll have to be careful and that means disassociating yourself from the Kreisau Circle. Wipe it from your mind.'

Von Menen shook his head in bewilderment. 'Rudolph, the Kreisau Circle might be a little too passive for my way of thinking, but at least it gives me *something* to cling to.'

Von Bauer leaned forward, his look intense. 'Forget it! Forget your association with me, too, and forget Gustav.'

'Why?'

'Because the idea of communicating with like-minded friends in Germany, especially through diplomatic channels, is too dangerous. If someone here, with proven links to you, were to be picked up by the Gestapo, Heydrich would have you hauled back to Berlin in chains.'

Von Menen's aspirations were shrinking around him. 'So, the message is: be a decent chap, go to Argentina and do a bit of spying for the Nazis. In the meantime, all I have to worry about is my conscience. Is that it?'

'Not exactly,' replied von Bauer, unmoved by the cynicism. 'You'll have more than your conscience to worry about.'

'Meaning?'

'I have four names for you, names you'd do well to remember. And I mean *remember*. Do not write them down. But first...' Von Bauer dipped into his briefcase, pulled out a small, brown paper package and slipped it across the table. 'Take this with you. You might need it.'

'What...?'

'It's a PPK and three cartons of ammunition.'

A look of sheer astonishment washed over von Menen's face. 'Surely you're not serious.'

'Oh, but I am, and you'll understand why when I tell you about three of these names.'

'I'm listening.'

'Müller, Schmidt and Jost. Müller and Schmidt are SD agents... Nazi Foreign Intelligence. They've been at the

Embassy in Buenos Aires since March, on a so-called fact-finding mission.'

'And Jost?'

'Gestapo, on a two-year secondment.'

'What the... is a Gestapo officer doing on a two-year secondment to Argentina?'

'Part of Heydrich's game plan. He wants a Gestapo/SD foothold in every German embassy we have. Very soon von Ribbentrop will be forced into accepting it. He'll have no choice. But where Jost is concerned, for now it's simply a way of monitoring the chatter of German expats. He feeds anything interesting back to Berlin, his cronies at Gestapo Headquarters get to work and if the dissident has relatives in Germany, they get a very frightening message...'

'Tell Felix to keep his mouth shut, or...?'

'Exactly. But the important thing for you to remember is that Jost is a dangerous man. Before his posting to Argentina, he was stationed at Gestapo Headquarters in Berlin, attached to...' – von Bauer paused, a grim look on his face – 'Section A3.'

'A3? They deal with—'

'Reactionaries; the likes of us. That's why you must forget the Kreisau Circle.'

Von Menen reeled back in his chair, his face creasing, one thought on his mind. *How long before Jost gags me, bags me and ships me back to Berlin?*

'Don't be fooled by the name, either,' resumed von Bauer. 'Erhardt Jost – not to be confused with Heinz Jost, who's in the process of being replaced as head of Nazi Foreign Intelligence by a young SS major, Walter Schellenberg.'

'So I've heard.'

'Well, hear something else... Müller and Schmidt are

from the highly polluted end of the SD sewer. The only thing going for Müller is his excellent command of the language; like you, his mother is half Spanish. But Jost is very different, a fervent Nazi, politically aware and highly dangerous, especially where the likes of us are concerned. To put it succinctly, he's completely lacking in any form of human compassion.'

'With respect, Rudolph, I know all I need to know about the habits of A3.'

'I'm sure, but you'll need to be especially cautious of Jost. Many a decent family in Germany has faced an unexpected funeral bill because of him. They call him "Mongoose, the snake-eater". You can't miss him. He's short and wiry, has straw-coloured hair, smokes cigars like there's no tomorrow and fancies himself with the ladies. He's a lone operator, too, works independently, doesn't trust anyone and shuns camaraderie. A little unusual for an SS man, wouldn't you say?'

Von Menen's mouth arched into a dry smile. 'Maybe it's his height.'

Von Bauer grinned. 'Whatever his height, if ever he found out about your real sympathies, believe me, he'd have no qualms about killing you.'

'*Killing* me?'

'Yes, and neither would Müller or Schmidt.'

Casting his eyes to the floor, von Menen looked uneasily at his valise, thought about the Walther and the ammunition and wondered if three cartons would be enough. He looked up and placed his elbows on the table, fisting his hands under his chin. 'The fourth name?' he asked wearily.

'Professor Franz Schröder, one of us, a kind of long-distance supporter. We were at Leipzig University together. We've always kept in touch and nowadays we communicate via my cousin's address in Gothenburg.'

'A professor of what?'

'Law, at the University of Buenos Aires. If you need to share your sentiments with anyone, he's your man. Be very discreet, mind – Franz's views about Hitler and the Nazis are well known throughout the entire academic community in Buenos Aires. And before you ask, he has no relatives in Germany. His family left for England in 1937.'

'How do I make contact with him?'

'The law faculty. It wouldn't be wise for you to be seen visiting his private address.'

'Description?'

'My age, slim, very tall, about a metre ninety, wears a monocle and, like most professors, has a penchant for quirky habits. Whatever the weather, or the occasion, he always wears a biscuit-coloured jacket.'

'He'll need proof of who I am.'

'That's in hand. Next Monday, I'm going to Sweden. I'll send a letter from Gothenburg to his post office box in Buenos Aires. I use the pseudonym Olof Carlsson. Franz uses the name Peter Nilsson. I'll refer to you as Nils Bildt and I'll give him some background information about your family – disguised, of course. With luck, he'll have the letter within two months.' Von Bauer dipped into his waistcoat pocket, pulled out a tiny photograph and gave it to von Menen. 'Show him that. It's a photograph of me and Franz, taken in the Bavarian Alps, spring 1914.'

'Seems you've thought of everything,' said von Menen. 'What can you tell me about the Ambassador?'

'Only that he's a career diplomat and an ardent Party man. I believe he went to Argentina shortly after Hitler came to power. My guess is he'll be highly suspicious of you at first, but I doubt he'll rock the boat. Ribbentrop wouldn't like it and Warsaw can be a very cold place in the winter.' A rueful smile drifted across von Bauer's face. 'There's something else,' he continued. 'How's your Shakespeare?'

'Awful.'

'Twelfth Night – "Thus the whirligig of time brings in his revenges"?'

'Sorry, Rudolph, not with you.'

'This morning I had cause to speak to someone from the *old* school. Word has it that some years ago your grandfather gave our Ambassador in Buenos Aires one hell of a haranguing; lasted the best part of an hour, so I'm told. Just thought I'd let you know.'

'But my grandfather was a von Schönberg. How would the Ambassador know about my connection to him?'

'The drums of the Foreign Office beat loud and clear, Carl, even as far as South America.'

Von Menen closed his eyes. 'Jesus; first Jost, then Müller and Schmidt, and now it's the Ambassador. I might just as well hitch myself to a granite kerbstone and hurl myself into the Spree.'

'There's one other thing,' said von Bauer, making ready to leave. 'Your new section chief, Günther Werner?'

'Yes?'

'He's not with us, but as far as I can gather, he's not against us, either. By that, I mean he's not a member of the Party; in fact, he seems a very decent sort of chap.' Von Bauer checked his pocket watch, mumbled something about his wife and pushed himself up from his chair. 'Time to say farewell, Carl. Before I go, though, I have two messages for you, the first from Field Marshal von Witzleben: he thanks you for your help and wishes you well.'

'The second?'

'From Helmuth von Moltke... whilst he does not share your proactive views, he respects your sincerity and wishes you God speed.' Von Bauer offered his hand. 'Well, enjoy the sea crossing, Carl, and do give my best to Franz... Oh, one last thing... the gun; take it with you. You might need it.'

Outside, dusk was gathering beneath a moonless sky. Streetlamps were unlit, windows hidden by close-fitting blackout curtains. Berlin would soon be a city of inky silence, a night for black-market racketeers.

Von Menen set off on foot, the weight of his valise telling as he crossed the Schloss Bridge and made into Unter den Linden. A lump rose in his throat as he passed the darkened image of the Zeughaus, the words of his dying grandfather echoing in his mind: *'Most Germans believe Hitler to be the great redeemer, Carl. He's restored their pride... given them something to crow about. But when the truth emerges, the people of this nation will realise that they've been duped by a despot. By then, of course, it will be too late; Germany will be in ruins.'*

In the distance, the Brandenburg Gate stood silhouetted against the pale afterglow of sunset, the scene blissfully tranquil. That Germany was at war was difficult to imagine. The crump of bombs, the wail of sirens and the smell of fire and cordite were rarely evident in Berlin. They were rarely evident in Germany.

The town house in Berlin's fashionable Mitte district was strangely deserted, and had been ever since von Menen's father had left his post at the headquarters of the German Army High Command to join the build-up of forces in the east. Frau von Menen, now ensconced at the family estate in Mecklenburg, had left many of the rooms mothballed, the furniture swathed in white beneath the heavy, pungent smell of camphor.

Von Menen sank into a deep armchair, the notion of informing his family about his impending departure to

South America uppermost on his mind. Since his father was on the Eastern Front, and his sister Katrina lost in the affections of her naval officer husband somewhere in the wilds of Tuscany, it brought the options down to one: his mother, who was spending a few weeks with his Aunt Ingrid at Flensburg.

It would not be easy. Like the rest of his family, she was mindful of his secret assignations and shared his staunch opposition to the Nazis, but von Menen knew instinctively that his posting to Argentina would provoke wild and worrying thoughts in her mind.

He walked to the far end of the drawing room, closed the blackout curtains, switched on the lights and studied the array of photographs on the lid of the Steinway grand, a snapshot gathering of pre-Nazi German elite: Colonel General Otto von Menen, Prussian to the core, uniform dripping with medals; Frederick von Schönberg, distinguished diplomat, arm-in-arm with his wife, formerly Maria Helena Devoto de Martinez, a dash of blue blood in her veins, the scandal of her marriage to a Protestant German diplomat still echoing through the ranks of Catalonia's high society; Klaus von Menen, youthful and dashing in the uniform of a lieutenant of the 3rd Royal Field Artillery Regiment, gazing admiringly into the eyes of his bride-to-be, the charming and radiant Anna-Maria Devoto de Martinez von Schönberg. And finally, Aunt Ingrid, glamorous and zestful, lolling on the arm of her wealthy playboy husband Baron Rudolph von Schneider, who was then killed in a flying accident in Austria in 1921. Aunt Ingrid had inherited everything and she'd never remarried, preferring instead to keep a drawer full of unwrapped affairs, her enduring relationship with a married Swedish diplomat still going strong after fifteen years.

The next day, von Menen took the mid-morning service to Hamburg. As Brandenburg rolled by beneath the clear blue sky, suburban woodlands gave way to long, low hills, pockets of marshland, streams and small, glistening lakes, dissolving beyond Wittenberge into an endless vista of fields burgeoning with potatoes and rye.

It made von Menen realise that he would miss the harvest – swathes of golden brown yielding to horse-drawn reapers, darting rabbits and the rhythmic clatter of threshing machines. It gave him to thinking about other things, too: *straw-coloured hair*, for one.

A nervous spasm raced through his stomach, the name leaping into his mind like a taunting Jack-in-the-box; a flaxen-haired Jack-in-the-box smoking a fat cigar. Erhardt Jost was just an image in his mind, but he was already beginning to haunt him.

He changed trains at Hamburg, made Flensburg a little after seven o'clock and arrived at his Aunt Ingrid's mansion a half-hour later, his first ever unannounced visit. He took the flagged footpath around the side of the house, past the stables and beyond the vegetable garden, the spicy fragrance of honeysuckle following his every step.

A maid greeted him at the scullery door and led him to the drawing room. He'd barely unbuttoned his jacket when the sound of footsteps came hurrying along the hall, his mother bursting through the door, a tense, nervous look on her face. 'I... I thought it was you,' she said, her voice quivering. 'Is it...?'

Von Menen shook his head. 'Father? No, Mother, it isn't.'

'Thank God. When I saw you, I—'

'Yes, yes, I know; I did try phoning you from Berlin last night, and again this morning, but I couldn't get through. It was the same when I tried from Hamburg this afternoon. Frankly, I was beginning to think...'

He realised instantly that his mother's thoughts were light-years from Flensburg. That Aunt Ingrid's phone had been out of order for the past two days was totally irrelevant. Anna von Menen's husband was safe. It was all the assurance she wanted.

At that, Aunt Ingrid, swathed in chiffon, a white fluffy pooch in her arms, glided through the terrace doors.

'Goodness, Carl, what a surprise. Is it my birthday?'

Von Menen smiled at the tease, reached into his pocket and pulled out his new diplomatic passport, his mother responding instantly.

'You've been promoted! How wonderful. For one horrible moment I thought you were going to tell us that you'd been conscripted.' She kissed him on the cheek and stood back apace, admiring him like he had just matriculated. 'Congratulations, darling, I'm so proud of you. Your father will be terribly pleased.'

'Champagne?' suggested Aunt Ingrid, lowering the pooch to the floor and ushering it gently through the doors with her foot.

'Thank you, Aunt Ingrid, but I haven't quite finished yet.'

'There's something else?' asked his mother.

'Yes, they're posting me abroad, sending me to...' Von Menen paused, exchanged a knowing look with his aunt. 'Well, to... Argentina, actually,' he said gently. 'I'm leaving in a few days.'

Frau von Menen shot him a piercing look, her shoulders dropping, a muscle pulsing in her cheek. Under the Nazis, such rewards did not come easily, or freely. The going rate was unquestioned allegiance to the Party and undivided loyalty to 'that maniac, Hitler'.

She rocked back on her feet, despairing of the thought buzzing through her mind, the notion that her only son had been coerced into joining the SS – or, worse still, given to grovelling at the feet of 'that conceited imbecile', von Ribbentrop.

'You haven't been taken in, have you?'

Von Menen's brow looked like a washboard emblazoned with question marks.

'Taken in?'

'Yes, taken in. As a family, we've always been at one in our thinking about the Nazis,' she snapped, as if he were a newly promoted Sturmbannführer of the SS. Then she saw the innocent look in his eyes and bowed her head. 'I'm so sorry, Carl,' she said. 'Forgive me. I don't know what came over me.' The muslin curtains billowed in from the open terrace doors and caressed her dress. 'What with your father in the east, Jürgen a week away from returning to Kiel, and now...'

Von Menen reached for her hands, looked into her eyes, her sandalwood face pained with worry. 'There's nothing to forgive, Mother,' he said. 'I understand your thinking, but my virtues and aspirations haven't changed and they're not likely to.'

They moved to the terrace, Aunt Ingrid's pooch watching suspiciously from the comfort of a wicker chair. Ingrid herself had withdrawn to the kitchen.

'When did you say you were leaving?' asked Frau von Menen.

'Sunday.'

'You'll be going by way of Spain and Portugal, I suppose?'

'Yes, sailing from Lisbon.'

'Will you have time to go to Zaragoza? It would be nice if you could visit Great-aunt Louisa. She'll be eighty-eight next month.'

'Afraid not, Mother, but I am hoping to stop off in Madrid for a couple of nights. I'd like to see Juan.'

'That's nice. Juan's a good, loyal friend.' She turned and ran a finger teasingly across the bridge of his nose. 'He did reshape this for you, though.'

'It *was* a boxing tournament, Mother, and Juan lost, remember?'

'Yes, of course, darling... Anyway, do give him my love. He's a charming man, so well-mannered and good-looking, too.' Her voice dropped to a low whisper. 'I rather think Aunt Ingrid had wished she'd been fifteen years younger when he visited us at Mecklenburg.' She reached up and patted down the edge of his collar. 'Don't forget to write. I'll expect a letter from you at least once a month.'

'I'll do my best.'

'No need to worry about Father and Katrina. I'll explain everything. They'll understand.'

'And Greta?'

'Greta, too. She's in Dresden, due back a couple of days after me. As for Hans, well, wherever your father is, he's right by his side. Have you spoken to Gustav and Lutzi?'

'Only Gustav. I've asked him to bring my car up, sometime after the 30th, if that's okay.'

'Yes, I'll be back from Flensburg by then. He and Lutzi can stay overnight, if they wish.'

Von Menen returned to Berlin on Thursday evening. On Friday, the transceiver and a spare set of crystals arrived by special courier. At nine o'clock in the evening, after six hours of frenzied packing, his trunk was en route to Tempelhof Airport. All that remained was his valise, the disguised transmitter and a medium-sized suitcase.

A little before ten, the telephone rang. Gustav Helldorf, stylish raconteur of the Foreign Office Press

Branch, genius of the high wire and expert on all things French and Russian, notably champagne and caviar, was in a colourful mood. Former Oxford scholar and best friend since childhood, Helldorf was the chief source of von Menen's eternal supply of non-German newsprint, which, by dent of his questionable dealings within the maze of Berlin's diplomatic quarter, included a regular supply of Britain's irreconcilable duo – *The Times* and the *Daily Herald*.

'About tomorrow evening, Carl…'

The thought of it rocked von Menen to the core of his senses. Helldorf had promised him the traditional 'send-off', Foreign Office-speak for an almighty hangover.

'Hell, Gustav, is it that close?'

'It is. You're still free, I hope, or do you have an appointment with that gorgeous Clarita Brecht?'

'That was just a fling. She's engaged to some dashing infantry captain, remember?'

'Good. We'll meet at the Adlon, seven o'clock… Lutzi's bringing Sigi.'

Von Menen did not respond.

'Did you get that? Lutzi's bringing Sigi, you know, legs all the way up to her—'

'Yes, yes, Gustav, I know… Fantastically good-looking and with the most divine figure imaginable, but…'

'But what?'

'She frightens me to death, that's what.'

'But you like her, don't you?'

'Of course. I'm very fond of her. The problem is, she's unnervingly unpredictable and her conversation rarely moves further than champagne, caviar and the ladies' fitting room at Wertheim's.'

'Don't know about Wertheim's, but I give her full marks for the other two. Anyway, it's your last night in Berlin.

She's great fun and *she's* not engaged. She adores you, thinks you're different. Ask Lutzi.'

'Different?'

'Yes, that adventurous bearing of yours. She keeps telling Lutzi that you're just what she wants: tall and strong-featured, with an inviting...' Helldorf restrained himself.

'Inviting what?'

'Rugged broken nose! Come on, Carl, it'll be great fun.'

'Gustav, you're impossible. At seven o'clock on Sunday morning, I'm catching a flight to Stuttgart, and you've agreed to take me to Tempelhof Airport. You'll have a head like a steam hammer.'

'I'll get you there. You have my word.'

'Okay, but as soon as midnight arrives, that's it. And Gustav...'

'Yes?'

'Please, be discreet. The Adlon might be some distance from the American Embassy, but it's well within hearing range, if you get my meaning.'

'I know where the American Embassy is, Carl. Where do you think all your foreign newspapers come from? Besides, we're not eating at the Adlon. I've booked a table at the Eden – lobsters and as much champagne as we can pour down our throats.'

Von Menen hung up with a sigh of misgiving. If he missed the Stuttgart flight on Sunday his whole itinerary would be thrown into turmoil, something he could ill afford. Tomorrow evening, Helldorf would have to be kept on a tight rein, and so would Sigi Bredow.

Von Menen homed in on the source of gaiety permeating from the American bar at the Hotel Adlon, where Helldorf, his girlfriend Lutzi and the vivacious, irrepressible Sigi Bredow were laying the tone for the evening, their laughter contagious, Sigi flirting openly with every man who dared steal her a glance, each of them wondering if her sapphire-blue eyes and pouting red lips were real.

Born in Leipzig, educated in Lausanne and groomed in every nightclub west of Wilhelmstrasse, Sigi Bredow had everything her rich industrialist father could give her: a ski lodge in the Bavarian Alps, fast cars and a wardrobe that would make even Greta Garbo bristle with envy. The only thing missing was intellect and her answer to that was fun, a figure like Aphrodite and a daring black dress in which only she could flourish, her self-perpetuated image of a sultry vamp of scant virtue roundly contradicted by knickers of Bredow steel.

Von Menen ambled into the bar wearing the one evening suit he hadn't sent to Tempelhof. He shook hands with Helldorf, kissed the two girls and sat down. Sigi moved quickly into mischievous mode, rubbed her hand lightly across the top of his thigh and fetched him an impish smile.

'Still playing with your anagrams, are you, Carl?' she teased.

Helldorf raced to his defence. 'Anagrams exercise the mind, Sigi,' he said. 'They make you think deeper.'

'Then perhaps *he* should try doing them,' replied Sigi, scornful eyes set firmly on a uniformed SS captain standing by the bar, hand on hip, a pompous look on his face. 'Bastard SS,' she whispered. 'Look at him, drunk on his own importance. I doubt *he'd* know the meaning of the word "anagram" even if someone quoted him the definition from the New German Dictionary!'

Exchanging a knowing look with Helldorf, von Menen took hold of Sigi's hand and gave her a gentle tug. 'Come on, Sigi, time to leave. Let's get something to eat.'

Dinner at the Hotel Eden drew to an untimely and inauspicious end at ten-thirty. Sigi, having consumed the best part of two bottles of champagne, rolled her eyes, fell forward across the table and buried her face in an elaborate cream dessert.

Von Menen lifted her up, wiped the mess from her face and carried her out into the warm night air. 'For you, Sigi,' he said, as if he was speaking to a tailor's dummy, 'the night is over. Time to go home.'

At Lutzi's apartment, just off the Kurfürstendamm, the lifeless Sigi was steered to the guest bedroom like an anaesthetised patient who had just left the operating theatre.

Von Menen retreated to the bathroom, sponged the cream from his jacket and repaired to the drawing room, only to find Helldorf and Lutzi resembling two entwined snakes. He coughed discreetly.

'Gustav, I'm on my way,' he said, in a loud whisper.

Helldorf, a lock of unkempt hair lying idly over his tightly-closed right eye, a half-empty bottle of champagne swinging in his hand, followed von Menen into the hall, legs in a knit-one, stitch-one, pearl-one gait. 'You're… not leaving… are you… Carl?' he stuttered.

Placing his hands squarely on Helldorf's shoulders, von Menen looked him straight in the eye – the one still open – and said calmly, 'Gustav, if you can hear this, I'd rather stay in Berlin for the rest of my natural life, but I'm under orders to be in Buenos Aires by the end of next month. If I stay here a moment longer, I won't make it to Argentina by this time next *year*!' He glanced along the hallway, a thin smile on his face. 'Besides, in the same room as you and Lutzi, I feel like a lump of coal on a fishmonger's slab.'

'So… what about… tomorrow?' burbled Helldorf, left eye now closed in blind partnership with the right.

'I'll be here at five-thirty. I'll drive to Tempelhof and you can bring the car back.'

A ball of orange rose lazily in the east, tracking the blue

Delahaye as it roared through the Brandenburg Gate, into Charlottenburger Chaussee and on towards the Zoological Gardens. Beyond the Grosser Stern, a flock of chaffinches, white wing bands flashing in the wakening light, streaked out from the Tiergarten, challenging the drop-head to a short race before peeling off into a dense canopy of green.

Buenos Aires cannot be better than this.

Rolled umbrella in hand, Helldorf was waiting by the door, trying vainly to amuse the two girls, his interpretation of Charlie Chaplin failing miserably. He and Lutzi looked uncommonly fresh, but Sigi, sheepish and forlorn in her stockinged feet, seemed as if she'd spent the entire night beneath a bush in the Tiergarten.

Tears welling in her eyes, she shuffled towards von Menen. 'I know you think I'm, well, not very lady-like, Carl,' she said, the palms of her hands flat against his lapels, 'but I didn't mean to cause you any embarrassment last night. You do forgive me, don't you?'

Von Menen bent down and kissed her forehead. 'Dearest Sigi, how could I possibly not forgive a sweet thing like you?'

Tears coursing down her cheeks, she stretched up on her toes and flung her arms around his neck. 'Love you,' she said, her voice trembling with emotion. 'Take care. I shall miss you.'

'And I shall miss you, Sigi. Promise you'll keep my seat at the Eden nice and warm?'

'I will – that is, if they ever allow me in there again.'

Lutzi stepped forward and bundled him into her arms. 'Love you, miss you, Carl. And don't worry, I'll keep in touch with your mother, I promise.' She beckoned his ear. 'And just in case he's too much of a man to say so, Gustav loves you, too. What he'll do without you, I simply do not know.'

'The same for me, too, Lutzi.'

The Delahaye rolled to a halt outside the main building at Tempelhof Airport. Von Menen and Helldorf walked through the departure lounge and onto the apron.

Helldorf offered his hand. 'This is as far as I go, Carl. Time to say goodbye, my friend. When we next meet, let's hope that this hideous war will be over and that Hitler and the Nazis will be just a damn awful memory.'

'I hope so, Gustav, I do hope so.'

Across the tarmac, the angular-looking Junkers 52 was a mere thirty metres away, corrugated fuselage glinting in the sunlight, the first of its three BMW engines spluttering into life.

'Before you go, Carl,' shouted Helldorf, voice rising above the noise, 'there's something you ought to know… I didn't mention it last night because I didn't want to put a dampener on things, but I know everything, Erhardt Jost included. You're a pretty tough nut, Carl, but so is Jost. Be careful. You might find yourself in the lion's den over there.'

'I know,' shouted von Menen, 'and I'm not looking forward to it. But Jost is not the only worry I'm wrestling with. It's more the notion of why they're sending me there. I mean, Christ, I'll be spying for those I want rid of!' He looked yearningly at the "Arrivals" sign twenty metres away, the doubts kicking in. 'I could easily change my mind, you know, even at this late hour.'

Helldorf shook his head. 'It's not worth it, Carl.'

Another engine whirled into life, the purser leaning through the cabin door, hand clasped over his hat, urging von Menen forward. Puffs of black smoke kicked out from the third engine, the purser waving frantically, von Menen wrestling with a crushing desire to make off, voices arguing inside his head. *Go! You have to. No! Make a run for it. You've all the money in the world. Konstanz tonight, Switzerland tomorrow.*

Helldorf saw the wavering look in his eyes. 'Carl, don't!'

Von Menen picked up the radio, grabbed his valise and inched towards the aircraft, each step more leaden than the last. He hesitated, then broke into a jog, the purser running to meet him. 'Take care of Lutzi!' he yelled over his shoulder. 'And make sure to keep Sigi out of trouble! Oh, and don't forget to give my very best wishes to your mother!' He reached the foot of the steps, turned, waved one last time and hurried into the cabin, the door closing behind him.

Von Menen looked out through the window, the Junkers starting to roll, his dreams, his hopes and his friends melting away. All he had now was a gun, a radio, a pile of money, a crazy assignment and the tormenting thought of a man called Erhardt Jost.

3

'Carl! Carl! Bienvenido, mi amigo!'

Dropping his valise to the ground, von Menen wedged the transceiver between his feet and braced himself for the inevitable Latin greeting.

Juan Cortes was in a jubilant mood. 'I can't believe you're here, Carl,' he said, his handshake finally coming to an end. 'And looking very important.'

'Me? You don't look so bad yourself.' Von Menen stepped back a pace, sunlight pressing through the windows, glinting on Cortes's oiled black hair. The moth-eaten sweater, flannelette shirt and scuffed suede shoes had gone, replaced by a sand-coloured suit, smart silk tie, crisp white shirt and crocodile skin shoes, a Fairbanks-style moustache adding to the affluent image.

'Positively prosperous,' said Cortes. 'Six months ago, Father made me a partner. Now, I have my own secretary *and* a clerk. But enough of that... I've a taxi waiting outside.'

Clambering into the back of a beaten old Citroën, they set off for downtown Madrid, a cooling breeze blowing through the open windows.

'It's been a long time,' said Cortes, voice still ringing with enthusiasm.

'Almost two years to the day,' replied von Menen. 'The war in Spain had been over for three months and I'd almost finished my first year with...' von Menen drew back, the driver all ears, '*la tenue sur Wilhelm rue*,' he whispered in French.

'A *grudging* first year, as I recall. Your only incentive being the wishful prospect that one day you might end up in Madrid. Well, here you are, the posting you've always wanted.'

'Not exactly; I'm only passing through, on my way to...' Von Menen reeled in again, inquisitive eyes reflecting in the cracked interior mirror. 'I'll explain later,' he winked.

Not until they had reached Cortes's apartment above the offices of the family law firm, off Calle Gran Vía, did von Menen explain his unexpected arrival from Germany.

'Sorry I clamped up so sharply in the back of the taxi, Juan, but I'm not staying in Madrid. I'm on my way to Lisbon.'

'Lisbon? You're kidding?'

'No.'

'Ah, well, even Lisbon's a damn sight nearer than Berlin. By train, I can be there in just over half a day; under three hours if I take the plane.'

Von Menen shook his head. 'Sorry, old chum, but I'm not staying in Lisbon, either. I—'

'You're not going to South America, surely?'

'Yes, Buenos Aires. Embarking at Lisbon on Wednesday, sailing on Thursday morning.'

'You lucky devil, how did you wangle that?'

'I didn't. I was ordered, with less than a week's notice; hardly had time to pack.'

'Must have taken your family by surprise.'

'Mother was a bit anxious, but Father doesn't even know. He's—'

'Somewhere east of Warsaw, I shouldn't wonder.'

'That's about the measure of it, yes.'

'Katrina?'

'She doesn't know, either. She and Jürgen are in Italy, due back any day now.'

'But your mother knows?'

'Yes, she's staying with Aunt Ingrid at the moment, at Flensburg. I took the train up there a few days ago. Remember Aunt Ingrid?'

'How could I forget?' smiled Cortes. 'Your Uncle Manfred's boat, a rough sea and Aunt Ingrid with a face as green as a cabbage!'

'Well, they send you their best wishes,' said von Menen, sharing the amusement. 'I'm sure Father and Katrina would, too, if they knew I was here.'

Von Menen's overnight suitcase was already lodged in the guest bedroom, but the valise and the disguised transmitter remained glued to his feet. Cortes was discerning enough to sense their importance. 'There's a steel cupboard in my office, Carl,' he said, flicking a glance at the valise. 'It's very secure and plenty big enough. If it would make you feel more comfortable...'

Von Menen welcomed the offer, the notion of a restrained evening in Madrid too much to contemplate.

Restaurant El Barquero was dim and discreet, full of shadows, flickering candles and the melodic sound of Spanish guitars.

Von Menen seemed relaxed, but Cortes was uncommonly edgy, the memory of Spain's civil war rising inside him; a ferocious, unreal past, father against son, brother against brother, Madrid crumbling to her knees, the flames of destruction fanned by Germany and Italy. He thought about the old Basque town of Guernica, destroyed by Hitler's Condor Legion, hundreds killed, two of them his grandparents. He would neither forgive nor forget it and he'd always believed that von Menen felt likewise. But von

Menen's new-found status puzzled him, and Cortes's mind was a maelstrom of doubt.

A good friend, an emissary of the Third Reich, no less, just arrived from Berlin by plane – by plane, mind – en route to the most glamorous city in South America, a first class ticket for a passage on Cabo de Hornos in his pocket; the same man who had been ushered, reluctantly, into the German Foreign Office by his illustrious grandfather at the expense of his long-held dream – 'I want an exciting life, Juan, adventure, discovery, journeys to the unknown. The humdrum of government is not for me. The thought of working for the Nazis abhors me. I can't abide them.' Cortes remembered the words as if von Menen had spoken them only hours ago.

The last spoonful of gazpacho brought the small talk to a halt. With the paella came the troubling topic of Germany's expansionist drive into Russia, which, for Cortes, meant only two things – Hitler and the Nazi Party! He ordered a second bottle of wine, watched the waiter leave, took a deep breath and averted his eyes in readiness for the answer he hoped he wouldn't hear. 'You've joined, then?'

Von Menen laid down his fork, a fat, juicy prawn impaled on the end of it. 'Joined? Joined what?'

'The Nazi Party... Hitler's hoodlum empire. "I can't abide them," you said, your exact words. And yet here you are, on your way to Argentina. I'd imagined that such jobs were for the Hitler-worshippers.' Cortes's tone bore the delicate weight of a sledgehammer.

Scarcely believing his ears, von Menen shifted uneasily in his chair. *Flensburg and Mother all over again.* 'Juan, there are many people at the Foreign Office who *are* members of the Nazi Party,' he said. 'Some are even honorary members of the SS, von Ribbentrop included, but me, definitely not. I can understand your scepticism, but believe me, my feelings now are the same as they were when I first realised what Hitler stood for. I despise him *and* his Nazi ideology.'

Reflecting pensively on his association with the Kreisau Circle, von Menen placed a finger on the base of his wine glass, inching it at a snail's pace across the white linen tablecloth. 'You might find this a little strange,' he continued, 'but I have no real enthusiasm about going to Argentina, no enthusiasm whatsoever. Given the choice, I'd rather stay in Berlin. To understand that, you have to appreciate how fervently I believe that the Nazi regime *will* come to an end eventually. It might take a few years, but it *will* happen, I know it will. But, please, this conversation is strictly between us. You're a good friend and I trust you.'

Cortes flopped back in his chair, cursing his impertinence. 'I'm sorry for being such a damn fool, Carl. Of course I understand. And, yes, you *can* trust me. It's just that, well, you know, the Nazis, the Fascists, call them what you like, they're all a bunch of gangsters.'

'In that case, seeing as we're at one on the subject, let's talk about something else… Argentina. You were there at the end of '35. Tell me, is it *really* the Paris of South America?'

'Most definitely. It's a wonderful place. The people are marvellous, very European, more so than the Europeans, if you get my meaning. It's a tricky place politically, though. Whilst most Argentines have little time for what's happening in Germany, there are those who are only two steps behind Hitler and Mussolini, and most of them wear uniforms. They're crazy about military expansionism and would love to see Argentina as a dominant pro-Nazi/ Fascist state in the Southern Hemisphere.' Cortes paused, shaking his head. 'As far as the war in Europe is concerned, Argentina might be neutral, but it's hardly Switzerland. It's a place where the unsuspecting could easily find themselves in deep trouble.'

Spain's newspapers were crammed with the news of Germany's amazing successes on the Eastern Front. Barely a week had passed and the German army was less than 450 miles from Moscow. Hundreds of thousands of Russian soldiers had been taken prisoner. West of Minsk, Stalin's soviet regime was bending to a new "system" of repression and terror. Hitler's extravagant concept of colonising the east was looking far less fanciful than anyone could ever have imagined.

Later that afternoon, Cortes drove von Menen to Barajas Airport, the Deutsche Lufthansa flight from Barcelona already on its descent as they pulled up outside the terminal.

'When I get back, Juan, I'd like you to come to Mecklenburg again. We'll sail the Baltic, visit Sweden, if you like.'

'I'd like that very much, Carl,' said Cortes, fumbling in his jacket pocket and pulling out a small pink stone, which he pressed into von Menen's hand.

'A boiled sweet?' joked von Menen.

'No, rhodochrosite. It's a semi-precious stone. The Argentines call it Rosa del Inca. It was discovered a few years ago in an abandoned copper mine in Argentina's Catamarca Province. I'd like you to have it. It's supposed to bring good fortune. If nothing else, it will remind you of our trip to Sweden.'

Good fortune?

Von Menen held no belief in the supernatural, but for some weird, inexplicable reason, his eyes remained riveted to the small pink stone resting in the palm of his hand, Helldorf's chilling warning ringing in his mind. *'Be careful. You might find yourself in the lion's den over there.'* He looked wistfully in the direction of the Sierra de Guadarrama, thought of Jost, Müller and Schmidt, saw his own ghost dancing in the clouds and asked himself if he would ever see Europe again.

Flicking the stone high above his head, he snatched it from the air and squeezed it tight shut in his hand. 'Thanks, Juan,' he said, forcing a smile. 'Luck is something I usually make myself, but on this occasion, I'll make an exception.'

★

Von Menen followed the porter into the passenger terminal, through the control point and along the quay, catching his first glimpse of *Cabo de Hornos*: a mass of twinkling lights, grey smoke lazing from her funnel and spiralling towards a crimson sky.

An eye-catching young lady, her dark brown hair trailing from beneath a floppy straw hat, stood awkwardly at the foot of the gangway, the hem of her dress snagged against a stanchion, two cumbersome hat boxes and a large travel bag more than she could cope with.

Von Menen laid down his valise and called the porter to a halt.

'Fala Portuguese?' he asked the lady, raising his hat.

'No, Español.'

Von Menen responded in flawless Spanish. 'You look as though you need help.'

'Thank you. I thought I could manage, but…'

Von Menen smiled, set free her dress and picked up her travel bag, grimacing at the weight of it.

'Books and instruments,' she said apologetically.

Von Menen concealed his curiosity. 'Right, you lead the way. I'll follow.'

They parted in the ship's lobby; she, grateful for his

help; he, smitten by her stunning good looks. 'Perhaps we'll bump in to each other again,' he said, tipping his hat.

'I'm sure we will,' she said with a smile.

Even before von Menen had removed the last of the three padlocks from his cabin trunk, Ramon, his cabin steward, an elderly, cheery individual with a shock of grey curly hair, launched into his well-rehearsed 'Welcome on board *Cabo de Hornos*' routine.

The unpacking finished, Ramon fished into his waistcoat pocket and plucked out a crumpled piece of notepaper. 'You have an item for storage in the ship's strong room, señor?'

'Yes, I do.' Von Menen reached for a weighty cardboard box, festooned in a web of string and dotted with large blobs of red wax. 'I was asked to deliver this to an address in Buenos Aires,' he explained. 'A family heirloom, I believe. Seeing as it's been entrusted to me…'

'Of course, señor, I'll see that the purser gets it.' Ramon referred to the notepaper again. 'When unoccupied, cabin door *and* portholes to remain locked at all times… all luggage, including your trunk, to remain in your stateroom?'

'That's right. I'll unpack my valise and small suitcase myself.'

Eyes brightening at the size of his tip, Ramon turned on his heels and departed.

Von Menen waited a while, locked the door, delved into his valise, pulled out a cigarette lighter and a stick of sealing wax. Stuffing the valise and the transceiver into the trunk, he locked the three padlocks, melted a blob of wax into each keyhole, then tossed the keys through the porthole.

Heaving a huge sigh of relief, he kicked off his shoes, flopped down on the bed and smiled. He'd made it, valise, radio, money and all. Next stop, Las Palmas.

She had no floppy straw hat and her long, shimmering brown hair trailed in the wind like the tail of a pony in full flight.

'Morning,' he greeted her. 'How are the books?'

The lady smiled. 'Fine thanks, as are the instruments.'

He held out his hand. 'I'm Carl Franz von Menen.'

'Maria… Maria Francesca Gomez. Thank you again for your kindness yesterday.'

'My pleasure. You're Spanish?'

'No, Argentinian.'

'Really? Señorita or señora?'

'Señorita.'

'Travelling alone?' he asked guardedly.

'Yes.'

'You've had breakfast?'

'Actually, no, I haven't.'

'In that case, if you'll forgive my boldness, would you care to join me on the promenade deck?' He saw the wavering look in her eyes. 'Of course, if you'd rather not…'

'Ten minutes?' she said.

'Ten minutes… And the name's Carl,' he reminded her.

She returned a short while later, wearing a simple shell-pink blouse and a swirling pastel-blue skirt, her hair piled up above her head, small pearl earrings the only sign of jewellery.

When they reached the promenade deck she sat down and removed her sunglasses, von Menen mesmerised by her perfect face: a soft, caramel colour, set with flashing brown eyes, an alluring smile and the longest, curling eyelashes he'd ever seen. She was beautiful, graceful and delightfully genial, and when she spoke, her voice was soft, unhurried and gently convincing. She was Doctor Maria Francesca Gomez.

'I would *never* have taken you for a doctor,' said von Menen.

'Ah, but a very junior one,' she smiled.

'Hence the instruments?'

'Quite.'

'Did you train at the Charité?'

'Yes, I finished my general clinical training about a month ago. Now I'm going home.'

'Has your family been in Argentina long?'

'On my father's side, since the sixteenth century. We're descended directly from a wayward Jesuit missionary, who arrived in San Juan province from Spain in 1595, kissed religious teaching goodbye and took off to the foothills of the Andes with a local Indian girl.' Her tone implied that the legend had been the source of much amusement in the Gomez family for centuries.

'And your mother's side?' asked von Menen, stifling his laughter.

'Of Italian descent… Her great-grandparents arrived in Argentina in 1845, settled in Buenos Aires for a decade or so and then—'

'Moved to Córdoba to open an ice-cream parlour?'

'Now you're teasing. Anyway, what about you?'

'Me? Not much to tell really. Until a few days ago I was living and working in Berlin for—'

'Let me guess… the Argentine subsidiary of IG Farben, or Siemens Schuckert? They sent you to work in Germany for a while and now *you're* going home?'

He laughed. 'Wrong. I've never been to Argentina in my life. I'm German.'

Her brow furrowed. 'German? But—'

'You thought I was Argentinian, with a name like *von* Menen?'

'It's not unusual. There are lots of *vons* in South America and you speak Spanish like a native.'

'Thank you for the compliment, but there's good reason for that. I was born in Spain, my grandmother was Spanish and I went to Madrid University. And my first name has

Spanish influence. My mother, you see, was intent on calling me "Carlos", after my great-grandfather, but my father wanted "Karl". In the end, they compromised and settled for "Carl", spelled with a "C".'

She smiled at the explanation. 'And when you left university?'

'I did some travelling, returned to Germany, enlisted in the army for three years and then I joined the German Foreign Office. Now I'm on my way to Argentina to take up the rather tedious post of Second Secretary at the German Embassy in Buenos Aires.'

'You must be very relieved.'

'Relieved?'

'To be leaving Germany.'

'Why should I be relieved?'

'The war! The Nazis!'

Her straightforward manner rocked him. The ship was only the length of the Tiergarten from the Portuguese coast and Cortes's cautionary advice was stabbing at his mind already – *Most Argentines have little time for what's happening in Germany.*'

'Do you not approve of what Hitler is doing?'

'Do *you*?' she replied pointedly.

'I'm a government officer, a servant of the German Foreign Office: apolitical, neutral and without attitude. My acknowledgement is to Germany.' He paused to take a sip of coffee. 'Besides, if I answered "no", you might think I was lying.'

'And if you said "yes"?'

'You probably wouldn't believe me anyway… In any case, I never discuss politics with beautiful ladies.'

She was not wont to give up easily. 'Yes, but—'

'Forgive me for enquiring,' he said, cutting her short, 'but I assume you've taken the Hippocratic Oath?'

'Of course.'

'To which extent you gave your solemn undertaking to observe certain codes?'

'Absolutely.'

'So, if Hitler were to faint at your feet, right now, would you attend to him… treat him in your capacity as a doctor?'

'Of course, it is my duty to care.'

'And in so *caring* for him, do you think you would be helping him in his cause?'

'Well, I…'

'Go on,' he prompted. Nonplussed, she reeled back in her chair, saw the mischievous look on his face and laughed. 'In the German Foreign Office,' grinned von Menen, 'we call it "diplomatic reasoning". Now, shall we talk about something else?'

'Okay,' she smiled. 'Tell me about your family, your parents. What does your father do?'

'He's a soldier, Prussian background, very military.'

'And your mother?'

'Half Prussian, half Spanish.'

'Any brothers and sisters?'

'A sister, Katrina, two years younger than me; she married a couple of months ago. Her husband's a lieutenant in the navy, which means that she'll be spending a lot of time with my mother, in Mecklenburg… And you?'

'I did have a younger brother, but he died when I was ten.'

'I'm so sorry to hear that.'

Their conversation continued well beyond breakfast, Maria adjourning briefly to her cabin to collect a large photograph album crammed with images of her parents, relatives, friends and the family's *estancia* in the Province of Córdoba.

'My main comfort in Berlin,' she said, laying the album

on the table. 'I went through the pages almost every day, imagining I was still at home, breathing the sweet smell of the Pampas and watching the sun go down beneath the Sierra Chica.' Enthralled by the thought of it, she looked out towards the horizon, felt the tremor of the engines beneath her feet and willed the ship to go faster.

'Who's the gentleman in uniform?' asked von Menen.

'Uncle Filipe. I doubt you'd like him, though, he's...' She paused, a searching look in her eyes. 'But perhaps you would, I don't know... Anyway, your turn now.'

'Sorry, can't equal your album. I've only got the one photograph.' He slipped a silver-framed photograph from its cardboard sleeve and handed it to her.

'Your sister's wedding?'

'Yes, taken after the ceremony, just the seven of us.'

'Your sister's very attractive. Your mother, too... That's her, isn't it? The lady with the light-coloured suit?'

'Yes.'

'Thought so. And the gentleman by her side, your father?'

Von Menen nodded.

'I'd say you look more like your mother.'

'So everyone says.'

'And the couple on the end, standing next to your father?'

'Hans and Greta; they're old friends of my parents. They live at the house in Mecklenburg.' A poignant lump rose in his throat, his eyes locked on the photograph.

'Something wrong?'

'A sad memory, that's all.'

'Nothing I've said, I hope?'

'Not at all.' Anxious to learn more about Maria, von Menen shrugged away the memory. 'What prompted you to study medicine in Germany?'

'Simple; I'd always wanted to attend the Berlin Medical Academy. Daddy studied there before the Great War. I wanted to follow in his footsteps, not that Daddy was overly keen on the idea.'

'Why not?'

'The ethics of medical science.'

'You're alluding to certain *events* at the Charité?'

'Yes. There was a time when I very nearly gave up and went home. Daddy found the whole business appalling. I doubt he'll ever forgive the Nazis for purging the Charité of many of its distinguished scientists, men like Selmar Aschheim, Bernard Zondek, Professor Karl—'

'Bonhoeffer,' supplied von Menen, 'the eminent psychiatrist.'

'You know of him?'

'Vaguely, yes.'

But *vaguely* was far from the truth. Karl Bonhoeffer was the father of Pastor Dietrich Bonhoeffer, a supporter of the Kreisau Circle and a founding member of the Confessing Church. He was something else, too – a colleague of Rudolf von Bauer's.

'Daddy really admires him, not just for his marked contemptuousness of Hitler's *Law for the Protection of Hereditary Health*, but for his outstanding clinical skill. But Dr Bonhoeffer's successor,' Maria shuddered, 'that cringing Doctor Maximinus de Crinis... more disposed to Hitler's cut-price mental welfare programme: the assassination of the mentally ill! I wonder if *he* ever took the Hippocratic Oath.'

Von Menen turned and closed his eyes. He wanted desperately to agree with her, but the words of von Bauer and Cortes held him back. He'd forced himself into a corner and somehow he had to get out of it. 'Many countries do have scandalous practices,' he said remorsefully. 'I suppose Germany is no exception.'

It was a faint-hearted riposte, yet somehow the pained look in his eyes and the shameful tone in his voice worked. Her hand slipped slowly across the table, her slender fingers reaching for his arm. 'I'm sorry,' she said, 'I wasn't being personal. And you're right, of course, many countries *do* have scandalous practices, Argentina included.'

That was the end of it. There was no further mention of Hitler or the Nazis.

Von Menen wooed her ceaselessly. As the days and weeks marched on, he sensed he had found the kind of woman he had always dreamed of and she felt the same about him, a man who respected her and valued her opinions, not some polo-playing, pleasure-seeking machismo searching for a marriage chattel.

In a strange kind of way they felt as though they had known each other for years; that they'd laughed together, cried together and, perhaps, even... But Buenos Aires was less than two days away and time was running out.

After dinner, they adjourned to the promenade deck. Von Menen ordered a bottle of champagne and they spent the evening gazing at a sky teeming with the jewel-like constellations of the Southern Hemisphere. Yet the stars were about as near to von Menen's thoughts as the distant galaxies themselves. Maria had captured his mind, his soul and his heart. All else seemed hopelessly irrelevant. Even the problems awaiting him in Buenos seemed light years away.

'Is there something wrong?' Maria asked.

'Only that we'll be arriving at Buenos Aires soon and...'

'Yes?'

'Well, the last few weeks have been very special for me,' he said quickly.

Maria was toying with the clasp on her evening purse.

She turned away and looked out across the vast, empty ocean.

'Sorry,' he said, 'I didn't mean to embarrass you. I just...'

She turned back and pressed a finger to his lips. 'Shush. I'm not embarrassed. It's been the same for me, but it's getting late and I'm feeling a little chilly.'

He walked her to the door of her cabin and kissed her gently on the lips. 'Sweet dreams,' he said. 'See you tomorrow.'

Her face held an expression he had never seen before, her eyes doing all the talking. *Make me feel I'm wanted. I need to know.* He drew her towards him, cradling her head against his chest. She could feel the beat of his heart against her face, a powerful, eager, inexorable feeling rushing through her body, her soul awakening to an emotion she'd never experienced before. Her mind made up, she pulled away. 'It's a long night, Carl,' she whispered. 'I'd rather not be alone.'

He lifted her head. 'You mean...?'

'I mean I'd like you to stay for a while – that is, if you want to.'

'If I *want* to? Of course I do, but are you—'

'Sure? I'm as sure as I ever will be.'

Von Menen lay there, mesmerised by the languid pace of the fan droning above the bed, moonlight splashing through the porthole.

The bathroom light dimmed, the door pushed open and Maria stepped out, a life-size Lalique figurine: lithesome, sensuous and oozing allure. She slipped in beside him, wrapped herself in his arms and fell madly in love.

They woke at six the next morning, happy, content and relaxed; he, not wanting to leave; she, not wanting him to go. 'Tonight's our last night,' he said. 'Tomorrow, we'll be in Buenos Aires... and you still haven't given me your telephone number?'

'I told you,' she giggled, 'we don't have a telephone, only a radio link with the next *estancia*.'

'In that case, I'll write to you.'

She yawned, nuzzled up against his shoulder and murmured, 'My address is on the dressing table. You'd best give me yours, hadn't you?'

'Er... I've no idea where I'll be staying.' When he thought about it, he realised he *didn't* have any idea where he'd be staying, and even if he did, he wasn't sure that he should tell her, not with Werner's cautionary advice ringing in his ears. Then, suddenly, he remembered. 'I've an account at the Banco de la Nación in Buenos Aires. You can write to me there.'

The next morning, von Menen called for the sealed cardboard box, which had been lodged in the ship's strong room since his embarkation at Lisbon. Inside was a set of bolt cutters – the "key" to the three padlocks he'd used to secure his cabin trunk. Soon, the radio was "free", and the trunk was packed and secured with three new padlocks, ready to go ashore.

He stood by the porthole, eyes glued to the quay, eager to catch a glimpse of Maria as she emerged at the foot of the gangway. Eventually, she did, arm-in-arm with her parents, a joyous event which von Menen had graciously declined. '*Sorry, but I have some urgent work to attend to before I leave the ship.*' It was a lie, of course, based on his awareness that Maria's father was a man of high moral principles, who despised Hitler's regime and quite conceivably saw every German as a heartless Nazi.

Maria slipped into the back of a waiting car, and without

a hint of a searching glance for the man whose heart she had captured, she was gone.

It was over, but something else was about to begin. *'Whatever his height, if ever he found out about your real sympathies, believe me, he'd have no qualms about killing you.'*

The menacing thought of Erhardt Jost was back.

4

A tall man, about thirty, with short, spiky brown hair, dull grey eyes and a long pointed nose swaggered across the lobby.

'Herr von Menen?' he enquired, in a clipped Swabian accent. 'I'm Heinz Neumann, from the Embassy. Heil Hitler.'

Ignoring the gesture of the raised right arm, von Menen nodded cautiously.

'I've a car down on the quay. You're ready?' he pointed.

'Just waiting on my cabin trunk,' replied von Menen.

'No need,' hastened Neumann, 'I've arranged for it to be delivered this afternoon. Shall we go?'

Von Menen lodged the disguised radio in the boot and climbed into the front passenger seat, resting his valise on his knees.

The car thundered along San Martin, horn blaring, Neumann yielding to no one. 'A present from the English,' he said, as the car sped past the English Clock Tower. 'On the right is Retiro Train Station.'

Slowing a pace, Neumann made a right beyond the Hotel Plaza, the horn silent for a moment. 'See that lot?' he said, flicking a glance to the left.

'Soldiers?'

'Yes, the Argentine army in all its fancy get-up. It's their Officers' Club. The jokers call it the National Congress!'

The Mercedes coasted to a halt outside a smart, honey-stone building on Esmeralda.

'This is it,' said Neumann. 'Your new home.'

Von Menen stepped from the car, collected the transceiver and walked into the lobby.

A man wearing a green satin waistcoat, shiny black trousers and an amber bow tie made to greet him, his oiled black hair glistening like newly-set tar, a wide, gap-toothed smile providing the comedy. 'Morning, señor, I'm Jose Fernandez, the janitor. Welcome to Buenos Aires.'

Von Menen stuck out his hand and introduced himself. Neumann, not wont for formality, tossed his head in the air and walked past in contemptuous silence.

The apartment was on the seventh floor, overlooking the gardens of Plaza San Martin, late-flowering acacias adding a touch of cheerfulness to the greyness of winter. In the distance stood the sumptuous Hotel Plaza and to the left, the towering Kavanagh Building.

Von Menen looked around the sitting room, a mirror image of the pictures he'd seen in the glossy magazines Gustav Helldorf had "borrowed" from the United States Embassy in Berlin: soft, neutral colours, polished wooden floors and a scattering of soft pile rugs. Amidst the stylised shapes of art deco furniture, a pre-war import from Germany stood on the sideboard – a neat Graetz radio.

In the kitchen, he found a plentiful supply of groceries – eggs, butter, milk, cheese, fresh fruit and preserves. Not a hint of austerity.

Neumann turned on the heating, gave a brisk guided tour, handed over the keys and headed for the door. 'The Ambassador is expecting you at ten o'clock tomorrow morning,' he said. 'In the meantime, if you want somewhere to eat, I'd suggest La Cabaña, at 436 Entre Rios, up by the Congress Building. They do the best steaks in town.'

'Thanks, but I'll stay in tonight. Maybe tomorrow,' replied von Menen, laying a discreet eye on the transceiver.

Von Menen rose early the next morning, a weak sun peeking through the curtains. After breakfast, he checked the contents of his valise, secured the transceiver and made ready to leave for the Embassy.

Downstairs, Jose Fernandez was immersed in the sporting pages of the tabloid daily, *El Mundo*. Von Menen cleared his throat and Jose slipped the newspaper discreetly into the drawer, uncoiled his wiry green torso and fetched himself up to his entire one and a half metres.

'The lock on my apartment door, Jose…'

'Yes, señor?'

'I'd like it changed, please. Can you arrange it?'

'Of course, señor.'

'No need to bill the Embassy, I'll settle the account myself.'

Jose skimmed through his diary. 'Tomorrow morning, señor, ten o'clock?'

'That'll be fine. I'll make sure to be around.'

Von Menen stood patiently in front of the desk, the sway of *Cabo de Hornos* still under his feet, an unwelcome atmosphere crackling around him – disquieted mutterings, deep sighs and the drumming of fingers on polished mahogany.

Perhaps I should have brought him an offering; a case of Deidesheim, maybe, or a string of Bavarian Milzwurst.

Toying with the starched winged collar of his shirt, the Ambassador finally looked up, the veins at the side of his face pulsing wildly.

'Sit down,' he said, with no hint of a welcome. 'I'm not given to mincing my words, so I'll tell it to you straight… I and the Chargè, d' Affaires are the only two people at this legation who know the *real* reason why you've been sent here and the *real* reason irritates me a great deal. In my view, this *new* information department is an unwelcome departure from the more conventional role of the Foreign Office. I caution you, von Menen, that I will not be placed in the invidious position of having to explain the use of any unorthodox activity to a certain department of the Argentine Military.'

'The Army Intelligence Service, Ambassador?'

'Exactly.'

'I understand, sir,' said von Menen, with studied dignity, 'and you have my word that I shall do my utmost to uphold the best traditions of the German Diplomatic Corps at all times and under all circumstances.'

'I'm sure you will, von Menen, I'm sure you will. Given your background I wouldn't expect anything less, but the fact remains, anyone with a nuance of sense knows that you're surplus to our legitimate requirements, including, I suspect, the Argentine authorities. Be under no illusion, I will not countenance any form of criminal or reckless activity. If you engage in anything akin to that kind of behaviour, you'll find yourself *persona non grata*, shamed, unwelcome and with a big Argentine boot up your posterior.' The Ambassador moved from behind his desk, walked over to the window and stood, arms folded, his back to the room. 'Nevertheless…'

Ah, the atonement bit, the submissive part, the 'since the Foreign Minister has decreed it' slant. Warsaw can be very cold in the winter.

'… irrespective of your *unconventional* role, you, like every other member of this legation, will have my full support, that is to say, as far as I can give it.' Hands in his jacket pockets, he made back to his desk, a sombre look on his face. 'Have I made myself clear?'

'Perfectly, Ambassador.'

'Good,' he said, returning to his desk. 'Any questions?'

'Just one, sir… Whilst I will be in regular contact, there are certain matters which require my urgent attention. Conceivably, they will necessitate my immediate and prolonged absence from the Embassy.'

The Ambassador leaned forward, shirt collar tightening against his neck. 'My dear von Menen,' he said, 'seemingly you are not *entirely* aware as to the extent of your own brief, so maybe I should enlighten you.' A gleeful smile trickled into his eyes, as if he were about to rid himself of some troublesome encumbrance. 'I have it on the very highest authority that you are to be left entirely to your own devices. Your reports will come directly to me, of course, but to put it simply, as soon as you leave this office you are on your own, the master of your own destiny!'

Furrows of doubt wrinkled across von Menen's forehead. 'But I do have my own office, sir?' he queried.

'You have your own office *and* your own safe,' retorted the Ambassador. 'In fact, you've got everything Berlin asked for. There's a safe in your apartment, too, behind a hinged panel at the rear of the wardrobe.' He reached over his desk and handed von Menen a small white envelope. 'You'll find the combinations and instructions in there.' A light knock sounded on the door. 'That'll be Neumann, but before you go, there is one last thing. There are a lot of people here who are very curious, even suspicious, about your position at the Embassy. A lot of questions have been asked about you. In fact, someone was making enquiries only this morning. He seemed very interested in you.'

'Interested in me? Might I ask who, sir?'

'A non-Foreign Office member of the legation, an attaché… name of Jost, Erhardt Jost.'

The name caught von Menen's breath, the late breakfast

he'd taken at a café on Florida backing up inside him, a cold feeling hurtling up the back of his neck. 'Is that… relevant, sir?' he asked, stifling his alarm.

The Ambassador shook his head. 'I've really no idea, but he did ask rather a lot of searching questions about you, especially about your family and your antecedents. Naturally, I told him nothing. I care rather less for his kind than I care for this new department of yours.'

Von Menen stared momentarily at the accustomed picture of Hitler hanging on the wall. His assignment scarcely begun, he sensed that Information Department Three had conceived its first prickly allergy already, an in-house allergy, so it seemed. The message was loud and clear: he was on his own, an envoy with a bogus remit, isolated, unprotected and plagued with the conjured image of a man with a shock of straw-coloured hair, a Gestapo agent with a burning hatred for anti-Nazis. Erhardt Jost was creeping up on him like an ugly virus.

The Ambassador offered his hand and bid him good day.

Von Menen walked across the room, pulled open the door and froze instantly. In the corridor, talking to Neumann, stood the student of evil himself: thirty-five, wiry frame, beak-like nose, pointed ears, close-set eyes, a complexion that resembled the flesh of a freshly-plucked turkey and straw-coloured hair cut to pudding bowl precision.

Erhardt Jost.

Jost fetched him an ice-cold look, said nothing, turned and headed along the corridor, leaving an anxious feeling tightening in von Menen's stomach.

He knows… He knows about the Kreisau Circle.

Neumann led the way to a large, airy room, explained the procedure for resetting the safe and cabinet combination locks, then left in his usual hurried manner.

Locking the door in his wake, von Menen drew the heavy inner curtains and switched on the lights. He rearranged the shelving in the steel cabinet, reset both combination locks and heaved a huge sigh of relief. At last, he was free of the radio, the ciphers, the Walther and the money, save for a fistful of pesos and a wad of US dollar bills.

After the gloomy hours of night-time Berlin, the Argentine capital was a kaleidoscope of vibrant colours, glittering shop windows and blazing streetlamps. It seemed almost artificial in comparison. Along dazzling, cinema-filled Corrientes, where men in smart suits tripped arm-in-arm with women in chic fashionable clothes, colourful posters of Spencer Tracy, Greta Garbo, Clark Gable, Vivien Leigh and James Stewart were as familiar as they were in Los Angeles, Chicago and New York City.

It seemed to von Menen that the glitzy, carefree world of the Hollywood he'd read about had rolled south to meet the haunting and evocative sound of the tango. The war in Europe was far, far away. It was just a banner headline in the international papers. Peering through the taxi window, his thoughts rolled back to what Cortes had said in Madrid: *'It's a tricky place… There are those who are only two steps behind Hitler and Mussolini'*. In such a bright, dazzling setting, it was difficult to imagine, but Hitler's Nazi regime had been difficult to imagine, too, and to that extent the notion that the lights in Buenos Aires might themselves go out, just as they had in Germany, was not an empty one.

The taxi headed towards Congreso, trailed by an unmarked Studebaker all the way down Avenida Corrientes and on towards the Congress Building, halting at Entre Ríos, where it did a hurried three-point turn and withdrew towards Avenida Callao. Werner's perception had been pretty precise. The Argentine Security Services had wasted no time.

After his third week in Buenos Aires, von Menen was almost on talking terms with the Policia de la Capital, he'd become familiar with the amateurish and sloppy surveillance techniques of Müller and Schmidt, and had perfected the art of countering the more qualified methods of Jost.

Each day, he spent several hours at the National Library, usually followed by visiting a newsreel cinema. He listened avidly to news bulletins on Radio Belgrano, read enough books, periodicals and newspapers to stretch the entire length of the River Plate and often roamed the streets until late at night; including the streets of the grime-stricken meat-packing and slaughterhouse district of Avellaneda, where grandiose buildings and manicured parks were as rare as a seven-peso note.

The learning curve was steep, but the reality closed in on him fast. Beyond the bright lights of Corrientes and the haute couture shops along Florida, there was a darker side to Argentina: endemic corruption, political injustice and social deprivation.

Status was the hallmark of existence. This was no more evident than outside the Military Officers' Club on Plaza San Martin, where braid and brass buttons added an ominous dimension – power! Von Menen reflected that Germany's National Socialist dictatorship was led not by a revolutionary general, but by a one-time corporal born in Austria. In Argentina, the idea of a politicised former corporal stalking the corridors of the Presidential Palace would have sent shockwaves throughout the entire officer corps of the Argentine military. The thought of him being a former Brazilian would have whisked the higher echelons into an apoplectic rage!

Yet whatever their misgivings about Hitler's credentials, Argentina's military stood in awe of his warring, expansionist achievements, a perception not shared by the man in the street, whose message was loud and clear: no one, other than Britannia, would ever reign over the United Kingdom! Von Menen sensed he had a mountain to climb. Finding a pro-German enthusiast amongst ordinary Argentines would be difficult enough; finding a *useful* one, almost impossible.

Casting a frown at his makeshift "DO NOT USE" note lying by the telephone, von Menen ambled over to the window and peered into the street below. The dark blue Studebaker was back, parked overtly in Esmeralda, windows fogged with condensation.

Condensation means limited visibility.

He grabbed his jacket, sprinted down to the ground floor and skidded to a halt halfway through the lobby. There was no sign of Fernandez and the small wooden janitor's cupboard affixed to the wall was open. Von Menen took one of the two keys hanging from the hook marked "tradesmen's entrance", exited the building through the back door and took a short taxi ride to the Hotel Plaza.

From a kiosk in the hotel foyer, he called the Faculty of Law.

'Yes, Professor Schröder is lecturing today... He'll be leaving at about four-thirty and he won't be back for another week.'

Just after four o'clock, a second taxi dropped him at Avenida Las Heras. Von Menen waited on the far side of the road, mindful of the notion that two trilby hats, or a mop of straw-coloured hair, might easily show up like genies from an oil lamp.

Half an hour later, a tall fair-haired man wearing a biscuit-coloured jacket emerged from the building, a monocle hanging from his left lapel.

Schröder!

The man crossed the road and headed in the direction of Recoleta, von Menen following at a cautious distance. Beyond Recoleta Cemetery, the man made a left, side-stepped a delivery wagon and disappeared. Cursing his own ineptness, von Menen drifted aimlessly along the sidewalk, mindful that Schröder would not be back for another week.

Damn!

A moment later, he saw it: a biscuit-coloured jacket in the window of a café on the far side of the road. He crossed over the carriageway and pushed through the door. The man was sitting side to the window, face hidden by the day's edition of *La Prensa*.

Von Menen ordered a coffee and sat down opposite him. 'I'm Nils Bildt,' he whispered in Spanish.

Silence.

Von Menen pushed back his chair and made to leave.

'Your mother's maiden name?' asked the man, speaking through the newspaper.

Von Menen inched back his chair. 'Devoto de Martinez von Schönberg,' he said.

'And your sister, Bettina... her date of birth?'

'26th February 1915... but her name isn't Bettina, it's Katrina.'

The man lowered his newspaper, smiled and stuck out his hand. 'Franz Schröder. I'm delighted to meet you, Nils, though I'm sure your name is anything *but* Nils Bildt.'

'No, I'm Carl von Menen, newly arrived from Berlin.'

Von Menen reached into his pocket, pulled out the photograph von Bauer had given him and passed it across the table. 'I'm at the Germany Embassy,' he said. 'Rudolph and I share the same sentiments.'

Schröder searched anxiously through the window, his eyes up and down the sidewalk.

'I wasn't followed,' hastened von Menen.

Schröder folded his newspaper and laid it on the window ledge. 'Good. It wouldn't bode well for you to be seen in my company.'

'Yes, Rudolph mentioned that you're, well, a bit open with your sentiments. But I'm relieved that you got his letter.'

'Five days ago. It arrived at my *overseas* mailbox,' whispered Schröder, seeming convinced that he'd fooled the eavesdroppers and sensors of the entire world. 'Anyway, now you're here, I suppose you'd like to talk, rid yourself of the inhibitions of the Embassy for an hour or two?'

'I would, yes.'

'The problem is,' murmured Schröder, glancing around the cramped little café, 'this is hardly the place.' He looked at his watch. 'Are you free this evening?'

'Yes.'

'Good; meet me at this address.' Schröder tore off a sliver from his newspaper and scribbled. 'It's a restaurant in San Telmo, owned by friends of mine. You can't miss it; it's like Italy revisited, all red, white and green.'

'*Il Pellicano*… Franco and Gina Saccani,' noted von Menen. 'They're Italian?'

'Yes, immigrated to Argentina eighteen years ago, just after Mussolini came to power. Nice couple, fervently anti-fascist, but not communists.'

'Trustworthy?'

'Totally, but we must keep our conversations in Spanish. The Saccanis are very discreet and I wouldn't want to compromise them. Every Wednesday and Friday I tutor their son, Giancarlo.' Schröder leaned a little further across the table. 'When you arrive,' he said softly, 'use the door in the alley, just around the corner. It leads to a small parlour at the back of the main restaurant.'

Tucked down a side street at the waterfront end of San Telmo, *Il Pellicano* was a modest, tiny place, buzzing with atmosphere.

Von Menen entered through the back door, made his way gingerly along a narrow passage and into an L-shaped anteroom, shelves creaking with dust-laden bottles of Chianti, smoked hams, salami and huge rounds of Parmesan cheese. It was pure Italian, the smell from the kitchen heavenly.

Schröder, sitting beneath a half-size portrait of Enrico Caruso, greeted him warmly. A moment later, a man the size of a small truck, with a large round face and wide smile beneath a huge bushy moustache, walked in from the kitchen carrying two large plates of pasta.

'Ah, Franco,' said Schröder, a hand on von Menen's arm, 'this is Carl, the friend I told you about.'

Von Menen rose to his feet, shook Saccani's hand and the big man sauntered discreetly back to the kitchen.

'As you can see,' said Schröder, 'there's only the one table. We're quite alone and we can speak freely.' He raised an eye. 'And since I'm anxious to know how things are in Germany...'

'They're difficult and very worrying,' said von Menen.

'For the likes of Rudolph, you mean?'

'And many others.'

Schröder poured two glasses of wine, eased one steadily across the table and took a deep breath. 'In my judgement, Carl,' he said with calculated solemnity, 'that evil little man has really over-stretched himself this time. I read in the press that the Eastern Front is just milk and honey for the German army. Perhaps it is, but Russia is a big country and as Napoleon discovered to his demise, the possession of territory alone does not guarantee victory.' Schröder reached for the wooden pepper mill standing like a sentinel in the middle of the table, gave it a few turns and watched the tiny black specks float down to his plate. 'Yes, the Russians are in retreat,' he said, shaking his head, 'but when they reach the outskirts of Moscow, Stalingrad and Leningrad, they'll stand firm and they'll fight like hell, because Stalin will make them fight... until they've spilled every last ounce of their blood. It will be very savage. Frankly, I don't see how the German army will be able to sustain momentum, not at that distance. It'll cost millions of lives.'

Von Menen shuddered at the thought that his father might be one of them.

'You know,' continued Schröder, pausing to stab at a square of ravioli, 'war is a history of mistakes, each side hopeful that they'll make fewer mistakes than the other. On that count, Hitler is destined to be a loser. Within a year to eighteen months, the Wehrmacht will be in full retreat, and if Stalin lives up to his name, the reprisals will be brutal and vicious. Hitler won't last more than two, maybe three, years.' A mischievous glint seeped into his eyes. 'Someone might even murder him before then.'

'I don't think there's much chance of that, Franz.'

'No, I suppose not... Anyway, let's change the subject. How are you finding Buenos Aires?'

'Exciting, interesting, confusing and... intriguing.'

'Intriguing?' frowned Schröder.

'In the political sense, yes.'

'Carl, the political scene in Argentina is about as complex and as mystifying as the steps of the tango itself, equally mesmerising and sometimes just as entertaining. Socialists, Anti-personalista Radicals, National Democrats and... the Military. Different names, but the same hidden agenda...'

'Corruption?'

'In a manner of speaking, yes. At the moment we have a National Democratic/Anti-personalista coalition, headed by a Conservative, Ramón Castillo; the stiffening, cogent figure of General Justo watching from the wings.'

'Which prompts me to ask: where, exactly, does the military stand in relation to Castillo?'

'Like a lamppost to a drunk, as they say; a lamppost which someone is certain to take away – in time.'

For once, von Menen felt relaxed, his sense of isolation ebbing away, the erudite Schröder reaching into his mind like a twentieth-century Plato. He was interesting, enlightening and persuasive, a great intellect, well-mannered, amiable and self-effacing.

'And what about this GOU organisation I keep hearing about?'

'Ah... the GOU,' smiled Schröder, 'the *Grupo de Oficiales Unidos*, a clique of pro-Axis military officers, about which we're *supposed* to know nothing.'

'Led by Colonel Juan Perón?'

'Yes... The GOU's aim is to reflect the political and military achievements of the Axis powers in Europe, elevate the military status of Argentina and dominate the whole of South America.'

'With or without the support of the people?'

'My dear Carl,' said Schröder, his look emphatic, 'for most Argentines, the concept of life has no relevance whatsoever to that which the GOU would have them endure. The man in the street has no taste for the politics of Hitler or Mussolini.'

'And Argentina's relationship with Germany?'

'Restricted almost entirely to the military. There's a commercial relationship, of course – banking, chemicals and the like – but the emphasis is largely on the sympathetic element within the Argentine military, mainly the younger, impressionable officers.'

'And the man in the street?'

'That's the job of the Nazi propaganda machine. The fanfare usually starts at the German News Agency, Trans Ocean, on Avenida de Mayo, from where it filters through to the German language newspaper, *Deutsche La Plata Zeitung,* and other Nazi/Fascist-sponsored news sheets, like *Momento Argentina.* I imagine there's an aspiring Goebbels at the Embassy who's oiling the cogs.'

'That reminds me,' said von Menen. 'Attachés at the Embassy... Did Rudolph hint at anything untoward in his letter?'

'Not that I could figure, but Rudolph's inclined to be very circumspect. I have to read his letters a dozen or more times before I get to the nub of what it is he's trying to tell me.'

'In that case, maybe you should know about a man called Erhardt Jost, a Gestapo agent. He arrived at the Embassy a few months ago, just ahead of me.'

'Is that significant?'

'In our case, yes. Jost has an avid aversion to anti-Nazis and his antagonism exceeds the bounds of indoctrination – he kills people!'

Schröder fell silent, his face the colour of stone.

'Something wrong?' asked von Menen.

'Not sure,' replied Schröder, clearly troubled. 'According to my secretary, a man telephoned the university about four weeks ago – twice, in fact – sounded a bit cagey, she reckoned, wouldn't give his name, didn't want to speak to me personally, just wanted my *home* address. Of course, she didn't give it to him and as far as I know he hasn't called since, but she thought he had a German accent.'

'Maybe it was just a coincidence,' said von Menen, 'but he's certainly active. He's followed *me* several times.'

There was a knock on the door. Franco walked in, muttered something in Schröder's ear and returned to the kitchen. Schröder looked anxious. 'Carl, you're sure you weren't followed here?' he asked.

'I'm certain. I took a very devious route… used three cabs, the first to the Colon Theatre, the next to the Congress Building and finally to Plaza Dorrego. I walked the rest of the way. Why do you ask?'

'Franco reckons that a car has been cruising up and down the street outside for the best part of an hour.'

'The Police de la Capital?'

'Possibly. Likely they're looking to harass Giancarlo, Franco's son, you know, the young man I tutor part-time. Nice fellow, but he's a bit of a fundamentalist, wants to set the whole world straight: no Nazis, no fascists, no communists, just utopia. Twice he's fallen foul of the police and twice he's been arrested.' Schröder looked at his watch. 'Should be home in about ten minutes. Chances are, he'll get the usual *words of advice* before he reaches the front door. Even so, I think we should call it a night. I'll get Franco to order you a taxi to the side entrance. But make sure to take the same, circuitous route back. Buenos Aires is full of unseen eyes.'

'And you?'

'I'll leave a few minutes later.'

'And our next meeting? I mean, how do we communicate?'

'Do you have a bank in Buenos Aires?'

'Yes, the Banco de la Nación on Plaza de Mayo.'

'Same as me… Let's agree to meet here in a fortnight's

time. I'll let Franco know to keep the room free. If I can't make it, I'll leave a message for you at the Banco de la Nación on the Wednesday before.'

'And if I can't make it?'

'Likewise, leave a message for me.'

If von Menen's spirits had been lifted by his first meeting with Schröder, then the letter he found waiting for him at the Banco de la Nación three days later filled him with a state of elation. By the time he'd reached his apartment, the light-blue envelope, bearing a faded whiff of perfume, had almost burned a hole in his pocket.

I miss you… I love you… I can't wait to get to Buenos Aires to be with you. Then, he reached the final page: *Saturday 23rd August is Daddy's sixtieth birthday… We're having a big party for him. And guess what – you've been invited, as a houseguest… My parents insist. PLEASE, do come. You can catch the El Cordobes Express from Retiro Train Station early on Friday morning. I'll be waiting to pick you up at Córdoba… All my love, Maria.*

He read the letter again. *My parents insist? How much has she told them?* 'He's German… a diplomat… comes from Mecklenburg?' Cautionary lights flashed on and off in his mind, teasing the memory of his last night on *Cabo de Hornos*, the passion, the closeness.

The lights were still flashing when he breezed through the door of Harrods department store, on Florida, the very next morning.

A voluptuous lady, about thirty, with mahogany eyes, dark brown hair and fulsome, scarlet lips gift-wrapped the crocodile skin wallet and matching hip flask for him, her crisp white blouse, a size too small, heightening the mountains of her D-size cups, von Menen's eyes transfixed on the dark, deep chasm.

She looked up and caught his gaze. 'Anything else I can do for you, señor?' she smiled.

He coughed nervously. 'Er, no, thank you... That is, unless you know where I might find a locksmith.'

'Avenida Santa Fe, beyond Pueyrredon... It's only a block from where I live,' she said, a helpful smile in her eyes.

'Thank you.'

'A pleasure, señor... If ever you need anything *specially* wrapped, just ask for me, Ana... Ana Pradera.'

'Thank you, Ana, I'll remember that.'

Beating a hasty retreat onto Florida, von Menen headed for the locksmiths on Santa Fe and left an hour later with a duplicate of the key he'd taken from Jose's cabinet.

The ground floor was quiet upon his return. Von Menen left the original key on the janitor's desk, along with a hurriedly scribbled note:

Dear Jose, key found on the first floor landing a couple of days ago.

Apologies for not returning sooner; quite forgot about it! Hope no inconvenience caused.

He returned to his apartment feeling that things might finally be starting to go his way.

5

After fourteen hours, 700 kilometres and what seemed to von Menen like as many stops, the *El Cordobes* Pullman finally pulled in at Alta Córdoba Station.

Maria was waiting on the platform, a movie star in all but name, the collar on her three-quarter-length ocelot coat pulled high above her neck.

'You look very glamorous,' he said.

She stretched up on her toes, fell into his arms and kissed him. 'I've missed you,' she murmured.

'The same,' he replied.

She pulled back a step. 'Let me look at you.'

'Nothing's changed,' he joked.

'Except you look very tired.'

'Tired? Anyone would look tired after fourteen hours on the slowest train in the Universe, chugging through the most impossibly flat land in the Universe, with nothing to look at but horses and cattle.'

'Well, you're here now, the Province of Córdoba – hills, valleys, meandering streams and the Sierra Chica.'

She took his arm and they walked towards the car in the evening twilight.

They drove north for an hour, Maria looking happy and content at the wheel of her new Chevrolet coupe. They turned off the main highway and climbed on to a narrow track, the beam of the headlights falling upon a large white sign hanging high above the entrance – *Estancia Sierra Chica*.

Some minutes later, the shimmering lights of the Gomez ancestral home came into view: a large lime-washed mission-style building with a pillared arcade, parapets and a bell tower rising high above the huge front door.

A tall, portly man stood waiting by the door, a glowing storm lantern in his hand.

'We're here, Daddy,' called Maria as they approached.

He offered his hand and smiled. 'Señor von Menen – or should I say, *Herr* von Menen – welcome to Estancia Sierra Chica. I'm Javier Gomez, Maria's father.'

'It's a pleasure to meet you, señor. Please, call me Carl.'

They moved into the wide flagstone hall. A lady stood at the foot of the staircase, elegant and radiant.

'Carl, allow me to introduce my wife, Ana,' said Señor Gomez.

Von Menen inched forward, reached for her hand and pressed it lightly, dipping his head in the process. 'Señora.'

'I'm so pleased to meet you, Carl.'

'My privilege, Señora Gomez. I'm honoured to be here.'

'A pleasant journey?'

'Long, monotonous and a little tiring, but educational.'

'Educational?'

'Yes, I sat next to a cattle farmer, a *gentleman* cattle farmer; very stylish, name of Valquez. Said he knew you; in fact, he said he would be here tomorrow.'

'Black jacket, bombachas, high boots and a belt studded with silver coins?' asked Señor Gomez, one eye balanced on his wife.

'The same,' von Menen smiled.

They moved to the drawing room, a large, stone enclave, the walls adorned with the artefacts of Spanish colonial rule – guns, swords, pikes, helmets, breastplates, shields and tapestries, an unambiguous reflection of seventeenth-century Spain.

'Dinner will be served in forty-five minutes, Carl,' announced Señora Gomez, glancing at the clock. 'We tend to eat very late here. First, I imagine you would like to freshen up. Your room is on the first floor... left at the top of the staircase and along the balcony. It's the third door on the right. You'll find plenty of hot water, towels and—'

'The generator, Mummy?' interrupted Maria.

'Oh, yes. Thank you, Maria. When the generator goes off, Carl, usually at midnight, everything switches to battery power. There's a separate switch just beside the bed. You'll find the lights a little dimmer, but quite bright enough.'

Von Menen adjourned to his room, soaked in the bath, then changed and rejoined Maria's father in the drawing room.

'Drink, Carl?'

'Thank you, sir. I'll have the same as you.'

'Sherry?'

'That's fine.' Von Menen raised his glass and took a short sip. 'Mm, very fine.'

'Can't beat a good *British* shipper, Carl.' Silence filled the room, Javier Gomez's face a picture of repentance. 'My apologies, Carl, I wasn't implying that everything British is best... Certainly didn't mean to offend you. It's the war in Europe,' he tutted. 'I'm afraid it's reached into my mind again.'

'No offence taken, sir; as it happens, I like sherry, British or otherwise.' Von Menen felt the instant comfort of his host's relief. 'You have a wonderful home,' he added.

'Founded in the mid-seventeenth century... been in the family for many generations. The origins are Jesuit.

Some of the original outbuildings are nearly three hundred years old.'

'But you don't farm it yourself?'

'That's right. My wife and I came to live here after my father died. We kept the house, but decided to lease out most of the land. The man you met on the train, Hector Valquez...?'

'Yes?'

'He leases about ten thousand hectares.' Señor Gomez settled back in his chair. 'Anyway, as much as I'd like to talk about *Estancia Sierra Chica*, Carl, I'd like you to tell me about Germany. It must be quite different now.'

'Very different,' replied von Menen.

'And Maria tells me that your father is a military man. Is that right?'

'Yes, a soldier.' It was, in fact, as much as von Menen had *ever* told Maria about his father. 'Sadly, I was unable to see him before I left for Argentina.'

'How very unfortunate.' There was a lull in the conversation. Gomez stared into the fire, gathering his thoughts, the question he *really* wanted to ask suddenly bursting out. 'Tell me, Carl, are you a Nazi?'

Von Menen fixed him with a cool, unmoved expression. 'No, sir, I am not. Neither are my parents; in fact, I can safely say that my whole family is *very* apolitical.' The ring of truth in his reply was unmistakeable.

'I'm pleased to hear that,' said Señor Gomez. 'Events in Germany have caused me a great deal of anxiety these past ten years. I still have this gnawing feeling that the Nazis will eventually bring Germany to her knees. I find that sad *and* frightening. Sad because Germany is a great country and frightening because there is a similar element at work in this country. It worries me a great deal.'

Sensing that it was hardly the occasion to be drawn into

a debate on the merits of the National Socialist German Workers' Party, von Menen said nothing, yet his reticence did little to stifle the slant of the conversation.

'Perhaps I should warn you about my wife's brother, Filipe. Like me, he's spent some time in Germany, but for entirely different reasons. The truth is, Filipe and I are separated by many different things, none more so than politics. He favours the politics of the extreme right.' The word "extreme" hung on his lips like a menacing black cloud. 'When he realises who you are, he will, I suspect, engage you in a deep, endless discussion about the values and attributes of the Nazi Party, not to mention the Italian fascists. I tell you this because he will be here tomorrow evening… en route from Mendoza to Buenos Aires.'

'Your brother-in-law,' said von Menen, as they made towards the dining room, 'what line of business is he in?'

'He's a colonel in the army, mixes with a pack of elitist officers who call themselves the GOU… *Grupo de Oficiales Unidos*, a bunch of politicised army officers, hell-bent on changing the whole political outlook in Argentina.' Javier Gomez smiled. 'The irony is,' he continued, 'none of us are supposed to know anything about it.'

'Changing the whole political outlook in favour of… what?'

'More State control and less democracy, if I know Filipe.'

A colonel in the GOU, and he'll be here tomorrow night. Interesting.

The Gomezes displayed a gracious, charming hospitality. Throughout the rest of the evening there was a conspicuous absence of any reference to the conflict in Europe, which von Menen attributed to the subtlety of Maria's mother.

Whilst she and Maria indulged him with the offerings from a table groaning with food and wine, Señor Gomez served up an educational insight into Argentina's last fifty years, from the "golden" twilight period of the nineteenth century to the more recent, turbulent years of the great depression.

'Argentina is a country of missed opportunities,' he told von Menen. 'It lacks a real sense of identity. The pitiful thing is, whilst soldiers play at being politicians and real politicians succumb to the temptation of fraud and corruption, we're never likely to gain one.'

Saturday evening arrived in grand style – an eight-piece orchestra, enough flunkies to staff the Hotel Plaza in Buenos Aires and more food and wine than any sane person could visualise.

Hair piled up in a mass of elaborate curls, Maria was at her stunning best in a peplos-style dress of sapphire blue.

'You're driving me to despair,' said von Menen, speaking through the corner of his mouth.

'Really?' she whispered.

'Yes, *really*. If I had my way, I'd...'

'You'd what?' she teased, waving to a lady in a black chiffon dress.

He nodded to the couch in the far corner. 'Well, I'd... to the stars and back.'

'To the stars *and* back? My, that is a long way. We'd...' – she halted, proffered another feigned smile at the lady in black and continued – 'best start first thing tomorrow morning, then. What say we ride out to the halfway house, at the head of the valley; it's where we used to have our summer picnics.' She smiled mischievously. 'Well, now we've sorted that out, I really ought to go and speak to Daddy's guests.'

The evening was one of elegance and sophistication, the guests numbering sixty, at least, including the stylish Señor Valquez and his beautiful young wife, Teresa, resplendent in an Andalucian-style dress of black and fiery red. They looked strictly flamenco, yet their display of the tango, with its sudden pauses and long gliding steps, was unmistakeably Argentine!

By the fireplace stood a man with the glow of importance: tall, slim, suave and athletic-looking; impeccable, almost artificial, in a white tuxedo, black silk tie and shoes so shiny they lit up the floor in front of him. Distant from the rest, he held an unflinching poise, his charcoal hair swept back from his forehead without a trace of a parting. He looked like a matinee idol and, as if nothing else seemed to matter, his narrow, suspicious eyes were fixed firmly on the young German diplomat in the far corner.

Colonel Filipe Vidal moved with the bearing of a cavalry officer, stiff, purposeful and imbued with pride, head held high, long wedge-shaped chin preceding all else.

'Carl, isn't it?' he asked.

'Yes,' replied von Menen, with erroneous surprise.

'Allow me… I'm Colonel Filipe Vidal, Maria's uncle.' Vidal's smile was discreet and cautious, his voice unhurried, each word exact, every syllable measured.

'I'm pleased to meet you, Colonel.'

Vidal palmed away the formality. 'Please, call me Filipe.'

A waiter stopped and offered him a glass of champagne. Vidal took a meagre sip, explored and played with the taste, then finally gave his approval. 'They know I only drink Dom Pérignon,' he said. 'It's the only decent thing *not* to come out of Germany. By that, of course, I mean Germany proper.'

If he has a genealogical link with Germany, it has to be Joachim von Ribbentrop.

'Maria tells me that you both came over from Europe on the same ship,' Vidal continued in his measured manner.

'Yes, we met after embarking at Lisbon.'

'You're German, I understand.'

'Yes.'

'From?'

'A small village north of Schwerin.'

'Ah, Schwerin, seat of the ducal Court of Mecklenburg... until the end of the Great War, that is... and you're an attaché at the German Embassy in Buenos Aires?'

'Second Secretary, actually.'

'Your first time out of Germany?'

'With the Diplomatic Corps, yes.'

'And what are your immediate impressions of Argentina?'

'It's a wonderful country. I like it very much.'

'Good, I'm pleased to hear it.' Vidal moved a little closer. 'Mark my words,' he muttered, 'it's going to get much better. One day it will be the equal of Germany.'

'Have you visited Germany?' enquired von Menen, knowing fine well that he had.

'Yes, in 1935. I spent twelve months there; a kind of military fact-finding mission, if you like.'

'You were impressed?'

'Very. I came back with lots of new and interesting ideas.'

'That's very reassuring.'

'And you, Carl? Ever do any soldiering?'

'Yes, I served with the 8th Infantry Regiment.'

'Interesting,' mused Vidal. 'Used to be commanded by Erwin von Witzleben, now one of your illustrious field marshals.'

'Seems you know quite a lot about the German army, Filipe.'

'It's a passion of mine. I hold the German army in very high esteem,' enthused Vidal.

The rarity I've been praying for?

They drifted towards the far side of the room, a swastika blazing eagerly in each of Vidal's eyes. 'Would you mind if we had a more meaningful talk, Carl?' he asked, ushering von Menen into the seclusion of the library.

'Of course not.'

'Splendid.'

Vidal cast a furtive glance around and pushed the door closed. 'Look,' he said, laying a friendly hand on von Menen's arm, 'I'd like you to know, Carl, that I have a great deal of respect and admiration for Germany's achievements. I and many of my colleagues find the current trend in your country very appealing. There's a lot we can learn from Germany.' He fixed a wary eye on the door and shook his head. 'Unfortunately, Maria's father doesn't share my sentiments. He's a nice enough man, but politically, he's completely out of touch. And from the *military* point of view, well,' Vidal shrugged and chuckled, 'he's got no idea at all.'

'I don't know where all this is leading, Filipe, but I'm afraid military matters in Germany are not my concern. I'm sure you appreciate that.'

'Of course I do, but it's not the military side of things I find important, not at the moment anyway. I'm more concerned with what drives the ideology, you know, the strategy, the general scheme of things.' He walked over to the window, hands behind his back, stopped and turned. 'When Hitler came to power, Germany was all but on her knees, but look at her now... the most triumphant army the world has seen, occupying, or influencing, practically the whole of Europe. She controls virtually every square mile of the North Atlantic and now she's in the process of colonising Russia. And to think, Hitler has achieved all of that in less than nine years! How?'

'Perhaps you should read the Führer's book, *Mein Kampf*,' suggested von Menen, hiding his cynicism.

'I have, several times, but rather than *read*, I'd prefer to *learn*, from someone who has a genuine feel for the wider, conceptual scheme of things, someone who understands the… shall we say… long-term plan of the German leadership?'

'Surely you don't mean me?' said von Menen, pointing a finger at himself.

'Why not? You know what's going on in Germany.'

'Of course I do, and I'm happy to discuss the events as I see them, but you must understand I am not party to any wide-reaching ideas that the German leadership may, or may not, have.'

'Yes, yes; but we shouldn't suppose that we can't mix and match a little, you know, meet now and again, exchange views and opinions.'

'Well, I'd certainly have no objection to that.'

Vidal moved towards the door, then paused. 'Good,' he said. 'But I think we should keep our little *arrangement* to ourselves. It would be most unwise of you to call me at the Ministry.'

Von Menen's eyes widened to the size of dinner plates. 'The… Ministry?' he ventured.

'Yes, the War Ministry… It would be prudent if my brother-in-law didn't know about our meetings, either. Don't you think?'

'In that case, maybe Maria should remain unawares, too.'

'Fond of her, are you?'

'Yes, I suppose I am.'

'In that case, let's keep it between the two of us. I'll

have a messenger deliver a personal note to you at the Embassy.'

'And if I'm not there?'

Vidal smiled. 'Simple; he'll keep trying until you are.'

Von Menen returned to Buenos Aires the following Tuesday, feeling like the cat who'd just eaten the cream and was only a whisker away from catching the fattest pigeon in the park. His relationship with Maria was assured, her parents had accepted him and Colonel Filipe Vidal seemed the needle in the haystack he'd thought he would never find.

His immediate concern now was his need to establish a "safe" house. *'Rent or buy, it doesn't matter. Just make sure that nobody knows about it, not even the Ambassador.'* Werner's directive had been playing on his mind since the moment he'd set foot in Argentina, von Menen's disquiet heightening daily by the systematic vigilance of the Policia de la Capital, a lack of personal transport, the "scent" of Jost and the seemingly unfathomable question of – *where?*

Buenos Aires was a big city with fine thoroughfares and grand boulevards, but elsewhere in Argentina it was very different. Autobahns did not exist, paved highways were scarce and metalled secondary roads were as rare as sheep with wings, as he'd discovered to the base of his jolted spine along the daunting washboard dirt roads of rural Córdoba.

His search began at a bookstore on Florida.

'Going somewhere interesting, señor?' asked the young assistant.

'Perhaps,' replied von Menen, unfolding a linen-backed map he'd plucked from a shelf in the "travel" section. 'This road,' he said, leading the young man's eye along a bold red line stretching from Buenos Aires. 'Is it paved?'

'All the way to the coast, señor.'

'And this one?' enquired von Menen, his finger on a thin black line.

'A dirt road, señor.'

'Passable by car?'

'Sometimes, depends on the weather... After a heavy downpour, it turns into glutinous mud, and when that happens you have to take the coach. But it's been fairly dry recently, so you might be lucky.'

'You seem to know the area well.'

'My grandfather lives nearby.'

'Hotels?'

'Some. But don't expect too much.'

The next day, von Menen found a letter waiting for him at the Banco de la Nación.

My apologies, Carl, but I must postpone our next meeting – I'm needed at the University of La Plata.
Keep in touch. Franz.

Von Menen headed home, stopping at the vendor by the Hotel Plaza to buy an armful of newspapers, hoping that one of them might hold at least part of the solution to his "safe house" quandary.

Flicking through the newspapers in the safety of his apartment, the classified pages of the *Buenos Aires Herald* held a glimmer of hope:

Ford T 79 shooting brake. $750. Must sell. Owner returning to US. Please ring...

He got up and looked through the window. The Studebaker was back, parked overtly in Arenales. Von Menen cursed at its presence and cursed further at the hazy silhouette beyond it. He fetched out his Zeiss binoculars, scanned the fringes of Plaza San Martín and sharpened up the image as the focus converged on the equestrian statue of General San Martín – a fat cigar, a slight frame and straw-coloured hair. Jost was "on duty" and he was as obvious as a Mexican red-headed parrot in Svalbard.

Von Menen's doubts were stacking up, his meeting with Schröder at *Il Pellicano* and the professor's suspicions playing heavily on his mind. Perhaps it hadn't been the police outside the restaurant after all. Maybe he *had* been followed, by someone much smarter than he'd thought – Jost!

His thoughts turned to the handwritten note he'd collected from the Banco de la Nación, wondering if someone else had written it, knowing that he had nothing to compare it with; the scribbled note bearing the address of *Il Pellicano* which Schröder had given him on their first meeting long since burned in the kitchen sink.

An anxiety hung deep in his stomach. Had Schröder *really* gone to La Plata?

Grabbing a wad of dollars from the safe at the rear of the wardrobe, von Menen raced down the staircase, fled the block by the tradesmen's entrance and headed straight for the telephone kiosk in the lobby of the Phoenix Hotel.

'Faculty of Law, University of Buenos Aires.'

'Sorry to bother you,' said von Menen, 'but I've missed a tutorial and I have a problem with some revision. Professor Schröder wouldn't happen to be around, would he?'

'Afraid not. He left for a meeting at the University of La Plata this morning and won't be back until next Monday.'

Drained and exhausted, von Menen almost slid to the floor with relief. Gathering his thoughts, he rang off, then called the number he'd taken from the *Buenos Aires Herald*.

Two hours and $750 later, a friendly and relieved American handed von Menen the keys to a black Ford T79 shooting brake.

Von Menen turned out the lights and peered through the curtains. It had rained during the early hours, a full moon reflecting an eerie sheen across the silent streets of Buenos Aires. There was no sign of the Studebaker and it pleased him to think that there'd been no sign of it for the last forty-eight hours. He picked up his bag, crept slowly down the stairs and set off at a brisk pace along Esmeralda.

Fifteen minutes later, the black station wagon edged up the ramp from the parking lot, nosed into North Alem and headed for the southern reaches of the city.

Downtown Buenos Aires was still sleeping, but as von Menen crossed the Riachuelo River, the slaughterhouses and meat-packing factories of Avellaneda were at full tilt, throbbing to the tune of despair and misery. He grimaced at the sight of it, stamped on the throttle and left the poverty and stench behind him.

After three days of searching, a chance conversation led von Menen to a holiday cottage 300 kilometres from Buenos Aires and a short drive from the ocean. The cottage was a short distance from the main compound of a large *estancia*, the location of which was remote. There was no electricity, but the transceiver could be powered by a six-volt car battery.

The manager, a likeable man, explained that the owners, Señor and Señora Braganza, spent much of their time in Buenos Aires. They had been trying to let the place for months. It was copiously furnished, had a fully-equipped kitchen, and linen could be provided at extra cost. Von Menen agreed on a renewable six-month lease and drove back to Buenos Aires.

Two days later, he returned to the cottage and unpacked the necessities. He adjourned to the drawing room, lit a roaring log fire and settled down to encrypt his message, recalling what Werner had told him: *'No extraneous rubbish. And remember the security code.'*

Darkness closed in, the minutes ticking by, a fierce wind gusting through the trees. When the clock struck ten, von Menen closed the curtains, lit three oil lamps and took two of them upstairs, returning to fetch the radio and the six-volt battery he'd bought from a garage in Buenos Aires. Connecting the battery, he bailed out the antenna, fixed it around the picture rail, tuned in the aerial and watched excitedly as the needle on the aerial current meter flicked to full power.

His message was waiting beside the "send" key. He was waiting, too, listening to the strange gurgling sound of the hot water system, eyes riveted to his watch, the luminous minute hand almost talking to him. As it nudged towards the full hour, 23h00, he reached for the Morse key, not forgetting the security code.

Attention... General Call... This is MEC9... End of Transmission... Go Ahead.

Switching to the listening section, he swept for a response, ears straining for the faintest bleep. Nothing. He tried a second time, a third, a fourth and then...

At the German Foreign Office's wireless relay station in Madrid, Albert Falk was in his sixth hour of duty when suddenly his hearing sharpened, his eyes narrowed and his pencil began dancing to the strained Morse bleeps of MEC9.

A moment later, relief swept across von Menen's face, the feeble staccato sound of his own call sign singing in his ears. Albert Falk was "talking" to him.

Joy o'joy, the miracle of Samuel Morse.

Von Menen's encrypted message was clear and concise:

SAFE HOUSE ESTABLISHED.
AKROBAT

By midnight, the transceiver and the rest of the radio equipment was lying beneath the kitchen floorboards, the encrypted message and expended one-time pad consigned to the fire.

The next day, von Menen was back in Buenos Aires, the shooting brake hidden in the basement lot on North Alem. The car and the cottage would remain an eternal secret. No one, not even Maria, would ever know about them.

6

The Embassy's receptionist sounded very uneasy.

'My apologies, Herr von Menen, but there's a boy downstairs, says he must speak to you urgently, something about a letter. I did try—'

'That's okay, Ilsa, I'll be right down.'

A young man in a reddish-purple tunic and matching pork pie hat was waiting in the foyer.

'Looking for me?' asked von Menen.

'Si, señor, the man who looks like a boxer.' Von Menen smiled as the young man handed him an envelope. 'The señor at the Alvear Palace Hotel said to give it to no one but you.'

The note was short and precise:

Meet me at Café Tortoni, nine o'clock tonight. Use the entrance on Avenida 25 de Mayo and go straight to the last private alcove on the left, past the main bar. F.V.

Café Tortoni was pure Buenos Aires: lively and noisy, an ambience of marble columns, dark wood panels, elaborate mirrors, faded theatre-red, and the evocative sound of the tango, riding on a haze of tobacco smoke and loud conversation.

Von Menen found the alcove, tapped on the panel at the side and peeked through the curtain. Vidal was alone, immaculate in a sombre grey suit.

'Welcome, Carl. Please, take a seat.'

Von Menen's eyes fell upon the bottle of Dom Pérignon sprouting from an ice bucket.

'Join me?' asked Vidal, nodding at the bottle.

'Thank you, that's very kind.'

Vidal charged two glasses, watched the foam disperse and smiled as the bubbles swam to the surface. 'Cheers, Carl... Champagne of the Greater German Reich.'

'Greater German Reich?'

'Joke of mine – you know, Germany's defeat of France? Anyway, please excuse the manner in which I got you here, but this city is full of people who not only *aspire* to being English, but actually think they *are* English. It's the same throughout Argentina.'

'You're referring to your brother-in-law?'

'Not necessarily, but since you mentioned it, Javier does like everything British... The House of Windsor, Winston Churchill, the whole damn gamut.'

'Whereas you...?'

'Despise them?' Vidal shook his head, his curious gaze softening to a weak smile. 'A man should never bear hatred, Carl. Even if he does, he should never avow to it. Besides, we Argentinians have a great deal to thank the British for: commerce, banks, railroads, electric power, water... everything.'

'But I suspect that you'd like to have a *great deal* to thank Germany for, too.' Vidal's sardonic chuckle incited von Menen further. 'Well, wouldn't you?'

'Eventually I hope we'll have *every* reason to thank Germany. This time next year, perhaps there won't be a Britain to be thankful *to*.'

'You think it will come to that?'

'I'd say it's a distinct possibility. Britain might be consoled by the thought of Germany's apparent inactivity in Western Europe, but when Hitler is done with Russia, well, then it will be different. Anyway, we can talk about that later. For the moment, I'd like to be assured that you're enjoying your stay here.'

'Yes, very much.'

'Especially now that you can move around more freely?'

The question sent a tingle up von Menen's spine. *The car? The cottage?* 'What do you mean, "more freely"?'

Vidal leaned forward, his finger beckoning von Menen's ear. 'Your two companions, in the blue Studebaker,' he said. 'This is Argentina, Carl. I'm a full colonel. I have influence. Besides, I want this little arrangement of ours to remain strictly private.'

'It's helpful that you should have such influence,' said von Menen, hiding his surprise. 'Being watched is one thing, being followed is positively predatory.'

The noise grew louder, the smoke denser, Vidal revealing a discerning, imaginative character: serious, but not lacking in humour. When he was serious, his voice sparkled with calculated reasoning, forceful ambition and strong opinion. When he was humorous, he was clever with it and while he was anything but self-effacing, he was not the egotist von Menen had labelled him following their meeting at the Gomez ranch.

But his obsession for all things German was infinite, his fanaticism passionate. Like Hitler, he wanted a regime of unfailing loyalty and unquestioned obedience, though strangely enough, he did not share Hitler's obsession for the persecution of the Jews.

'The Jews have a lot to contribute,' he argued, 'provided they do not impede the progress of Argentina's destiny... On the other hand, communists, homosexuals and those of an extended liberal persuasion, well, they're a different matter.'

Vidal's enthusiasm chaffed at the very core of what von Menen stood for, but he listened all the same, and he listened because he *had* to listen. Vidal wouldn't stop. He lauded Hitler's achievements, vented a phobic dislike for Stalin, questioned the competence of Churchill and poured scorn upon the Americans. Yet his perception of the wider concept of things – politically, socially and economically – was well-balanced and eloquently argued, and in that sense he *sounded* very impressive. But so, thought von Menen, had Hitler in 1933. And Vidal wanted big strides for his country, too: military power, social and economic reform and an education system that would be the envy of the world.

'What we have at the moment,' he argued, 'is an economy dictated by people who see their vast tracts of land, and the profit they derive from it, as the only commodity Argentina has to offer. We have to change that. We need to industrialise this nation, build our own cars and trucks, locomotives, ships and planes.' All of this Vidal saw through the ideology of National Socialism, an ideology that would ignite in Buenos Aires and burn across the whole of Argentina with such intense ferocity that eventually the whole of South America would dissolve into one dominion – 'the Argentine Empire!' He wasn't impatient for it, either. 'Deliberate and cautious, Carl,' he kept saying. 'We have no reason to be hasty.'

'From what you have told me this evening, Filipe, I get the distinct impression that you would wish to endear yourself to Germany in a more *positive* fashion?'

'I don't think Argentina would ever endear or attach herself to any one state, Carl, not in the complete sense. We have no intention of losing our sovereignty or our independence. Certainly not. What I have in mind at the moment is some form of *unofficial* liaison with Berlin. It would have to be very discreet, of course, and I would have to remain entirely anonymous, for the time being, at least. I'm sure you understand that.' Vidal reached for another bottle of champagne, which had appeared through the curtain as if by magic. 'What I'm trying to say, Carl, is that we, in the military, would wish your government to know just how much we admire Germany's accomplishments; in fact, we would like to see a similar direction in Argentina. That's what I'm saying.'

'A change of administration?'

'In time, yes, but as I said earlier, there's no reason to be hasty.'

'But you mean a form of National Socialism.'

'Of course.'

'Endorsed by the GOU?' suggested von Menen, with candid perception.

Vidal smiled sardonically. 'It doesn't necessarily have to be that way, but if that's what it takes. You see, it's all a matter of conviction. If we can convince the people of Argentina that this country is capable of accomplishing great things, as it surely is, and that every Argentine will benefit from its achievement, as they surely will, then there's no reason why democracy shouldn't prevail.'

'But, Filipe, you're talking about the *ascendancy* of National Socialism. For that to succeed you need a significant power base. Where will you find it? Not from the landowners or the industrialists, that's for sure.'

'Out there, Carl,' replied Vidal, gesturing with his glass, 'there are millions of people who want a share of the spoils of this country. They have a vote, yes, but it's rarely reckoned with, not in the way *they* would choose, anyway. That's because there's too much chicanery. We have to deal with that, sweep away the corruption and the dishonesty, give the people a *real* vote. The rest is simple. If we can win *their* trust, National Socialism in this country will have found its power base, the mightiest political power base Argentina has ever seen. Many think it's just a pipe dream, including some of my colleagues, but believe me, one day it *will* happen.'

Staring at the ice bucket, von Menen leaned back in his chair, his face full of quandary.

'Something worrying you, Carl?' asked Vidal.

'I'm just a little perplexed, that's all.'

'About a man's ambition for his country?'

'No, about your confidence in *me*.'

Vidal pulled himself forward, leaned across the table and laid his hand on von Menen's arm. 'There's a reason for that, Carl,' he said softly. 'You see, I want you to be the key to the liaison I spoke about.'

'Me!'

Vidal's face was ablaze with awareness. 'Yes, you; it *is* why you're here, isn't it?'

'But, Filipe, I'm merely a Second Secretary. I'm not the German Ambassador.'

'My dear Carl, you don't paint a very flattering picture of yourself.' Vidal sat back in his chair, folded his arms, a relishing glint in his eyes, his face full of knowing. 'Perhaps I should remind you of who you *really* are… You are an agent of the German Foreign Office, an agent of von Ribbentrop's Information Department Three. And you have been sent here *specifically* to assess the proactive viability of certain elements in Argentina, elements sympathetic to the Axis cause. Oh, and something else…' Vidal paused, took stock of the disquieted look on von Menen's face and poured another two glasses of champagne. 'I'm also aware that you are not a member of the Nazi Party. But that doesn't concern me. As for your father, *"not so distinguished"*? That *is* what you told my niece, isn't it?' Von Menen's eyes were back on the ice bucket. 'Your father may be modest in some directions, Carl, but come now, he's *very* distinguished… a military genius. I admire him immensely. I suspect you do, too.'

Von Menen felt paralysed from the neck down, his breathing shallow, his eyes closed. Vidal knew far too much, and now, in what seemed like a state of suspended animation, he was waiting for the rest of it.

Vidal shot forward, lauding von Menen's silence, smiling like a man who had check-mated his opponent for the tenth consecutive time. 'Don't look so sullen, Carl. There's no point in denying it. Just think about it for a moment… Germany has an intelligence operation in Argentina and Argentina has something similar in Germany, although on a much smaller scale, I agree. But they both serve the same purpose – to focus on people with weaknesses. It's an accepted fact. We know it is, so let's be realistic… Let's be honest with ourselves.' Vidal jabbed his finger repeatedly at the table. 'Listen, I know for a fact that there are certain people in Germany who doubt Hitler's political wisdom. There are some who doubt his ability to win the war, even.'

A veiled reference to the Kreisau Circle?

A lump rose in von Menen's throat. Suddenly, he was alive again, anxiety ripping through his body. 'I'm not sure what you mean, Filipe.'

'Look, Carl,' said Vidal, almost climbing over the table, 'I have personally authorised the issue of over fifty Argentine passports to people in the German government, many of them senior Nazis, some of them members of the German Foreign Office. Perhaps you're familiar with one of them,' he said teasingly, 'Doctor Alfred Wehmen?'

Shocked to the soles of his Eduard Meier shoes, von Menen's eyes lit up like searchlights. He could scarcely believe his ears.

The conceited, double-dealing fat bastard.

'You see, Carl, I knew all about you even before you set foot in Argentina. That you happened to meet Maria was just a coincidence, although a very welcome one. It saved me the trouble of having to look for you.'

Resigned to the inevitable, von Menen held up his hands. 'I don't doubt your idea would make my life a lot easier, Filipe, but I'm at a loss to understand why you have picked me, when there are others at the Embassy who are much better equipped to deal with such matters.'

'By that, I presume you mean one of the military attachés, or perhaps one of Heydrich's lot?' scoffed Vidal.

Von Menen's neck sank into his shoulders. 'Why not?'

'Carl, I wouldn't touch the Abwehr if they were the only German organisation this side of the Atlantic. I met Canaris in 1935 in Berlin. He's as slippery as an eel. He didn't impress me at all. As for that other lot,' he grimaced, '*dense* isn't the word. I don't suppose they've got a single matriculation certificate between them.' Vidal thumped the table, his features hardening. 'No! This is a political matter. It requires someone with a real sense of diplomacy, someone with acumen, someone I can trust.' He spoke as if it were a matter of providence, as if von Menen had no choice in the matter. 'I cannot afford any mistakes, and more importantly, I cannot afford any leaks.'

Von Menen's attention on the ice bucket remained absolute.

Vidal rocked back in his chair and fixed him with a long, hard gaze. 'I'm giving you what von Ribbentrop wants, aren't I? The fact that I know *who* you are and *why* you're here doesn't concern me.' He held out his hands in treaty. 'There's no catch. I'm not asking your government for anything – other than, perhaps, some kind of sympathetic, moral support. Think of it as a matter of...' the word was dancing on the tip of his tongue, evading him, almost irritating him.

'Expedience?'

'Yes, expedience. It's appropriate, an arrangement that fits our individual circumstances, wouldn't you say? Anyway, another glass of champagne... *Salud!*'

The chink of glass resounded in von Menen's ears like the cry of Jonah.

★

'You didn't give me much time, Carl,' said Schröder, pulling a notebook from his jacket pocket. Von Menen wondered if it was the same biscuit-coloured jacket he'd worn at *Il Pellicano*, or whether he had a wardrobe full of them.

'Yes, sorry about that, Franz, but I drew a blank at the National Library and since it's rather urgent...'

'Mine is not to reason why, Carl. You don't have to tell me anything. In truth, I'd rather not know. It's best that way. Anyway, the profile you asked me for: Filipe Hernando Vidal, a colonel in the Argentine army, born 1887 in Buenos Aires, son of an army general who died about twenty years ago. His mother, of French extraction, died last year.' Squinting at his near-illegible handwriting, Schröder peeled back the next page of his notebook. 'Seems he's a very bright man... Graduated from the University of Buenos Aires in 1912, double-first in economics and law... Enlisted in the army six months later. The following year he was wedded to Isobella Stern.'

'Stern? Jewish?' queried von Menen.

'Yes, a very prominent family in Buenos Aires.'

Interesting. 'The Jews have a lot to contribute...'

'Is it relevant?' asked Schröder.

'In the sense that it explains a somewhat puzzling line of thinking, yes.'

'Anyway, her father, Joshua Stern, is still alive, heads the

102

family business, a merchant bank in Buenos Aires.'

'Children? Vidal, I mean?'

'One, a son; he works for his grandfather. Family-wise, there's not much more I can tell you, other than the fact that Vidal's sister is married to Professor Javier Gomez, an eminent surgeon. He lectures at the Faculty of Medicine in Buenos Aires. As for Vidal himself, well, seems to be a scholarly individual, astute and very shrewd... Something of a radical during his university days, so one of my colleagues told me, and he should know – he and Vidal studied economics together.' Schröder scrolled further down his notepad, a glint in his eye.

'There's more,' intuited von Menen.

'Yes... the GOU, the organisation we spoke about previously?

'Go on.'

'My colleague says it's got Vidal's thinking stamped all over it; that is, the thinking of the Vidal he knew over thirty years ago. While others might be driving it forward, he wouldn't be surprised if Vidal was giving the directions.'

'And at fifty-four he's still only a colonel. Why?'

'Given his intellect, I suppose the logical answer to that question is that he's too clever by far; probably frightens the likes of General Justo to death. Anyway, where politics are concerned, particularly of the extreme kind, there's invariably a significant, sometimes anonymous, figure behind the scenes. In the GOU, perhaps that figure is Vidal.'

'I wonder just how radical is he?' mused von Menen.

'There's certainly no evidence of extremism,' said Schröder. 'He seems happily married, leads a very sedate life and keeps himself to himself.'

'That's not to say that there isn't a more sinister element to his character.'

'Absolutely. You only need look at some elements of the

Nazi Party for proof of that – von Ribbentrop, to name but one.'

'So, he's an intellect, he's inventive, he's wealthy and he's happily married; there's no sign of impropriety, no evidence of *extreme* radicalism and he prefers to take a back seat.'

'I'd say that's a fair appraisal,' agreed Schröder.

'Meaning his attributes don't mark him out as a fast-track political reformer?'

'Either that or he's got the constructive ingenuity of a beaver, the silent cunning of a fox and the composure of a stalking lion, patiently—'

'Biding his time for the right moment?'

'Or living a life of misplaced optimism.'

'Perhaps, but whichever way you look at it, he's obviously nobody's fool.'

Like the last of the winter snow in a warm Alpine meadow, von Menen's doubts were dispersing fast. If Vidal's ideology were a true reflection of what was really fermenting within the ranks of the GOU, then the dark clouds of revolution were gathering above Argentina again.

The question was: when would the storm clouds break? Two years at most, thought von Menen, which is precisely what he committed to paper.

★

'So, von Menen, you have been here barely two months and in that short space of time you *think* you have acquired sufficient knowledge to envision the destiny of Argentina?' sneered the Ambassador. 'I hope you have not based this…' – he paused, nodded at von Menen's report – 'ridiculous judgement of yours *solely* on the whims and aspirations of this GOU organisation. You'll need more evidence than that.'

Von Menen gestured towards the window. 'The evidence is out there, sir,' he said calmly. 'It's all around us.'

'*You* might believe that, but what you're suggesting is damn preposterous. This man, Perón, for example, he's only been back in the country a short while… I mean, what credentials does he have?' He frowned at von Menen's report. 'A revolution? Within two years? Give the country to the proletariat? Share the wealth? Good God, man, it's impossible.'

Von Menen's eyes fell on a small bronze casting of a pedigree Friesian bull standing proudly in the middle of the Ambassador's desk. A gift from some German ex-patriot, no doubt.

'This country is *owned* by a select few,' the Ambassador continued, 'and that select few will *never* allow this to happen.' His hand fell sharply upon von Menen's report.

'I appreciate what you are saying, sir, but it *is* my opinion and I'm standing by it.'

The Ambassador picked up his pen, wavered a second and finally added his signature. 'Know this, von Menen. Having read your report, I have no option other than to sign it, but I do so with grave misgivings. You are ploughing a very lonely furrow. In two years' time I don't doubt that you will be standing before me receiving another well-deserved admonishment – *before* being shipped back to Germany. Good day to you.'

★

With Maria still in Córdoba, von Menen was fated to endure another lonely Sunday lunch in downtown Buenos Aires – two hours spent gazing through the window of a tiny café on Florida, listening to the gurgling "music" of a Gaggia coffee machine and the background lyrics of Bing Crosby's "Only Forever".

At first, he could scarcely believe his eyes. He turned, shook his head, waited a second, and then looked again. But it was no apparition. Jost was sitting in the window of the restaurant opposite, his companion large and affectionate, mountainous bosoms almost halfway across the table, challenging the salt cellar, a picture of sweet perfection.

Von Menen choked on his espresso. At one metre seventy and barely ten stone, the wiry Jost would need scaffolding, ropes, pulleys and another serving of grilled beef to meet the challenge of the woman sitting opposite him, about whom there was a certain familiarity.

Suddenly, it dawned – a crocodile skin wallet, a matching hip flask and a chest the size of the Matterhorn. Ana Pradera had found her next eager man.

Von Menen finished his coffee, put on his hat, pulled down the brim and sneaked out onto Florida, a plan fermenting in his mind.

Apart from the doorman snoring heavily beneath a sheet of newsprint, the Embassy was empty. Upstairs, the door to the shared Gestapo/SD office was unlocked.

Von Menen crept inside, sat down before Müller's Adler and allowed his imagination to run wild:

Dear Señora Pradera,

Saw you in Harrods the other day... Noted the name on your blouse... Thought perhaps you might like to join me for dinner, take in a show. Please give me a call on...

Yours, Heinz Müller

Next, he typed out the envelope – *Private and Personal: For the attention of Ana Pradera, c/o Harrods Department Store, Calle Florida, Buenos Aires.* Sealing the envelope, he placed it in the Gestapo out tray, knowing that Jost, by habit, would beat Müller to the Embassy on Monday morning.

Von Menen arrived at the Embassy at seven-thirty, Jost a half-hour later. Müller followed at nine. Within minutes, the row of all rows erupted along the corridor; two raging stags locked in a cage with a doe on heat, spit, accusations and denials flying in all directions, the maelstrom carrying through the entire building.

'Look, I'll prove it!' screamed Jost. Von Menen caught the sound of a typewriter, the *click, click* of keys, followed by the whine of the platen as the paper was snatched from the machine. 'Look, it's *your* damn typewriter, Müller, no mistake about it!' Von Menen couldn't see it, but the real fireworks began when Jost tore open the envelope and read the script.

Then came the pleading voice of Müller: 'But...'

'No *buts*!' yelled Jost. 'I warn you, stay clear!'

The cacophony brought down the Naval Attaché, the First Secretary and finally the Ambassador himself.

Von Menen smiled, walked nonchalantly past the mayhem and out into the street below. *Thank you, Müller.*

★

At the end of September, Maria arrived from Córdoba, moved into an apartment near Plaza Lavalle and settled into a regime of long hours at the Hospital de Clínicas, with few days off.

Von Menen, meanwhile, maintained his bi-weekly meetings with Schröder, made frequent trips to the safe house and developed a burgeoning rapport with Vidal.

By the end of November, Vidal had become increasingly concerned by events in the Pacific.

'The Americans are very jittery about the threat of Japanese expansion,' he told von Menen, during a lunch-time meeting at the Jockey Club. 'I'm fearful that they won't stand for it much longer.'

'I agree, Filipe; a military conflict between Japan and the United States would have devastating repercussions.'

'Worse than that, my friend. My sources in London say that Churchill has already given a commitment that if Japan goes to war against America, Great Britain will declare war against Japan. If that happens, Germany will inevitably declare war on America, with obvious consequences: Roosevelt will put immense pressure on Central and South America to reject the Axis coalition and break off diplomatic relations with Germany. He might even insist that they declare war against her, which would place a huge question mark over Argentina's relationship. You might care to think about that, Carl.'

A few days later, news vendors throughout Buenos Aires were bellowing the message that neither von Menen nor Vidal wanted to hear. 'The Japs have bombed Honolulu! The Japs have bombed Honolulu!'

The international situation quickly became a depressing, chaotic mess. Britain and the United States were at war with the Axis partners, Russia was at war with Germany, Hitler was at war with the whole damn world and Argentina was in conflict with… herself!

Vidal watched in horror as the states of Central America folded to the power of the US dollar and declared war on Germany. Much to his relief, though, South America held firm, in spite of Roosevelt's threats. Von Menen saw an immediate change in Vidal's thinking, his hitherto cautious approach replaced by a compelling urgency: 'I'm going to give you the GOU's entire agenda,' he informed von Menen. 'Make sure that it reaches Hitler. And do not, under any circumstances, divulge your source, otherwise our arrangement is finished.'

Vidal remained as fanatical about his own anonymity as he was about his belief in the GOU, or his unwillingness to discuss Perón. He sought no favours and demanded nothing, except trust and secrecy, and in that sense his motives remained a complete enigma to von Menen. But von Menen played along with it, if only to satisfy the appetite of von Ribbentrop, whose enthusiastic praise for *his* agent in Argentina had caused the Ambassador in Buenos Aires to adopt a more mellow posture.

Jost, meanwhile, remained "lost" on the north face of Ana Pradera's bosom; Müller and Schmidt stepped back a pace and von Menen soaked up the freedom, enjoying the comfort of a small apartment near Plaza Lavalle, waiting, watching and keeping von Ribbentrop at arm's length.

7

Reinhard Heydrich was dead, assassinated in Prague by Czech agents. Von Menen was elated, yet the black armbands worn by Jost, Müller and Schmidt sent out a sobering warning. Sensing that his period of respite was about to end, he left his office, locked the door and stayed clear of the Embassy for the next four weeks.

The soil around Heydrich's grave had barely settled when a political earthquake thundered across the entire sub-continent of South America – Brazil declared war on Germany. Yet in spite of Berlin's anxiety, the Argentine government held firm.

Vidal stayed true to his word and his information kept flowing, without even a hint of an appeal for anything in return. Von Menen could not fathom it. *'Constructive ingenuity. Silent cunning. The composure of a stalking lion.'* Schröder's words kept ringing in his mind.

Some months later, Hitler's luck finally ran out – the German 6th Army collapsed before Stalingrad. The beginning of the end. A mood of defeat and bitterness swept across Germany and Hitler did not like it. Ernst Kaltenbrunner, appointed by Himmler to fill the vacant role of leader of the Reich Security Administration, soon got to work.

Von Menen's dormant anxieties about the Kreisau

Circle were back with a vengeance. They deepened when news arrived from Berlin that Pastor Dietrich Bonhoeffer had been detained by the Gestapo, and General Hans Oster, deputy head of the Abwehr and a confidant of Rudolph von Bauer, had been dismissed. At a hastily arranged meeting at *Il Pellicano*, he urged Schröder to be doubly vigilant.

A few weeks later, an urgent message was waiting for von Menen at the Banco de la Nación.

'Vital that we meet tonight, ten o'clock. PLEASE, make sure that you're not followed.'

Schröder had changed the venue to a bar two blocks up from *Il Pellicano*. Von Menen followed his usual, circuitous route: he changed cabs twice as far as Plaza Dorrego and completed the rest of his journey on foot.

Tailed by the murky shadows of night, he passed *Il Pellicano* on the far side of the road. The restaurant was closed, a black curtain draped inside the window, the backcloth to a framed picture, a crucifix and two flickering candles. A confusing scene of serenity and gloom. Von Menen slowed, checked his urge and flitted past like a moth in the night.

Schröder was sitting at a table in the far corner, his face like a weathered tombstone, solemn and expressionless.

'Franz?' enquired von Menen, stretching out the word. 'I've just passed *Il Pellicano*. What…?'

Schröder palmed away the question, opened up the late edition of *La Razón* and pushed it across the table.

Von Menen's eyes settled on the headlines, his face paling. 'Good God… When?'

'Six o'clock this morning. His father found him in the alley at the back of the restaurant.' Schröder heaved a deep sigh. 'He sent someone to the university to tell me early this morning.'

'I don't understand,' said von Menen. 'Why?'

'The politics of youth,' replied Schröder. 'He'd become more and more reactionary and, like many a decent Italian living in Argentina, he sensed that Germany and Italy were all but finished in North Africa and they might soon be done in Sicily. Giancarlo saw that as a new beginning for Italy and he made no secret of his views.' Schröder sighed again. 'He'd received several warnings. Anonymous, of course, though I suspect they came from the Italian Embassy.'

'But *killing* him. I—'

'The Italians have got their own answer to the Gestapo, Carl.' Schröder dipped into his pocket, pulled out a spent cartridge case and passed it to von Menen. 'Take a look.'

Von Menen studied the embossing around the base of the casing. 'Nine-millimetre... Definitely Italian.'

'Franco found it by the side of the boy's body.'

'Why didn't he hand it to the police?'

Schröder shook his head. 'Wouldn't be interested. They'll be happy enough that they've got one less radical to keep an eye on.'

Von Menen read the newspaper article again, a thought piercing his mind. He leaned forward, grabbed at Schröder's arm and shook it. 'Franz,' he said earnestly, 'I don't figure the Italians for that kind of thing, not in Argentina, anyway. But Jost, the man I warned you about, I haven't seen him in ages.'

'Meaning?'

Von Menen looked earnestly at Schröder. 'He's got every excuse, Franz. The Gestapo's tearing Germany apart at the moment. Remember Rudolph's friend, Oster? He's been dismissed. You've got to be careful. Believe me, Jost would have no scruples about killing you... Me, too, if he knew I'd been seeing you.'

'I was coming to that, Carl. *I've* been taking risks ever since Hitler came to power and I won't change. I won't be silenced, not now, not ever. But it's different for you. You *have* to keep your views secret. I don't like it, but I think we should stop meeting like this, at least until things improve.' A thin smile brushed across his face. 'That is, if ever they do improve.'

★

Thursday 6th May 1943

Maria took the early morning train to Córdoba, the arrangement being that von Menen would join her on the following Monday and they would return to Buenos Aires the next weekend. 'If anything changes, I'll leave a message for your father at the Hospital de Urgencias,' he told her.

Von Menen saw the headline as he walked into the daylight from Retiro Station: ANTI-NAZI FOUND DEAD. *La Nación* had the whole story:

Last night, Professor Franz Schröder, an outspoken critic of Hitler's regime, was found dead outside the door to his apartment in central Buenos Aires. Police say he was killed by a single gunshot wound to the head...

The colour drained from von Menen's cheeks, beads of sweat peppering his forehead, a knot of suspicion tightening in his stomach, Schröder's image running wild in his mind.

Jost, it can only be Jost.

Suddenly, Jost's face held a constant presence in his mind, a torturous core of terror. The guessing was over. Von Menen knew that the next bullet was heading for him.

He hastened across Avenida del Libertador, heart thumping, stride quickening, Schröder's face staring at him from every newspaper vendor's billboard. He felt like a man

113

on a fast train; the brakes had failed and the end of the line was looming up fast. *What to do? Where to hide?* He needed an answer and he needed it fast.

It came to him as he crossed into Maipu: he would go to Córdoba.

He turned on his heels, headed straight back to Retiro and booked an entire compartment on the night sleeper, leaving for Córdoba at five o'clock that evening.

Back at his apartment, he washed, changed, packed an overnight bag and spent the rest of the day by the drawing room window, eyes peeled for the faintest sign of the blond malevolent. He saw nothing.

At four o'clock, he departed the building by his usual route and headed straight for Retiro Station.

The knock on his compartment door grew steadily louder until the noise eventually woke him.

'Yes?' called von Menen.

A muffled voice.

Von Menen eased up the blind and peered through the window. A tall man, dark hair, a clipboard under his arm, his back to the door.

Von Menen pulled back the privacy catch. The figure spun round and the door flew open, a silenced pistol leading the way. Jost leapt down from the suitcase he'd used as a stool, booted it inside the compartment and threw the clipboard down on top of it.

'Quick, inside!' he ordered.

Not wont to argue with a gun, von Menen backed inside, heart beating at the cyclic rate of a machine gun.

'Stop!' barked Jost, footing the case to one side. 'Sit down.' Feeling behind his back, he slid the door shut and reset the catch. 'Swing your feet up, put your arms beneath your back and lie still.'

Von Menen did as ordered.

'Like it?' sneered Jost, his free hand tugging at the black hair piece.

'It's hideous… Black hair and blonde eyebrows? You look like a Friesian heifer.'

Jost struck von Menen's face with his left fist, a throbbing red patch rising on his cheek. 'You're in no position to joke, von Menen. Besides, whatever I look like, it got me this far.'

'I wouldn't argue with that,' said von Menen, wanting desperately to soothe his cheek, 'but the question is, *why* are you here?'

'I'm here because I can smell your kind a mile away. You're a resister, an anti-Nazi,' replied Jost, spite burning in his eyes, his face twisted with hate and malice. 'I'm here to commend you to that big von la-di-da estate in the sky. But before I send you on your way, I need to ask you a few questions.'

'About what?'

'The Kreisau Circle.'

'The what?'

Jost wasn't fooled by feigned innocence. He brought the gun down and struck von Menen on the side of the face. 'The Kreisau Circle,' he repeated. 'I searched the apartment of that friend of yours, Schröder, found something very interesting… a letter, sent to him in 1941.' Jost pulled out the letter and shoved it in von Menen's face. 'It refers to the impending arrival in Buenos Aires of one *Nils Bildt*, and I believe you and Bildt are one and the same. Your arrival in Buenos Aires corresponds exactly with that of Bildt's. Why don't you make it easy for yourself and tell me who the hell Olof Carlsson is?'

Face throbbing like bubbling lava, von Menen shook his head, as much as the gun would allow. 'Haven't a clue what you're talking about,' he said. 'Never heard of the Kreisau Circle, never heard of Nils Bildt, never heard of Olof Carlsson.'

Jost jabbed the pistol hard against von Menen's neck. 'I can almost feel the beat of your carotid artery through the barrel,' he sniggered. 'I'll ask you again. What do you know about the Kreisau Circle? Who is Olof Carlsson? I haven't got all night. I want names, contacts in Germany, everything.'

'I've told you, I don't know what you're talking about.'

'Then why have you been meeting with Franz Schröder?'

'Franz who?'

Jost's face filled with a sickly grin. 'Schröder, the man you've been meeting at a small Italian restaurant in San Telmo, *Il Pellicano*, I believe it's called; the man who would have our Führer "committed to a lunatic asylum", as he was quoted as saying in *La Prensa*. I still can't believe my luck,' he said, shaking his head. 'The irony of it is, I did that young Saccani lad as a favour. He squealed like a stuck pig in that alley. Before I finished him off, he was singing like a canary. *"Señor Schröder and the man with the broken nose,"* Jost mimicked. *"Very well-dressed, very refined."* He meant you, von Menen, didn't he?' He pushed the pistol harder into von Menen's neck. 'Let's try again: What do you know about the Kreisau Circle? Who is Olof Carlsson?'

'Even if I knew, there'd be no point in my telling you, because you'd kill me anyway.'

'Yes, but as a reward, I'd make it quick.'

'And…?'

'If you don't tell me, it'll be slow and very painful.'

Seeing his life streak by at the speed of a Katyusha rocket, von Menen had all but surrendered himself to the inevitable. All he could think of now was Maria, his parents and the rest of his family. He thought about death, too, about the family tomb at the local church in Mecklenburg, the final resting-place he was about to be denied. What would death be like? *Should I pray?* he wondered. *Our Father...*

And then he thought about the pain and how long it would take him to die with a round of hot, nine-millimetre lead flying through his neck, severing his carotid artery and zipping through the other side. Seconds, a minute, five minutes? No, Jost wouldn't wait that long. It would be straight through the head and he'd be out of the door in a flash.

'So, you killed Giancarlo *and* Franz Schröder,' he said, after some hesitation.

'You get no prizes for guessing right, von Menen.'

'With a silenced nine-millimetre Italian Beretta. Using Italian ammunition?'

Jost grinned. 'You don't think I'd be so stupid as to use "Made in Germany" stuff, do you? As for the Beretta... It was a present from a friend of mine in the OVRA.'

'Ah, the *Organizzazione per la Vigilanza e la Repressione dell'Antifascismo* – Mussolini's answer to your lot.'

Jost was losing patience, his eyes smouldering like the Devil's own. The end seemed near. And then, as if an angel had carried it mercifully through the carriage window, fortune dawned. Von Menen's eyes strained down at the small Italian pistol. The safety catch was on! If he could free his left arm before Jost's thumb could reach past the trigger guard, he might have a chance. 'What is this Kreisau Circle, anyway?' he asked, playing for time.

The question had barely left his lips when the engine's whistle emitted a piercing shrill. The noise startled Jost, his eyes darting sideways for a second. But a second was all von Menen needed, his left arm arcing beneath the top bunk, his huge fist smashing against the side of Jost's face. Jost stumbled, the Beretta skimming across the floor.

The wiry Jost stretched out for the gun, but before he could reach it, the heel of a size-ten shoe swung down from the bunk and crushed his hand. Von Menen dived for the pistol and tossed it onto the upper bunk. Grimacing in pain, Jost scrambled to his feet and leapt into the air, his head striking the roof of the carriage as he groped blindly for the weapon.

But the athletic von Menen was too quick and too strong for him. He grabbed Jost's arm, locked it hard behind his back and pinned him by the neck to the carriage window. Jost's damaged hand was useless, the veins in his neck enlarging, his face turning a livid pink. He wanted to kick out, but he couldn't. Von Menen had got him rigid; his grip tightened.

All Jost wanted was air and at that very moment he would have betrayed even Hitler for one last gasp of it. His evil, narrow eyes, wider than they'd ever been in his entire life, rolled slowly heavenwards, his struggling ceased and his body went limp. The hushed siren of death had beckoned. Von Menen stepped back and sank to his knees, Jost wilting to the floor, inert and lifeless.

Von Menen stared at the locked compartment door, asking himself if Jost had been alone and praying that what von Bauer had told him, almost three years ago, was true: *'Works independently, doesn't trust anyone and shuns camaraderie.'*

Convinced or not, von Menen had to get rid of the body. Checking his watch, he calculated that the train had already passed through San Francisco and would soon be approaching the wide open spaces south of Laguna Mar Chiquita. He doused the light, eased up the privacy blind and peered through the window. Outside, the night was a wilderness of raven black, moonless, skyless and groundless, with no hint of the horizon.

Von Menen pulled down the blind, switched on the light and began the gruesome task of removing Jost's clothes and personal effects. Allowing him the dignity of his *"Fabricado en Argentina"* underwear, he removed all else, including a watch and cheap ruby ring. He checked the entire body for tattoos, but found none.

Switching out the light, he lowered the carriage window, hoisted the body to its feet, heaved it onto his shoulders and fed it, head first, through the open window, like an ox shedding its yoke. Jost slipped silently into the night.

Von Menen did not know it, but at that very moment the train was passing over an elevated section of track, the body plunging down the incline and rolling to a halt at the edge of a thicket. Come dawn, the giant caracaras would be on the wing, scenting for breakfast. An hour after sunrise, Jost's remains would be nothing more than picked bones.

Dazed with exhaustion, von Menen slumped to the floor and rested awhile. Then he gathered up the clothes, the watch, the ring and the gun and stuffed them into Jost's overnight case, knowing that he had to get rid of them.

When the train pulled in at Alta Córdoba, von Menen made for the station buffet, resolved that he would not go to the Gomez *estancia* after all. Jost was dead. There was no need to hide. He took a taxi to the city centre, bought a new bag, put Jost's bag inside it, and returned to Córdoba Central Station in time to catch the daytime Pullman service back to Buenos Aires.

On Tuesday morning, he telephoned the Hospital de Urgencias at Córdoba and left a message for Maria's father, cancelling his proposed visit. That same afternoon, he left Buenos Aires for the safe house.

By ten o'clock the next morning, Jost's clothes were nothing more than a smouldering pile of ashes, the Beretta, watch and cheap ruby ring at the bottom of the River Plate. Jost's "disappearance" sparked little interest amongst his colleagues, especially Müller, who was interviewed at some length by the Ambassador.

Von Menen, meanwhile, stuck with the general consensus. 'Evidently, he was a bit of a womaniser, sir… Been venturing south of the city for his pleasures, so I understand. Perhaps he'd ruffled the feathers of one irate husband too many. In La Boca and Avellaneda they have their own way of dealing with such matters.'

★

The Alvear Palace Hotel was scarcely eleven years old, yet the private dining room of the Presidential suite, with its soft shades of peach, russet and oyster, was the unequivocal reflection of timeless luxury: tulip wood furniture, gilded bronze mounts, neo-classical paintings and an exquisite Aubusson carpet that even the lavish and egocentric Marie Antoinette would have killed for.

Vidal was at his courtly, elegant best – sparkling black shoes, glistening black hair, a dinner suit with satin lapels and a crisp white shirt fastened with jet-stone buttons that winked in the light of a huge candelabra.

'Forgive the presumption, Carl, but I've already ordered for you – oysters, *poisson* and crème brûlée; my usual champagne, an elegant Puligny-Montrachet and for a lazy conclusion, a fine Madeira. I do hope you approve.'

'Sounds very nice.'

Vidal beckoned the waiter. 'Please serve the first course, Luis, after which, you may leave. I'll call you when I need you.'

The waiter drifted across the room, served the oysters and departed, secreting his gratuity with all the artistry of a magician. Vidal waited a moment, checked the door leading to the anteroom and locked it.

'Well, Carl,' he said, returning to the table. 'Good of you to come at such short notice.'

'Your note did express a degree of urgency, Filipe.'

'Yes, I've a very important announcement to make. I am about to…' Vidal paused, flicked open the lid of his cigarette case and snapped it shut again.

'About to what, Filipe?'

'Disclose to you something of the utmost secrecy, something I want you to communicate to your friends in Berlin. Under no circumstances are you to divulge it to anyone else, not even the Ambassador.' He paused, a hint of conniving in his eyes. 'I trust you can do that – I mean, you must have your *own* ciphers.'

'Er…'

'Carl, please,' insisted Vidal, 'this is no time for German subterfuge. The future of Argentina depends on it.'

'Well, if it's *that* important, I'm sure I could arrange *something.*'

'Good, now we can proceed.' Vidal inched his chair nearer the table. 'As you know,' he whispered, 'President Castillo has endorsed the National Democratic Party's nomination of Robustiano Costas as the next President.'

'And he *will* be appointed. It's inevitable, isn't it?'

Vidal smiled. 'My dear Carl, the word "inevitable" has no place in Argentine politics. Costas is a very wealthy land-owner and a committed Anglophile. His views are immeasurably at odds with the GOU. Believe me, his appointment would not, shall I say, be *good* for Argentina? It would not be good for Germany, either. By the end of next week, Argentina *will* have a new President, but it will not be Costas.'

Von Menen's neck shot out from his shoulders, his

voice low. 'Filipe, are you saying that there's going to be a coup, a revolution?'

'That's precisely what I'm saying. Come 4th June, the military will be in full control. Take my advice: a week tomorrow, keep off the streets of Buenos Aires.'

'But if Costas isn't going to be the new President, then...'

A smile broadened across Vidal's face. 'Some think it will be General Arturo Rawson. Even Rawson thinks so,' he chuckled; 'but I can tell you with absolute certainty that he will not. There's an element of uncertainty about Rawson, you see. One minute he's this and the next minute he's that.' The words almost sang from his lips. 'The only *real* certainty about Rawson is that he's in favour of this United Nations business, you know, "let's all sit around a big table and agree to everything the Americans want". He thinks Argentina should join. Not a chance. If we go down that route, the Americans will demand that we relinquish our stance on neutrality and that would be a complete disaster, not just for Argentina, but for Germany, too. Anyway, it's all rather academic... The GOU would never allow it.'

'Even at the expense of Argentina being barred from membership of the United Nations?'

'Even that,' replied Vidal, forcefully. 'Neither our membership of the United Nations, nor the reversal of our policy on neutrality, will usurp Brazil's position as America's most favoured ally in South America.'

'Meaning Argentina would have forfeited her prestige for nothing,' suggested von Menen.

'Exactly; leaving the Brazilians laughing all the way to the United States Federal Reserve Bank. You see, Carl, we don't want a close relationship with the Americans, but we don't want Brazil to have one either. Anyway, we're losing the main thread of the debate, which is: *we*, the GOU, will decide who the next president of Argentina will be, not the Americans.' Vidal countenanced a look that disposed von Menen to thinking that he was entirely privy to the precise order of play. 'Carl,' he said, pausing to glance at the locked door, 'the next President of Argentina will be…'

Von Menen's eyes were almost out of their sockets.

'…General Pedro Ramírez.' Vidal winked, reached across the table and patted the back of von Menen's hand. 'You see, Carl, where Germany is concerned, you have absolutely nothing to worry about.'

It was a little after midnight. Dinner was over and the small talk had finished. Von Menen made to his feet and was about to leave. 'Oh, nearly forgot,' said Vidal. 'I hear you're one down at the Embassy.'

'One down?'

'Yes, a fellow called Jost, the Gestapo attaché. Hasn't been seen for over a month, so I'm told.'

Von Menen's heart skipped a beat. 'Er… yes, that's right. Bit of a mystery, really.'

'Did you know him?'

'I knew *of* him, but I wouldn't say I *knew* him, as such.'

'Any idea what might have become of him? I mean, do you think he's defected?'

'Defected? No, some reckon his fate was a little more final than that.'

'Meaning?'

'He was a philanderer, having an affair with a married, fiery Italian woman – down in La Boca, so rumour has it.'

'Naughty, naughty. He's probably in bits and pieces at the bottom of the River Plate by now.'

'Perhaps. Anyway, why do you ask?'

'I'm merely curious, Carl, that's all.'

I wonder.

Von Menen left for the safe house the very next morning. At eleven o'clock that evening, his encrypted signal was whizzing through the ether.

★

In Berlin, Günther Werner, a thick red folder beneath his arm, looked tired and worn.

'Have we received confirmation from any other source?' enquired a jubilant von Ribbentrop.

'No, Minister, this is the very first we've heard of it.'

'You're saying that there's been no word from the Abwehr *or* the SD, no word from anyone, other than von Menen?'

Werner shook his head. 'Nothing, Minister, but that doesn't surprise me. If I'm correct in my assumption, von Menen's information is from his usual high-grade source, a reliable and well-placed informant who still wishes to remain anonymous. Von Menen has always respected that.' Werner hunched his shoulders, held out his hands. 'He's never been wrong before Minister, not once.'

'I don't care if the source is a horseless, drunken, one-legged gaucho,' contended von Ribbentrop, 'as long as the information is accurate… I will not have the Foreign Office being made a laughing stock.'

'With respect, Minister, I don't think there's any fear of that. I've studied all of von Menen's recent reports and they all point to an event of this nature.'

'A revolution? In Argentina? Next Friday?' Von Ribbentrop was desperate to believe it.

'That's what von Menen has predicted, Minister, yes.'

'And this Ramírez individual?'

'Well, given his history, Minister, his elevation to President makes sense to me.'

Perceiving the almost certain acclaim of Hitler, von Ribbentrop sprang instantly from his chair, waving the signal in front of him. 'I hope you're right, Werner, because I'm leaving for the Führer's HQ immediately. This is the kind of heartening news the Führer wants to hear.' He paused, pressed a button on his intercom and barked out a string of commands. 'Cancel all appointments... Tempelhof in thirty minutes. Phone my wife, and instruct my valet to pack enough clothes for three days.'

Cheeks flushed with anticipation, von Ribbentrop started across the room. 'When the revolution has evidenced itself, send a wire of congratulations to von Menen,' he said over his shoulder, 'and be certain to include my signature. If there isn't a revolution, tell him that he'll be on the Eastern Front in double-quick time, even if I have to send a U-boat to bring him back! As for you, Werner,' he added, nearing the door, 'until next Friday, I suggest you sleep in your office! This information remains in-house, not a word to anyone, including Canaris, and especially that young upstart, Schellenberg.'

★

Von Menen arrived back in Buenos Aires the following Thursday afternoon. He called first at his apartment and then headed straight for the Clínicas Hospital to collect Maria.

They had planned a late-night cinema outing, followed by supper at the Pedemonte Restaurant on Avenida de Mayo, though in light of the bombshell that was about to rock Buenos Aires, he doubted the wisdom of it. Vidal had not said *when* the revolution would begin, but the

Pedemonte was only two blocks from Government House, and Government House would assuredly be a hotspot. Feigning a stomach upset, von Menen convinced Maria that they should stay at home.

As the hours ticked by, the night remained surprisingly uneventful. By Friday morning, von Menen was beginning to think that Vidal had got it wrong. Then, just as Buenos Aires was coming to life...

'What's all that noise?' asked Maria, her face full of alarm.

Von Menen opened the balcony doors and saw crowds of jubilant, flag-waving people in the street below, singing and dancing. 'I tell you, it's true,' yelled a taxi driver, 'I've just come from Rivadavia... There's a lot of gunfire up there, soldiers everywhere.'

Maria leapt from her chair, tightened the cord of her dressing gown and rushed to join von Menen at the balcony.

'From what I can make out,' he related to her in his calmest tone, 'it seems the army is involved in a gun battle, over at Rivadavia.'

'Carl!' she exclaimed. 'What do you think's happening?'

Von Menen saw the frightened look in her eyes. 'I'm not quite sure,' he said, biting on the lie. 'Could be some form of an uprising – a military coup, maybe.'

'Oh, no!' cried Maria, hands clasped to her cheeks. 'Do you really think so?'

Von Menen leaned over the hand-rail, a surging crowd below. 'If the excitement down there is anything to go by, it certainly looks like it.'

Ashen-faced, Maria walked back into the lounge. 'They've done it,' she gasped, slumping back into her chair. 'They've actually gone and done it.'

'Done what?'

'Taken over. After thirteen years, the generals are back, only this time it'll be much worse, just like…' She paused, remembering the taboo subject they'd agreed never to discuss.

'You mean, just like Germany?' he said, woefully aware of his bogus ignorance.

'Since you mention it, yes… I don't want *that* kind of existence in this country, or any other country for that matter. It isn't right… It isn't decent!' She was almost shouting.

He listened, of course, but von Menen's mind, already a warehouse crammed with remorse, was back at Zur Letzten Instanz tavern in Berlin, searching for the fading memory of Rudolph von Bauer's "consoling" advice – *Just act out the part…*'

What would you think now, Rudolph?

Von Menen knelt down beside her and took hold of her hand. 'Maria, even if it is the military, there's no reason to suspect that—'

'That they won't force their will upon the people, like the Nazis are doing in Germany? You're being unusually naïve, Carl, aren't you? Read the newspapers. *They* know what's in store for us, even if no one else does. I'll tell you something, if it *is* a military coup and Uncle Filipe has had a hand in it, Daddy will make sure that he never shows his face in Córdoba again, ever!'

She jumped to her feet and stormed towards the bathroom, leaving von Menen kneeling on the floor, wondering whether or not he'd sold his feigned integrity.

In Avenida de Mayo, a column of tanks and armoured cars made towards the Presidential Palace, led by the man who aspired to be President, General Arturo Rawson, escorted by General Pedro Ramírez.

At the Naval Mechanical Training School, the army

encountered some serious opposition from a faction of naval cadets, unaware that a revolution was in the making. Some lost their lives, but eventually the guns fell silent and the ousted Castillo chugged his way to asylum across the River Plate.

Like Vidal had predicted, the blue and white sash of Argentina proved a temporary adornment for Rawson. Days later, in a farce of theatrical proportions, the hapless would-be President was spirited out of the tradesmen's entrance of the Casa Rosada and replaced by the man the GOU wanted – Pedro Ramírez!

Watching the spectacle from Plaza de Mayo, von Menen likened it to the extravagant proclamation Hitler had made in 1933 and drew the same conclusion – the road to a New Jerusalem was still closed!

★

Vidal was already halfway through a bottle of his usual champagne when von Menen breezed into Café Tortoni.

'You're looking very triumphant, Filipe. Still celebrating, I see?'

'I've been celebrating for some days, Carl.'

'And deservedly so. You got it right; your prediction, I mean.'

'Pleased, was he?'

'Who?'

'Von Ribbentrop.' Vidal reached calmly for his glass, took a sip of champagne, raised his eyebrows and said calmly, 'I imagine he felt very proud of himself, being able to give Hitler such high-grade political information.'

'Well—'

'The truth is, Carl,' interrupted Vidal, 'if we're to

compete with Brazil, and thus stand up against the Americans, we're going to need lots of help, in the materialistic sense, you understand.'

Von Menen guessed what was coming next. All he could see in Vidal's eyes was brass and armour plating. 'By help, I take it you mean—'

'Field guns, tanks and half-tracks, heavy machine guns and thousands of machine pistols.'

'That's quite an order.'

'Maybe, but it's no more than Brazil's getting from the Americans under their land-lease agreement.' Vidal's eyes were full of cunning.

'There's something else?' asked von Menen.

Vidal gazed steadfastly at the ceiling. 'Yes, one of those new electro U-boats you're developing.'

Von Menen knew the square root of nothing about the development of the so-called electro U-boat, but he was not wont to reveal his ignorance. 'Forgive my curiosity, Filipe, but why are you telling me this, when you should be talking to the military attaché?'

'With the greatest respect, Carl, this matter requires an entirely different approach. Your military attaché, General Wolff, is a little too close to a man I don't care for – Canaris. I need someone more removed, someone who appreciates what the GOU has achieved, someone who, shall we say, has been kept appraised of the delicate political situation in this country for the past two years, preferably someone who has the ear of Hitler.'

'You mean, von Ribbentrop?'

Vidal bounced forward. 'What a marvellous idea, Carl,' he said, a note of cynicism in his voice. 'How astute of you to suggest your Foreign Minister.'

Payback time.

Von Menen was on the back foot and he knew it. 'You

do appreciate that this will require very careful research, Filipe. Approval will have to come from the highest level. There'll be lots of complications – payment, delivery; it could take several months to arrange.'

Vidal held up his hands in agreement. 'Delivery will, inevitably, present some difficulties for you, but for us, payment isn't a problem. Tell von Ribbentrop that Germany can have as much in export credits as she likes – wheat, beef, anything. We'll also throw in something else you're short of – gold! Bear in mind, though, that these negotiations are *strictly* a matter between you and me. I have the trust of a small, albeit very powerful, circle of colleagues; but even so, it would be in everyone's interest, particularly your own, if this did not go any further. There are a few headstrong members of the GOU who would be more than happy to court the help of the SD, which is something I do not care to think about. The last thing we need is to raise the suspicions of the Americans.'

'But if you take delivery of a U-boat, the whole world will know what you've been up to.'

'Yes, but then it would be too late for the Americans to do anything about it. The fact is, Argentina is still a neutral country. We can trade with whom we like, including Germany.' He paused, took a sip of champagne and shrugged. 'You know what it is about the Americans, Carl. They have this anxiety about not having any influence in Argentina, and their anxiety has increased dramatically since Ramírez took over.' A poker-face smile rose in his face. 'Seemingly, they have this ridiculous notion that we're hell-bent on subverting our neighbours – Paraguay, Bolivia and Chile.'

'Well, aren't you?'

A smile and silence.

After nearly two years, the deeply enigmatic Vidal had

finally asked for something, though von Menen suspected that the *real* Vidal was still yet to emerge, quite possibly with a flush of aces up his sleeve.

8

Decrees poured out of the Presidential Palace like confetti. Congress remained in dissolution; the promise of Presidential elections sank to the level of a farcical joke. Industrial action was rife. In Avellaneda, the meat-packing industry ground to a halt.

Ramírez needed a miracle, but if Ramírez needed one miracle, Hitler was desperate for ten. The Italians had swapped Mussolini for Churchill and Roosevelt, and the once-invincible German army was in steady retreat through Italy. On the Eastern Front, the Russians pressed on remorselessly, while in the skies above Germany, the combined allied air offensive was hitting the very epicentre of Hitler's Nazi empire – Berlin!

Von Menen needed a miracle, also. Vidal was impatient for his tanks and guns, his intolerance growing – *'It's been months, Carl. What's happening? My colleagues are getting edgy. You must give me some assurance. When? When? When?'* Worse still, Maria's increasingly hostile attitude towards the military regime was irritating Vidal. *'She must keep her views to herself... I cannot be expected to provide protection for the entire Gomez family indefinitely!'*

Then von Menen received an urgent note which took him to the phone booth at the Hotel Phoenix at break-neck speed.

'It's as well you phoned. I have some very grave news... We must speak, urgently. It's vitally important.' Vidal's tone was brusque and frosty.

'I could meet you this evening. Say eight o'clock at the Tortoni, your usual table?'

'Make it seven-thirty. And don't be late!'

Vidal had a face like an impoverished mortician. Not a hint of a smile.

'What, exactly, *is* the situation with the arms shipment?' he asked angrily.

'No news yet, Filipe, I'm afraid. Berlin is preoccupied with other matters at the moment. I'm sure you know that.'

'I might have damn well guessed,' cursed Vidal, closing his eyes. 'Berlin might be preoccupied with *other* matters, but *we* have other matters to contend with, too.'

'We?'

Vidal regarded the question with some disdain. 'Yes, *we*, you and me! One of my impetuous colleagues thinks we've waited long enough. He says he knows a quicker way. He's…' There was an awkward pause.

'He's what?'

'Made contact with someone in your Foreign Intelligence outfit, someone who's promised to speed things up. He thinks there's a chance we might receive the first shipment before Christmas.'

Von Menen reeled back in his chair, a desperate look on his face. 'I know how disappointed you are, Filipe, but if you follow that route, the only thing you're likely to receive before Christmas is—'

'Yes, yes,' snapped Vidal, 'the wrath of the Americans. I know that. But I *did* tell you… I've been warning you for weeks.' He shook his head in despair. 'Frankly, I feel very let down.'

'I'm very sorry, Filipe. All the same, you need to be aware of the likely consequences.'

'I am!' said Vidal sharply. 'The unfortunate thing is

that this problem, which should *never* have arisen in the first place, has come at a time when we have more pressing matters to contend with at home!'

'The growing civil unrest?'

'Yes. Some measures introduced by Ramírez are causing widespread dissatisfaction.'

'Even among the GOU membership, I hear.'

'That too,' confessed Vidal. 'Some are already calling for changes.'

'In the leadership?'

'Possibly.'

'They'll have to be careful,' warned von Menen. 'If Ramírez finds himself threatened, he'll turn to the Americans out of sheer desperation.'

'Everything's possible, but not even Ramírez has reached the stage of dependency on the Yankee dollar.'

'Well, he would need to change public opinion first, which isn't easy.'

'Public opinion means *nothing*,' retorted Vidal. 'Eventually, you'll understand that. In the meantime, perhaps your masters in Berlin might care to salvage something out of this mess. Now, if you'll excuse me, I must go.' Vidal rose from his chair and headed for the door, taking with him what remained of their friendship.

Now, it was solely business.

In spite of the late hour, Jose was frantically polishing the large brass number plaque at the entrance to the apartment block. He called out when von Menen was halfway through the door.

'You had a couple of visitors earlier, señor.'

'Visitors?'

'Yes, two men, about three hours ago, went straight up to the seventh floor.' Jose stroked his chin, a vague look on his face. 'Come to think of it, I don't recall seeing them leave.'

Von Menen made his way up the stairs, walked quietly along the corridor, and stopped at his door. The short length of matchwood, which he always wedged between the frame and the face of the door whenever he left the building, was lying on the carpet.

A ponderous weight crept into his stomach. Quietly, he inserted the key, eased back the latch bolt and slowly pushed open the door. The apartment's hall was enveloped in darkness, the silence absolute.

Von Menen made for the sitting room, pushed open the door, groped for the light switch and flicked it. The room stayed black and silent. A prickly feeling crept across the back of his neck. Two paces forward and the door slammed shut behind him.

A standard lamp in the far corner came on, a face grinning beneath it.

Heinz Müller had a malevolent reputation and "a cut above the rest" was no idle figure of speech. Neither was his derisory nickname, "The Bavarian Meat Slicer", which bore no relevance to his family's delicatessen business in Munich. Müller dealt strictly in blood, mucus and sinews of the human kind.

Von Menen glanced over his shoulder, his suspicions confirmed. Wherever Müller was, Schmidt was never far away.

'Evening, von Menen; nice of you to come home at last,' drawled Müller, lazing comfortably in von Menen's favourite armchair, his feet on a stool, his pistol waving menacingly before him.

Shoes creaking, Schmidt moved forward. Von Menen inched away, but Müller's harsh command left no room for compromise.

'Stay where you are!' he barked. 'We need to ask you a few questions.'

Von Menen looked calm, but his heart was almost in his mouth. 'About what?' he asked.

'About a proposed arms shipment... and don't give me that casual look. You know what I'm talking about.'

Von Menen shrugged in mock ignorance. 'But I don't.'

'I think you do,' insisted Müller, grinning like a well-fed hyena as he rose to his feet. 'What's more,' he continued, 'we'd like to know who told you about the coup last June. You see, we suspect it was you who informed Berlin, when it should have been... *us*! You'll never know how embarrassing that was.'

'I'm merely a Second Secretary, Müller. Such matters do not form part of my remit. I've no idea what you're talking about.'

Müller flashed a wide smile at Schmidt, revealing teeth that looked like two rows of blank dominoes. 'Oh dear, Schmidt, he's merely a Second Secretary,' he sneered sarcastically, 'and, would you believe, he doesn't know what we're talking about.' Schmidt said nothing, but in his mind's eye von Menen could see the ear-to-ear smirk across his face. Müller's voice moved up an octave. 'Perhaps we should stimulate your memory, then, Herr *Second Secretary*.'

Stashing his Walther beneath his belt, Müller pulled out a switchblade and moved forward, trailing the body odour of an overworked carthorse. Soon, the two men were no more than a foot apart, face to face, eyeball to eyeball. Alarm had found a new home in Buenos Aires, thought von Menen, confronting an image that ought to have been set in formaldehyde and donated to a museum of horror years ago, a face lined with terror, yet somehow tempered by a hideous, crinkly black hair that sprouted from Müller's left nostril and curled up beneath the tip of his nose.

'It's never easy to psychoanalyse someone who has a gun,' said von Menen, 'but I'll ask you, all the same: Do you believe in reincarnation?'

Müller reached hold of von Menen's tie, yanked it down and sneered. 'Why do you ask?'

'Because you look as though you might have been something else.'

Müller, an inch or two shorter than von Menen, stood in arrogant pose, head held back, eyes blazing with malice, nostrils widening like an enraged bull, the distance between them closing to the width of a dinner plate.

Through the mirror on the far wall, von Menen could see that Schmidt was closing from behind. Any second now he would have a hold on von Menen's arms, Müller carving a signature on his face that would need at least a dozen stitches.

His forehead covered the ten or so inches to Müller's nose at what seemed like the speed of light, the switchblade falling to the floor. Müller's gun sprang from his belt as von Menen's right knee flashed up, catching Müller in the groin. He fell heavily to his knees, one hand clutching his face, the other, the most treasured part of his anatomy.

Von Menen spun round. Schmidt, caught unawares by the lightning speed of the incident, carelessly forgot to duck, a steam-hammer fist rocketing into his face. As he lifted his hands to cup the blood gushing from his nose, von Menen struck him a vicious blow to the kidneys. The hapless Schmidt dropped to the floor in a crumpled heap, blood everywhere. Von Menen snatched Schmidt's pistol from its holster, stuffed it in his pocket and kicked Müller's gun to the far side of the room.

Looking like a pilgrim facing Mecca, Müller, already contemplating the potential loss of fatherhood, felt the full force of von Menen's fist crack against his jaw, stars sailing across his eyes. He was out. Von Menen retrieved the Walther, emptied the chamber, ejected the magazine and threw it across the room. Writhing on the floor like a snared animal, Schmidt raised a limp right hand in surrender. He'd had enough.

Coaxed by a litre of stagnant water from a vase of flowers, Müller began to stir. He dragged himself to the far side of the room and sat with his back against the wall, legs akimbo.

Von Menen leaned over him. 'Müller, you're about as subtle as the Devil in a monastery,' he said calmly. 'Regarding the events of last June, I think it is fair to say that I know rather less than you. As for the so-called "arms shipment" you mentioned, I've really no idea what you're talking about. Maybe you could find a way of understanding that.'

Müller stayed mute, Schmidt likewise.

'Obviously you don't agree,' said von Menen. 'Well, have it your own way.' He reached into his pocket, pulled out Schmidt's pistol and jammed the muzzle into Müller's ear. Müller snapped shut his eyes, his brow creasing in fright, his heart racing madly.

'Heinz, for Christ's sake!' cried Schmidt. 'Say something. He's going to kill us!'

Müller opened his eyes. 'Okay, okay!' he screamed. 'There's...' Müller's tongue seemed riveted to the roof of his mouth. 'There's probably been a misunderstanding.'

'*Probably?*'

'Yes... I mean... *definitely* a misunderstanding. We... We got it wrong, didn't we, Willie?'

'Of course, of course,' agreed Schmidt, spitting out the words without even a thought.

'Good,' said von Menen. 'Now, as for this evening's little incident, I'm sure we can come to some kind of *private* arrangement.'

'Pri-vate?' stuttered Schmidt.

'Yes… You dismiss this arms shipment nonsense, allow me to get on with my real business as a Second Secretary, and I'll forget about this little incident.'

'And if we don't?' asked Müller.

Von Menen bent down to impart a fierce whisper. 'If you don't, I'll see to it that Kaltenbrunner learns about your dismal performance tonight. It will not be you who'll be embarrassed; it'll be your boss, Walter Schellenberg. You can work out the rest for yourself.'

Müller glanced ruefully at Schmidt. 'Okay,' he nodded, 'you have a deal. Can we go now?'

'Of course. But first, the switchblade… Take it from your jacket pocket, slowly, and toss it to the far side of the room.'

Hauling himself painfully to his feet, Müller did as instructed. 'And our guns?' he asked.

'Sorry,' replied von Menen. 'On that count, you *will* have some explaining to do.'

★

Vidal's covert appeal for arms had finally boiled dry, yet the GOU would not give in. In a desperate petition for help, his more eager colleagues turned to Walter Schellenberg.

Arms or no arms, Argentina's brazen offensiveness towards the United States had stretched Roosevelt's patience to the limits. Von Menen knew that if the merest snippet of information about the GOU's negotiations with the SD reached the American President's ears, it would send him into an apoplectic spin: Argentina would be *forced* into isolation, Germany would lose another "friendly" state and von Ribbentrop would spit blood. If the dwindling empire of the German Foreign Office was to avoid another diplomatic door being slammed in its face, Schellenberg would have to be stopped. But von Menen sensed that Schellenberg would fail, anyway, like von Ribbentrop had failed, and for the very same reason – Hitler needed every tank, gun and artillery shell for himself.

Von Menen cleaned up his apartment, snatched a couple of hours' sleep and left for the safe house at three o'clock in the morning.

After two years, the journey to his secret retreat had become almost second nature. Usually, it took five to six hours, but on that crisp spring morning the weather was fine and dry, and when the shooting break turned off the metalled highway, it cracked along the dirt track road at a blistering pace.

A sliver of amber fringed the eastern skyline. As dawn came up, a heavenly blue sky revealed an endless vista of quagmires, ditches and lagoons, a place where the wind blew ceaselessly and the vegetation rarely exceeded a blade of grass or a spear of marshland reed. It wasn't exactly Mecklenburg, but von Menen had found an affinity with the lonely, desolate and silent Pampa, a place where motorised transport was as rare as a three-legged horse and the trappings of modern-day life ended at the dirt track highway.

He arrived at the cottage at eight o'clock, encoded his message, retrieved the transceiver from beneath the floorboards, changed the crystal arrangement and radioed his signal.

A while later, with the radio back beneath the floorboards, von Menen headed for the main house, a strong sun hovering in the cloudless sky. From the shady opening of its kennel, a large black dog watched him suspiciously as he approached the front door. But the Braganzas were not at home. 'They've gone to their lodge in the foothills of the Andes,' a maid told him; 'won't be back for at least a month.'

Jorge Rosas, a young, reclusive gaucho, with flashing dark eyes, black wavy hair and a bashful smile, was away, too. *'He's twenty-two, has an unfortunate speech impediment, the mentality of a twelve-year-old and the horse skills of a Mongolian warrior...'* the camp manager had once told von Menen, *'talks with his hands and rarely opens his mouth. When he does, his speech is almost impossible to fathom. Sad history, really. When he was eight years old, he saw his father gored to death by a Hereford bull... Very traumatic... Never got over it... Thought you should know.'* After two years, the impediment was still there, but thanks to the slavish patience of von Menen, Rosas had improved immeasurably and now he could read and write Spanish. But like the rest of the gauchos, he was twenty miles to the south, trooping 2,000 head of cattle to the nearest terminus.

Engulfed by the heady fragrance of false acacias, Persian lilacs and white magnolias, von Menen made his way back to the cottage, reflecting on the good fortune that had come his way when he'd found the place. He'd made good friends and the owners liked him. But in the depths of the Pampa, von Menen was someone else. He was Carlos Menendez, a name that had slipped from his lips with consummate ease. *'I'm Spanish... I teach languages, privately, in Buenos Aires. I'm looking for peace and solitude.'* That was the story he had told the Braganzas. Since then, he'd lived with the fear that one day he might bump into them in Buenos Aires, perhaps in the company of Vidal or, worse still, Maria. Yet his life of duplicity had held out and he prayed it would stay that way.

After lunch, von Menen drove to a small fishing village twenty miles to the east, where red and yellow boats nestled along the quayside like a flock of exotic birds.

He parked by the quay and headed straight for the nearby hotel, the centre of all life, rumour and gossip. Having stayed there on his first visit to the village, he remembered the occasion well. The advice and the grappa had flowed like a river in full flood: *'This was once Argentina's third largest port. Ships came here from all over Europe, collecting hides and wool. You've seen the length of the quay, surely? We had our own Customs House. The building's still there, just along the road. Have another grappa, Carlos...'* He did and he suffered for it, much to the amusement of the locals.

The bar was full, yet freakishly quiet, the dice still, the dominoes silent and the green baize of the billiards table empty; no raucous laughter, no hissing and crackling from Radio Belgrano. The wireless was switched off. All eyes and ears were on two men sitting next to the door, one about forty, the other a deal older, the barman, Luis, pretending not to notice as their voices grew louder.

'Something wrong, Luis?' von Menen asked guardedly.

Luis flashed a discreet glance in the direction of the two men, the conversation reaching fever pitch, the young man's fist crashing down upon the table, a glass falling to the floor, tiny fragments splintering everywhere. Everyone turned and watched. The young man scowled and a dozen pairs of eyes searched for a vacant space on the ceiling.

'The older of the two is Enrique Rivera,' whispered Luis. 'The younger one is his son, Diego.'

'Father and son? They seem more like Cain and Abel.'

'They will be, before the night's out.'

'Why?'

Luis stuffed a white cloth inside a glass tumbler, rotated it briskly and then held it to the light. 'Family matters,' he said quietly, 'a fishing family, very close.'

'Fishing? But... the older one looks like he must be at least seventy-five. Surely he still doesn't go to sea, does he?'

'No. That's the problem. Diego wants to throw it in. He's had enough. His wife is from Buenos Aires and her mother is ill. She wants to go and look after her. Sad thing is, the old man's wife died just over a year ago, so it looks as though he'll be left on his own.'

Suddenly, Diego sprang to his feet and stormed towards the door, knocking over a stool in the process. 'That's the end of it, Papa. Josefina and I are leaving!' Reaching the door, he turned sharply. 'As far as I'm concerned, you can sell the damn boat.' The door slammed shut and Diego was gone.

Enrique Rivera looked woefully at the ceiling and shook his head. The dice began to roll and the dominoes started clicking again.

'Where does he keep the boat?' asked von Menen.

'Down at the end of the road, where the Naval Prefecture is...?'

'Yes.'

'Turn right and you'll find her moored about a hundred metres up the quay. She's called *Margarita*.'

Later that evening, von Menen signalled Berlin again. The transmission was acknowledged, but without instruction.

Low clouds scudded in from across the bay. The smell of rain was in the air and reed beds on the far side of the inlet were dancing to the tune of the wind.

Enrique Rivera was a picture of sadness, leaning against the wheelhouse of the stationary *Margarita* and staring aimlessly across the quay.

'Not a day for sailing?' offered von Menen as he approached.

Rivera looked skywards, sniffing the wind. 'Used to be in my day,' he replied.

'Mind if I come aboard?'

'Help yourself, nobody else wants to.'

Even before he'd set foot on the deck, von Menen had reached his decision. 'Had her long?'

'About ten years.'

'What is she, nine metres?'

'Just over; beam is three. She's a sturdy old girl, takes a mean sea,' Rivera boasted, warming to his theme.

'She can be rigged for sail, then?'

'A single gaff... Can't always trust an engine, you know, not even one as good as that.' He pointed to the engine cowling.

'Diesel?'

'No, petrol, thirty horse... single screw.'

'What does she burn, say, at seven knots?'

'About two and a half gallons an hour... Range is about a hundred and thirty.'

Von Menen made a quick mental calculation. 'Tank holds two hundred and twenty-five litres?'

Rivera was impressed. 'You seem to know quite a lot about boats, Señor...?'

Von Menen stuck out his hand, felt Rivera's hard, knurled skin. 'Carlos Menendez,' he said, 'but please, call me Carlos. And yes, I've done quite a bit of sailing. I'd consider it a pleasure if you would join me for a drink. That is, if you can spare the time.'

'I have all the time in the world, young man.'

A kindly, weather-beaten old soul with a blue-print of veins on his cheeks, Rivera had seldom recounted his sixty-plus years at sea with such enthusiasm. He talked for hours, von Menen on the edge of his chair, listening with boundless interest as he scrutinised a moth-eaten chart held in place by two heavy ashtrays.

'The reason you need a high tide to get in and out of the port,' explained Rivera, 'is this sandbank. At low water it's shallow enough to paddle in.'

'And that's the lighthouse?' asked von Menen, pointing to a star-like symbol.

'Yes, every sailor's mother...' Rivera's words suddenly dried up, his eyes moistening.

'Look,' said von Menen, placing a hand on his shoulder, 'I was in here last night and couldn't help overhearing the conversation you had with your son. I really am very sorry.'

Rivera sighed wearily. 'I suppose the whole damn town knows about it.'

'That's not important,' reasoned von Menen, engaging the old man's eye. 'The fact is, I think I can help you. More importantly, I think *you* can help me. You see, I'd like to buy *Margarita*, that is, if you want to sell her.'

'But why would you want to do that? You're not a fisherman... You're not even a local.'

'True, I'm not a fisherman and I'm not a local, either. I'm Spanish. I teach languages in Buenos Aires, but I do come down here quite often. Well, what do you say? I'll give you a fair price.' He went on to name it.

Rivera pondered the idea. He stared forlornly at the charts, stroking his chin as he reflected on the memories of a lifetime.

Von Menen waited patiently. Eventually, Rivera lifted his head, jerked himself free of the past, smiled faintly and slapped his hand on the table. 'Okay. If you want her, she's yours. Pay me on your next visit.'

'Thank you,' beamed von Menen. 'You'll have the cash within the next few weeks.'

They shook hands and the deal was sealed.

'There's just one other thing,' said von Menen. 'I'll still be spending most of my time in Buenos Aires. What say you keep an eye on her for me, maybe spruce her up a bit, give her a lick of paint, if you like? I'd be more than happy to pay you for your trouble.'

'I'd be pleased to,' smiled Rivera. 'It'll keep me occupied. And since you've been so generous with your offer, you're welcome to have the old hut by the quay.'

Von Menen remained at the safe house for the next two nights, waiting for the signal from Werner he knew would never arrive. On Monday morning, he drove back to Buenos Aires, another element added to his life of duplicity.

9

Von Menen hastened into the drawing room, turned up the radio and caught the latest bulletin on Radio Belgrano:

One of the government's new measures is the appointment of forty-eight-year-old Colonel Juan Domingo Perón as head of the National Labour Department. It is hoped that Colonel Perón, who is currently serving as an under-secretary at the War Department, will bring...

It was no surprise to von Menen. Perón's political aspirations had been an open secret for months, just like his unquestionable authority within the GOU.

What did surprise him was Vidal's mystifying reluctance ever to discuss the man, even in the vaguest sense. Whenever von Menen enquired about the prospect of meeting Perón, secretly, Vidal routinely dismissed the idea – *'Wholly inadvisable, Carl. He's merely a colleague, that's all.'* It was the greatest understatement ever: Perón and Vidal were as parallel as the railway lines between Buenos Aires and Córdoba.

Von Menen hadn't heard the phone ring, but when he returned to the bedroom he saw the distraught look on Maria's face, the receiver pressed against her ear.

'What's wrong?' he whispered.

Maria waved the question away. 'But he's all right, isn't he?' she said, speaking into the phone. The creases below her eyes smoothed out. Relief washed over her face. 'Thank God for that. For a moment, I thought… Yes, I will, Mummy, I promise. I'll phone the Clínicas and explain… Yes, I'll be there as soon as possible… No, I don't know what Carl's doing…' Shameful of the lie, she stared helplessly at von Menen and shrugged. 'Yes, I'll try and get a message to him. Give Daddy my love and try not to worry… Love you, too. Bye.'

Von Menen watched anxiously as she replaced the receiver. 'What's wrong?'

'Daddy, he's had a heart attack. Thankfully, a minor one, so Mummy says. He's at the Urgencias Hospital in Córdoba… They're doing the usual tests. I've told Mummy I'll be there tomorrow morning.'

Von Menen placed his arm around her shoulder and kissed her. 'I'll go with you,' he said. 'I'll get tickets for the night train.'

They soon found out that Maria's father's condition had done little to suppress his increasing worries about the ruling *junta*. Mention of the name "Perón" caused him great anxiety. When the family gathered on the terrace for a cooling drink on the very afternoon of his release from hospital, Javier Gomez unleashed another tirade of scorn.

'The man's a damn fraud!' he said, throwing down his copy of *La Prensa*. 'He may be a colonel and he may have read a few books, but for him to suggest that he has the answer to the ills of this country is, frankly… Ah, the man's an imbecile.'

'Javier!' exclaimed his wife.

'Well, he should stick to soldiering – as should your brother.' Señor Gomez wormed deeper into his cushioned wicker chair.

'He's ended the strikes,' she said quietly.

'Oh, he's done that all right... Locked up a few people in the process, too. Trade unionists, the lot... In fact, he's locked up most of those he disagrees with.'

'I'm not *agreeing* with him, darling. I'm merely saying that he's succeeded where others have failed... He's ended the strikes *and* got the meat-packing industry back to work again.'

'But—'

'Yes, I know what you're going to say, Javier... He's given the workers more money, promised them improved living standards, better working conditions and a greater political say. Whether he has a motive for that, I don't know, but he *has* got them back to work. That's all I'm saying.'

'Speaking as an outsider, he seems very ambitious to me,' said von Menen, not wanting to join the conversation, yet not wishing to be seen as having no opinion of his own.

'You're right about that, Carl,' agreed Señor Gomez. 'He *is* ambitious, beating his own self-seeking path to the Casa Rosada, I shouldn't wonder. As for the workers,' he said, jabbing his chin at his wife, 'he's bribed them!' Señor Gomez forced himself to his feet and walked slowly up and down the terrace like a fox stalking a hen house, stopping only to thrust home his point. 'Don't you see he's merely using them?'

'Using them?' echoed Señora Gomez. 'For what reason?'

'Because he has to. He's been spurned by the leading industrialists and he's been spurned by the traditional overlords. He's simply made a 180-degree turn and targeted the under-classes, the poor and the disadvantaged. He's shrewd, I'll give you that. He's not only won their hearts and minds, he's gained—'

'A power base?' supplied von Menen.

'*Exactly*, Carl, a power base, built on impassioned allegiance. The best power base a dictator can have.' He shook his head and added, apologetically, 'Sorry, Carl, but Hitler is proof of that.'

'Well...'

'But he is, Carl,' hastened Señor Gomez, freeing von Menen from his moment of awkwardness. 'So is Franco and so *was* Mussolini...' He bent down, picked up his discarded *La Prensa* and slapped his hand across the front page. 'Look what we have now. Our own *brown shirts*, a bunch of thugs hell-bent on taking to the streets and fighting Perón's cause for him. The only difference is, Perón's brown shirts have no shirts at all...'

'The *descamisados*,' muttered Maria.

'Yes, the *descamisados*,' agreed her father, his face reddening with rage. 'The shirtless ones. If you listened hard enough, you could hear them chanting from the summit of Mount Aconcagua – "PER-ÓN! PER-ÓN! PER-ÓN!".'

'Darling, I think that's enough,' said Ana Gomez. 'You're getting too emotional. It's not good for you.'

'Mummy's right, Daddy. It isn't good for your blood pressure.'

Defeated by his wife and daughter, he sighed, tucked his newspaper under his arm and headed back to the house.

Von Menen had said little, but he knew Javier Gomez was right. Peronism had arrived.

★

Argentina tipped into 1944 with the new year almost unnoticed. Perón's burgeoning army of supporters had gained some benefits, but across the wider domestic spectrum, the political situation was worsening. Imported goods were difficult to find, fuel was getting scarcer and what remained of democracy was fast disappearing down the plughole of inequity.

Resolved to create one mass labour movement, Perón continued to crack down heavily on the few remaining non-conformist elements within the various unions. The *junta*'s hand of contempt swept over every aspect of Argentine life.

For the impotent Ramírez, a threatening realisation hovered above the rooftops of the Presidential Palace. The *real* purpose behind Perón's snug relationship with the labour masses was shining like a beacon all the way from his Labour headquarters straight through the windows of the Casa Rosada. Ramírez had lost his way, his political stature was weakening and Perón's charisma was growing. Soon, someone would have to give way.

Von Menen, meanwhile, had seen nothing of Vidal for almost five weeks. Their next meeting – arranged in haste by Vidal – did not come until the third week of the year.

Saturday 15th January 1944

Austerity had not yet reached the Alvear Palace Hotel, where steamy government scandal was traded for the latest rumours to emerge from the Jockey Club. But Vidal was given to unmitigated discretion, and von Menen knew where to find him – in a small, private dining room on the second floor, Dom Pérignon at the ready.

'Given the worsening political situation, Filipe, you look, dare I say, like a man without a worry in the world.'

'Oh, I have plenty to worry about, Carl, but as I've told you before, politics is like a game of poker. Some would like to win every hand, but in reality they know they can't.

As for me, I only ever play what the British call "patience" – I keep the whole pack to myself. But I suppose you're wondering why I've asked to see you.'

'More guns, more tanks?' replied von Menen, with daring impudence.

'Your witticism does you credit, Carl, but I doubt you'll have time for wit when you hear what I have to say.'

'It must be serious?'

'Very serious. The Americans are claiming that they have knowledge of our *attempts* to obtain arms from Germany, which, given Argentina's net proceeds from the venture, serves to heighten my own personal resentment.'

'If you had stuck with me, Filipe—'

'I doubt we would have got even one Luger pistol,' interrupted Vidal.

'Maybe, but the Americans wouldn't be pawing at your back.'

'Perhaps,' retorted Vidal, fumbling for his cigarette case.

'Am I to understand that you've brought me here to tell me that the Americans are putting pressure on you?'

'To put it in its proper context, yes. They're making threats… veiled threats, of course, but threats all the same. They insist that we renounce our position of neutrality and break off diplomatic relations with Germany.'

'And has Ramírez reached a decision?'

'Not yet, but the indications are that he *will* comply, perhaps within the next ten days.'

Von Menen was visibly shocked. 'You mean he'll go against Germany?'

'Most definitely… Not solely to appease the Americans, either.'

'Meaning?'

'Ramírez is obsessed with Perón's growing influence.'

'If you're talking about *the* Perón, the man I never got the chance to meet,' said von Menen caustically, 'then I think Ramírez's obsession is well-founded.'

'Whatever you think, Carl,' Vidal countered, 'Ramírez *knows* that Perón is posturing for the presidency and that he has the full support of the GOU.'

'Are you suggesting that Ramírez would use the issue of the arms deal as an excuse to sever relations with Germany, just to spike Perón's guns and maybe provoke some form of reaction?'

'Yes.'

'That's crazy.'

'I agree, but desperate men do crazy things.'

'But surely, in order to subdue Perón, Ramírez would need the support of at least one faction of the military, wouldn't he?'

'Remember last June, Carl, the gun battle outside the Naval College?'

'The navy? Surely not... Ramírez was at Rawson's side last June. He's just as answerable for what happened at the Naval College as Rawson, probably more so.'

'All the same, within the next ten days he *will* issue a decree severing diplomatic relations with the Axis powers, and in so doing, he'll have the backing of the navy. It's not guesswork, Carl, it's a statement of fact.' Vidal's voice was full of certainty.

'It takes an awful lot of believing, Filipe. I mean, the navy allied to Ramírez? It's unthinkable.'

Vidal grinned. 'Carl, after two and a half years you have yet to come to terms with the fact that the political forum in Argentina is a place where the Ethiopian *does* change his skin and the leopard its spots.'

'Your knowledge of *Jeremiah* does you credit, Filipe, but I'm not convinced about the navy's support for Ramírez. It doesn't add up. Surely the GOU would never allow it?'

'You're still missing the point.' Vidal placed his glass on the table, beckoned von Menen's ear and, with a smile in his eyes, whispered, 'Ramírez will not be in office much longer.'

'What!' Von Menen's eyes were ablaze with intrigue.

'Leaving the navy out of it for a moment, the GOU will never allow the Americans to have it all their own way. There *will* be changes, though.'

'Sorry, Filipe, you'll have to explain.'

Vidal hunched his shoulders. 'It's obvious, isn't it? Perón is emerging as the major player within the GOU and the GOU will have the final say.'

'Are you suggesting that Perón will be the next President?'

'No, but that's not to say that he won't be instrumental in selecting the man who will be the next President.'

'What you're saying, then, is that Perón will remain a powerful figure, come what may.'

'I wouldn't argue with that. Whatever Perón does now, he's smiling all the way to the Casa Rosada.' Vidal picked up his glass and studied the lost look on von Menen's face. 'You do realise what all this means, don't you?'

'Of course. America will not only insist that you relinquish your neutrality against Germany, they'll demand that you declare war against us, too.'

'They will. They'll make all kinds of promises and offer all sorts of assurances, but in my opinion, the only thing Argentina is likely to accomplish from it is membership of the United Nations. If that necessitates Argentina declaring war against Germany, I give you my word... it will never happen – *never!*'

Von Menen's anxieties were piling up, his mind a torrent of emotions. The idea of leaving Argentina was bad enough;

the idea of leaving Maria, too difficult to contemplate. 'Whatever happens now,' he said, after a lengthy silence, 'the future doesn't augur well for a German diplomat in Argentina.'

'Sadly, that's true. Your Ambassador and his underlings will soon be on their way home.'

'Me included,' added von Menen, blandly.

'Are you saying you don't like it here?'

'Of course I like it here, but—' Marrying the tone in Vidal's voice to the mischievous look in his eyes, von Menen stopped abruptly.

'I'm glad of that,' said Vidal, now at full stretch across the table, 'because you won't be going anywhere. You're staying here. Call it an invitation, if you like.'

'An invitation? You do realise what you're saying, Filipe. When Argentina severs relations with Germany, my status here will change immediately. I'll have no diplomatic protection whatsoever. I'd be seen as an enemy of the State.' He shuddered at the very thought. 'And what if Argentina *does* declare war against Germany? Hell, Filipe, given the volatile situation here, even you could find yourself in a difficult situation.'

'With respect, Carl, I think you're over-reacting. Neither of us has anything to fear in that direction. The fact is, I *must* maintain some form of contact with Germany and my best hope of achieving that is through you.'

'Of achieving... contact with Germany?'

'Carl, don't give me that innocent look. I've heard all the excuses from Maria and her parents. They may have been, shall we say, *taken in* by your seemingly innocent activities, but not me.' Vidal placed his elbows on the table, cupped his face in his hands and fixed von Menen with a rigid stare. 'I know you have a radio,' he said, sounding almost apathetic. 'Frankly, I couldn't care less if you've got ten. I couldn't care less where you keep it, either.'

Bells were pealing in von Menen's head. Vidal had always been an eager, predisposed source, discreetly, albeit officially, as it were, conveying the notions of a powerful clique of idealists, of which he was undeniably one – and in all probability, still was. But von Menen had sensed a shift in Vidal's thinking. He seemed to have divested himself of collective representation and was now appealing for himself – not *we*, but *I*.

Vidal tapped out a slow, relentless tempo on the lid of his cigarette case, watching the dying end of a crumpled, half-smoked cigarette smouldering in the ashtray. He waited for von Menen's response.

But von Menen would not be rushed. Vidal's proposal had all the hallmarks of doubt and uncertainty. He needed only to think of the weakening Presidency to realise that: first it had been Castillo, then Rawson and now Ramírez. If there was no security of tenure for the President, what hope was there for a defunct German diplomat, illegally at large in a country that might yet declare war against Germany?

'I appreciate that you can't give me any *written* assurances,' said von Menen, 'but how do I know that I won't end up languishing in Villa Devoto Prison?'

Vidal's face wrinkled like an old newspaper. 'The only assurance I can give you, Carl, is based on the conclusion you came to earlier.'

'And that is?'

'If you end up languishing in jail, it follows that I will be in the next cell.'

Von Menen fetched him a look that nigh on drilled a hole straight through his skull. 'Filipe, I'll consider what you've had to say. But whatever my decision, you will receive neither a negative nor an affirmative response from me. To put it succinctly, you will not know if I've agreed to your request or not; that is, until you try to contact me. It's a gamble you'll have to take.'

'You mean, if *Berlin* agrees to it,' smiled Vidal.

'Whoever, whatever, you'll still be faced with a gamble.'

'It's a bit loose, Carl, but... I accept.'

'What now?' asked von Menen.

'Well, assuming that you *do* stay, when I need to contact you I'll place an announcement in the obituary column of Wednesday's edition of *La Nación*. To avoid any misunderstanding, I'll repeat the announcement the very next day.'

'And if, by then, the newspapers have been so heavily censored that *La Nación* doesn't appear, or even exist, then what?'

'It *will* appear, I promise you.' Vidal dipped into his jacket pocket, pulled out an envelope and slid it across the table. 'You'll find the precise text of the message in there. When the announcement appears, we'll meet at Café Tortoni at nine o'clock on the following Monday. There's something else in there, too,' he continued, gesturing at the envelope, 'something to help you with your transport needs. Petrol coupons. Any points you wish to make?'

'Two... First, you must give me your word that you will afford full protection to Maria and her family, that there will be no harassment by the Federal Police and—'

'Maria and her father hold strong views, Carl,' interrupted Vidal. 'As I've told you before, I can't go on protecting them forever. But I will try, I promise.'

'I have your word on that?'

'Yes.'

'I hope so... Secondly, it beholds you to ensure that

no attempt will be made to find me. If I have the slightest inclination that my presence here is the subject of any attention by the Federal Police, I'll be out of this country quicker than you can blink.'

Von Menen left the Alvear Palace at eleven-thirty, the night air as still as the inhabitants of Recoleta Cemetery, the humidity unbearable.

Harbouring a condemned man's share of anxiety and oozing sweat like water from a burst pipe, he set off towards Plaza San Martin, his shirt clinging irritatingly to his back, his trousers sticking to his clammy legs.

'Just act out the part.'

Von Bauer's words still haunted him, but it was too late to judge the morality of it now. Too much had happened, the whole dubious venture a non-stop roller coaster of deceit, intrigue and machination, his conscience weighing him down like a blacksmith's anvil: failed allegiance, questionable integrity. Who was he working for? Who did he really personify – the Kreisau Circle, von Ribbentrop or Vidal?

As he approached his apartment, one thought was uppermost in his mind – his love for Maria. The question of what he would tell her was tugging at his heart like a drag anchor.

The following morning brought clear blue skies. In the east, where the chocolate-brown waters of the River Plate dispersed into the marshlands of Magdalena, a shimmering haze peeled over the horizon. Another stiflingly hot day was brewing.

Von Menen cracked on at a storming pace, the dirt road as dry as a tinderbox, the shooting brake trailing a huge ball of dust as it thundered east.

He arrived at the cottage at nine-thirty, his eagerness to visit *Margarita* and check the progress made by Rivera outweighed by his pressing need to contact Germany. If Vidal's scheme met with von Ribbentrop's disapproval, he would have to move quickly, retrieve the transceiver, destroy all evidence of his presence at the cottage and return immediately to Buenos Aires. *Margarita* would be written off and Rivera's work would have been in vain.

Von Menen parked at the rear of the cottage, rushed upstairs to draw the curtains and fetched up the radio. The text of the signal would be crucial — no suppositions, no buts, no maybes; a message that would incite an explicit, unambiguous answer – *stay* or *leave*.

He encoded the message, checked it carefully and changed the lead heading from URGENT to MOST URGENT.

Meanwhile, Germany was shivering in temperatures below freezing, coal was scarce and heating was a luxury. Walther Richter, a bespectacled sixty-one-year-old telegraphist, wearing two layers of clothing and a pair of fingerless woollen gloves, had just poured a steaming hot drink from his thermos flask when he picked up von Menen's signal from the Madrid relay station:

MOST URGENT
GERMANY/ARGENTINA. RELIABLE SOURCE INDICATES DIPLOMATIC RELATIONS WILL CEASE IMMINENTLY. SOURCE REQUESTS CONTINUED LIAISON. DEEP COVER ESSENTIAL. HIGH REWARDS. LOW RISK. ADVISE.
AKROBAT

Richter dismissed all thoughts of the biting cold and set to work. He sent von Menen an acknowledgement, then set the encoded message on its long and complex route through the channels of Nazi bureaucracy. It would reach von Ribbentrop by late afternoon.

Von Menen burned the paperwork, flushed the charred remains down the toilet and stashed away the equipment until evening.

It was a long, tense and lonely wait, but at eleven-thirty that evening, von Menen received the briefest of signals from Germany.

ENJOY THE SUNNY ARGENTINE WINTER.
GOOD HUNTING. W.

★

Thursday 20ᵗʰ January 1944

Back in Buenos Aires, von Menen found the German Embassy sizzling with rumours. Reports were still unconfirmed, but the question on everyone's lips was: *When will the Argentine government shut us down?* Neumann, already feeling the discomfort of a standard-issue Wehrmacht helmet on his head, complained bitterly.

Later that morning, von Menen submitted his four-page assessment on the latest political situation in Argentina, asserting that there would soon be a cessation of diplomatic relations with Germany and a change in the Argentine leadership.

An hour later, the report was in front of the Chargé d'Affaires. So, too, was von Menen.

The Chargé d'Affaires sighed wearily. 'I've read your report,' he said, 'and I agree with your assessment. Inside a week, I suspect that we'll all be on our way home – that is, if we can get home.' He peered over the top of his spectacles.

'I have not been specific about the date, sir, but my instinct tells me that Ramírez will make the announcement within the next few days.'

'I'd sensed that. I'm still not entirely convinced that Ramírez *will* be replaced, but as your *friends* in Germany are always wont to remind me, you're probably right.' A submissive smile flickered in his eyes, a hint of repentance in his voice. 'You know, von Menen, when you first arrived here, I think, perhaps, the Ambassador misjudged you. If it's any consolation, I'm happy to put that right.'

The Chargé d'Affaires leaned over his desk and passed von Menen a memorandum, marked *MOST SECRET.* 'This arrived by wire less than an hour ago. It suggests you'll be leaving ahead of the rest of us.'

'Yes, sir, I—'

'Please, no need to explain. Your work here has been exemplary. Is there anything else I should know before you leave?'

Von Menen indicated his bulging briefcase. 'Only that I've cleared my desk, sir. The safe and cupboards in my office are empty and all classified material has been destroyed. There's just the matter of the keys to my apartment – in particular, the safe. If you agree, I'll package them securely and leave them with the janitor. When I'm about to leave, I'll phone your secretary, Fräulein Hein, and inform her that they're ready for collection.'

They shook hands. Von Menen picked up his briefcase and bag, and made towards the door.

'Oh, I very nearly forgot,' called the Chargé d'Affaires. 'A moment, if you please.' Von Menen turned and placed his luggage on the floor. 'Do you...' The Chargé d'Affaires paused, reached for a sheet of paper lying on top of his desk and looked at it before trying again. 'Do you know of a Count von Moltke?' he said quietly.

A lump rose in von Menen's throat, his heart palpitating wildly. He tried to swallow, but couldn't. 'Beg your pardon, sir?' he said, in a cracked voice.

'Von Moltke... Count Helmuth-James Graf von Moltke, to give him his full title.'

Von Menen spawned a phoney look of calm, all too aware that beads of sweat were peppering his neck. He cleared his throat nervously. 'Well, er... obviously, I'm familiar with the name. They're descendants of Field Marshal von Moltke, I believe. If my memory serves me right, they have an estate somewhere in Silesia.'

'At Kreisau, I believe.'

The word *Kreisau* clanged in von Menen's head like a church bell. 'Really?' he said. 'Well, I can't say that I've ever met any of the family; at least, not to my knowledge.'

'So, I can safely say that you're not acquainted with them?'

'Definitely not, sir. Might I ask the reason for your interest?'

'He was arrested by the Gestapo yesterday.'

'Arrested? What for, sir?'

'Subversive activities, I believe, the suggestion being that he'd been associating with a number of like-minded individuals; people who, for want of a better expression, are *well connected.*'

'Well connected?'

'Yes, families of standing... you know, people in government, including the Foreign Office.'

'And I suppose you thought...' Von Menen pointed a finger at himself.

'I didn't suppose anything. I'm merely doing as I've been asked to do... speak to those individuals at the Embassy who were at Wilhelmstrasse in...' – he paused, raised his spectacles and glanced at the sheet of paper again – '40, '41;

people who, it can be said, are from… well… distinguished backgrounds. You were at the Foreign Office during that period and it could hardly be said that your family is not distinguished.'

'Yes, but…'

'But nothing, von Menen, that's the end of it. I'm perfectly satisfied with your explanation.'

Tormented by the horrifying thought that perhaps von Moltke had not been the only one to have lost his freedom at the hands of the Gestapo, von Menen took his leave.

Von Menen headed immediately for the Banco de la Nación, closed his account and opened another at the Banco de Boston, using the name Carlos Menendez. With the money hidden beneath the floorboards at the cottage added to that in the safe at his apartment, he had the equivalent of over $30,000 USD, a fortune by anyone's standards.

By late afternoon, he'd packed his trunk and two suitcases and removed all evidence of his German origins from his clothing. The next phase of his duplicitous life was about to begin. He penned a short letter to Maria, shook off the sentiments of gloom, stuffed the envelope in his pocket and headed for her apartment.

Maria had left a note on the dining room table.

Sorry, Carl, but I've been called to the Clínicas. Hope to be with you by seven. There's a cold drink in the icebox.

See you soon.

Love, Maria.

He was sitting next to the balcony window when the taxi pulled up in the street below. Maria rushed into the building and sprinted up the ten flights of stairs to the fifth floor.

Von Menen looked at his watch. *One, two, three, four, five… twenty, twenty-one, twenty-two…* A key went into the lock. As the door flew open, he checked his watch one final time. 'Twenty-eight seconds, darling. Your best time ever!' he joked.

Breathing heavily, she fell into his arms. 'I'm sorry,' she gasped; 'thought I could beat the lift. Anyway, I'm not too late, am I?'

'No, it's only just turned seven.'

She billowed out the top of her dress. 'Phew, I'm so hot… Can't wait to get under a cold shower.' She headed for the bathroom.

'I've booked a table for eight-thirty,' he called, as she stepped into the shower.

'I can't hear you… Open the door.'

He did, and saw her hazy image behind the screen, a stirring reminder of what he was walking away from. 'I've booked a table for eight-thirty at *El Tropezón*. It's a little early, but seeing as you've got to be back at the Clínicas by seven in the morning…'

'That's fine,' she replied.

A few minutes later, Maria paraded into the sitting room, did a quick twirl and halted beside the coffee table. 'Do you like it?' she asked.

'Very much. The colour suits you.'

She stepped forward, took hold of the pale blue material and flared out the hem. 'I bought it in Córdoba… Thought I'd treat myself. It's not very showy, but it's nice and cool and seeing as the weather has been so hot and sticky…'

'It's very nice.'

Dinner was a silent, sombre affair, von Menen's mood deeply morose, his mind full of turmoil. *How to tell her... When to tell her?*

In a perverse kind of way, her presence served merely to heighten his anguish – the touch of her hand and smell of her perfume constant reminders of the daunting, awful moment of truth. Yet von Menen's main worry was the lie: deception and sheer dishonesty. In Maria's eyes, he would be back in Germany, when, in truth, he would be a mere three hundred kilometres from Buenos Aires.

He now questioned the value of Vidal's shadowy scheme, wondering if it was worth all the anxiety. He was minded to tell Maria there and then, spurt it out and get it over with, but he decided to wait until they were back at her apartment.

Two hours later, Maria was standing by the drawing room window. Holding her snug around her waist, her hands clasped on top of his, the moment of truth had arrived.

'There's something I have to tell you,' he whispered. Von Menen was perfectly still. All he could feel was the beat of her heart.

'I think I can guess what it is,' she murmured. 'I wanted to ask you about it earlier, but I thought it might spoil the evening.'

'You know, then?'

She turned and faced him, her eyes full of tears. 'I think so. You only have to read the newspapers — the rumours, the innuendoes... You're leaving, aren't you?' Her voice trembled, her eyes almost inside his head.

Choking on his own sentiment, von Menen could feel the pain that had been threatening to overwhelm him for days. 'Yes, it's inevitable,' he stuttered.

A look of forlorn hopelessness reached across her face,

tears flooding from her eyes and trickling down her cheeks. As he brushed his fingers soothingly across her face, she stared at him, her eyes pained and embellished with redness.

'Take me with you, *please*!' she pleaded.

'I can't, Maria, you know I can't.'

'But why? I'm a doctor… Germany needs doctors,' she said hurriedly.

'You're also Argentinian, and Argentina needs doctors, too – good doctors like you. In any event, I want you here, where it's safe. I'm coming back, I promise.'

'Coming back?' A glimmer of hope sprang into her eyes.

'Yes, by any means possible. I give you my word.' He kissed her tenderly on the forehead. 'There's something else I have to say to you, something I want to *ask* you, really.' There was a look of seriousness about him, a look she had never seen before. She listened intently, searching his eyes for the words she had been aching to hear for so long. 'I don't just want you to wait for me,' he said, 'I want you to be my wife. Will you do me that honour?'

Charged by a sudden torrent of joyfulness, she gazed deep into his eyes, wrapped herself about him and shouted, 'YES! The answer is YES!'

In the few precious hours that remained, not a hair's breadth or a whisper of warm night air came between them.

Maria woke as the first light of dawn filtered through the curtains. She slithered her feet over the edge of the bed and crept from beneath the sheets.

Wiping the sleep from his eyes, von Menen motioned to join her, but she shook her head. As he lay there, in a muddled half-sleep, she leaned over him, smiled and kissed him softly on the lips. He pulled her close and wrapped her in his arms, but said nothing. The message was in his warm embrace. He would not be there when she returned and she knew it.

'No need to get up,' she whispered.

The door closed shut and as he lay there, gazing silently at the ceiling, he could hear the faint noise of her footsteps as she made her way along the corridor.

The alarm went off at seven thirty. Von Menen sprang out of bed, called out her name and then remembered... she was gone.

He found the letter on the bedside cabinet, alongside a photograph and a pretty white handkerchief, embroidered in pink. It carried the unmistakable fragrance of her perfume and the imprint of a fresh, red kiss.

My Dearest Carl,

Knowing how much you hate doorstep goodbyes, my heart told me instinctively that you will not be here when I return. I give you my undying and deepest love. Please take it with you. All I ask in return is that you PLEASE, PLEASE come back. Wherever you are, whatever you do, my love will be with you, always.

Your loving and affectionate Maria.

In a moment of panic, he reached for the telephone, then thought better of it and replaced the receiver. He picked up the handkerchief, replaced it with his own and exchanged his letter for hers.

After depositing his apartment keys with Jose, von Menen snatched a late breakfast at the Hotel Plaza, telephoned the Embassy and left a message with the receptionist: 'The package for Fräulein Hein is waiting for collection.'

The next day, Buenos Aires was a cauldron of intrigue,

the city buzzing with rumours that Ramírez was not only preparing to sever diplomatic relations with Germany, but he was about to declare war against her, too! The pressure was escalating.

10

Von Menen hurried along the quay, the smell of paint and varnish rising as he neared *Margarita*.

'Mind the wheelhouse door,' said Rivera. 'The paint's still wet.'

Von Menen glanced around the deck. 'It's unbelievable,' he said. 'You must have been here—'

'From eight in the morning 'til six at night, except Sundays.' Ushering von Menen to the back of the wheelhouse, he gestured to the engine. 'Had someone down from the local garage to look her over.'

'And?'

Rivera swung the handle, the engine coughing into life, puffs of grey smoke billowing from the exhaust. 'As sweet as the day I bought her.'

'What say we give her a run out in the morning?' suggested von Menen. 'If there's enough wind, we can put her under sail.'

A light crept into Rivera's eyes. 'Fine by me. There'll be some rain, mind, but there's a spare set of oilskins in the hut.'

'Gasoline?'

Rivera lifted his beret, scratched his head. 'Only a guess, but I reckon the tank's about two-thirds full; should take another fifty litres. We won't need coupons, though; fishing boats are exempt. We'll leave just after six... High tide is at seven. By the time we reach the confluence, there'll be enough water under the boat to clear the sandbanks. We'll make north-east across the bay, skirt the lighthouse and head out into the Atlantic. By then, we'll have enough wind to stretch the canvas.'

★

In Buenos Aires, Ramirez had failed to get rid of Perón and now Ramirez was gone, replaced by another GOU marionette, General Edelmiro Farrell. Perón's political star was rising. It was rising in his private life, too: a dazzling lady, young enough to be his daughter, tall, slim and attractive, with unnaturally blonde hair and a passion for fame and prominence, had stepped into his life. Her name was Eva Duarte.

★

Von Menen explained his lingering stay at the cottage by the simple expediency *'I'm writing a book'*, which everyone seemed to accept. He went unshaven, wore simple clothes, spent much of his time aboard *Margarita* and became a willing hand at the *estancia*.

Keen to add the rudiments of English and German to his new-found literacy in Spanish, Jorge Rosas became a frequent visitor and often joined von Menen on his sailing trips.

But von Menen was far from content. The constraints of his prolonged seclusion, lack of news about his family and enforced separation from the outspoken Maria were a constant reminder of his bizarre and precarious circumstances. His anxiety for Maria's safety deepened with every snippet of information arriving from Buenos Aires, where a full-blown dictatorship was burgeoning, fuelled by the growing stature of the infant Federal Police.

Von Menen continued to make his weekly transmissions to Germany, but the only information they contained was that which he'd read in the press, and he received only a customary acknowledgement by way of reply. But it was more than he ever heard from the dormant Vidal who, for all his insistence that von Menen should remain in Argentina, was as noticeable as a solitary grain of sand on the beach at Mar del Plata. Had it not been for the weekly pile of *La Nación* newsprint, which he burned in the garden of the cottage each Friday, von Menen might well have forgotten all about him.

★

Hitler's grip on the war was weakening: the Allies had landed in Normandy and the German army was now on the defensive in France, Italy *and* Russia.

Meanwhile, in Buenos Aires, Perón was getting busy. His sweeping reforms of the Labour Movement were apace, trade unionists forced to accept them. Those who refused joined their like-minded friends in Villa Devoto Prison or found themselves shoved aboard the "last train" to the infamous Neuquén concentration camp. The sale of one-way tickets across the River Plate increased dramatically, while the less fortunate simply "disappeared".

★

Thursday 20th July 1944

Half a dozen people were gathered in the hotel bar, von Menen drinking his afternoon coffee.

'Quiet!' shouted Luis, turning up the radio.

'I repeat,' said the announcer, *'we are interrupting this broadcast with an important news bulletin… Adolf Hitler is dead. Unconfirmed reports say that the German leader was killed during a bomb attack at his military headquarters in East Prussia earlier today. A further bulletin will be issued later.'*

A maid, wide-eyed and confused, rushed in from the kitchen and straight into a wall of silence. Transfixed and dumbfounded, von Menen looked like an alabaster figure cemented to the floor, the news slowly sinking in.

Suddenly, the bar erupted. Luis turned down the radio. Rivera looked at the ceiling, crossed his chest and said, 'Mary, Mother of Jesus, a miracle.'

'Did… I… hear… correctly?' von Menen asked, stretching out the words. 'Is… Adolf Hitler… dead?'

'Seems like it,' said the barman.

'A brandy, please, Luis, a large one.'

Von Menen swallowed the measure in one, euphoria threatening to consume him. He placed the empty glass on the counter and walked calmly out of the bar.

The shooting brake had barely reached the end of the road when von Menen let out a loud, joyous cry. 'It's over!' he bellowed, as if the whole world was listening. 'No more Hitler, no more Himmler, Goebbels, Göring; no more von Ribbentrop!' And if there was no more von Ribbentrop, it followed that there'd be no more Information Department Three and no more Vidal! The scent of triumph was in the air.

Already, he imagined himself back in Buenos Aires, collecting Maria, explaining everything, whisking her away to the theatre, a late-night dinner at *La Cabaña* and… freedom.

Back at the cottage he sat glued to the radio, ceaselessly tuning in the aerial, never daring to venture out of the room. *'I must emphasise that these reports are still unconfirmed,'* the newscaster kept repeating.

Later that afternoon, Radio Belgrano issued a further news bulletin.

'German radio station Deutschlandsender has broadcast an announcement throughout Europe that Adolf Hitler is alive. I repeat, Adolf Hitler is still alive. A plot to kill him at his headquarters in East Prussia failed. Several people are understood to have been arrested.'

Von Menen collapsed into a chair, face flushed with torment, his body numb with disbelief. Suddenly the collective madness of Hitler, Himmler, Goebbels and the rest had returned, bringing with it a question of torturous magnitude – *who* had been arrested? It was answered at eleven o'clock that evening, in a final bulletin from Buenos Aires.

'In a broadcast at nine o'clock local time, Adolf Hitler confirmed to the German nation that he was still alive. The Führer blamed today's events on "a tiny clique of ambitious, irresponsible and at the same time, stupid and criminal officers." A number of senior officers are reported to have been shot, amongst them, General Ludwig Beck, former Chief of the Army General Staff, and Colonel Claus von Stauffenberg, the officer who is alleged to have planted the bomb—'

Grim-faced, von Menen switched off the radio. He paced the full length of the room, out into the hall, through to the kitchen and back again, all the while agonising over the repercussions that were sure to follow.

In the ensuing two weeks, the names of eight others who had fallen from the scaffold at Plötzensee Prison spilled from the radio like an excerpt from a military *Who's Who*; among them, Field Marshal Erwin von Witzleben and Lieutenant Peter Yorck von Wartenburg.

Von Wartenburg's name stoked pains of anguish in von Menen's stomach. A cousin of von Stauffenberg, he had been von Moltke's closest Kreisau Circle conspirator.

In Argentina, von Menen was safe, at least from the clutches of the Gestapo, but in Germany, the net would be closing in. He prayed that it would not close in on his family.

In Europe, the Nazis were in deep crisis, but in Argentina, a new political will was blossoming. The imminent liberation of Paris and the uprising of the French Resistance sent a tidal wave of strong sentiment sweeping across Buenos Aires, the city wrapped in red, white and blue, the French tricolour hanging from every window. Few had ever seen so much of France in their entire lives. Stirred by the events in Paris, the people of Argentina joined in a spontaneous display of civil disobedience.

Perón responded. Thousands of paramilitary Federal Police, supported by thuggish elements of Peronist nationalists, swept into action with brutal efficiency.

Meanwhile, the message von Menen had been waiting almost seven months for appeared in consecutive editions of *La Nación*:

DI FRANCO Rodolfo, husband of Carmela Anna Margarita, died peacefully in his sleep…

11

Monday 28th August 1944

Buenos Aires

Impeccably dressed in a dark chalk-stripe suit, von Menen checked in at the Hotel Plaza, drove to Retiro Station, parked the shooting brake and headed straight for the Alvear Palace Hotel, taking a small overnight suitcase with him.

'I'd like a suite,' he announced at the reception desk. 'The best you have.'

The man in full morning dress fingered through a large blue ledger. 'I can offer you the Presidential suite, señor?'

'That will do fine.'

'How many nights, señor?'

'One.'

'Do you require dinner?'

'A cold supper, served in my room – sandwiches, canapés and two bottles of Dom Pérignon, on ice. Instruct the waiter to deliver everything at *exactly* five past nine. And since I'll be leaving early in the morning, I'll settle my account now.'

'Very good, señor. I'll arrange for someone to take your bags upstairs.'

'That won't be necessary,' hastened von Menen. 'I've

only the one small suitcase.' He peeled off a handful of notes to settle the bill, then headed for the elevator.

Leaving nothing to chance, von Menen worked out his plan with meticulous care. Except for a brown paper bag, two envelopes and a knife, which Jorge Rosas had honed to razor-edge sharpness, his overnight suitcase was empty.

Soon, all that remained of the suitcase was a heap of leather, two hinges, two locks and a handle. Von Menen stuffed the pieces into the brown paper bag, took the elevator to the ground floor and returned to the Hotel Plaza.

Standing forlornly by his bedroom window, the weight of deceit bearing down on him like a foundry press, he gazed out across the wintry form of Plaza San Martin, eyes reaching for the Clínicas Hospital. Maria was just a heart-stopping ten-minute taxi ride away, yet completely unreachable. An impossible dream, stolen by lies and deceit, the questionable aspirations of the ruthless Vidal and – he muttered aloud – *'that damned war in Europe'*.

At eight forty-five, von Menen took a taxi from the Hotel Plaza and headed for Avenida de Mayo, instructing the driver to park just west of Calle Piedras. He waited, his Walther in one pocket, two envelopes in the other — one addressed to Vidal, the other left blank.

A black Packard pulled up on the opposite side of the carriageway, thirty yards ahead of the taxi. Vidal stepped out, glanced furtively along the sidewalk then hurried into Café Tortoni. Von Menen leapt from the cab, dashed across the road and made for the newspaper vendor pitched at the junction. Handing him the blank envelope, he hastened back along the sidewalk to meet the doorman standing by the entrance to the Café Tortoni. Money changed hands and the second envelope was soon on its way to Vidal.

A minute later, Vidal emerged from the Tortoni, collected the second envelope from the newspaper vendor and read it beneath the light of a street lamp, his face a web of confusion.

I can see you quite clearly.

Do not speak further to the newspaper vendor and do not re-enter the Tortoni.

Proceed directly to the vehicle with the flashing headlights.

Von Menen ordered the driver to flash his lights. Vidal looked up, walked quickly towards the taxi and climbed into the back.

'Carl?'

'Yes, it *is* me, Filipe.'

'What a transformation. I do believe it suits you. The beard, I mean.' He beckoned von Menen's ear. 'Why the clandestine bit?' he whispered.

'These days one can never be too careful.'

Vidal smiled, sank back into his seat and slapped his hands on his knees. 'So, you decided to stay after all.'

'Looks that way, wouldn't you say?'

'Yes. And I don't mind admitting that I'm very grateful. Sorry you've had to wait all these months, but there were certain matters I had to be absolutely certain about. Anyway, where are we going?' he asked, wiping the condensation from the taxi window with his gloved hand.

'To your favourite hotel, but first, I'd like to know how Maria is.'

'Oh, she's fine, still at the Clínicas and still talking about you. She's in Córdoba, by the way, so there's no fear of you bumping into her tonight, which is just as well, really, since she thinks you're in Germany. Everyone does.'

'Given the circumstances, I didn't have much of a

choice. I told you I didn't want her implicated' – he looked suspiciously at Vidal – 'or endangered. And her father?'

'Much better. He's finally learned the art of relaxation.'

It was exactly nine-ten when the driver dropped them at Callao & Posadas. They walked around the block and entered the Alvear Palace via the entrance in Ayacucho.

By the time they had reached the suite, the waiter had been and gone. The scene was set.

Vidal poured himself a glass of champagne and settled into a deep leather chair, watching the condensation trickle down the side of the ice bucket. 'So, where've you been hiding?' he teased. 'Córdoba?' But he shook his head at his own suggestion. 'No, couldn't be. That would have been very foolish. Rosario? Mendoza?'

Von Menen remained expressionless.

'Not Buenos Aires, surely?'

'You must be joking. There are more Federal Police crawling these streets than you could get inside the Boca Juniors' football stadium.'

'That's because we *need* the Federal Police on the streets… They help to keep the walrus academics of the military in check.'

'They keep the public in check, too,' said von Menen sharply.

'If you're referring to the events of the past few days… yes, some of us did find it a bit depressing, but freedom must be limited for the sake of the cause. Too much liberty brings chaos and disorder.'

'Is that what Perón thinks?'

The question alarmed Vidal.

'Well?' pressed von Menen.

'Best ask *that woman*,' Vidal mumbled.

'I see… Well, since your eminent Vice President isn't

on the agenda, maybe you should tell me why you made contact with me.'

Vidal fumbled with his monogrammed silver cigarette case, pulled out a chunky Saratoga and lit it, the smoke leaving his lips in a long, grey plume. He took another long draw and then, as if inspired by the intake of nicotine, jerked forward.

'Carl, about last January… Ramírez was a little hasty, I'm sure you know that.'

'Certainly. It was a foolhardy gesture, even for a President.' The joke was lost on Vidal. 'In his efforts to outwit Perón, his actions recoiled on him. Now he's joined the ranks of the other failures… but the situation would never have arisen if your meddling Colonel Sanchez hadn't poked his nose into the arms deal.'

Vidal raised his brow. 'How did you know it was Sanchez?'

'Easy. *La Nación* said his wife had reported him missing, so I put two and two together, arriving at the only logical conclusion – murder!'

Vidal picked up his glass. 'Come, come, Carl… the man went *missing.*'

'Well, whatever happened to Sanchez, *I'm* still here. So, let's try again. What is it you want to speak to me about?'

'I'm getting there,' said Vidal. 'Ramírez's backers had the misguided notion that, having severed diplomatic relations with Germany, America would supply us with arms.'

'Enough to have put you on a par with Brazil, appease the more militant element of the army and silence Perón?'

'Maybe.'

'But it didn't turn out like that?'

'No, because the Americans have the ridiculous notion that we're still hell-bent on subverting our neighbours, especially Chile.'

'Filipe!' snapped von Menen. 'You *did* ask for a submarine, and that would have given the Americans a great deal to be anxious about. I mean, I can almost hear Roosevelt's thinking – *They'll coerce the Chileans to give up the area south of the fiftieth parallel. They want control of the Cape.* Forget the Americans; threatening the Falklands would have brought the whole of the Royal Navy's South Atlantic fleet to your doorstep!' He shook his head. 'But that's all academic. What are you *really* trying to tell me?'

Vidal reached for his handkerchief, dabbed an unwanted segment of tobacco from his tongue and pulled himself forward, his manicured fingernails digging into the arms of his chair. 'Carl, there's a lot of talk in the media about Germany being finished. I do not share those sentiments. Germany is unconquerable! Victory is just around the corner.'

Suddenly, Vidal's voice was brimming with conviction; his cheeks, normally smooth and pale, flushed red, the veins at the side of his face looking like lengths of purple spaghetti, his eyes glazed with excitement.

He actually believes it, thought von Menen. *He really believes that Germany will prevail.*

'Hitler is a soldier of providence,' said Vidal, 'manifested by a power the likes of which Churchill, Roosevelt and Stalin do not understand. He's an invincible genius. Believe me, Germany *will* win the war.'

Such sentiments were cold comfort for von Menen. 'If what I've read in the Argentine press is true, Filipe, Germany's cause looks pretty damn bleak to me. The Allies have a firm foothold in France, our westerly counter-attack has failed and the German army is in retreat. The Russians have already reached the East Prussian border, and at Kishinev we are completely surrounded. Considering all that, I'm heartened to know that you're still so confident.'

'I have every reason to be,' enthused Vidal. 'Germany's so-called "miracle" weapons will lead her to victory: her new jet-propelled aircraft, long-range ballistic rocket missiles and revolutionary electro U-boats!'

'Your analysis of Germany's situation is very reassuring, Filipe, but I'm sure that you didn't go to the trouble of keeping me here all these months just to give me a lecture on how Germany is going to win the war. I'll ask you again, what do you want? Why am I here?'

Vidal sucked in his breath through clenched teeth, a slight twitch appearing at the corner of his mouth. 'All right,' he sighed. 'I need arms. Two thousand MP-40 sub-machine pistols and 200 light machine guns, MG-42 Spandaus.'

'Is that with or without the ammunition?' asked von Menen sardonically.

'I'm being earnestly serious, Carl, but since you mentioned it...' – a faint smile fed into his eyes – 'a token amount of nine-millimetre wouldn't go amiss. There's something else, too.'

Von Menen listened with heightened awareness.

'We have a couple of submarines laid up with defective periscopes.' Vidal pulled a notebook from his pocket, flicked open the first page and studied it briefly. 'By *periscopes*, I don't mean the whole periscope mechanism, I mean the prism element. Your people in Germany will know what I'm talking about.' He glanced at his notebook again. 'Periscope seals have a limited life span; they rupture, seawater gets into the chamber and the prisms get damaged. When that happens, the whole periscope is rendered ineffectual.' Vidal leaned over the table, his eyebrows almost touching the ceiling. 'Without a periscope, a submarine is useless. I *need* those prisms.'

'Hold it, Filipe,' said von Menen. 'I'm not so sure about this. If I'm not careful, I could end up in the same situation as some of my compatriots.' He fixed Vidal a piercing glance. 'Are you *sure* you can't do this some other way?'

A devious smile burgeoned across Vidal's face. 'There *is* nobody else. You're the only one left. If you've been reading the newspapers, you'll know that we've rounded up every German agent in Argentina.'

'I read about that, and I couldn't help thinking how perverse it was, given the relationship some of your colleagues had with certain elements of the German legation.'

'But we had to do *something*, Carl. There were more German agents in Argentina than you could shake a stick at... and I use the term *agent* loosely. Some of them might just as well have had their occupations tattooed on their foreheads. But I deliberately gave you free rein. Why else do you think you're still here?' Vidal lit up another cigarette. 'So?'

'What does Germany get in return?'

'Immediately, nothing, but eventually, the same as I offered you before: gold and export credits. And *if* things do go drastically wrong for Germany, which I doubt, I'm prepared to throw in a little sweetener – some *additional* benefits, if you like, for anyone who might be interested in, shall we say, relocating.' Vidal laid a sealed envelope on the table, tapped at it with his finger. 'That's the order list.'

'It's more achievable than tanks and artillery pieces, but there's still the logistical problem of getting it here.'

'Allow me to enlighten you.' Vidal glimpsed quickly at his notebook. 'You have any number of U-boats with the capacity to carry several tonnes of cargo and they're quite capable of reaching the South Atlantic. Type 1XC cargo carriers, for example; range, nearly 17,000 miles... Type 1XD U-Cruiser; range, over 32,000 miles... Type XB, cargo-carrying minelayer; range, 21,000 miles. And, of course, the electro U-boat; range, 15,000 miles.'

Vidal had done his homework, or someone had done it for him.

'I can't argue with those figures, Filipe, because I don't know. But as for this new electro-submarine, well, it's probably still on the drawing board.'

'Wrong,' replied Vidal, with a huge grin. 'Several have been commissioned already, at Hamburg *and* Bremen.'

'There's an additional problem – the Atlantic is bristling with Allied warships.'

'Maybe, maybe, but that isn't to say that the Allies could find one of your new electro U-boats.' Vidal pulled a second envelope from his pocket and dropped it on the table. 'You may need that. And to convince you that my motives are genuine, I've arranged for the all-important page at the front to be left blank. Fill in whatever details you like. If it helps, you can tell von Ribbentrop that, if all goes well, he has my word that diplomatic relations between Argentina and Germany will be restored within weeks.'

'You said that with great conviction, Filipe. What makes you so sure?'

'Trust me.'

Von Menen thought a while. 'This will take time,' he said, shaking his head, 'and even then, I'm not so sure that...'

Vidal fixed him with an implacable, threatening gaze, leapt forward and banged his fist loudly on the table, a smoked salmon sandwich rising from the silver salver and dropping to the floor. 'Time is something you *don't* have! You *must* be sure. You have no choice.'

Von Menen's lengthened silence provoked him further, forcing him to reveal his last hand, the flush of aces.

'You ought to be thinking about Maria, you know, the two of you getting married. It's what you want, isn't it? I mean, anything could happen to her. Remember Colonel Sanchez?'

Von Menen reached calmly into his jacket, pulled out the Walther, released the safety catch, drew back the breech and fetched the first round into the chamber.

Vidal stared brazenly at the muzzle. 'I should warn you, Carl,' he said calmly, 'if I do not make a certain telephone call by midnight, Maria, who is already being watched, will have her name in the obituary columns of *La Nación* within forty-eight hours.'

'Your own niece? You'd kill your own niece? You're mad!'

'Caligula killed most of his relatives,' replied Vidal, cold and expressionless.

Von Menen reined in his repulsion, reset the safety catch and pocketed the weapon. Reaching across the table, he took hold of Vidal's wrist and squeezed it. Vidal grimaced as he felt the pressure increase, the same pressure that had crushed the life out of Erhardt Jost.

'Filipe,' von Menen said quietly, 'if anything happens to Maria, I promise you, I *will* kill you, even if I have to circumnavigate the globe ten times to find you.' He released Vidal but continued to stare coldly into his eyes.

'I get the guns, you get Maria,' said Vidal, rubbing his wrist. 'I get what I want, you get what you want… everyone's happy.'

'And if I don't?'

'You know the answer to that question.'

'How much time do I have?'

'Even I realise that you cannot do it in a month, or even two months, but I wouldn't wish you to think that you have all the time in the world.'

'And if I *do* put forward your proposals to von Ribbentrop, and von Ribbentrop succeeds in convincing Hitler, then what?'

'You get a message to me through a contact in Germany.

You'll find her address in the envelope. Her name is Grace Martens.'

'Grace Martens!' Von Menen stifled his laughter. 'Don't you mean Graciela Martinez, or maybe Graciela Gonzalez?'

'No need for the cynicism. She's Argentine, of German origin. Her parents live in Rosario. She used to be a secretary with Deutsche Bank in Berlin.'

'And now she works for you and her only companion is a radio.'

Vidal restrained his annoyance. 'I told you when we first met: you have, or did have, people in Argentina; we have people in Germany.'

'So, if and when I have some positive news for you, I get in touch with this Grace Martens, and she does the rest?'

'In a manner of speaking. But you must not impart anything other than a "yes" or "no". If the answer is "yes", include an approximate date of delivery, in code.'

'A code of which she, no doubt, is completely unaware, and only you will understand?'

'That's right,' smiled Vidal. 'Take the word MOTHERLAND. "M" equals zero, "O" equals one, and so on. If, for example, you anticipate that delivery will take place approximately fifteen weeks *after* the date of the signal, the message will read, "YES – O.R." Only then can I proceed with forward planning at this end.'

'And when I arrive at the address, how do I identify myself to Grace?'

'Give your name as Javier Maria Gomez, a Spanish expatriate.'

'Your permanent reminder to me of why I'm doing this?'

'Perhaps,' shrugged Vidal. 'Anyway, you're to explain that you're collecting on behalf of wounded members of the Spanish Blue Division serving on the Russian Front.'

'And how will she reply?'

'That her husband was with the same division and that he was killed in June.'

Von Menen picked up the envelope. He was about to take his leave when Vidal reached out and lightly took hold of his arm.

'There's just one other thing,' he said solemnly. 'Something I should have mentioned earlier; a bit of news which you would certainly not have picked up from the radio or the newspapers. It's to do with Kaltenbrunner's Reich Security Administration, the RSHA.'

Von Menen stiffened his gaze. 'What about it?'

'Kaltenbrunner's taken control of the Abwehr,' replied Vidal, in a kind of sardonic throw-away. 'Hansen, who succeeded Canaris, was kicked out some time ago. My understanding is that he and Canaris have been arrested in connection with the plot against Hitler.'

Von Menen's eyebrows shifted up a notch. In the weeks leading to the severing of diplomatic relations, there had been unconfirmed reports that Canaris had been sacked and that Hitler was about to sanction the unification of the Abwehr *and* the foreign intelligence element of the RSHA, placing the Abwehr under the control of Himmler's SS. 'How do you know this?' he pressed Vidal.

'Herr Schellenberg. He's now running the whole of your foreign intelligence service.' Vidal stood up, a wry smile on his face. 'If you'll excuse me for a couple of minutes…'

Von Menen waited until the bathroom door closed, then rose quietly to his feet and slipped away.

Outside, an unmarked chauffeur-driven Chrysler was parked in Ayacucho. In the back was a man wearing a distinguished uniform of the Argentine navy, shoulder epaulets braided with a gold crossed anchor and a single star.

Von Menen knew the face instantly. It was Rear Admiral Ricardo Ortiz, a man with an ardent disdain for the GOU and burning hatred of Juan Domingo Perón, a malice born of the bitter memory of what had happened at the Navy's Mechanical Training School in June 1943.

Von Menen walked on, side-stepped into a doorway and waited, a hunch playing on his mind. Minutes later, Vidal appeared, made along Ayacucho and climbed into the back of the Chrysler. Von Menen's jaw dropped like a lead weight. Vidal and Ortiz? It didn't ring true.

As the Chrysler roared away, a light dawned – Schmeissers for Vidal, periscope prisms for Ortiz, a very cosy conspiracy. The veil of mystery had lifted. Everything was beginning to make sense: Perón was holding the GOU's strings, but the shadowy and anonymous Vidal had been pulling them.

It wasn't Peronism at all. It never had been. It was Vidalism. But Vidal had been marginalised, pushed aside by *"that woman"*, as he'd vehemently described her. Now, he wanted control back, only this time, he wanted everything, even if it did mean enlisting the help of Ricardo Ortiz. To hell with Perón and to hell with Eva Duarte.

The GOU's ideology was Vidal's ideology. No doubt he felt it was his providence, too, just like his hero, Hitler; the people's impostor, half-crazed, half-demented, the supreme broker of power, wanting to rule the whole damn world. But Vidal wasn't so greedy; he only wanted part of it – South America!

Back at the Plaza Hotel, von Menen was full of hushed panic, his face a tortured mess, Vidal's words grinning at him insidiously – *'I get what I want, you get what you want.'*

Maria wasn't his only worry. If Vidal's wild and adventurous scheme wasn't crazy enough, his bombshell statement about the Abwehr was nothing short of a nightmare. Just as Heydrich had thrived on malevolence, Kaltenbrunner flourished on hatred and the darker side of mischief. If he *had* seized control of the Abwehr, then next on his shopping list would be... Information Department Three!

The very notion of it sent von Menen's mind into deeper turmoil. The Abwehr had been an integral part of the German military which, like the Foreign Office, was, and always had been, a *government* organisation. But the RSHA was different. It was strictly *Nazi.*

Von Menen's mouth went dry, a strange nausea reaching into his stomach. He felt like a man in a lead suit who'd just bought the Devil's own jigsaw puzzle; two puzzles, mixed up in the same box!

He paced about his room, cursing the idea that he couldn't get a message to Maria. That Vidal was having her watched, even in Córdoba, was no wild conjecture. Her phone would be tapped, her mail censored.

His mind was full of aching questions. Was it safe to use the radio? Who had he been signalling these past six months, Information Department Three or the RSHA?

He thought about Werner's security code, an air of hope settling over him. If what von Bauer had told him about Werner all those years ago – '*he's not a member of the Party; in fact, he seems a very decent sort*' – was true, and Kaltenbrunner had seized control, Werner would have left out the code. But the code was still there and he had received the last message just two weeks ago.

The thought half-calmed him, but his limited composure was soon overshadowed by the daunting prospect of returning to Germany – if, indeed, he could get back to Germany. With the mess the Kreisau Circle was in, the odds that he would be picked up by the Gestapo had increased dramatically. It was a risk he would have to take. There was no alternative.

The envelope which Vidal had given him remained unopened on the bedside table. Weighing it in the palm of his hand, von Menen sat down, recounting Vidal's words. *'And if things do go drastically wrong for Germany, which I doubt, I'm prepared to throw in a little sweetener – some additional benefits, if you like, for anyone who might be interested in, shall we say, relocating.'*

Inside, there was a second envelope, together with a message in Vidal's own hand.

If you're wondering where I got the photograph from, I "borrowed" it from Maria!

Von Menen tore open the flap and tipped out the contents. Six blank identity cards fell onto the bed, along with a pristine Argentine passport. Leafing through the pages, he noted that it had been "issued" in Buenos Aires four days previously. It contained Spanish, Portuguese and Swiss visas and a blank descriptive page. *Fill in whatever details you like.*

Vidal had thought of everything.

12

Von Menen sat by the bedroom window, eyes dancing between his watch, a plateful of scrambled eggs and the gloomy front-page headlines of the *Buenos Aires Herald*.

ALLIED FLOOD LAPS AT WEHRMACHT'S HEELS.
US "Fliers" Reportedly 90 Miles from Reich Frontier.

He shaved off his beard, slipped into a sober grey suit and placed a call to the newspaper, which was also a useful source of shipping movements.

'Good morning, Buenos Aires Herald,' said a female voice.

'I'd like to know if there are any sailings to Europe within the next week or so,' enquired von Menen.

'Just a moment, please… If you hear a click, don't hang up. I'll be answering another call.'

Von Menen held his breath, crossed his fingers and prayed.

'Hello?'

'Yes, I'm still here.'

'Sorry, but I can't find anything.'

'You're sure? Only it really is very urgent,' he pressed.

'Absolutely. Oh, just a moment…' She sounded less sure – which was potentially promising. 'Still there?'

'Yes,' said von Menen anxiously.

'This is all very confusing,' she said, her reply punctuated with uncertainty. 'I've found something which suggests that *Cabo*…'

Without warning, the line went dead, then came back again.

'Are you still there?'

'Yes, but I didn't quite catch what you said… "Cabo" something?'

'Yes, *Cabo Espartel*, part of the Ybarra Line… scheduled to depart for Lisbon on 5th September.'

'That's next Tuesday, isn't it?'

'Yes, a week today. Strangely, though, I can't find any reference to when she arrives.'

'But she's part of the Ybarra Line, you say?'

'Yes. I can give you the name of their agent in Buenos Aires, if you like.'

He assented and scribbled down the details.

Von Menen planned to leave Argentina in exactly the same way as he'd left Buenos Aires seven months previously – disappear like the snow in spring and leave Vidal guessing – only this time, it would not be so easy.

Vidal would be keen to know when, and under which pseudonym, von Menen had left the country. A blank passport was all very well, but the unique number on every page would be a sure giveaway, and that same number would be in the hands of every official at the Port of Buenos Aires – except, perchance, those at the Uruguay ferry terminal.

By taking the overnight steamer to Montevideo and waiting for *Cabo Espartel* to arrive from Buenos Aires, von

Menen hoped it would lessen the risk of being identified by some vigilant immigration official. Even then, the passport would not see him beyond the borders of Switzerland, since Kaltenbrunner's frontier police would be naturally sceptical about an Argentine travel document. Somehow, he had to get a second passport, to which extent Werner was his only hope.

Navegación Transatlántica – Agents for Ybarra & Compañia, Companhia Colonial de Navegação, Naviera Aznar – so read the relief inscription across the length of the plate-glass window. Von Menen stepped inside, made his way down a long, narrow corridor and knocked on the door marked *Navegación Transatlántica*.

'It's open,' called a voice from within.

He pushed open the door and saw a relic of a teleprinter chattering incessantly in the far corner, churning out an endless stream of paper. A man of at least seventy, with silvering hair, gold-rimmed spectacles and wearing a pair of black mufflers over the cuffs of his crisp white shirt, stood before it, collecting and folding the paper as it jerked from the carriage.

The clerk raised his sad sensitive face, etched with lines of worry. 'Can I help you?'

'The sign outside says you handle Ybarra & Company...' began von Menen.

'That's right.'

'I believe *Cabo Espartel* is due to arrive from Europe within the next few days.'

'You believe correctly, señor. She should be steaming towards the River Plate right now.' He peered over the top of his spectacles. 'Are you expecting a consignment?'

'Er, no,' replied von Menen, feigning sadness. 'I'm trying to get back to Spain. It's my grandfather... he's seriously ill.'

The clerk smiled sympathetically and moved towards his desk, pointing to a stack of letters impaled on a thin, six-inch spike. 'Sorry, but these are just a few of the letters we receive from people who want to reach Europe. Would you believe, there was a lady in here the other day offering four thousand pesos to get to the top of the queue? It's the war, you see.' Supposing that to be the end of the conversation, he buried his head in a thick leather-bound ledger and began writing.

'I'd pay twice as much!' said von Menen.

The gold nib pen, hitherto moving at a purposeful pace along a faint red line, came to an abrupt halt; the clerk was motionless for a while, the notion of eight thousand pesos soothing the thought of his forthcoming retirement. Slowly, he raised his head, a dubious look on his face.

'My, you *must* be desperate, señor. That's a great deal of money.'

'I'm anxious to see my grandfather, before it's too late.' Von Menen cast a long, quizzical gaze around the office, walked his fingers along the edge of the clerk's desk and looked nonchalantly towards the ceiling. 'I'd hazard a guess it would take a hard-working man some considerable time to earn that kind of money.'

'A *very* considerable time,' agreed the clerk, wondering how many more days he would have to spend in his cluttered office, filling in ledgers, answering queries, sifting and filing papers ten hours a day. He glanced at the inner door to check it was closed. 'How would you pay this, er... eight thousand pesos?'

'Cash, of course. Four thousand for the ticket and four thousand for...'

'You do realise that, even at that price, you would have to use the pilot's cabin?'

'I wouldn't much care if I had to sleep in the hold,' replied von Menen.

'I'd have to telex Ybarra and get their approval...'

'Of course.'

'And most importantly, as far as this agency is concerned, you would deal *only* with me. Not a word to anyone else, understand?'

'Certainly. And your name?'

'Cueto, Marcelo Cueto.'

'Seems like a fair arrangement, Señor Cueto. But there's just one thing I need to clarify... I have some business to attend to in Uruguay. It would be useful if I could join the ship in Montevideo. Can you arrange that?'

'Yes, though it will mean you boarding a day later.' Cueto cast a wary eye at the closed door. 'Look,' he whispered nervously, 'it will take me a day or two to sort things out. If you could leave me your name and a number where I can contact you...?'

'Of course. My name's Carlos Menendez and you can reach me at the Hotel Toscano, at Dolores.'

'Good. With luck, I should have some news for you tomorrow afternoon. I take it you have a passport?'

'Yes, an Argentine passport,' said von Menen, and quickly furnished Carlos Menendez with a suitable backstory. 'I was born here. My grandfather was a Spanish immigrant. He settled here in 1880, but returned to Spain just before the Great War.'

He engaged in a few moments of small talk with Señor Cueto before leaving, just to make sure the old clerk was firmly on his side.

Back at the Hotel Plaza, von Menen filled out the blank Argentine passport, using the name Carlos Menendez and a place and date of birth he would never forget: Córdoba, 7th December 1915 – Maria's birthday.

He settled his bill and set out for Dolores, taking a minor detour south of La Plata.

It was the *Telegraph* sign hanging clumsily above the shop door that caught his eye. He brought the car to a halt and scribbled down a brief message.

To: Señor Carlos Menendez… Grandfather dangerously ill…

The bell clanged incessantly as the door scraped along the harsh flagstone floor. Inside, the air was thick with tobacco smoke and the stench of stale green vegetables, overripe fruit and strong, black coffee.

Weaving through a stalactite mass of brushes, pans and shovels, von Menen made his way gingerly towards the far end of the store. The telegraph clerk, as the sign above the counter described him, beckoned him forward.

'I'd like to send this,' said von Menen, feeding the note through the grill. 'It's rather urgent.'

The telegraph clerk – a grubby white shirt and two days of stubble adding to his dark, unkempt appearance – took a slurp of coffee from a chipped mug, reached for a pair of bifocals and studied the note with all the importance that went with his title. 'Anything else you'd like to add?'

'No thanks, but you could tell me how long it will take to get there.'

'Should be there tomorrow morning.'

Von Menen paid the fee and departed, knowing it would bypass the cottage and go straight to the camp, adding drama and substance to his contrived story about his ailing grandfather.

He checked in at the Hotel Toscano at eight o'clock. The next day, just after breakfast, there was a knock on his bedroom door: 'Señor Menendez, there's a telephone call for you, downstairs.'

Von Menen raced down to reception and picked up the phone. 'Señor Menendez.'

'This is Marcelo Cueto, from the shipping agency in Buenos Aires. I've got some good news. You have a passage on *Cabo Espartel*, boarding at Montevideo on 6th September.'

'That's wonderful!'

'Does our arrangement still stand?' Cueto's voice was barely audible.

'Yes, of course it does. When can I come and see you?'

'Saturday? The office will be closed, but I'd rather meet you somewhere else, in any case. Shall we say eleven o'clock, at the Confiteria Ideal?'

'At Suipacha and Corrientes?'

'Yes, next to the cinema.'

'Fine, I'll be there.'

He rang off with a sigh of relief, feeling he had moved a little closer to Germany.

Von Menen was barely through the front door when the sound of a horse in full stride broke the routine silence of the cottage.

Jorge Rosas leapt from his saddle, rushed up the footpath like a whirling dervish and pressed the telegram into von Menen's hand. 'Se...Se...Señor.' Breathless, agitated and wholly frustrated, Rosas couldn't get his words out.

Von Menen tore open the envelope, studying the message with feigned despondency. Humphrey Bogart could not have done better.

'It's my grandfather, Jorge,' he said, hand on forehead. 'He's seriously ill. I must return to Spain, immediately.'

Rosas held out his hands, von Menen interpreting the signs.

'Thank you, Jorge, but I don't need any help. Maybe you could let Señor Braganza know that I'll be leaving for

Europe in a couple of days and I will not be back for quite a while.'

Rosas shook his head.

'You mean Señor Braganza and his wife are not at the house?'

Rosas nodded furiously.

'They're in Buenos Aires?'

Rosas nodded again, two fingers held up before him.

'For two… weeks?'

Another nod.

'In that case, Jorge, you'd best tell the camp captain.'

The following morning, von Menen called to see Enrique Rivera. He told him about his "ailing grandfather" and asked him to keep an eye on *Margarita*. Next, he visited the hut, where he collected a huge square of canvas and a long length of rope.

Back at the cottage, he signalled Germany.

ARRIVING LISBON ON CABO ESPARTEL EARLY OCTOBER.
HAVE URGENT INFORMATION. NEED PASSPORT AND FUNDS.
AKROBAT

There was no time to wait for a reply; it might easily take three days and von Menen needed to be back in Buenos Aires inside forty-eight hours. He wrapped the radio and the rest of the paraphernalia in the canvas sheet, secured it with the rope and pushed it way back beneath the floorboards, making sure to leave enough rope showing to enable him to drag the radio out, if and when he ever returned.

The next day he drove back to the quay, intent on "mothballing" *Margarita*, but the helpful Rivera had been there before him. The wheelhouse had been covered with an old canvas sail, the deck equipment and disconnected engine battery transferred to the hut. All von Menen had to do was carefully store his radio battery and lock the hut.

He returned to the cottage and counted out the money – eight thousand pesos for Señor Cueto and enough personal currency to lend substance to the reason for his prolonged visit to Spain. He wrapped four thousand pesos in a dark blue neck scarf and stuffed another four thousand into a brown paper bag. Everything was in order.

'Keep up with the studying, Jorge,' said von Menen, as he boarded the train to Buenos Aires on Friday afternoon. 'I want to see a marked improvement when I get back.'

After an uneventful journey, von Menen checked in at the Hotel Phoenix on San Martin. He dined late and slept well.

The following morning, a deluge of rain swept across Buenos Aires, the sky almost black. Von Menen found a taxi and eventually made the Confiteria Ideal just after eleven-thirty. Cueto had arrived ahead of him, looking like a well-trodden bath mat.

'Sorry I'm late,' apologised von Menen, peeling off his raincoat as he sat at the table, 'but the weather…'

'I know,' replied Cueto, 'I've only ju—' Cueto paused, dipped hurriedly into his pocket and pulled out a blue polka-dot handkerchief, catching his sneeze in the nick of time. 'Damn this weather! As I was about to say, I've only just got here myself.'

'You have the ticket?' von Menen asked anxiously.

'Right here,' said Cueto, reaching inside his jacket and pulling out a sodden brown envelope. 'Sorry, but the rain went straight through my coat.'

'Just as long as the ticket's okay.'

'The ticket's fine, I assure you. The ship is on schedule and is due to arrive tomorrow. I'll speak to the captain personally and inform him that you'll be boarding at Montevideo. On her return voyage, she'll be calling briefly at Las Palmas, but you should still be in Lisbon within about thirty days.' Cueto opened the envelope and laid the documents out on the table. 'It's all in there,' he said, indicating with an open hand. 'Ticket, itinerary, everything.' Slipping the documents back into the envelope, he stuffed it back in his jacket pocket.

Von Menen reached for his briefcase and rose to his feet. 'If you'll excuse me for a moment,' he said, 'I need to visit the cloakroom.'

Minutes later, he returned, and pushed a dark blue neck scarf across the table. 'My payment for the ticket,' he whispered. 'Four thousand pesos... and you can keep the scarf.'

Cueto stared nervously at the folded scarf, his hand wavering as he reached to pick it up. Stuffing it into his pocket, he glanced furtively around the room. 'I need to, er... visit the cloakroom myself,' he said in a strained voice. 'If you'll excuse me a minute...'

Von Menen knew that counting four thousand pesos would take rather longer than "a minute" – in fact, when he next looked at his watch, it had already taken seven – but he wasn't concerned. He had checked the cloakroom. There was only one way in and one way out and he was sitting next to it.

Cueto emerged almost ten minutes later. 'My apologies, Señor Menendez, but I had to be sure. Company money, you know.' He retrieved the envelope from his jacket pocket and passed it across the table. 'And our little arrangement?'

Von Menen fished in his suitcase, then passed the brown paper bag discreetly around the side of the table.

Cueto leaned cautiously to one side and dipped his hand inside the bag, feathering the thick wad of notes.

'It's all there,' said von Menen; 'four thousand pesos, as promised.'

The picture of weariness was gone, emotion reaching into the old man's eyes, his bottom lip quivering slightly. 'I've worked for that company for fifty-six years,' he said, nodding aimlessly in the direction of the street, his voice faltering, 'ever since I was fourteen... sweeping floors, making tea and now, doing the ledgers. In all that time I've been scrupulously honest. I've never done anything like this in my entire life, not once.'

Von Menen reached across the table and touched his saviour's arm. 'Your secret is safe with me,' he said. 'As for the money, well, spend it wisely.'

Von Menen spent the next thirty hours in self-imposed exile at the Hotel Phoenix, brooding about Maria, thinking about the worsening situation in Germany and worrying about the last obstacle that remained between him and the gateway to Uruguay – the Argentine frontier control.

At eight o'clock on Sunday evening, he paid his bill and took a taxi the short distance to the ferry terminal. The steamer, *City of Buenos Aires*, casting a thick plume of smoke into the damp night air, was making ready for her return trip across the wide, murky expanse of the River Plate. The queue was long and slow, the control a mere twenty metres away, taunting him to take the last tantalising step.

Yet something held him back: a man in black, whose mean, dark eyes roamed up and down the snaking queue with the frightening solemnity of an executioner. He wore the uniform of the Federal Police and he was carrying a Moschetto Beretta sub-machine gun.

Von Menen calculated, his eyes on the one immigration

officer for whom the sight of a passport seemed nothing more than a troublesome interlude.

'We thrashed you fair and square,' the officer was saying with a laugh, teasing the man sitting next to him. 'One–nil!' *El Superclásico*, the one-day soccer war, had spilled into the late shift of the Argentine Immigration Service.

Cautiously, von Menen approached the desk. 'Marvellous game. Did you catch it on the radio?'

'Catch it on the radio! I was there… Wouldn't have missed it for the world.'

'Lucky you. Varela scored a great goal, I hear.'

'Fan-tas-tic,' replied the man, who had as much appeal for von Menen's passport as he did for his much-loved Boca Juniors' adversary, River Plate. He picked up the document, flicked through the pages and, without even a cursory glance, banged it with his stamp.

Von Menen scooped up the document, nodded politely and moved towards the exit.

'A moment, please, señor!' The voice was low and harsh.

Von Menen froze and turned slowly to face the source of the bidding – the man in black, Moschetto Beretta sub-machine gun and all. A muffled drum was beating inside von Menen's head.

'Yours, I believe,' said the officer. 'Very nice, too,' he winked, as he handed von Menen the small portrait photograph of Maria. 'It fell out of your passport.'

Von Menen breathed a sigh of remission, thanked the officer and hurried away.

Monday 4th September 1944

City of Buenos Aires arrived at Montevideo at eight o'clock in the morning. Von Menen took a taxi to Calle Ituzaingó and checked in at the Pyramide Hotel.

He drifted aimlessly around Montevideo, dragging the burden of anxiety and misgivings with him. *Is my ticket genuine? Will I ever reach Lisbon?* During lunch at the Café Oro del Rhin, his uneasiness stepped up a gear. The kitchen door was open, grim news spewing from the radio inside.

'Among the more recent executions in Berlin,' said the announcer, *'are those of General Carl-Heinrich von Stülpnagel, until recently the Military Governor of France, Adam von Trott zu Solz, a senior Foreign Office official, and Major Rudolph von Bauer.'*

Von Menen's body fell limp, his face draining to a pallid grey, an icy chill rushing up his spine. Full of trepidation, he waited nervously for the name of his friend, Gustav Helldorf, but it never came. Nevertheless, his doubts had multiplied. The odds that he would be picked up by the Gestapo on his return to Germany had shortened dramatically.

During the next twenty-four hours, von Menen's nerves refused to settle. On Tuesday he kept his eyes glued to the sea-bound approaches to Montevideo. It was late afternoon when he spotted the stack of smoke, about six miles out, the outline of the vessel growing steadily larger, the white intertwined monogram of Ybarra & Company unmistakable.

Back at the Hotel Pyramide, he telephoned the Port Captain's office.

'Yes, it's *Cabo Espartel*. Due to berth later today... sails for Europe at seven o'clock tomorrow evening.'

At five o'clock on Wednesday evening, von Menen boarded *Cabo Espartel*, smoke kicking from her smudged, black funnel. An hour later, the deep, rich voice of the Master boomed out from the bridge:

'Bo's'n, we're ready to leave. Inform the Port Captain's office that we require a tug.'

After three years and two months, Carl Franz von Menen was returning to the Fatherland.

13

Friday 6th October 1944

Lisbon

Von Menen watched anxiously as the Portuguese immigration officer scrutinised his passport.

'Are you staying in Portugal, Señor Menendez?'

'No, I'm going directly to Spain.'

'Your purpose?'

'My grandfather… he's seriously ill.' Von Menen offered him the spurious telegram. 'My apologies, but I do not have a copy in Portuguese,' he explained.

The officer, whose linguistic skills went slightly further than Portuguese, read the telegram, nodded sympathetically and wished him well.

Von Menen's plan was to reach Madrid as soon as possible, fall on the help of his friend Juan Cortes, and take the first available flight to Berlin.

The questions that had tormented him in Buenos Aires followed him all the way along the quay at Lisbon's Alcântara Dock. *Has Information Post Three survived? Has Werner acceded to my request? Will there be a new identity document waiting for me?*

From a bar by the waterfront, von Menen called the

Wagons-Lits office at Rua do Carmo, inquiring about flights to Madrid and Germany. The news was cruel: a plane, en-route to Germany, had left for Madrid the previous day.

'I've no idea when the next service will be,' explained the agent. 'These days it's hit and miss. Some Deutsche Lufthansa flights don't even come to Lisbon; they terminate at Madrid.'

Disheartened, von Menen set off for Rossio Station.

The realisation struck him the moment he stepped from the tram at Rua do Arsenal – the man in a smart grey suit, newspaper tucked under his arm, had been following his route for quite some time. He stayed close, too close. *Has he been sent by Werner, or Schellenberg?*

Beyond Rua da Betesga, von Menen ducked into a café. The room was hot and airless. A stout old lady with a good start on a moustache and thighs so fat that they hung over the seat of her chair was sitting at the next table, a large sticky cake on her plate. Two waitresses, giggling uncontrollably, watched her from the far side of the confectionery cabinet.

Von Menen might have laughed, too, but the image of Salazar that adorned the kitchen door reminded him of the irony of his circumstances: he'd left one dictatorship behind him and, in his striving to reach another, he had to pass through two more – Portugal and Spain!

A moment later, the same man in the same smart suit stepped through the door, intent on sharing von Menen's table. He sat down, placed his folded newspaper next to the sugar bowl, ordered and paid for a coffee, drank it without another word and departed, leaving the day's edition of *Diário de Notícias* staring von Menen gloriously in the face.

Palming the newspaper into his bag, von Menen picked up his suitcase and left.

The cubicle in the men's toilets at Rossio Station was no place for a traveller *and* his luggage, yet somehow, much to the amusement of the lavatory attendant, von Menen wormed his way in, suitcase, handgrip and all.

Hidden inside the newspaper, the passport very nearly commended itself to the gaping wide pan of Shanks porcelain, but von Menen managed to snatch it clear.

His own photograph stared back at him. Kurt Lindemann; Swiss; occupation: banker; arrived in Spain from Germany on 2nd October, or so the passport indicated. Folded inside its pages, he found a well-thumbed letter of introduction from Dresdner Bank, an "open" Deutsche Lufthansa ticket for the Madrid/Berlin service, Portuguese, Spanish and Reichsmark bank notes and a typewritten note in Spanish.

Use only this passport. Destroy all other means of identification and destroy this note.
Take the first flight from Spain to Berlin.
Good Luck. W.

Is the message genuine? As he despatched the note to the sewers of Lisbon, von Menen prayed that it was.

Monday 9th October 1944

Madrid

Smartly dressed and oozing importance, Juan Cortes was sitting at his desk dictating a letter to his secretary when, slowly, the door pushed open.

'Yes, Emilio, what is it?' asked Cortes.

Emilio Gazala, general factotum, maker of coffee, fetcher of this, that and the other, and licker of stamps and all else, stood bewildered at the threshold, wringing his chubby hands and humbling himself to the point of extreme.

'Begging your pardon, Señor Cortes, but there's a man downstairs. He insists on seeing you personally, says it's *very* urgent. He, er… claims to be a *friend*, sir…' The word *friend* hung on Gazala's lips like a septic sore. 'Said to give you this, señor.' He walked the length of the office and placed a tiny object on the lawyer's desk.

Cortes stared at the small pink stone, leapt to his feet and spoke hurriedly to his secretary. 'That's all, Isabella. I'll call you if I need you.'

Collecting her pencil and pad, Isabella glided out of the office.

Cortes hurried from behind his desk, took hold of Gazala's arm and almost frog-marched him to the door. 'Show the gentleman in, at once! And see to it that you bring some coffee.'

Von Menen looked clean, tidy and well-groomed, but he did not reflect the image of the sparkling young diplomat who had passed through Madrid in 1941. Cortes's greeting was warm, lavish and unending.

'My God, Carl, it's good to see you. Where have you been? I was beginning to think you were…'

'Dead?'

'Well, not exactly *dead*, but I did expect to see you back in Europe some time ago.'

As they sat down, there was a feeble knock on the door. Von Menen gestured with a finger to his lips. Gazala walked in, placed a pot of coffee and two cups on the table and left.

'Where've you come from?' whispered Cortes.

'Lisbon, this morning.'

'Lisbon?'

'Yes, I arrived in Portugal yesterday.'

'From…?'

'Buenos Aires, of course.'

'But I thought... well, you know, last January... I assumed you would have come straight back to Europe. I've been waiting for you to phone me for months!'

'Sorry, Juan, it's a long story. I *had* to stay behind. The situation dictated it. What's important now, vitally important, is that I get back to Germany as soon as possible. I'm hoping to get a flight, but I'm told the service is very unreliable. I might have to wait as much as a week.'

'Well, you can't be wandering all over Madrid for a week. Best you come and stay at my place. It's only a short ride away and there'll be no awkward questions. My folks are with the rest of the family at the villa in Granada. Do you have money?'

'Plenty, thanks.'

Cortes checked his watch. 'Look, I have a meeting with a client in Colmenar Viejo at three o'clock this afternoon. But I'll be back around six-thirty. Take a cab, try and get some sleep. You look exhausted.'

'It's me, Carl. I'm back,' shouted Cortes, walking through the door.

'I'm in the bedroom, changing,' shouted back von Menen. 'Won't be a second... I gather from this obvious independent lifestyle you lead that you're still unmarried. Right?'

'Yes, but only for a year. I've just got engaged. Getting married next October, the twenty-seventh.'

Von Menen hurried into the drawing room and heartily shook his hand. 'Congratulations! Who's the lucky girl?'

'Her name's Fabia, Fabia Figuera. She's a teacher. Say, how'd you like to be my best man?'

'Sorry, Juan. I'd love to, but my future right now is a

little uncertain. What's in store for me when I get back to Germany is anyone's guess.'

Cortes noticed the worn expression on von Menen's face, the listless tone in his voice. 'Is there something wrong?' he asked.

'I'm just a little tired, I suppose.'

'I know you as well as anyone, Carl. There's something on your mind. You're in some kind of trouble?'

Von Menen wandered over to the window and stared out across the bright lights of Madrid. Somehow, it reminded him of Buenos Aires. Then everything came racing back – Maria, Vidal, von Ribbentrop, the Kreisau Circle, the Gestapo and that sinister building on Prinz Albrecht Strasse. 'The truth is, Juan,' he said, speaking with his face pressed against the glass, 'I'm in a mess, a gigantic mess.'

'Can you talk about it? I might be able to help you.'

For the next two hours, von Menen related the whole tale, ending with the fact that he was convinced Vidal was trying to seize power and that Maria's life was at stake because of it. Fascinated by the entire story, Cortes listened like the astute lawyer he was, not missing a word. He said nothing until the moment von Menen fell back in his chair, exhausted.

'Let me get this straight, Carl. If you can't persuade von Ribbentrop to agree to this Colonel Vidal's demands, you think Maria will end up...?'

'I'm certain of it.'

'Even though he's her uncle?'

'Where Vidal is concerned, Juan, family doesn't come into it.'

'Did you warn her about him before you left?'

'No, she only would have challenged him, which would have been highly dangerous. She's a singularly-minded individual, too forthright for her own good.'

'A bit like Fabia,' grinned Cortes. 'But… the Kreisau Circle. Surely, going back to Germany will be an even greater risk?'

'That's the dilemma, Juan. If I don't appease Vidal, Maria's at risk; if the Gestapo know about my connections, *I'm* at risk, as will be my entire family.' Von Menen buried his face in his hands. 'Whichever way you look at it,' he mumbled through his fingers, 'it's a damn mess. Even if I escape the Gestapo, there's always the possibility that von Ribbentrop won't agree to Vidal's request. Then it's almost certain that I'll end up on the Russian Front!' He took a deep breath, forcing himself to regain his composure. 'But… if the Nazis *do* buy into Vidal's scheme, then you might, *perhaps*, be able to help me.'

Cortes shook his head. 'But what can *I* do that the German authorities can't?'

'If I return to Argentina, I'd like it to be on my terms, via Madrid and Lisbon. No submarines, thank you.'

'Using a false identity?'

'Yes… an identity which not even the German Foreign Office would know about.'

Cortes drew the cork from a bottle of von Menen's favourite Vega Sicilia and poured two glasses. 'Carl, I'll do anything humanly possible to help you. And if you're concerned about my discretion, don't be. As a Cortes, I give you my word that whatever you confide in me will remain locked in my head.'

'I know that, Juan. I appreciate it greatly.'

'So, what do you want – another false identity, one you can fall back on the moment you arrive in Spain? A Spanish or Portuguese passport, maybe?'

'No, that won't be necessary…'

Von Menen popped into his bedroom, brought back his Argentine passport and dropped it in Cortes's lap. 'All I need to get back to Argentina, Juan, is that and a ticket in the same name.'

Cortes opened the passport, noted the name and laughed. 'Carlos Menendez? Did you use this to cross the Portuguese border?'

'No, I used a Swiss passport, which I obtained in Lisbon.'

'So, you smuggled this one into Spain? Where did you hide it?'

'Between two pieces of bread, a slice of cold ham and some lettuce!'

Cortes laughed loudly.

'What I'd like now,' said von Menen, 'is for you to keep it in a secure place until I get back.'

'I'll keep it in my safe.'

'Maybe you could keep an eye on shipping movements to the South Atlantic, also.'

'That shouldn't be too difficult.'

'But we're still left with the problem of communication.'

'Well… we still receive airmail from Germany. It's fairly infrequent, but it *does* happen. It's a service we provide for a few very special clients, if you get my meaning. The difficulty is, it can take anything up to four weeks and when it does arrive, invariably it's been opened by the censors.'

'I assume you use a post office box?'

'Yes.'

'Who picks up the mail?'

'Emilio Gazala. He takes charge of it until the client collects it. It's quite legitimate. We keep proper records, a ledger, everything.'

Von Menen wrote down a name on a piece of paper and handed it to Cortes, who studied it with some amusement.

'Who the hell is Señor Marante?'

'He plays full back for the Boca Juniors,' grinned von

Menen, 'but from now on, he's you! Tell Gazala that if he receives any mail in the name of Marante, he's to hand it directly to you, no one else.'

'Anything you write will have to sound meaningless and very innocuous,' advised Cortes.

'It will. If any of my correspondence contains a reference to Vasco da Gama, in whatever context, you can take it as meaning that I'm on my way back.'

★

On 15th October, Spanish radio announced the sudden death of Field Marshal Erwin Rommel. Once described by von Menen's father as *the* soldier of unprecedented military intellect, Rommel was reported to have suffered an embolism on the previous day.

★

After four days of waiting, a clerk from the Wagons-Lits office at Madrid's Palace Hotel telephoned to say that he had received confirmation of a Deutsche Lufthansa Focke Wulf 200 leaving Munich for Barcelona and Madrid.

'When is it scheduled to return?' asked von Menen.

'Saturday 21st… It leaves Madrid at two o'clock in the afternoon, calls at Barcelona and Munich…'

'*Calls* at Munich?' asked von Menen frantically.

'Yes, señor, it terminates at Berlin.'

Heart thumping, von Menen dare hardly ask the next question. 'Is there a reservation in the name of Lindemann?'

'Yes, señor, initial "K".'

A taxi was waiting outside, but von Menen was adamant he would go to the airport alone. Glancing at his watch,

212

he held it to his ear, tapped the face with his finger and frowned. 'What time do you make it, Juan?'

'Eleven fifty-five.'

'Thought so. My damn watch is kaput.'

Cortes disappeared into his room, returning with a silver fob watch. 'Here, take this. It keeps excellent time.'

'But Juan, I couldn't… I remember you inheriting it from your grandfather, in your final year at university.'

Cortes pressed the timepiece into von Menen's hand. 'No arguing. Take it. Think of it as an added incentive to get back to Argentina – not that I think you need an incentive.'

Von Menen picked up his bags and made his way along the hall, hesitating at the door. 'You know, Juan,' he said, 'it's ironic, really. When I left Berlin for Buenos Aires in '41, someone warned me that I might be walking into a lion's den. Here I am now, going *back* to Berlin, plagued by the thought of being thrown into a snake pit.' A strange look fed into his eyes. He reached out and shook his friend's hand. 'Frankly, I think I prefer lions.'

14

Zossen

One metre ninety and with a face like the north side of the Matterhorn, Hans Otto Steiger, the highest-decorated warrant officer in the entire German army, stood with his hand on the open door of a black Mercedes, waiting for a man he had served under for twenty-eight years.

General Klaus von Menen made his way towards the Mercedes as quickly as his lame gait would allow. Returning Steiger's salute, he threw his walking cane and cap into the back of the car, then slipped into the front passenger seat.

'I'm redundant, Hans!' he said, as the car swept through the gates of the German Army High Command HQ.

Steiger grinned, supposing the General to be joking.

'I'm through, my friend, finished, washed up. As of today, I'm another name on the *Führer* Reserve – that is, until they *officially* retire me.'

Sensing that it was no joke, after all, the amusement drained quickly from Steiger's face. 'Seriously, sir?'

'General Guderian told me an hour ago. Never liked Zossen, anyway.'

'I suppose that means *I'll* be heading back to the Eastern Front, then, sir.'

General von Menen fixed Steiger with a devilish smile. 'The only front you're heading for, Hans, is in Mecklenburg. You're staying with me. Guderian's orders.'

'Heavens. No more soldiering. What will we do?'

'There's a one-off job for us sometime in the next few weeks, but Guderian doesn't know what it is.'

Steiger followed his usual route, through Steglitz, Wilmersdorf and on to Charlottenburg, dodging the legacy of the latest air attack – piles of rubble, potholes, makeshift barriers and the bewildered souls of Berlin. Beyond the southern fringes of Spandau, the Mercedes gathered speed, racing into the rain-swept darkness.

Lulled by the comforting purr of the engine, the General succumbed to his weariness and fell asleep, head flopping forward like a rag doll. Alone in his thoughts, Steiger's mind delved back in time: the Somme, a moonless night, a badly wounded officer and a death-defying sprint across no-man's-land, bucking the menacing threat of machine gun fire, a hushed, cheering chorus spurring him on. *'Run, Hans, run, run, run.'*

Somehow, he had made it back to the German line, the young Oberleutnant Klaus von Menen across his back, lucky not to have lost his life, let alone his badly wounded leg. The deed of heroism earned Corporal Hans Otto Steiger the *Pour le Mérite,* instant promotion to sergeant and an undimming friendship with the man whose life he had saved.

Steiger pushed on through Perleberg, the memories still rising – the Armistice; a weak and exhausted Germany; an army in disarray; an empire gone, cities and towns in disorder and the ever-increasing threat of Russia's new Red Army. He looked at the sleeping General and smiled. *It's been a long road, Klaus.*

Beyond Dassow, a high stone wall came into view; up

ahead, a wide open entrance flanked by two stone pillars. Steiger made a right, rumbled across a cattle grid and swept up the long tree-lined drive, gliding to a halt before the horseshoe flight of steps which curved down from the huge brick-built edifice.

The General stirred. Steiger leapt out of the car, hurried to the far side of the vehicle, held open the door and waited, umbrella at the ready. General von Menen climbed out of the car, field-grey topcoat draped over his shoulders. Steiger stepped back, stood rigidly to attention and saluted, military fashion. For the General, and Steiger, the "party" salute held no place in German military etiquette.

General von Menen waved his stick and smiled approvingly. 'Thank you, Hans. I don't need the umbrella. I'll call you in the morning. We have a lot to discuss.'

A white-jacketed orderly rushed down the steps, beaten to the car by an excited black Labrador. 'Evening, General… Evening, Sergeant Steiger.'

'Evening, Schwartz,' said Steiger. 'The General's bags are in the back.'

Schwartz collected a large leather suitcase from the boot, leaving the General to fuss over the dog and say his goodbyes to Steiger.

'Have a pleasant evening, Hans, and give my love to Greta. Come on, Yeremenko.'

The Labrador ran ahead, the General taking considerably longer to join Schwartz at the top of the fourteen steps.

'How's my wife?' he asked, as they entered the house.

'Much better, General,' replied Schwartz, closing the door and switching on the lights. 'She retired to bed a short while ago, saying she would wait up for you. Oh, and cook has prepared a cold supper for you, sir. Would you like me to serve it in the dining room?'

'Thank you, Schwartz, but I think I'll skip supper. I'll catch the news on the radio and retire.' *Retire?* The word was already beginning to haunt him. 'Perhaps you could arrange some coffee in the morning – not too early; say about eight-thirty.'

'Very good, General.'

Steiger turned through a high arched entrance into a cobbled courtyard the size of a tennis court, where stood the fading remnants of German imperial greatness: obsolete stables, deserted groom's quarters, storerooms, laundry house, boiler house, fully-equipped workshop with its own blacksmith's forge and enough garaging for six limousines.

He coasted into the garage, parking the Mercedes between a BMW saloon and his own pride and joy – a Steyr 1500 command car.

His wife was standing by the front door, waiting to greet her "hero". Greta Steiger was a solid, matronly lady, with prominent cheekbones, a glowing complexion and thick, shoulder-length flaxen hair. She had a warm, radiant face, amethyst eyes and looked younger than her forty-six years.

Steiger smiled, dropped his case to the floor and threw his arms around her. One heave and his wife was suspended, her feet barely touching the floor.

'I've missed you,' he said.

'Hans!' she giggled. 'I'm not nine stone anymore!'

'No, but you're just as nimble.' He lowered her to the floor and closed the front door behind them, breathing in the smell of home. 'How've you been?'

Greta Steiger could contain herself no longer, her eyes moistening, a tear trickling down her cheek. 'Oh, Hans…'

'I know. It's fourteen years to the day.'

'You remembered. Fourteen years… It seems like only yesterday.'

'Come on, let me give you a cuddle.' He squeezed her tightly, then let go to get another good look at her face. 'That's better,' he said, brushing away her tears.

She forced a smile into her eyes. 'I'm okay.'

'And Anna?'

'She's much better.'

'Good… Klaus has been very concerned about her.'

'She's still a little weak, of course, but improving. And you?' she asked, leading him by the arm into the parlour.

'Tired, but otherwise fine.' Steiger shook his head. 'Klaus, though. He's so morose these days, rarely says anything, hardly a word, no jokes, nothing.'

'It's the worry, Hans, the responsibility.'

'That's another problem,' sighed Steiger. 'It's not *his* responsibility anymore. He's been transferred to Führer Reserve, awaiting retirement.'

'*Retirement?*'

'Yes; as far as the General is concerned, the war is over.'

Greta Steiger stared at her husband in utter amazement. 'You can't be serious.'

'Oh, but I am. No more Zossen, no more Russian Front, no more anywhere… except here, of course.'

Greta steeled herself to ask the question. 'And… you?'

'I'm finished, too.'

'You mean…?'

'I mean from now on, you've got me all day and every day.'

She flung her arms around him. 'Oh, thank God, Hans… thank God.'

General von Menen pushed open the bedroom door, a faint glow washing across the landing. His wife was still awake, her face bathed in the soft light of a bedside lamp, her much-treasured copy of Miguel de Cervantes' *Don Quixote* in her hands.

He sat down on the edge of the bed and kissed her. 'Schwartz tells me you're a lot better.'

'Much better, darling, thank you,' she smiled.

'That's good, but you really need to be careful, Anna. Remember what the doctor said the last time: bronchitis can easily turn into pneumonia.'

She looked lovingly at him. 'Klaus, darling, please, stop worrying about me. Greta has taken very good care of me. She's been marvellous, so kind. She's such a good friend. I don't know what I would do without her.' Anna touched his brow, her hand drifting slowly down the side of his face. 'You look so tired,' she said.

That night, Frau von Menen slept the sleep of the blissfully content, but not so her husband.

The burden of command had been lifted, but General von Menen still felt the agonising torment of the Russian Front, where German soldiers – cold, hungry and weary – faced the insurmountable odds of the Red Army: enough T-34 tanks to line the autobahn between Berlin and Hamburg, more YAK fighter planes than a flock of starlings on a migratory flight south, and enough troops to fill the Berlin Olympic Stadium over and over and over again. Yet Hitler continued to complain that *his* armies were not doing enough.

The rain had stopped, the silence broken only by Anna's hushed breathing. Exhausted, with all hope of sleep abandoned, the General slipped silently from his bed, sat down by the window, parted the curtains and peered out across the dark, vast expanse of his beloved Mecklenburg.

His wife stirred just as dawn broke. 'What's the matter, Klaus?'

The question went unanswered. General von Menen was lost in an ocean of misery, his mind tangled by the thought of a future where only agony and despair would exist. Anna slipped out of bed and hurried across the room, the light of day settling on a tortured face, a husband she hardly recognised. Kneeling beside him, she placed her arm around his shoulder.

'What is it, Klaus?'

'I'm not so sure you'd want to know,' he said.

'I do. Please tell me… I'm your wife, I love you.'

He looked at her pensively. 'I'm finished, Anna. They have no further use for me. I've been transferred to the Führer Reserve.'

She stared at him, a hail of conflicting thoughts rushing through her mind. 'And Hans?' she asked carefully.

'The same.'

'Couldn't Heinz have done anything for you? I mean…'

A wry smile slipped across the General's face. 'Guderian may be a little unconventional, my dear, but these days, he's as invalid as the rest of us. Three more months and he'll be the same as me – gone! In any case, it's all rather academic.' Gently squeezing her hand, he looked into her eyes. 'Anna, my dear, we've lost. Germany cannot hope to stem the tidal wave of defeat. The Allies are unstoppable… It will all be over by next spring. And when it *is* over, we won't just be beaten, we'll be humiliated.' He sighed heavily. 'My greatest fear is that the Russians will be at the gates of Berlin before either the Americans or the British. At the rate they're going, they could easily occupy the whole of Mecklenburg.'

'Which means we'll lose everything.'

'Everything.'

'You're sure the Russians will get here first?'

'We are their main political objective, Anna. They have a burning desire to punish us.'

At that moment there was a faint knock on the door.

'That will be Schwartz. I asked him to serve coffee at eight-thirty.'

Frau von Menen rose to her feet, adjusted her dressing gown and made to open the door. 'Leave it on the table, please. I'll serve it myself.'

Schwartz took his leave and left them to their privacy.

Anna von Menen poured coffee for both of them and sipped hers, staring pensively at a photograph of her parents on the dressing table. 'Seems my father was right, *"Hitler will ruin this country."* He said it often.'

'It's not just Hitler, Anna, it's this whole, rotten stinking ideology they call Nazism. We should have done something about it... I mean, me and others like me.' He shook his head, appalled at his own dereliction. 'We saw it happening and we did nothing about it. *"Hitler was elected to power democratically,"* they said. *"Using force to depose him would be contrary to the high principles and traditions of the German military."* I said it myself just three months ago: *"Prussian officers do not mutiny."* And now, I'm ashamed of what happened to those who *did* try to change things – von Witzleben, Beck, Olbricht, Stauffenberg, von Stülpnagel, Speidel, Canaris...' He paused, uncertain that he should say anything further, but he trusted his wife. 'As for that evil organisation of Himmler's... heaven alone knows what will happen when their vile, inhuman perversities come to light.'

'What do you mean?'

The General buried his face in his hands and rubbed his eyes. 'Do you recall me telling you about what had happened in Poland... and afterwards, in Russia? Units of Himmler's Einsatzgruppen followed on behind the army, carrying out their so-called ethnic cleansing operations. General Blaskowitz tried to stop it, remember?'

She shuddered at the recollection. 'Yes, I do. It was ghastly, quite ghastly.'

He reached out for her hand. 'Anna, in the occupied territories, that kind of thing has been going on for years. And if we're to believe the rumours about what's been going on inside the so-called concentration camps, it's been happening here, too, in Germany.'

Anna von Menen, a woman of charm, culture and great compassion, clenched her fists, pain rushing across her face. 'We've heard the *rumours*, yes,' she stuttered, 'but surely, they... they can't be true, can they? I mean, how could they do that to *anyone*, let alone their own countrymen?'

'*They*, Anna, are not ordinary people; they're crazed fanatics, madmen. Believe me, when this country finally falls, as it surely will, there'll be widespread retributions, especially at the hands of the Russians. The Americans and British will insist on a more judicial approach, proper courts and proper trials.' His eyes peeled wide open. 'But you can be sure of one thing; some *will* pay the ultimate penalty.'

★

A light knock on the door and Schwartz walked into the dining room.

'Sorry to disturb your lunch, General, ma'am, but there's a gentleman on the telephone. Gave his name as Baumer, says it's *very* important, sir.'

'Very well, Schwartz, I'll take it in the library.'

General von Menen looked at his wife, rolling his eyes in exasperation.

'Who's Baumer, darling?' she asked.

'Gestapo... A bumptious SS captain on Hitler's staff... arrogant, conceited, coarse and not very intelligent.

Does a lot of hawking for Bormann. He's certainly no *gentleman*.'

Even though the door was closed, Frau von Menen could hear her husband's fiery side of the conversation.

'What! No, it's not convenient. Can't it wait a few days? You're damn right I'm annoyed.' There was a lull in the exchange. 'Right, have a plane collect me at Priwall, tomorrow morning, ten o'clock sharp. And make sure it isn't a Storch – I want to be there and back on the same day, with no stops! Really? Well, aren't I the lucky one.'

General von Menen returned to the dining room, *fait accompli* written all over his face. 'Sorry, Anna,' he said, 'but I've got to go to Rastenburg... Hitler's headquarters. Nothing to worry about. I'll only be gone for one day.'

★

Deep in the Görlitz Forest, a hundred kilometres south-east of Königsberg, Hitler's Supreme Headquarters made for a dismal and ominous setting; a series of purpose-built wooden huts and fortified concrete bunkers surrounded by impenetrable barbed wire fences.

Baumer, thirty-two years old, one metre seventy-five, with a bull neck and a face like a fairground boxer, walked into the room. The three-inch scar along his left cheek lent him the image of a foil-parrying member of the German aristocracy, but in truth, it was the mark of a chiv, put there by a left-wing agitator during his street-brawling days with the Nazi SA.

'Ah, General, you've arrived at last.'

General von Menen regarded the insult calmly, peeled off his gloves and laid them on top of the desk. 'Hauptsturmführer Baumer,' he said quietly, 'if you can find time to restrain your effrontery for a moment, you will see that I am not a figment of your imagination, I am actually standing here, before you, in reality – *an infantry general of the German army!* Why I'm here, I do not know.'

'I know who you are, General,' replied Baumer, eyes riveted on the large brown envelope that he pushed disdainfully across his desk. 'You're here to see the Head of the Party Chancellery.'

'Herr Bormann?'

'Yes, but he's otherwise engaged with the Führer, discussing certain matters with some of your... er... *former* colleagues. You are to read the contents of this in my presence, memorise the instructions and then' – he flicked a glance at the fire which was crackling furiously at the far side of the room – 'burn them!'

General von Menen lifted the envelope, seated himself by the fireplace and sliced it open to reveal two sheets of paper, each marked TOP SECRET. He had just reached the foot of the second page when the door to the adjoining office pushed open, revealing the clockwork figure of an SS Standartenführer. Baumer stood, saluted the Standartenführer and gestured discreetly in the direction of the seated General von Menen.

The Standartenführer proceeded towards the fireplace. 'Good day, General von Menen, I am Standartenführer Keppler. Herr Bormann sends his apologies, but he is otherwise engaged, hence he has instructed me to speak to you. I trust you had a good flight?'

The General looked up. 'I did, thank you, but having read this, I'm not so sure that I should be here. I am a General of Infantry, *not* a transport sergeant.'

Keppler regarded the distinguished infantry commander with some reverence. 'I am aware of your legendary deeds, General, but you will note that the order has been signed at the very highest level. We are not talking about a simple matter of transportation; we are talking about a very special convoy.' He reclined into the chair on the other side of the fireplace. 'You are about to assume responsibility for a highly secret operation, General, an operation which is of vital importance to the future of the Third Reich. I'm—'

Keppler broke off abruptly. The door to the room from which he had emerged was still ajar and from it spewed the high-pitched shrill of a man who, by some fluke of history, had endeared a maniacal, disciple-like following, his ranting cutting through the stillness of the Görlitz Forest, the words *'betrayal'*, *'disloyalty'*, *'duplicity'* and *'treason'* peppered with frequent utterances of *'useless'*, *'craven'* and *'renegade'* reaching through to the anteroom. Two morose-looking generals emerged, smiled weakly and headed straight for the door.

Sighing in dismay, General von Menen picked up the order and turned back to Keppler. 'There's no mention of logistics.'

'I'm working on that right now. As soon as I have the information, I will contact you. You'll then have two days in which to report to Berlin for a second briefing.'

'Berlin – what's left of it – is a big city,' retorted the General. 'Where and to whom do I report?'

A wry smile adorned Keppler's face. 'You will receive that information ahead of your departure. Hauptsturmführer Baumer will be there to meet you. He will explain everything.'

'Why the delay?'

'It's a question of storage. I'm hoping to resolve it within the next couple of weeks, but it could take a little longer.'

The General replied with weighted cynicism. 'Standartenführer Keppler, I can wait as long as you like, but I doubt the Russians will afford you the same amount of patience!'

225

15

Saturday 21ˢᵗ October 1944

As twilight settled over eastern Spain, the four-engine Condor airliner raced down the runway at Barcelona Airport and clawed its way into the firmament. Ahead lay over 600 kilometres of hostile skies.

At eight o'clock, an announcement echoed through the cabin. *'Ladies and Gentleman… Captain speaking. Perhaps you sensed our last manoeuvre… We have crossed the Italian Riviera.'* The announcement was greeted with spontaneous applause.

Von Menen settled back in relief and drifted into a deep sleep. The plane rolled down the runway at Munich's Riem Airport, made a half-hour stop-over and then took off again. Still he didn't stir.

'Carl… Carl… Carl.'

The incessant whispering in his ear and the repeated nudging at his arm finally roused him. Von Menen opened his eyes to see a face leaning towards him. He shook himself from his daze and sat bolt upright.

'My God, Ulricht? Ulricht Hoffman?'

'Yes,' smiled the man in the seat across the aisle.

'Goodness, I haven't seen you for—'

'Six years, just after I left the army,' supplied Hoffman.

'What are you doing here?' asked von Menen, as they shook hands.

Hoffman laughed. 'The same as you; going to Berlin!'

Von Menen stared at his dark blue uniform. 'But I thought you were serving with the Luftwaffe?'

'I was, until I was shot down over France... May, '40. They gave me a medal, a small pension and then kicked me out. Since then, I've been a pilot with this outfit.'

'Deutsche Lufthansa?'

'Yes, for over three and a half years. And you? I heard you'd joined the Foreign Office?'

'That's right. I've been away for the past three years — Argentina...' – von Menen halted, his covert past pricking at his mind – 'and then Madrid for a year,' he added hurriedly.

'Lovely city; I've been on the Madrid route for the past month. Going there again next week.'

Von Menen was now wide awake, eyes as bright as beacons.

'Must be all of three years since you last saw Berlin?' mused Hoffman.

'June, '41. Evidently, I'm in for a bit of a shock.'

'You certainly are. Married?'

'No... you?'

Hoffman steeled himself to reply. 'I was,' he said, his smile melting away. 'My wife was killed in an air raid last March. I was on a trip to Stockholm at the time.'

Von Menen leaned across the aisle. 'Ulricht, I'm very sorry. It must have been a dreadful shock to you. Do you have children?'

'Yes, a little girl. Miraculously, she survived. My mother looks after her.'

The pitch of the engines changed as the airliner altered course, Tempelhof just a few kilometres away. They flew over the Havel and the Berliner Forest. Up ahead, the sprawling conurbation of Berlin, dotted with a patchwork of glowing fires, came into view.

Hoffman noted von Menen's look of unease. 'Don't even think about it, Carl. You'll get used to it.'

'Will I?'

'Everyone does, in time. Where are you heading when we arrive?'

'I'll check out my parents' house first. If I can't get in, I'll find a hotel.'

'I'll give you a lift into town,' said Hoffman. 'There's no public transport at this time of night and finding a hotel just isn't that simple. If the worst comes to the worst, you can stay at my place. I live with my mother, back in Dahlem.' Hoffman flicked his head over his shoulder, as if Dahlem was at the rear of the cabin. 'When we arrive at Tempelhof, I have to report to crew scheduling, so I won't be taking the same route into the building. Give me twenty minutes and I'll meet you outside.'

Von Menen ambled towards the terminal with a growing unwillingness, his only solace being that he would not be asked any searching questions about "Herr Lindemann" in the company of Ulricht Hoffman.

He was the last in the queue, the crushing image of the Gestapo's Frontier Police already in sight – two desks, two officers, two Walther P38s and all the paraphernalia of Nazi bureaucracy.

'Next!' called the officer on the left. Von Menen closed the last three yards with all the enthusiasm of a schoolboy heading for a caning, the hairs at the nape of his neck bristling like the needles on a porcupine's back. 'Passport!' ordered the officer gruffly. Von Menen coughed nervously, laid the document on the desk and waited.

'Ah, so *you* are Herr Lindemann?'

Von Menen swallowed hard. 'Yes.' The officer turned and raised his hand. A man in a dark brown suit hurried across the hall, footsteps ringing on the marble floor. *This is it. Werner's coded signal was a dupe. No more worries about accommodation; next stop, Gestapo Headquarters. Today I have a full set of teeth, tomorrow…*

'Herr Lindemann?'

'Yes, I'm Lindemann,' confirmed von Menen.

'SS Captain Josef Daufenbach, Gestapo Frontier Police.' His voice was staid, his face void of expression. He reached into his pocket, von Menen unmoving, waiting for manacles. 'I've been asked to give you this,' said Daufenbach, handing von Menen a wax-sealed envelope. 'An official from the Foreign Office delivered it this afternoon.'

Relief zipped through von Menen's body. He felt weak and mentally battered but his heartbeat was normal again.

'Thank you,' he answered politely. He picked up his passport and walked away. Through the swing doors at the end of the hall, he ripped open the envelope and read the handwritten message.

Welcome home. Go to Wilhelmstrasse tomorrow morning. W.

Hoffman picked his way cautiously through the darkness, a fine sickle moon in the sky. Von Menen sat motionless, eyes glued to the windscreen, the sight spearing his mind like a red-hot needle. It was worse than he'd envisaged, much worse.

Even in darkness, the destruction was mind-numbingly visible: burned-out carcasses of cars, trucks and trams; bombed-out buildings and flattened streets; mountains of debris everywhere.

Along Wilhelmstrasse, the scene was one of widespread devastation. The Foreign Office, bleak and desolate, looked like an unfinished building smothered by a patchwork of tarpaulin sheets, flapping in the wind like the sails of *Mary Celeste*. Ahead lay the ruins of the

Hotel Bristol, and opposite, the gutted shell of the British Embassy. The Hotel Adlon, a relic of its majestic past, was a pitiful sight.

Hoffman made a right into Unter den Linden. Its destruction was unimaginable. The once magnificent avenue looked like the aftermath of an earthquake, the smell of tragedy rising from every pile of rubble. Von Menen jabbed at Hoffman's arm, urged him to make a left. A hundred yards further, his face turned ashen grey.

'Ulricht, STOP!' He gaped silently at the scene across the road, cold beads of sweat emerging from his brow. 'Please, God, no!'

Leaping from the car, he raced across the street. The once elegant town house lay in ruins, the whole front missing. All that remained was the rear wall. Numbed by the sight, von Menen clasped his hands to his face.

'I'm sorry, Carl. Someone you know?' asked Hoffman.

'My parents,' choked von Menen.

Ulricht took hold of his arm. They scrambled towards a piece of timber, standing starkly upright among a pile of debris at the back. On it, in smudged white paint, was the inscription: *"Von Menen family – all safe."*

Gasping a long sigh of relief, von Menen flopped down on a slab of concrete. 'Thank God... Thank God, they're safe. You know, Ulricht, I was so damn naive, I'd no idea it would be so bad.'

Hoffman sat down beside him. 'The major raids started last November,' he explained. 'The Royal Air Force sent 750 bombers in just one night. It was like Armageddon... Huge blankets of fire and smoke over much of Berlin... The fires burned well into the next day. Wilhelmstrasse, Unter den Linden, Friedrichstrasse, all badly hit. Nowadays, they send Mosquitos. There's no warning, they just appear, anywhere, anytime. It really plays on the nerves. By day there are also

the Americans, wave after wave, like birds migrating south.'
Hoffman was lost in thought, recalling the bombs that fell
like blossom in an orchard. Then he shook himself and
jumped to his feet. 'Come on, let's go. We've been brooding
for long enough. And I've just thought where you'll find a
room.'

'Where's that?'

'The Savoy.'

'Off Kurfürstendamm?'

'Yes, wonderful place, even nowadays. I stayed there on
the first night of my honeymoon. I know the front of house
director, Johann Ritter, splendid chap. I'm sure he'll find a
room for you.'

'I recall staying there myself,' said von Menen. 'New
Year's Eve, '38, I think. A group of us had been to a dance at
the nearby Delphi.'

'You won't be doing any dancing tonight, Carl,' said
Hoffman. 'Dancing in public has been banned for over two
years.'

'You're joking?'

'No. There's nothing left to joke about these days.'

Through the Brandenburg Gate the picture was surreal,
like a scene from the battlefields of the Great War – bombed-
out buildings, craters and weird, skeletal silhouettes of
splintered trees. It looked like another planet. Hoffman made
a left at the Grosser Stern, skirted around what remained
of the zoo, and headed off along Kurfürstendamm. A right
turn at Fasanenstrasse brought them alongside the Savoy.

'Wait here a second.' Hoffman popped inside and was
back in a minute, a large smile on his face. 'You're in luck;
they have a room.' He lifted von Menen's luggage onto the
sidewalk, scribbled down a brief note and pushed it into his
hand. 'It's been great seeing you again, Carl, really it has.
Here's my address and telephone number. Let's not wait

another six years before we meet again, okay? Life's too short. In the meantime, if you need anything, anything at all, please call me.'

There was something... ah! *'Madrid... Going there again next week!'* Von Menen could scarcely believe his luck; Hoffman, the ideal intermediary, a chance he could not give up. Cortes, the epitome of discretion, would see it that way too, von Menen knew he would.

'As a matter of fact, Ulricht, there is something, if you'd be so kind. Do you have another piece of paper?'

'Sure.'

Von Menen scratched down Cortes's name and address, plucked the pocket watch from his breast pocket and held it in his hand. 'You might think this a bit of an imposition, Ulricht, but my watch gave up on me yesterday and the fellow whose name I've just given you lent me this. He's a good friend and I'd like to get it back to him as quickly as possible. He's a lawyer. We went to Madrid University together and we've kept in touch ever since. But if you think that it's, well, irregular...'

'No, that's quite all right, Carl, leave it with me. I'll deliver it personally.'

'Thanks, Ulricht. I owe you.'

Even in its less functional state, the Hotel Savoy was an oasis of calm and organised efficiency, a citadel of welcome relief amid the desert of chaos and mayhem. The feeling of warmth and invulnerability was immediate.

In the lobby stood the graceful and polished front-of-house director, Johann Ritter, himself the symbol of five-star luxury, stylish in a half-morning suit, two centimetres of starched white cuff peeking from below the hem of his sleeves, his beard and moustache clipped to mathematical precision.

'Good evening, Herr von Menen, welcome to the Savoy. I believe I know your father, General von Menen?'

'That's right, yes.'

'Your parents stayed here last May. It was after the air raid, terrible business. Your father was on leave… And you, sir, have you been here before?'

'Yes, about six years ago; 1938, I think it was.'

'Well, you'll find things a little different nowadays. We're a bit lacking in certain quarters, but we do our best. It's the war, you know.'

'Yes, I understand.'

'I've put you in room 501. It's on the top floor, directly ahead of the staircase, overlooking Fasanenstrasse. Problem is, we're not allowed to use the lift, and we're short of staff… bellboys, porters, all gone, all conscripted… so I'll give you a hand with your luggage. Herr Hoffman mentioned that you'd been away for a while?'

'Yes.'

'Then perhaps I should give you a few words of advice about air raids. First, do you have a flashlight?'

Von Menen fished in his bag, pulled out a torch he'd bought in Buenos Aires three years previously, and gave Ritter a quick "on/off" demonstration.

'Good, then you won't need a candle. If you hear the siren, make your way directly to the shelter in the basement. No need to change out of your pyjamas, just put your jacket and trousers on over the top. It can be quite chilly down there.' The conversation continued all the way up the staircase. 'There's plenty of hot water,' said Ritter, 'but the rules here are just the same as those outside – only one bath per week, on either Saturday or Sunday.'

At the second floor, a group of chattering Orientals passed them on the landing. Ritter noted the bemused expression on von Menen's face.

'Japanese,' he whispered. 'They've been here since their Embassy was bombed.'

Reaching the fifth floor, von Menen's thoughts turned to his parents. 'What about telephones? I'm very anxious to get in touch with my mother.'

'There's a telephone in each room, sir. You'll have to go through the switchboard, of course, but if you give me the number, I'll get Frau Horstmann to place a call for you tomorrow morning.'

They reached the room. Ritter unlocked the door, went in first and placed the two suitcases by the side of the dressing table.

'The bathroom is over there, sir; telephone by the bed; light switch above the headboard. If you require an extra blanket, there's one in the wardrobe. Oh, and this is very important... the curtains *must* be closed *before* you switch on the lights. The police are very strict about blackout procedures.'

Ritter took his leave and von Menen switched out the light. Peering through a chink in the curtains, he saw the vague outline of the Delphi Dance Palace, the past engulfing his mind – Saturday night gaiety, joyous amusement; Sigi Bredow, Lutzi, Gustav Helldorf and himself, swaying to the big band sound of Teddy Stauffer. Now, it was only a memory. Even the Kreisau Circle was just a memory, buried beneath the failed attempt to topple Hitler. Berlin was being swept away, and with it would go the rest of Germany.

Von Menen saw a desperate future, all the more fearsome by the biting anguish at the back of his mind. *How long will it be before my links with the Kreisau Circle emerge?* His life was more precarious now than it had ever been.

16

Selling Vidal's scheme to von Ribbentrop would not be easy, still less von Ribbentrop convincing Hitler that there was sufficient merit in it for the Nazis. Yet with Germany almost on her knees, von Menen was confident that some elements of the Nazi hierarchy would trade even Bavaria for a safe haven in Argentina, let alone a shipment of arms. For them, Vidal's hare-brained scheme would prove too tempting by far.

At five-thirty in the morning, after an anxious, sleepless night, and with a desperate craving to explore the streets of Berlin, von Menen left the Savoy and headed towards Kantstrasse. It was still dark, but the light cast by the crescent moon was enough to make him gasp in horror at the ghostly, darkened shapes of burned-out buildings.

Hurrying along Fasanenstrasse, he passed the Kurfürstendamm, eyes falling upon a scene of biblical proportions, the ruination horrific, the air a fusion of charred wood, damp rubble, gas and putrefied flesh. He felt like a man in an alien land. Further along, he stopped at a place he'd known so well, but no longer recognised.

Where once had stood Lutzi's apartment, a rusting, jagged piece of metal reached up from a high pile of masonry, looking like the outstretched arm of a drowning man. Von

Menen's mind spun back to his last night in Berlin, the memory of Lutzi, Sigi and Gustav echoing inside his head, a lump rising in his throat, tears coursing unashamedly down his face.

Pushing the memory to the depths of his mind, he wiped the tears from his cheeks, headed towards Budapester Strasse and began the long trek to the Foreign Office. But a short diversion to Lützowstrasse fetched another anguishing sight: The Bredows' sumptuous villa, where the "gang" had often partied until the early hours, had vanished. All that remained was a huge mound of rubble. Von Menen froze at the vision, the tension in his chest almost squeezing the life out of him, his grandfather's words tolling in his mind like the bell of death: *'Hitler will lead this country to ruination.'*

It was nearing light when he reached Wilhelmstrasse, the skyline a profile of destruction. Beyond the Reich Chancellery stood what remained of the Foreign Office, the main entrance flanked by two SS guards. One noted his name and escorted him inside.

Von Ribbentrop's one-time grandiose headquarters looked like an abandoned building site, heavy oak timbers forming a jumbled architecture of shored-up walls, ceilings, doorways and windows. It was damp and cold. Marble floors that had once resounded to the footsteps of German and foreign dignitaries lay fragmented, cracked and splintered. The lavish fittings and plush carpets had gone, and with them, the feeling of splendour and richness.

Only a small number of staff were on duty, the bulk of the organisation now operating from the safety of a cluster of villages in Silesia. A thin, gaunt man with bulbous, watery eyes announced himself as the Duty Officer. He handed von Menen a travel warrant, a wad of coupons and a typed itinerary.

'You're to travel to Krummhübel tomorrow morning,' the Duty Officer said. 'A certain von Althoff will be waiting to meet you at the station.'

'Von Althoff?'

'Yes, he phoned yesterday.'

Von Menen looked heedfully at the SS guard. 'I don't suppose there's any mention of the name *Werner*, is there?'

'Afraid not, just von Althoff. You're to take the courier train from Görlitzer Station at six in the morning, change at Hirschberg and take the local train to Krummhübel. Von Althoff will be waiting for you on the platform. And don't lose the rail warrant. Without it, you won't get on the train.'

Von Menen made his way back to the Hotel Savoy, his mind full of renewed suspicion. *Who is von Althoff? Who will be my host at Krummhübel – Werner, Schellenberg or Kaltenbrunner?*

★

It was an ecstatic meeting. Klaus and Anna von Menen hadn't seen their son in over three years, and it showed. A full thirty seconds passed before Anna finally untangled herself from her boy. She moved back a step, reached out and touched his face, as if not quite sure that he was standing there.

'We couldn't believe it when we heard your voice on the phone,' she said excitedly, the questions coming in quick-fire succession. 'Where've you been? What have you been doing? Will you be staying?'

'I flew in from Madrid on Saturday and stayed with Juan for a couple of weeks. Sorry I didn't phone, but it was quite impossible. He sends his very best wishes, by the way. Now... tell me about Katrina and Jürgen.'

'They're both fine. Katrina is...' – Anna saw the General

glancing her a caution – 'well, she's staying with Marlena in Hanover. She'll be home in a few days. Jürgen, too, we hope.'

They sat down, listening attentively as von Menen recounted his nauseating experience along Kurfürstendamm.

'I went round to Lutzi's place, or what was left of it. Afterwards, I passed by the remains of the Bredow villa. Are they...?'

'Sigi and her mother were out during the raid, but Herr Bredow was killed,' replied his mother, 'and the news about Lutzi isn't so good.' She turned, looked searchingly at her husband. 'Klaus, I think *you* should tell him.'

'Tell me what?' asked von Menen anxiously. The General gestured to the two adjoining rooms. 'It's all right, Father, I've checked. Both rooms are empty and the light fittings are clean.'

Inching himself a little nearer to the edge of the bed, Klaus von Menen gathered himself. 'Carl, a lot has happened since you left. Life in Germany is not what it used to be, not even in 1941.'

'I know, Father. I've seen it outside and I've read about it in the foreign press, though I suspect I've seen and heard only the half of it.'

'Remember Lutzi's brother, who worked at the War Ministry?'

'Konrad?'

'Yes. He was arrested a few days after the attempt on Hitler's life. His immediate family was arrested. Lutzi was one of them... and Sigi, too. The Gestapo refer to it as "kith and kin" detention. Lutzi was held at Lehderstrasse Prison. The last we heard was that she'd been moved to a concentration camp; Flossenbürg, we think.'

'And Sigi?'

'They kept her at Gestapo headquarters for a few days and then released her. No one knows where she is now.'

'And… what became of Konrad?'

'He was hanged at Plötzensee Prison last month.'

Von Menen took a long gulp of air, his face white with rage.

'Many suffered the same treatment,' explained the General. 'You knew Adam von Trott zu Solz, didn't you?'

'Yes, I heard about his fate. I heard about Helmuth von Moltke, too.'

'Gottfried von Bismarck fared a little better. His name saved him, but only as far as a concentration camp. As for Helmuth von Moltke, he's still being held, as is General Oster, Canaris's number two. Word has it that they're in Ravensbrück. You've heard about Rommel, I suppose?'

'Yes, the Spanish newspapers carried the story… Embolism, wasn't it?'

'That's how it was reported. Truth is, *he* was alleged to have been involved in the plot, too, but he chose the alternative to a show trial. Shortly after being visited by two generals, he poisoned himself.'

Von Menen got to his feet and paced back and forth between the door and the window, his mind about to explode. He sat down again, turned to his father and said, 'You haven't mentioned Gustav Helldorf.'

His mother rose from the edge of the bed and gently took hold of his arm. 'Gustav is dead, Carl. He was killed on the Eastern Front at the beginning of August. There was no way we could let you know. All the non-conformists in Government posts were called up a long time ago. They caught up with Gustav just after he and Lutzi were…' She paused, her lips quivering.

'After he and Lutzi were what?'

'Married, last June. Five weeks later, Gustav was in

uniform and on his way to the Eastern Front. We didn't find out that he'd been killed until September. I tried to get in touch with his mother, but we heard she'd gone to stay with her sister at Hanover. As far as I know, she's still there. I tried phoning the house at Schwerin several times, but the calls were never answered. It's doubly sad for Frau Helldorf. You see, Gustav's older brother, Friedrich… he was shot down before Stalingrad, almost two years ago.'

Numb with grief, von Menen dropped back in his chair. He clenched his fists, pressed his eyes shut and shook his head slowly in disbelief. 'I can't believe it. The whole of the Helldorf men-folk, dead: first, Gustav's father in 1917, and now Gustav *and* Friedrich.' Von Menen got to his feet again, grief overtaken by a fusion of frenzied thoughts. Dazed, he walked over to the window, looked out across Fasanenstrasse, probing the burned-out husks on the opposite side of the road. 'Father,' he said in a hushed voice, his back to the room, 'I could see *some* merit in a limited action against Poland, just to regain unrestricted access to East Prussia. But the rest of it… I mean, what was the *real* purpose in attacking Russia?'

'Hitler's demented obsession, Carl, his mindless determination to smash communism and colonise the east.'

'Colonise the east? Colonise the whole damn *Universe*, more like it. For nearly three years, we've been fighting the whole world: the British Empire, the Americans and the Russians. Now we're fighting the Italians and meanwhile we've lost our influence in Latin America. It's been a complete catastrophe! Perhaps you could tell me, Father, how the hell we allowed ourselves to get into this mess?'

Disabled by the directness of his son's question, the General looked helplessly at his wife, searching for a modicum of inspiration. Their eyes staged a brief discussion.

'I suppose it's because I, and others like me, allowed it to happen,' he replied, in a voice full of remorse.

'You *suppose*, Father? Then why didn't the likes of you and the *others* – by which I presume you're referring to your Prussian colleagues – join with Beck, von Witzleben, Stülpnagel and Rommel? It would have been the proper thing to do!'

'Carl!' cried his mother, noting the General's look of despair. 'You know our position as far as the Nazis are concerned. We despise them, just as much as you do. Our views have not changed and neither have your father's principles – Prussian officers do not mutiny.'

'Mother, mutiny is open rebellion against *constituted* authority! The Nazis do not have constituted authority.'

General von Menen endeavoured to calm the situation. 'But in 1932, Carl, the electorate of this country presented Hitler with a massive democratic mandate.'

'Thank you, Father, but I know all about that – if you're hungry, you'll vote for anybody and if you're very hungry, you'll vote for the Devil. And that's what most people did, they voted for the Devil!'

'I wouldn't argue with that, but when Hindenburg died, ninety per cent of the electorate of this country, *ninety per cent*, mind, voted to support Hitler's notion that he should become Head of State, as well as being Chancellor.'

'But that was over ten years ago – since when he's received no votes at all, because no one's *allowed* to vote. How many votes do you think he'd have got after Stalingrad?' Von Menen, his anger spent, caught the dejected look on his father's face. Then, when he thought about his own, feeble, miserly role with the Kreisau Circle, the memory of Vidal and all that had happened in Argentina, he was sickened by his own sanctimony. 'I'm sorry, Father,' he said, his voice loaded with regret,

'I wasn't intending to be personal. You know how much I love and respect you.'

'I know, Carl, and I accept that much of what you've said is true.' The General looked at his wife, who nodded her agreement. 'We both do. Hitler's fight is no longer for Germany. It's not even for the preservation of the Nazi Party. It's for himself. He's trying to stave off the impossible; save his own neck! We cannot possibly win the war. In my opinion, all we have left is about six months.' The General rose from the edge of the bed, walked over to his son and placed his hands about his shoulders. 'But you must realise, Carl, that while we, the family, can talk like this, defeatist talk will not be tolerated by the Nazis. There are still many people who would willingly denounce those with such views and the penalties are very severe. The fact is, it's not just Hitler; madness is endemic throughout the SS.'

Von Menen couldn't argue with that, but his own involvement weighed heavily. 'Father, you mentioned on the telephone that a man visited Mother last February.'

'Yes. Werner, I think his name was. That's right, isn't it, Anna?'

'Yes,' agreed Frau von Menen. 'He didn't say a great deal, just that you were doing something *very special*, as he put it. He was very discreet. We thought you might possibly have gone to Paraguay, Chile, or even Peru.'

Von Menen nodded and gave his father a significant look.

'Does this relate to what you wanted to ask me?' enquired the General.

Noting the immediacy of something sensitive, Frau von Menen, the lifelong epitome of discretion, made towards the door.

Von Menen stretched out his arms. 'Mother, please. You don't have to leave. If I can't trust you, who can I trust?' He

242

turned to the General. 'In assessing my own situation, and by that, I mean the reason I am back in Germany, I need answers to some very pertinent questions.'

'Go on.'

'The Abwehr is no longer part of the Wehrmacht, right?'

'True. It's been dissolved. The function of the Abwehr comes under the umbrella of the RSHA, Kaltenbrunner's outfit. The man who now runs the foreign intelligence service is Walter Schellenberg, an SS Brigadier, a bright, scheming individual, only thirty-four and very slippery. Rumour has it he has immediate and unrestricted access to Himmler.' He noted the searching look in his son's eyes. 'Sorry, Carl, I've no idea if he's procured your outfit.'

'Well, I have a meeting with someone tomorrow and I'm hoping he won't be wearing the uniform of the SS.'

'You do know that the whole of the Foreign Office has moved south?' asked Frau von Menen.

'Yes, Mother, that's where I'm going tomorrow, Krummhübel.'

'Any idea when you're likely to be back? Only we've decided to stay in Berlin for a few days. It's Great-aunt Helga's ninetieth birthday tomorrow and since we're here, we thought we'd pay her a surprise visit.'

'By the end of the week, I hope, but I really can't say for sure.'

Frau von Menen glanced hurriedly at her watch. 'Goodness, it's nearly five o'clock. Hans and Greta will have been waiting downstairs for the past hour.'

Von Menen picked up the phone, then stalled, tapping the handset slowly in the palm of his hand. 'Tell me, Father... von Moltke...'

The General saw the aching look in his son's eyes and perceived the question instantly. 'I knew all about your involvement with the Kreisau Circle, Carl,' he said. 'Your mother did, too. Call it intuition, if you like, or even a father's expectation of his son. Had I not been a professional soldier, I'd have done the same.'

'But—'

'I know… you're concerned that your name might eventually come up… but I doubt it will. They're all honourable men, and besides, you've been away far too long.'

Unlike the view he held of his adopted uncle Manfred, Carl von Menen had never regarded the Steigers as anything other than an older brother and sister. It had been that way for over twenty years.

Mesmerised by the sight and smiling eyes of her "little brother", Greta Steiger stood motionless in the doorway, tears of joy welling in her eyes. Suddenly, she could wait no more. Throwing down her coat, she ran to him like a woman hurrying to catch the last bus. 'Missed you,' she whispered.

'Missed you, too, Greta, and your apple pies.'

'Oh, you…! You haven't changed a bit.'

'Neither have you, Greta. You look marvellous. It's so good to see you again.'

Greta Steiger moved aside, allowing the massive frame of her husband to envelope the "boy" he had taught to box almost twenty years ago. 'Good to see you again, Carl.'

'You, too, Hans. It's been a long time.'

'Yes, we've got a lot of catching up to do.'

'A few rounds in the courtyard?'

'Look, I'm an old man now,' joked Steiger.

'A little heavier, too, I'd say, but I'd wager you haven't changed.' Von Menen flicked a quick glance at Greta. 'Tell me, is this husband of yours still up to his old pranks?' The two men exchanged a few playful punches.

Greta, stunned with joy, brushed a tear from her cheek and nodded. 'Your father thinks he's a bit of a magician... can't for the life of me think why.' She flashed a smile at the General.

'Best you don't know, Carl,' said the General. 'I don't. I'd rather not.'

'Well, Hans?' asked von Menen.

'Your father gets very concerned about where all the extra petrol, wine and food comes from, but as I keep telling him, they're presents from General Montgomery.'

The room resounded with raucous laughter. It was the tonic everyone needed.

They retired early that evening, but a little after ten o'clock, Berlin resounded to the sound of wailing sirens.

Von Menen clambered from his bed, slipped on his clothes and headed for the basement, his parents and the Steigers already there, along with many others, including what looked like the entire staff of the Japanese legation, all sitting calmly on long wooden benches.

No one spoke; the only noises an occasional cough, the shuffling of feet and the babble of overhead water pipes. Two candles flickered on an old table, the glow dancing on the brown-painted walls. An elderly man, the legs of his blue-and-green striped pyjamas showing beneath the hem of his coat, pulled out a half-bottle of schnapps and took a long swallow.

Moments later came the incessant crack of flak and the crump of high explosive incendiaries, bells ringing, sirens howling. Von Menen looked up and held his breath, the walls trembling, dust fluttering down from the ceiling. Overhead, a water pipe began to hiss until finally it started to leak, a fine spray of water falling on the table, just missing the candles.

'British Mosquitos, Carl,' commented Steiger, 'here to liven up the sirens, disrupt night-time factory work, cause as much mayhem as they can and get the emergency services flying around Berlin like racing pigeons.'

At one o'clock, the "all clear" sounded. The Savoy was still standing. So was von Menen. His Berlin baptism was over.

Welcome to the war.

17

At the untimely hour of five o'clock, Steiger dropped von Menen at Görlitzer Station, the platform teeming with hundreds of cold and desperate people, their whole lives crammed into battered suitcases, prams, pitiful makeshift trolleys, crates and tattered cardboard boxes.

A long line of carriages stretched down the platform, a giant locomotive at the front, hissing and spitting steam, the hazy orange hue radiating from its open firebox blissfully comforting.

For most of those lucky enough to have a ticket, it was the train to salvation: an escape from the relentless Allied bombing offensive, the shortening odds of death and the unforgiving demands of Hitler's heartless and brutal regime. For von Menen, it was the train of tormenting uncertainty.

At the break of dawn, the train pulled out, every carriage packed, the corridors choked with people, arms outstretched through open windows, a cacophony of last farewells, the tears plentiful. It crossed the Landwehr Canal at walking pace, all eyes on the widespread destruction as it lumbered slowly through Treptow, the silence of incredulity almost palpable.

Von Menen peered disconsolately through the window, his mind darting back to his grandfather's advice again.

'When the truth emerges, the people of this nation will realise that they've been duped by a despot. By then, of course, it will be too late; Germany will be in ruins.' Now the reality was staring him right in the face. Berlin was on her knees. The unmistakeable signs of defeat were everywhere.

When von Menen alighted at Hirschberg, he had been standing for eight hours. He was tired, hungry and numb with cold, but he cheered at the sense of calmness and the clean, crisp air that greeted him at Krummhübel. The carnage and misery of Hitler's war was somewhere else; it was not in Krummhübel's back yard.

To the south, a mantle of smoky grey mist covered the high peaks of the Giant Mountains. It was too early for snow, but the sudden snap of cold weather gave rise to the thought that it must only be a few days away.

A man in a full-length astrakhan coat greeted von Menen on the platform. 'Helmut Maier, Foreign Office,' he said, his voice as deep as a tuba. 'Herr von Althoff sends his apologies, but he's been called to Prague.'

Von Menen stuck out his hand. 'Pleased to meet you, Herr Maier.'

They drove to the edge of the village, halting outside a neat little chalet, part-hidden by a planting of pines; a crisp, white building with brown-varnished windows, a studded oak door and ornate wooden window boxes.

'We've requisitioned most of everything around here,' said Maier: 'hotels, guest houses, chalets, anything with a bed and a front door. They keep telling us that it's only temporary, but I can't see us ever going back to Berlin. Anyway, you've been billeted here. It's comfortable and quiet, but Frau Hirscher has a reputation for being frugal with the heating.' Maier stole a glance at his watch, reached over to the passenger door and pushed down the handle.

'Sorry to have to dash,' he said, 'but I've an appointment elsewhere.'

'I won't be seeing anyone today, then?' asked von Menen.

'Ah, should have mentioned. Herr von Althoff said to tell you that you're expected at nine in the morning.'

'I'm to see Herr von Althoff tomorrow morning?' asked von Menen.

'No, sir, he won't be back for another three days.'

'Then who?' asked von Menen, cautiously.

Maier shrugged. 'Sorry, I'm only the driver. I know *where* to take you, but who you'll be seeing I've no idea. I'll call for you at eight.'

It was, as Maier had hinted, as cold as an icebox. No heating, no hot water and no hot food. Even the "welcome" was icy. Frau Hirscher was a stern-looking woman, about sixty, tall and slim, with features so sharp she looked like a stick insect in half-moon glasses.

Exhausted, von Menen managed as best he could on a dinner of one cold sausage, a portion of cold potatoes and a lukewarm beverage that the frosty Frau Hirscher called coffee. In bed, he wore long johns, pyjamas and two sweaters. Even with his topcoat flung over the duvet, he still shivered.

But it was not the cold that kept him awake. It was the thought of who he would face at nine o'clock in the morning – the likeable and amiable Werner, the unknown Schellenberg or the malevolent Kaltenbrunner?

Tuesday 24th October 1944

They pulled up beside a large wooden chalet, fronted with ornate shuttered windows and a heavy green door.

249

'This is it, sir,' said Maier, casting an eye over the crumpled piece of paper which bore the address.

Von Menen took a deep breath, tightened his stomach and stepped from the car. 'Thanks,' he said, staring up at the high stone chimney. He walked up to the door and pressed the bell, a deep ominous chime sounding inside.

A woman of about forty, with cold grey eyes and an austere look, wearing tweeds, thick brown stockings and lace-up brogues, answered the door. Von Menen wagered with himself that she would have a Kalkhoff bicycle around the side, a wicker basket at the front and a dress guard over the back wheel.

'Yes,' she said, brusquely.

'I'm Carl von Menen. I believe I'm expected.'

'Come in.'

Another icy welcome. Von Menen followed her along a narrow hallway until they reached an open door on the right.

'You're to wait in here,' she said, with not a hint of civility. 'There's coffee in the thermos flask, milk and sugar by the side. Be sparing with the sugar, mind, *and* the milk!'

'Who—?' The door closed shut at the start of his question.

He sat by the hearth and waited, his anxiety deepening, the pressure building.

Some minutes later came the sound of muffled voices in the hall outside, the high monotone of the woman who had met him at the door and someone else, a man. *Which man?*

The door pushed open, a hatless head appeared, its face wrapped neck-to-nose in a thick woollen scarf, a mystery on two legs.

'Sorry I'm late,' muttered the man through his scarf, 'but I had an urgent dental appointment. Damn tooth.'

Peeling off his scarf, he draped it over the back of a chair, von Menen seeing his face for the first time: old and drawn, eyes heavy and listless. At first, he was none too sure, but slowly, a face from the past emerged. Von Menen restrained himself, an inner feeling of joyous relief nigh on consuming him.

Werner walked across the room, placed a hand on von Menen's shoulder and shook him warmly by the hand. 'It's very good to see you again, Carl.'

'It's good to see you, too, sir.'

'Fortunate that Hausser spotted you.'

'Hausser? The man in Lisbon?

'Yes.'

'Fortunate indeed. The passport came in very handy, as did the air ticket.'

'Hausser's a good man,' said Werner. 'Works solo and follows his nose.' He shot von Menen a dry smile. 'On this occasion, he followed *yours*. Anyway, can't be too careful. In Lisbon, Schellenberg's spies are all over the place, shipping agencies included.'

'Then am I to understand that Information Department Three is still part of the Foreign Office, sir, because—?'

'Because you've heard that Schellenberg has taken over the Abwehr,' interrupted Werner, 'and you thought, maybe, he'd suddenly become your new boss?'

'Something like that, yes.'

'Well, no need to concern yourself on that account. Information Department Three remains completely autonomous.'

Thank God.

Werner moved to pick up the thermos flask, cursing his tooth in the process. 'So, how was Argentina?'

'Enterprising and adventurous, sir.'

Werner poured the coffee and beckoned von Menen to

the fireside. 'Forgive me for asking to see you so soon,' he said, 'but I'm curious to know the reason for your urgent return. The Minister would like to know, too. In fact, he wants a full report by this evening. But first, I'll deal with the laudatory bit. I've been instructed by Minister von Ribbentrop to offer you his warmest congratulations. He thinks – and I agree with him – that your product has been the best we've had. Well done.'

'Thank you, sir.'

'Something else, too… You're anxious to see your family, I expect?'

'Yes, I was going to ask you about that, sir.'

'No need… Everything's arranged. There's a courier bus leaving Krummhübel for Berlin at two o'clock this afternoon. You will be on it. You've been ordered to take a spot of leave.'

Von Menen was scarcely interested in tributes, but the word "leave" and the notion that he would be returning to Berlin that afternoon prompted a new thinking: he could accompany his parents back to Mecklenburg.

Finishing his coffee, Werner leaned back in his chair. 'Well, shall we begin?'

Von Menen raised an eyebrow, looked over his shoulder and gestured in the direction of the door.

'Our conversation will not carry as far as Fraulein Feitz's office.'

Von Menen hesitated, Maria flashing through his mind, chased by the image of his dear friend, Gustav Helldorf, Lutzi's incarceration at Flossenbürg, the executions, the demise of the Kreisau Circle and the wreck of his beloved Berlin. Then he considered Werner. He wanted to believe Werner was one of the many who didn't like what he was doing, yet did it all the same because he wanted to survive, care for his family and live to a ripe old age.

'Well?' prompted Werner.

Von Menen drew himself forward, the script already written in his head, his sights set firmly on the gathering weakness of the Nazi hierarchy and their need to escape, the manner in which he was about to portray Vidal fit only for fiction.

'It is my considered judgement, sir,' he began, 'that it is only a matter of months, perhaps weeks, before Argentina declares war against Germany. Doubtless, Farrell and Perón will try to avert it, but the United States will, eventually, force it upon them.'

'Can't say I'd argue with that.'

'But, it *can* be avoided, sir.' Werner's look brought von Menen to the edge of his chair. 'You see, there's a very interesting scenario fermenting in Argentina. If we coax it along, I'm sure it will avert the threat of a declaration of war against Germany and, perhaps, lead to the restoration of diplomatic relations between our two countries.'

Werner's head shot forward, his eyes narrow. 'Are you serious?'

'Very. You might find this difficult to believe, sir, but I have irrefutable evidence of a coalition between the Argentine navy and a disillusioned element within the army. Together, they have one aim – to seize power from Farrell and Perón!'

Looking like a man who'd just been given a route map to salvation, Werner rose from his chair, picked up a long, brass poker and began re-arranging the embers in the hearth. 'I'm not divulging any great secret,' he said, speaking over his shoulder, 'when I tell you that Minister von Ribbentrop was outraged by the turn of events in Argentina last January. As for the Führer, well, "a great betrayal", I think his words were.'

'I can imagine.'

'This latest information, is it reliable?'

'Absolutely, sir. It's the brainchild of my source.'

'Do you believe him? I mean, it's a grandiose scheme…
but if he's capable of pulling it off, well…'

'I have enormous trust in him, sir, and yes, he *is* capable
of it.' Von Menen almost choked on his own assurance. 'But
he has a rather big problem. In my reports last January, I
informed you that Farrell was merely a puppet. Well, he's
still a puppet. The *real* power lies in the hands of Perón, and
Perón will not abandon his power as easily as Castillo or
Ramírez did. He'll fight!'

Werner's face was full of puzzlement. 'What is it with
this man Perón? I find him an unfathomable individual.
Why on earth didn't he seize power for himself last January,
or for that matter, last June?'

'Because he wants to achieve power in a way that will
silence his critics forever, especially the United States,'
replied von Menen.

'Through the ballot box?'

'Yes. He has total control over the entire Argentine
labour movement and the under-classes worship him.'

'But that doesn't answer the question about his
relationship with Germany.'

'He has a great deal of empathy for Germany,' said von
Menen, 'but as you once told me, politically he's more
inclined to the ideology of fascism. Nonetheless, he's clever
enough to recognise that the hearts of most Argentines
beat in unison with the Allies. In that sense, he knows that
if he's to achieve meaningful political status, his long-term
prospects will depend on a healthy relationship with the
United Nations, meaning that Argentina will disassociate
herself from Germany.'

'And your source opposes those views?'

'Most definitely.'

'It seems like an almost impossible task. How on earth is your source going to achieve it?'

'I'm not familiar with the strategy, sir, but he'll have to stifle Perón's supporters. If he doesn't, they'll swamp the streets of Buenos Aires before the first shot has been fired.'

'You mean, the *descamisados*, as they're called?'

'Yes, they'll have to be kept out of central Buenos Aires.'

'Is that possible?'

'I believe so. Within the upper echelons of the Argentine military, there is more disunion than the GOU would have us believe. Some of the officer class are adamant that Germany will, eventually, achieve victory and *some* would like to see an end to Perón. The main problem lies with the Federal Police. Their loyalty to Perón is unbending. Numerically, their strength poses a thorny problem for *any* would-be revolutionary. But given his position, I'm sure my source can assemble enough heavy armour to stifle every key location in Buenos Aires – the radio station, the Federal Police Headquarters, the Presidential Palace and every main Government installation. By then, the doubters will have lost their timidity and be right behind him. After all, like Mardi Gras, revolution is practically an annual event in Argentina.'

'But where do *we* come in?'

'He needs weapons. The latest variant of the Schmeisser machine pistol, the MP-40.'

'Ah. Anything else?'

'MG-42 Spandaus and...'

'Yes?' inquired Werner, hurriedly scribbling down the details.

'Prisms.'

Werner looked up from his notebook. 'What?'

'Prisms... submarine periscope prisms. He assured me that our people would know *which* submarines.'

The look on Werner's face implied much doubt. 'Even

if we accede to his request, we're still left with the task of getting it to Argentina.'

Von Menen was ready with his answer. 'To be honest, sir, his knowledge of our submarine fleet embarrassed me.'

'Obviously, he's been well briefed by his friends in the navy,' deduced Werner.

'Perhaps, but it doesn't say a great deal for the security in German shipyards.'

Werner was in deep thought, von Menen sensing that he was warming to the idea. Eventually, he smiled. 'We could always hand this over to Schellenberg... but we won't. The Minister wouldn't hear of it. Neither would I – in which case, I'll be recommending that you should handle everything. Can I assure Minister von Ribbentrop that you're capable of it?'

'I've a plan formed already, sir.'

'Well, you've convinced me, Carl. Now it's up to me to convince the others. Bear in mind, though, it will certainly go to the very top.'

'The Führer?'

'Yes. It will not be easy, either. Admiral Dönitz will never countenance the idea of releasing a submarine for an operation he's certain to see as foolhardy and adventurous. Then there's the matter of the Schmeissers. These days, the Wehrmacht needs as many guns as it can get its hands on, hence we couldn't oblige your source the last time. On the plus side, however, the restoration of diplomatic relations with Argentina would be a very prestigious achievement.'

'There's something else, sir,' said von Menen, about to reveal his last, sweet ace. 'The man I'm dealing with... Whilst he's convinced that Germany *will* win the war, he accepts that things *could* go wrong. He'd like it understood that, if we help him now, he's prepared to guarantee safe haven in Argentina for members of the German leadership.'

'That could be construed as defeatist talk, Carl. All the same, I will mention it... in a low whisper. By the way, Carl, tell me, how did you get out of Argentina?'

'I convinced a shipping clerk in Buenos Aires that my grandfather was dying in Spain. Then I bought him his pension!'

'How much? No, don't tell me! Best if I don't know.'

'The rest was fairly straightforward. Getting into Spain couldn't have been easier, thanks to Herr Lindemann.'

Werner grinned. 'Anything else?' he asked.

'Yes, I need a favour, sir. I'm concerned about a girl I know, Lutzi Mayr – sorry, I mean Lutzi Helldorf. Her husband was a friend of mine, killed in Russia a few months ago.'

'Go on.'

'I really don't know how to put this, but I gather she's in a concentration camp — Flossenbürg, I think.' Von Menen watched Werner's brow crease like a concertina. 'Something to do with her brother, who was executed last August, allegedly for being implicated in the plot against... well, I suppose you can guess the rest.' Werner puckered his lips, sucked in deeply, an exaggerated shudder passing through his shoulders. 'It's just that I'd like to know what's happened to her, sir. I thought maybe...?'

'I appreciate your concern for your friend, Carl, but I'm afraid such matters are for the Gestapo, and the Foreign Office has no influence over any part of Kaltenbrunner's regime.' Suddenly, Werner got to thinking, a hopeful glint in his eyes. 'Perhaps there is one avenue I could explore,' he said, 'but I'm not making any promises. Anyway, before you go, best take this with you.' He passed over a small booklet. 'Try not to lose it. It's an authorisation for petrol, a hundred and fifty litres a week – enough to take you to the moon and back!'

'That's very generous, sir.'

Werner offered his hand and showed him to the door, hesitating as he reached for the handle.

'One more thing, Carl... Your old friend, Müller... he's back in Berlin. Doesn't know you're here, of course, but perhaps it would be wise if you stayed clear of Gestapo Headquarters on Prinz Albrecht Strasse.'

'*Gestapo* Headquarters?'

'Yes; the moment Müller arrived back in Germany, Schellenberg wasted no time in getting rid of him. He's now with the Gestapo, where his talents are more appreciated.'

I might have guessed. 'And Schmidt?'

'In Denmark, I believe.'

'Thanks for the tip, sir.'

18

Schwartz pulled open the heavy front door and Katrina stepped inside, the two large parcels she was carrying tumbling unceremoniously onto the polished oak floor.

'Carl!'

'Yes, your big brother, home at last!' He lifted her clear of the floor.

'Careful,' she laughed; 'haven't you heard?'

'Heard what?' Von Menen lowered her to her feet, stepped back and eyed her closely. 'You're…?'

'Yes,' she beamed. 'You're going to be an uncle.'

'Fantastic! When's the big day?'

'22ⁿᵈ March.'

He flicked away the fringe from her porcelain blue eyes, cupped her face in his hands and beamed. 'You look radiant,' he said, 'still full of girlish innocence.'

'Thank you, kind brother. At twenty-nine, I'll take that as a compliment.'

After a late lunch, von Menen and the General left for a short stroll across the terrace.

'There's something on my mind, Father. Last Sunday, at the Savoy, I… well, I was a bit hasty. I know it's no excuse, but I wasn't prepared for the kind of devastation

I found in Berlin. I still haven't come to terms with it.'

'It hurts me too, Carl,' replied the General. What you said about von Witzleben and the others, trying to stop the Nazis, was right. Truth is, I very nearly joined them.' He paused, finding it difficult to revisit that episode in his life. 'I can understand your bitterness. It's your generation that will have to pick up the pieces.' They stopped just short of the orangery and looked out towards the fading light in the west. 'You know, Carl, there's a shadow of darkness descending over Germany, a darkness that will last for a generation or more. In the east, the Russians are converging upon us like a pack of ravenous hyenas. When they get here, they'll exact an orgy of vengeful retribution upon us.'

Just as Schröder had predicted.

'Believe me, we're at the mercy of the obituarists,' concluded the General.

'Do you think the Russians will be here before the Allies?'

'I'm convinced of it.'

'As far as Berlin?'

'Yes. In the north, they might even end up beyond Lübeck, and believe me, when they arrive, no amount of bargaining by the Allies will induce them to give up one square metre of territory.' He turned, fixed his son with a rigid stare. 'Remember what Lenin said, "Whoever has Germany, has Europe"?'

'There's no way of stopping them?'

'There's all this talk about miracle weapons, and perhaps some of it's true, but it's all too little, too late. Eventually, most Germans will be scrambling for the things that will keep them alive – food, warmth, shelter and a good night's sleep.'

'How does Uncle Manfred view all this?'

'He's a realist. From behind his desk at U-boat Headquarters, he sees the same gloomy picture as I do. Reckons that Dönitz is just another fanatic, not as excessive as some, but a believer, all the same, someone who still sees Hitler as the great redeemer… His mother is still alive, by the way.'

'Whose? Dönitz's?'

'No, Manfred's.'

'Goodness, she must be over ninety.'

'Ninety-one, still living with her housekeeper – and *she's* seventy-five!'

'Near Königsberg?'

'Yes, at Marienburg. The Russians will be past there before the year's out. I'm convinced of it. So is Manfred. He's been trying for months to persuade both of them to come this way, but his mother will not listen. *"Damn the Russians,"* she keeps telling him. Anyway, you'll see Manfred on Saturday when he and his lady come to dinner. Jürgen, too.'

'You mentioned that he'd been given a new command?'

'Yes, one of the new generation electro-submarines.'

Just as von Menen was beginning to think that he'd found some meaningful discourse with his father, mention of electro-submarines brought Vidal's treacherous little scheme rushing back to his mind.

'Might this new submarine… turn the situation, do you think?' he asked cautiously.

'No, and neither does Jürgen. Those at the top are in too much of a hurry, he says, trying to push things forward, making too many mistakes. He's mightily impressed with it, though; says it's the first truly submersible warship. Reckons it can cruise submerged on silent-running electric motors further and faster – seventeen knots, I think he said – than any conventional submarine. I'm not a technical man, as you know, but to think that it can breathe, top up its batteries and dispense its exhaust fumes at periscope depth, well, that really is something.'

'How on earth does it do that?'

'Some revolutionary snorkel system, so Jürgen says. Anyway, time we went back inside. Your mother will be wondering what's become of us.'

'You go ahead, Father. If you'll excuse me, I'm going to see Hans and Greta.'

Von Menen walked into the Steigers' parlour feeling like a man who'd been asked to drain the Atlantic.

'You look like an out-of-work mortician, Carl,' quipped Steiger.

'It shows, then?'

Steiger turned to his wife, who was busying herself around the fireplace. 'I'd say so, wouldn't you, Greta?' Greta smiled sympathetically.

'Mind if I stay for a few minutes, Greta?'

'Of course not. You're welcome here anytime, Carl, you know that.' She plumped up the cushion on a nearby chair.

'You'll have a drink?' asked Steiger.

'Thanks, I need one.'

Von Menen gazed around the parlour, admiring its neat, cosy simplicity. 'I love this room,' he said. 'It's so homely, so welcoming.' He walked over to the sideboard and stared blankly at the two large photographs of the late Steiger children – Heinz, wearing his short black Panzer jacket, and Anna, all of eight years old, smiling playfully on the back of a donkey at Travemünde. It was the last photograph taken of her. He reached out and brushed his finger poignantly across her face.

Greta moved quickly to his side, reached up on her toes and kissed him on the cheek. 'Come and sit down,' she said softly.

'She was so young, Greta, and I was so damn foolhardy. I should never have been so far out at sea.'

'It wasn't your fault, Carl,' said Greta. 'It was an accident. You did everything you could. You were *all* young. How could you possibly have known that the weather would change so suddenly? Come on now.' She took him by the arm and led him back to his chair. 'We saw you and your father at the back of the house a short while ago; seemed you were having a profoundly deep discussion. My instinct tells me that it's Hans's turn next,' she smiled, 'or am I mistaken?'

Von Menen smiled and nodded. 'You can read me like a book, Greta. You always could.'

They moved to a small oblong table covered with a brown, tassel-frilled counterpane. Steiger poured three glasses of Juniper schnapps. 'Here's to you, Carl,' he said. 'Prost!'

'Prost!' Greta and von Menen chorused.

Following the toast and first sip, there was a hushed quiet, Steiger rolling his glass slowly between the palms of his hands. From the thoughtful look in his eyes, von Menen knew he was in for some *brotherly* advice. Greta must have sensed so too, as she found a subtle moment to leave the table and return with her knitting.

'You know, Carl,' said Steiger, 'apart from your mother, I think I am better acquainted with your father than anyone – with the greatest respect, that includes Manfred *and* you.' He looked fondly at Greta, then gestured to a photograph of the General and himself in full battle-dress. 'Your father was the best man at our wedding,' he said. 'Your parents stood sponsor for Heinz and Anna when they were baptised. When we lost Anna, it was they who stood by our sides. Then, when Heinz was killed, they insisted that we should come and live here. Not that it

263

made much difference, because, as you know, we were practically living here anyway.'

He paused, looked at his glass and drained the rest of its contents. 'I've served alongside your father all my adult life, from the battlefields of the Somme to the suburbs of Moscow. I am immensely proud of that. When you left for South America, we'd just invaded Russia and we were gloriously triumphant. But when the Russian winter arrived... well, your father knew instinctively that the whole damn war would end in disaster. And he was right. Last week they announced that 50,000 German *officers* had been killed in action since the start of the war – over 130 of them generals! Difficult to believe, isn't it? The recurrent theme now is retreat, retreat and retreat. It's been that way for some time. It's a living hell for any German soldier in the east. Trying to stop the Russian advance is impossible!'

Steiger recharged the glasses, then continued. 'Your father is a brilliant infantry general, the very best, an inspiring, courageous and daring battlefront commander, a man who's worshipped and admired by all those soldiers privileged to have served with him; brave soldiers, tired soldiers, frightened and confused soldiers; men who need leaders like your father, not leaders who spend their time back at staff headquarters. When he was forcibly transferred to a desk at Zossen, it was the worst thing that could ever have happened to him, but he had no choice – his leg had given up completely. He just couldn't walk anymore...'

In the silence, all they could hear was the click, click, click of busy knitting needles, as Frau Steiger, seemingly oblivious to the gist of the conversation, nodded approvingly at her husband's words.

Von Menen buried his head in his hands. 'Christ, Hans, what the hell has happened to us all?'

'Carl, you're talking in the past when you should

be thinking about the *future*. That's what your father's concerned about right now: the future of German youth, and that means Katrina, Jürgen – and you. That's the stark reality. What we have to do now is *survive*. Maybe it's not for me to speak to you like this, and if you think I've been lecturing you, I'm sorry, but a lot has happened these last few years. Times have changed, people have changed – it's inevitable. Whatever your father told you out there, Carl, and whatever he said back in Berlin, give credence to it. I'm sure it was sound advice.'

'Thanks, Hans. I just needed to hear it from someone else. It's just that, well, Father doesn't seem right. He's okay when you're talking to him, but when you catch him alone, he looks entirely lost. Mother's noticed it, too.'

'We all have,' replied Steiger.

'I thought maybe it was because he'd...'

Steiger raised an eyebrow, 'Flipped his lid? Hell no, not your father. He'll still have his sanity long after the rest of us have been carted away.'

'I wasn't suggesting that he'd lost his head. It's just that he seems to have given up... lost his will to fight. It's not like him.'

'Your father hasn't given up, Carl, he's simply come to terms with the inevitable. He realises that if we carry on like this, the only route to salvation for Germany is through defeat and ruination. What's going on back east is wholesale slaughter. It's a hopeless cause. Soldiers are dying for no reason at all. Your father's a professional soldier, a loyal one, too, but ever since Stalingrad he's been in a state of perpetual torment.' Steiger saw the puzzled look on von Menen's face. 'Oh, I know all about the conversation you had with him at the Savoy Hotel. He was half expecting it. The truth is, your father *would* have backed von Witzleben, Beck, Rommel and the others, but if he had done, he and I would have been on the gallows months ago, and possibly, by association, Manfred and Jürgen, with your mother, Greta, Katrina and Aunt Ingrid languishing in Flossenbürg. You must understand that?'

Von Menen looked blankly at the floor. 'Sorry, Hans. You're right, I know you are.'

'Carl, you and your father are like two peas in a pod,' exhorted Steiger. 'Whatever it is that has *officially* brought you back to Germany, I wouldn't mind betting that it's only the half of it. I suspect the other half is locked away in your conscience... von Moltke, Adam Trott, von Bauer and the rest of them. You were worried that your name might appear, and in your absence you thought that your parents might, perhaps, be used as scapegoats. Right?'

'That's about the way of it, yes.'

'Well, you're safe, Carl... We're all safe... We're still alive. What we have to do now is make sure we stay that way.'

'You won't mention to Father that I...?'

'Spoke to me about him? Of course not; I respect him too much.' He reached across the table and gripped von Menen's wrist. 'I respect you, too, Carl – it's good to have you back.'

'It's good to *be* back.' Von Menen smiled at them both, then glanced at the clock on the mantelpiece. 'Look, I really must get going. I'll see you tomorrow night.'

Greta exchanged a difficult look with Hans. 'Er... afraid not, Carl,' she said.

'You mean you won't be there?'

'We'd love to be with you, Carl,' explained Steiger, 'you know that, but it's my brother's sixtieth birthday and our plans to visit him were made some weeks ago.'

'Harald, sixty?'

'Yes, tomorrow.'

266

'Is he still farming, over at Bützow?'

'Yes, still struggling with three hundred acres. He's got the old band saw working again and I've promised to give him a hand sizing down some timber. You wouldn't believe the amount of wood up there, and these days, there's quite a demand for it.'

'Well, wish him a very happy birthday from me.'

Saturday 28th October 1944

Von Menen's sudden and unexpected appearance left his brother-in-law, Jürgen Lanze, completely bewildered.

'What the...?'

Oily rag in one hand, starting handle in the other, von Menen made his way across the courtyard, an ear-to-ear smile across his face. 'No jokes about Diegos, Inca tribesmen or the long-lost sons of the Conquistadors,' he warned jovially, 'otherwise...' – the greasy end of the handle was perilously close to Lanze's nose – 'I might just try and crank you up!'

Lanze grabbed him by the shoulders. 'Why, you...! When the hell did you get back?'

'Landed in Berlin last Saturday night, arrived here yesterday.'

'Well, it's terrific to see you, Carl,' smiled Lanze. 'You look marvellous. You've heard the news, I presume?'

'Yes, congratulations! I'm delighted for both of you. Seems that congratulations are in order for other reasons, too,' he added, casting an eye on the three gold braid rings around the sleeves of Lanze's tunic and the black-and-silver cross dangling below his neck.

'Oh, that... It's nothing, really.'

'Come on, Jürgen, it's the Knight's Cross. You don't get

a Knight's Cross for *nothing*. I suppose you're one of those *aces* I've been reading about – a tonnage king, right?'

'Something like that. Anyway, what about you? Here for good, or are you just—'

'Goodness, Jürgen, you're no different to the others! Here I am, just back, and already you want to know how long I'll be staying.'

'Uncle' Manfred von Leiber, a confirmed bachelor whose hair had turned prematurely grey at the age of thirty, was a handsome, robust and genial individual with a sharp and incisive wit.

In the new era of National Socialism, his balanced and logical thinking had long since marked him out as an overcautious realist, his views bringing him into conflict with a certain contemporary, Grand Admiral Dönitz. In January 1943, after Dönitz's promotion to Commander-in-Chief of the German navy, it was no coincidence that Manfred von Leiber's future followed a banal route, languishing in a mundane and nondescript post at Danzig, until he was transferred unexpectedly to the new U-Boat headquarters at Bernau.

It was von Leiber who had instilled in von Menen his love for the sea, taught him how to sail, explained the complexities of terrestrial navigation and instructed him in the use of nautical instruments. It was a very special relationship, yet the beautiful lady at von Leiber's side was hardly von Menen's image of a potential 'aunt'. The dazzling Eva Schilling was a tormenting reminder of someone more than 11,000 kilometres away.

'Manfred tells me that you have just returned from Madrid,' said Eva, 'and before then you were in Buenos Aires.'

'That's right.'

'Ah,' she sighed, 'Buenos Aires. What a beautiful city.'

'You've been there?' asked von Menen eagerly.

'Yes, in '31; September, I think it was. I'd just made my first appearance in Paris and a few days later I boarded *L'Atlantique* on her maiden voyage. I was supposed to appear at the Colon Theatre, but I went down with a severe throat infection and ended up spending the best part of two weeks in bed at the Hotel Plaza.'

'So you didn't see much of Buenos Aires, then?' asked von Menen.

'Not as much as I'd have liked. By the time I was well, I had to leave for New York.'

Eva had so much to say it seemed she would never stop talking. Von Leiber had heard it all before, yet the others found Eva's spell-binding exploits fascinating, with Al Jolson, Paul Robeson, Irving Berlin, Fred Astaire, Ginger Rogers and even the Duke and Duchess of Windsor acclaimed as personal friends, as no doubt they were. Theatre had found a new dimension on the von Menen estate. Whenever Eva halted to take a sip of wine or pick at a morsel of food, everyone waited patiently for the next chapter. In the chronological sense, she soon arrived at 1938 and her meeting with "that horrible little man" in Berlin.

After dinner, the men adjourned to the library, leaving the three ladies to embark on the next part of Eva's global merry-go-round. Katrina's brief absence to freshen up gave her mother the chance to broach the delicate question of matrimony.

'Eva, what you were telling me on your last visit... I don't suppose Manfred has...?'

'No, he hasn't said anything. If you ask me, Anna, I suspect he thinks our age difference is too much. Personally, I think it's nonsense. I'd marry him tomorrow, but *I'm* not doing the asking.'

In the library, the only topic of conversation among the

men was the war, the consensus unanimous: time was running out and Germany's prospects looked bleak. An apocalyptic future was bearing down from the east. The Russians were on their way, bringing with them a regime that would condemn Germany to another period of tyranny and oppression.

★

Sunday 29th October 1944

Von Menen was sitting with his mother on a wrought iron bench at the edge of the rose garden, enjoying the calm sunshine. He told her all about Maria, though made no mention of the danger she was in.

'Is it a serious relationship?' asked Frau von Menen.

'About as serious as it could be – I've asked her to marry me and she's accepted.'

Just then, the sound of footsteps could be heard approaching along the gravel path. The General was soon upon them, his wife full of eagerness.

'Klaus, Carl's asked a lady to marry him. Her name is Maria.'

'Where did you meet her – Krummhübel?' joked the General.

'Hardly. I've known her for over three years; met her on the boat going over to Argentina. She's a doctor, trained at the Charité.'

'Did she accept your proposal?'

'Yes, she did.'

'Well, there's a thing. Never had a doctor in the family before.'

'She's Argentinian, too,' hastened Anna, thrilled at the news. 'Looks like we're going to keep the Spanish language in the family after all.'

'And her father?' asked the General.

'He's a surgeon, owns a large estate in the Province of Córdoba.' Noting the excitement building in his mother's eyes, von Menen was quick to quash any hasty conclusions. 'For the moment, I'd rather you didn't say anything to the others. My future looks decidedly shaky and it's not inconceivable that I might never go back to Argentina, which means—'

'We understand, Carl,' she reassured him. 'We won't say a word.'

Von Menen embraced her and received a hearty pat on the back from his father. Anna von Menen, her eyes still bright, proceeded to potter around the rose garden whilst he and the General repaired to the house.

'Are we likely to be disturbed, Father?' von Menen asked as they reached the drawing room. 'Because I need to talk to you about something very important.'

'I shouldn't think so. Your mother will be out there for some time. Since the departure of the last gardener, she's given to tidying up the roses herself. And Katrina and Jürgen have gone for a walk. What's the problem?'

'Do you remember, in January, when Argentina severed diplomatic relations with Germany?'

'Yes.'

'Well, I didn't go to Paraguay. I didn't go anywhere. I stayed in Argentina, with Foreign Office approval.'

'Seems a bit strange, given the circumstances,' said the General.

'Yes, but there was a reason for it. A certain Argentine colonel, a man I'd been dealing with since my arrival in Buenos Aires, was anxious to maintain contact with Germany. *I* was that contact.'

'In that case... why have you come back?'

'Because the colonel wants to get rid of Perón and he wants Germany's help.'

The General gave a dry laugh of disbelief.

'It's true. He needs modern weapons and that's why I'm here, to try and organise a shipment of arms to Argentina. I'm waiting on a decision from von Ribbentrop... and I imagine *he's* waiting on a ruling from...'

'Hitler?'

'That's what I suspect, yes.'

'That could take some time.'

'I know, but that isn't my biggest worry. You see, this surge of so-called Peronism, in Argentina?'

'Yes.'

'Well, it isn't Peronism at all. It's the ideology of the man I've been talking about. Colonel Filipe Vidal. He's a colleague of Perón's, but Perón has side-lined him.'

'He wants to regain his influence?'

'No, he wants more than that – he wants the Presidency. If he gets it, he's promised the resumption of full diplomatic relations between Argentina and Germany.'

'A bit presumptuous, isn't he?'

'That's the way I see it, too, but Vidal doesn't. He fervently believes that he can rule Argentina, and Germany *will* win the war.' Von Menen's eyes glittered. 'The only division between Vidal and Hitler is that Vidal's uniform is more stylish... *and* he's got brains.'

'A Nazi with brains? Now that makes him a very dangerous individual.'

'Dangerous *and* cunning. You see, if Hitler does fail to stop the Allies, Vidal is offering safe haven in Argentina for members of the Nazi hierarchy.'

'But... surely... you don't *have* to co-operate with him.'

There was a brief silence. 'I have no choice, Father.'

'But... why?'

Von Menen clamped his hand to his forehead, a desperate look in his eyes. 'Because Vidal also happens to be Maria's uncle. He has made it plain that, if I don't co-operate, Maria…' His voice broke slightly. 'Well, she'll come to some harm.'

'His own niece! He really *does* sound like a Nazi.'

'That's only the half of it. Having witnessed the state of Berlin, I just couldn't countenance that kind of thing happening in Argentina. I couldn't live with it.' Von Menen slowly clenched and unclenched his fists. 'The fact is, whichever way I turn, I'm trapped. If Hitler agrees, the consequences don't bear thinking about: there'll be untold bloodshed, and I don't want that on my conscience. And if he doesn't agree, Vidal *will* kill Maria. I know he will.' His face was a patchwork of indecision. 'At first, I thought I could handle it… I had a few ideas… but now I'm not so sure.'

'Ideas?'

'Spike the whole operation. Place a bomb in the arms shipment timed to detonate *after* the arms have been transferred. Abort the whole operation on some trumped-up pretext… Denounce Vidal… *Anything*, anything at all to resolve it. The problem is, it's *not* resolvable!'

The General gripped his son by the shoulders. 'You're working ahead of yourself, Carl,' he said quietly. 'Personally, I wouldn't be trying to reach a decision just yet.'

Von Menen met his father's eyes and made an effort to calm himself.

'This man, Vidal, *might* be a bit like Hitler, but Hitler has been in power for over eleven years. Such things do not happen in Argentina. It's quite conceivable that by the time you return, both Vidal *and* Perón will have been consigned to the history books. If you want my advice, pray that Hitler will sanction it, get back to Argentina and worry about the rest later.'

Von Menen made to speak, but the General raised his arm to forestall the question.

'Dump the arms at sea, if need be. Take Maria to Brazil, lay low for a while, then head for the United States. But whatever you do, get the hell out of Germany. There's no future for you here.' Concealing the moisture welling in his eyes, the General turned away. 'If you doubt my sentiments, don't…' – his voice, cracking with emotion, grew quieter, until it was almost a forlorn whisper – 'because the end of the von Menen dynasty in Mecklenburg is only a winter away. I have absolutely no illusions about that. Believe me, if Katrina and Jürgen had a similar chance, I'd give them exactly the same advice: leave Germany!'

'What about Mother and yourself?'

'Your mother and I are a little too old for that, Carl. We'll probably move to Flensburg with the Steigers. The British and Americans wouldn't dare allow the Russians to get that close to the Danish border.' The General ambled over to the window and smiled at the image of his wife, busying herself in the garden. 'Looks like your mother's not short of a thorny problem herself.'

Peering through the window, von Menen caught a glimpse of his mother, the hem of her coat entangled in a rose briar. He saw the sad smile in his father's eyes and realised that everything really was coming to an end.

On Monday morning, von Leiber returned to Bernau, Jürgen headed back to Lübeck and Eva took off in the general direction of Geneva. In the evening, with the Steigers back from Bützow, Frau von Menen arranged a farewell party for Fritz, the handyman, who was leaving just ahead of his eightieth birthday.

With Fritz gone, all that remained of the original staff was Schwartz, Ursula – a burly, fifteen-stone cook from Munich – and the housekeeper, Elizabet, not far short of Fritz's years herself. Just like the entire east wing, which had been closed since Christmas 1942, a large part of the west wing was mothballed.

As winter approached, Frau von Menen continued with her struggle to create some semblance of order in the rose garden, the General forever telling her that her efforts were futile. 'The Russians won't appreciate it one bit,' he kept saying.

Meanwhile, in order to conserve what was left of the latest, and perhaps final, load of solid fuel to be delivered, Steiger and von Menen busied themselves transferring a mass of logs from the rear of the stable block to the relative dryness of the old laundry house.

In mid-November, just as everyone was coming to terms with the sinking of the German battleship *Tirpitz*, a motorcycle courier arrived at the von Menen estate carrying sealed orders for the General.

Rendezvous with Major Baumer
Wednesday 15th November at 10h00
Keppler.

Making a mental note of the accompanying address, General von Menen set off across the courtyard in search of Steiger. He found him in the garage block, tinkering beneath the bonnet of his treasured Steyr command car, Greta nearby, dutifully holding a spanner.

'Excuse me, please, Greta. Anything fixed for this Wednesday, Hans?'

Steiger lifted his head from the engine compartment, exchanged a quizzical look with his wife and shook his head. 'No, can't say as I have, General.'

'Good, then we're off to Berlin, on business.' At that, Greta made a tactical withdrawal to the house.

'Where in Berlin?'

'Jägerstrasse, number thirty-four to thirty-six.'

Steiger picked up a piece of rag, wiped his hands and thought deeply, conjuring the hazy memory of a good-looking girl, an ornate, grandiose building with diamond-patterned brickwork and a pair of griffin-like creatures perched on the roof top. 'Number thirty-four? That's the old Reichsbank building.'

The General, already two slow paces out of the garage, stopped and turned, his face a picture of bewilderment. 'What was that you said, Hans?'

'Thirty-four Jägerstrasse. It's the address of the old Reichsbank.'

'I don't know about the number, but you're right, the old bank *is* on Jägerstrasse... and Jägerstrasse runs into Kurstrasse—'

'Which is where the new Reichsbank is,' interrupted Steiger.

'Right again, Hans... and the two buildings are connected by an enclosed pedestrian walkway. But how do you know the street number?'

'Easy. Do you recall me telling you about the time after I'd matriculated, when my father sent me down to Berlin to stay with my Uncle Frederick, the brains of the family, the one who worked in the office at the AEG works?'

'Fixed you up with some sort of an engineering apprenticeship, didn't he?'

'Yes. I stayed with AEG until I enlisted.'

'But what's that got to do with the Reichsbank building?'

Steiger poked his head outside the garage and looked up and down the courtyard, checking that Greta had gone. 'When I was staying with my aunt and uncle,' he whispered, 'I used to date a girl who worked there, really good looking, she was, but very aloof – *'I work at the Reichsbank, thirty-four Jägerstrasse,'* she said, all very self-important like. It was well before I met Greta.'

'You're sure about the number?'

'Positive.' Steiger stuffed the piece of oily rag into his overall pocket and smiled. 'Perhaps they want our photographs for the next issue of Reichsmark notes,' he said cynically.

'It's an interesting concept, Hans, but I rather think not. Anyway, we're to be there at ten in the morning. What say we leave around five and stop for breakfast at the Hotel Gröbler, in Perleburg?'

'Sounds fine, General. Full uniform?'

'The whole lot,' winked the General. He was about to take his leave when, with one hand on the front wing of the Steyr, he said, 'Shouldn't you have got rid of this by now?'

'I've tried, twice, but you know what the army's like – if there isn't a piece of paper to fit the purpose, nobody wants to know.'

'Yes, but…'

'General,' interrupted Steiger, 'I drove her all the way from Bialystok, through Warsaw, Poznan and finally to here. It was over a thousand kilometres. Besides, in a few months, she might come in handy.'

Shaking his head, the General waved away the excuse. 'Another thing… something I've been meaning to ask you for some time. Where the hell did you get all the petrol from for that journey?'

'Well, it was like this…'

The General threw up his hands in resignation, turned and hastened back to the house as fast as his crook leg would carry him.

'Don't tell me, Hans, I'd rather not hear,' he bellowed over his shoulder. 'I don't need any lessons in sharp practices, thank you.'

Steiger dived back beneath the bonnet, still laughing.

19

Steiger crossed the Weidendammer Bridge, made a left into Unter den Linden and turned right beyond the Opera House, edging his way gingerly past the mounds of rubble in Oberwallstrasse.

'Nine-fifty, General,' he said, checking his watch. 'Jägerstrasse is next on the left.'

'Stop just after the turning, Hans,' the General instructed.

Steiger made a quick left, brought the Mercedes to a halt and switched off the engine. On the far side of the road stood a figure in the sinister garb of the SS, flanked by two men in dark suits, one about sixty, the other much younger.

'Rumour has it that this is where they keep the bullion – in the new building, I mean,' said Steiger.

'It's not a rumour,' replied the General, intrigued by the figure on the far side of the road. 'For the moment, though, I'm more concerned about that man in the SS uniform… It's not Baumer, it's Standartenführer Keppler!' He nodded to Steiger. They got out and crossed the road at a steady pace.

'Morning, General,' said Keppler. 'Allow me to introduce Herr Fischer and Herr Voigt.'

Fischer, the older of the two men in dark suits, stood with his heels together and dipped his head sharply. 'It's an honour to meet you, General. I've read a great deal about you.'

Keppler edged a little nearer to the General, mumbling a few words in his ear.

'Warrant Officer *Steiger*,' replied the General, loud enough for all to hear.

Voigt pricked back his ears, his eyes alight with excitement as they homed in on the black-and-white ribbon of the *Pour le Mérite* and the red, white and black of the Knight's Cross.

'*The* Sergeant Steiger?' replied Keppler.

'There's only one,' replied the General, 'and before you ask, wherever I go, *he* goes.'

'Er... of course,' replied Keppler, patently aware that two years previously, Goebbels, at the insistence of Hitler, had organised a personal photoshoot of Steiger, his image appearing on the front page of *Das Reich*.

'Right, gentlemen,' said Fischer. 'If you'll follow me, please.'

Across Kurstrasse and into Reichsbank Platz, they saw the new Reichsbank building on the right, half of its windows blown out, piles of debris everywhere. Fischer led the way through the main entrance. Steiger kept a watchful eye on the labouring Voigt, whose orthopaedic left shoe with its two-inch sole rendered a painfully awkward gait. But when he gave the young man an encouraging pat on the back, Voigt obstinately picked up his stride.

They arrived at a twin arrangement of steel barred gates, set six metres apart, each with a wicket-type entrance. Fischer unlocked the first gate, re-locked it after everyone had stepped inside and repeated the process at the second gate.

'Ideal place for a few people I know, Hans,' whispered the General.

Steiger nodded towards Keppler. 'I think one them is here, General,' he muttered.

Along the corridor stood a massive polished steel door, set with three keyholes, a graduated dial, two chrome levers and a spoked brass wheel. They watched as Fischer worked methodically through the opening process – a click, another click, down with one lever, up with another, a clunk, a seemingly endless spin of the wheel – and finally pulled open the door, revealing a dimly lit room.

On the left, stretching for all of ten metres, was a barrier of floor-to-ceiling steel bars, lined on the inside by a continuous length of black curtain. No one could see inside. Fischer unlocked the door opposite and pushed it open.

Steiger wrinkled his nose, a familiar smell invading his nostrils. 'Resin,' he said, 'new timber, pine.'

The room was large, cold and austere, lit by a solitary shadeless bulb hanging from the ceiling. A neat arrangement of small wooden boxes with rope handles attached to each end reached up from the stone floor.

Leaving Keppler and the two officials in muted conversation by the door, Steiger and the General circled the boxes, one slow step after the other. Feigning a cough, Steiger covered his mouth and mumbled through his fingers.

'If this is what I think it is, General, there's enough to finance a whole Panzer army!'

The General nodded aimlessly. A moment later, Keppler and Fischer joined them.

'Herr Fischer tells me that there are 820 boxes,' said Keppler, 'each weighing *slightly* more than thirty-two kilograms. And you, General von Menen, will have full responsibility for their safe passage to…' Restraining himself, he looked guardedly at Fischer. 'Well, we'll discuss that later.'

Ten minutes later, Fischer and Voigt departed, leaving Keppler, the General and Steiger to confer in a smaller room.

'Let me make one thing clear, General,' said Keppler. 'You may have your ideas about the content of those boxes back there, but I make no comment. Your only remit is to ensure that the consignment reaches its final destination – without incident!'

The General tapped the floor with his stick, his patience waning. 'We have a long journey ahead of us. If we are not to discuss the *contents* of the consignment, can we at least speak plainly about the destination?'

Keppler pulled a map from his attaché case, opening it out across the table. 'There,' he said, jabbing his finger against a pencilled cross. 'Priwall, which, if my limited knowledge of the region serves me right, is not too far from where you live, General.'

'Where, exactly, in Priwall?' asked the General.

Keppler pulled out a second map, so detailed that it showed the outline of roads and buildings. 'Your journey will end here,' he said, pointing to a rectangular figure-of-eight outline. 'It's just back from the…'

'Submarine base?' discerned the General.

'Yes,' agreed Keppler, 'but the submarine base has no relevance to this operation.' Refolding the map, he pushed it across the table. 'You'd best take that with you. I've got another copy.'

'What about access to the Reichsbank, loading procedures, that kind of thing?'

'All streets in the immediate vicinity – Kurstrasse,

Unterwasserstrasse, Reichsbank Platz, Jägerstrasse – will be closed. Pedestrian and vehicular access will be strictly forbidden.'

'Logistics?'

'I'll leave that to you,' said Keppler.

General von Menen looked searchingly at Steiger. 'Warrant Officer Steiger, your opinion on logistics, please. You're the expert.'

Steiger was no more a logistics expert than he was a ballet dancer, but he somehow managed to contain his surprise at his sudden appointment to quartermaster.

'Let me see,' he mused. 'A consignment of 820 boxes, you say?'

'That's right,' confirmed Keppler, referring to his notes. 'Weighing a total of 26,400 kilograms.'

'Near enough 26.5 tonnes,' said Steiger, thinking out loud. He pulled out a pencil from his tunic pocket and jotted down some figures. 'I'd say we'll need ten Opel Blitz trucks, the three-tonne model… covered, of course… allowing for eighty boxes, something over 2.5 tonnes in each truck…' He paused and thought for a moment. 'Six men in each truck, two up front and four in the back, plus two motorcycle combi outriders and two Kübelwagons. Excluding General von Menen and myself, I'd say we're looking at something like seventy men.'

'My God,' said the General. 'Seventy men, ten trucks, two motorcycle combis, two Kübelwagons *and* fuel… There are commanders on the Russian Front who'd give their right arm for that equipment.'

'Maybe,' replied Keppler, seeming more concerned about Steiger's calculations than the plight of German soldiers on the Russian Front. 'I make that only 800 boxes, Warrant Officer. What about the other—?'

'Standartenführer!' snapped the General. 'We're talking

about twenty boxes. If needs be, we'll put the damn things in my command vehicle.'

Keppler responded with a hard stare. 'General von Menen, when you speak to me, you are speaking to a representative of the Führer's Secretary, Herr Bormann. I am well aware of your illustrious career, but be under no illusion, I have been *ordered* to impress upon you that mistakes will not be tolerated. *Will. Not. Be. Tolerated.* Do you understand?'

His blood almost boiling, General von Menen fixed the SS man with a steadfast look. 'Have you ever been a real soldier, Keppler?'

Keppler shook his head.

'No, I thought not. Then let me enlighten you. Orders are for the compliance of idiots and the guidance of prudent, sensible men. Which one are you?'

Disarmed by the question, Keppler fastened his attaché case. 'The requisitioning is my responsibility, General,' he said. 'You'll find men and transport waiting at the Reichsbank on the appointed day, at the appointed hour.'

'And *when* is that likely to be?' asked the General.

'In about ten days, but I can't give you an exact date. You will be informed in advance by special courier.' Keppler rose to his feet. 'Anything else before we leave?'

'Yes, two things: I'd like a field kitchen to be in situ at the market place, in Perleburg, at least two hours ahead of the column arriving.'

'And the second?'

'Hauptsturmführer Baumer – he was supposed to be here today, which begs the question, what is his part in all of this?'

'Hauptsturmführer Baumer has *certain* new responsibilities in the Mecklenburg region. At the moment, he is otherwise engaged at Schwerin. But he has a house between Bützow and Schwaan – a huge, white-painted place; I've been there many times – and he will be at Priwall to meet you on the day of the operation.' Keppler's voice took on a tone of caution. 'It strikes me, General, that you have the same regard for Hauptsturmführer Baumer as you do for me, but you'd best be aware that he has some very influential friends. In fact, he's only recently returned from Gestapo Headquarters in Berlin, having been posted there to help with the interrogation of some of the suspects involved in the plot to murder our *glorious* Führer.' A sickening smile appeared on Keppler's face. 'His success rate was very high.'

'I know what he is,' said the General. 'I'm well versed with the significance of the black diamond on the left sleeve.'

'Maybe, but I know him much better than you do. Where Hauptsturmführer Baumer is concerned, fools and prisoners are not an option. Before his posting to Supreme Headquarters, he served with Department E5, as part of Einsatzgruppe A, in the Baltic States. Before that, he was with Department B4. Jews.'

Suddenly, Keppler's face turned a peculiar shade of grey, his breathing erratic, his right hand beginning to shake. He reached for the back of his chair and sat down.

'Are you all right?' asked the General.

Frantically opening his attaché case, Keppler fetched out a small glass bottle, hurriedly shook out three pills and threw them into his mouth, jerking back his head in the process.

It struck the General like a lightning bolt. 'You were with him, weren't you? You were with the Einsatzgruppen, one of the killer squads.'

'Only for three months,' stammered Keppler. 'I couldn't stomach it a moment longer. It… made me ill.'

'Have you any idea what's happening to *real* German soldiers in the east, because of what you did?' demanded the General.

Keppler closed his eyes and lowered his head.

'Not to mention the fate that awaits countless German families, women *and* children.' The General hammered his fist loudly on the table. 'Just think about it, *Stand-ar-ten-füh-rer*. The reprisals, which many Germans are suffering right now, due largely to *your* evil deeds, are just as gruesome and just as vile as anything *you* ever meted out, *if* that's possible.'

The room fell silent, the General studying the sad and pathetic figure before him.

'Do you know something, Keppler,' he said softly; 'people like you and Baumer sicken me. You have done this country the greatest disservice in its entire history.' He turned to Steiger. 'Warrant Officer, we're leaving. There's an awful smell in this room. I need some fresh air.'

Heading north-west through the ruins of Berlin, the General and Steiger were in a sombre mood, the reality of Hitler's war all around them. Only the remnants of healthy normality remained, and soon, even the remnants would be gone, swept away by a regime hell-bent on destroying not just the material substance of Germany, but the very fabric of her nationhood.

In his euphoric rise to power, Hitler had promised a 1,000-year Reich, yet in less than twelve years all he had achieved for Germany was ruination. A once-great country was spiralling down the plughole of Europe, and with it would go one of Mecklenburg's most distinguished families.

As the Mercedes sped through Nauen, General von Menen was in deep thought, beset by a notion as alien to him as the far reaches of the universe. And yet, as much as he searched his conscience, the same question came hurtling back. *Why should they have it? Why?*

They had just passed through Friesack when he finally emerged from his deep state of mental absorption. Steiger had not uttered a word since they had left the suburbs of Berlin, but when the General spoke, he knew he had won the bet with himself.

'What did you think about that business back there, Hans?'

'I presume you're referring to the *gold* we're not supposed to know about, General?'

'Yes. What's your opinion?'

'Well, the way things are going, sir, the British and Americans will be shaking hands with their Russian counterparts in less than six months. Back there,' he continued, jabbing his thumb over his shoulder, 'there's enough gold to finance a new beginning for someone, a beginning that's set to start at a place where there's a harbour, an airstrip and a float plane station – Priwall!'

'Meaning?'

'Meaning someone's planning on going away for quite a long time and they're not taking Reichsmarks as spending money. When the war's over, gold will be the most widely negotiable commodity in the world, aside from the US dollar.'

'Hans, your analysis is well conceived and very precise. You should have been a Field Marshal.'

Steiger laughed. 'You know, the other evening, Greta and I were sitting in the parlour wondering how we'll cope with the inevitable. Oddly enough, she is almost resigned to it. In a way, I suppose it's different for us, not having any children. We'll just take our chance with whatever comes along.'

'Anna and I have already given that some thought, Hans.'

'You mean, what you'll do when the Russians arrive?'

'Yes, we've discussed it frequently. When the time comes, as it most certainly will, we'd like you and Greta to come to Flensburg with us.'

'Well, I…'

'Don't argue with me, Hans, I'm a senior officer of the Wehrmacht! Besides, Ingrid's as keen as anyone to get you up there. It's a big house; there's room for all of us, Jürgen and Katrina included.'

'Thank you, General. Talking of big houses… I didn't say anything at the time, but I think I know the place Keppler was boasting about. It's not a house, it's a mansion; north-east of Bützow, used to belong to the Gluecksmanns. It's about ten kilometres from Harald's farm.'

They sat quietly for a while, neither saying anything. Then, as if prompted by a psychic consensus of thought, both spoke in unison: 'We could always…'

Steiger laughed. The General smiled and stroked his chin.

'What was it you said, when we first walked into that vault … something about the wood?'

'It was pine. I noticed the smell of resin immediately.'

'You're sure it was pine?'

'Positive. When I was at Harald's the other week, I helped him size down a large load of timber. All pine.' Steiger briefly took one hand off the wheel to show the General his right palm. 'That's how I got the blisters.'

'And this timber, is there any left?'

'Mountains of it.' Steiger was still on the General's train of thought. 'General, are you seriously suggesting that we should…?'

'At the moment, Hans, I'm not suggesting anything.

I'm merely thinking, and I always think better with a large brandy. Let's stop off at the Gröbler for a drink. Oh, and by the way, you know the arrangement we have when we're alone; cut out the *general* bit, otherwise I'll address *you* as warrant officer.'

Frau von Menen was busy penning a letter to her sister, Ingrid, when the General walked into the drawing room. He bent down and kissed her on the forehead.

'The Delahaye... it's not in the garage. Is Carl out?'

'Yes, gone to Berlin. Someone phoned him this morning, about eight-thirty. Seemed strangely pleased with himself when he left.'

'Interesting,' muttered the General. 'Did he say when he'd be back?'

'Tomorrow, hopefully... Which reminds me, do you recall Ulricht Hoffman, served with Carl in the army? Tall, good-looking young man.'

'Yes, nice fellow... transferred to the Luftwaffe, I think.'

'Yes. Sadly, his wife was killed in an air raid last March... He's been left with a young daughter to bring up.'

'Dear me, how awful.'

'Carl said they were on the same flight to Berlin. He's hoping to see him again this evening.'

'Very well,' said the General. 'Give my regards to Ingrid.'

He left his wife to her letter-writing, reflecting that the talk with his son would have to be put off for a day. But perhaps that was for the best. There was a lot to think about.

20

Thursday 16th November 1944

The full misery of winter weather had descended upon Mecklenburg. It was wet, windy and bitterly cold.

In the half-light of early morning, General von Menen bundled Yeremenko into the back of the Mercedes and set off along myriad rain-soaked country roads. By eight o'clock, they had reached the foot of an incline rising steadily in the direction of Holdorf.

A motorcycle, closing fast from behind, flashed by at high speed, crested the horizon and disappeared. The General pulled up, reversed down the road and steered the car on to the verge, a thought pricking at his mind.

On the right was the Radegast River, flanked by the Gadebusch–Rehna railway line; on the left, a pocket of dense woodland, which followed the road to the point where the motorcycle had vanished over the horizon. Though hard to detect, a track, part-hidden by a clump of elderberry, led into the wood.

Yeremenko sat obediently beside the car, waiting for the General's command.

'Go!' The dog shot across the road and scampered into the wood.

Stark, leafless shapes of oaks, false acacias and beeches stretched towards a threatening leaden sky. It was a damp, cheerless place, the silence broken only by the General's footsteps swishing in the long, wet grass and the sound of Yeremenko rummaging in the distance. Fifty metres from the road, the track funnelled out into a wide clearing, where stood an abandoned makeshift shelter.

Charcoal burners.

To the south, across open farmland, the road to Gadebusch stretched out like an arrow for at least a kilometre and a half. The dog came bounding back, sat to heel, panting heavily, a long pink tongue dangling from his open jaw.

'This is it, Yeremenko,' said the General, gently patting the dog's head. 'This… is… it.'

Gone to Lübeck South Hospital with Katrina and Greta – visiting the wounded brought back from Memel. We've taken the BMW. Back about three.

Love Anna.

P.S. Carl phoned. He'll be back at seven tonight; mentioned something about having to call at Borsigwalde (?) first.

General von Menen studied the note, picked up the telephone and called Steiger. A few minutes later, a knock sounded on the drawing room door.

'Come in, Hans!' Standing by the cocktail cabinet, the General held a glass of brandy in each hand. 'One for you and one for me.'

'Thank you, General, but isn't it a little—'

'It's *Klaus*, Hans,' said the General, cutting him short. 'You know the rules. And yes, it *is* a bit early, but you might feel the need for it later. For the moment, a toast: to brave and absent friends.' Their glasses met with a chink. The

General paused, then looked straight at Steiger. 'How long have we known each other, Hans? Twenty-eight years?'

'Give or take a few months,' agreed Steiger. 'And I'd do it all over again.'

'Likewise.' Taking a sip from his glass, the General settled into his chair, Steiger sitting opposite. 'The unfortunate thing is, my friend, age aside, we're not likely to get the chance to *do it all over again*. For us, *and* for Germany, the future is very grim. When the Russians get here, the events of 1918 will seem like a tea party. Now—'

'First, Klaus, if I might be so bold,' interrupted Steiger. 'Yes?'

'As I was saying to Carl the other day, I believe I know you better than any other person... except, of course, Anna...'

'I wouldn't argue with that, Hans.'

'So before you say what I suspect you're about to say, I wonder if I might save you the trouble?'

'Go ahead.'

'Just how do you propose we should do it?'

Five seconds elapsed before the General's stoical expression broke into a smile, replaced quickly by a look of solemnity. 'You do realise that if we're caught, we'll be shot,' he said grimly.

'If we're lucky,' contended Steiger.

'There'll be no hiding behind service records.'

'We won't be caught, Klaus. We'd have to be pretty damn dumb to be outwitted by that bunch.'

'I know, but it's not just the two of *us* I'm thinking about; it's Anna, Greta and the others. If there's the slightest indication that things are going wrong, I propose that we pack them off to Flensburg at once. Agreed?'

'Absolutely. So, when and where do we start?'

'All in good time, Hans. For the moment, we have a

sticky problem. You see, for what I have in mind, we'll need an extra...' Without warning, he suddenly switched tack. 'Borsigwalde, in north-west Berlin...'

'Yes?'

'Do they still produce ordnance at the munitions works there?'

'As far as I know they do, yes.'

'Even after the October raid?'

'I believe so. Is it relevant?'

'Oh, just a feeling I have. Anna left a note... Carl telephoned that he'd be home about seven, had to call at Borsigwalde first. I have a sneaky suspicion that he meant he was heading for the munitions works... but more about that later. Now, where was I?'

'You said, *"we'll need an extra..."*?'

'Oh, yes... We'll need an extra pair of hands.'

Steiger's eyes were like two large question marks. 'Who do you have in mind?'

The General answered in a very quiet voice. 'Carl.'

Steiger inched to the edge of his chair. 'Will he agree?'

'Well, if he doesn't, we'll abandon the whole idea. There's no one else we can ask... Manfred is tied up at Bernau and Jürgen is at sea most of the time. Carl's our only hope.'

'And assuming he agrees, then what?'

'How much could we get in the Steyr?'

'Over half a tonne, at least.'

'You're sure?'

'I'm certain.'

'In that case, what I said to Keppel about the odd twenty boxes wasn't far short of the truth. Twenty should be enough. We shouldn't be too greedy.'

'So, what do you have in mind?'

'A simple plan – we'll just switch the boxes. Twenty of theirs for twenty of ours... Now, the boxes—'

Steiger jumped in. 'They'd have to be exactly the same, Klaus. We can't simply guess the measurements.'

'We're not going to. Let's start with the thickness of the timber. What's your opinion?'

'I'd say two centimetres.'

'That's what I thought.'

'But the depth, width and length, well, I don't know,' said Steiger, shaking his head.

'I do,' hastened the General. 'When the tip of my cane was touching the floor, the handle was level with the top of the highest box; I counted the number of boxes and I know exactly how long my cane is. The rest was easy to work out.' He handed Steiger his cane. 'Draw your hand along the lower part of it. Can you feel the two indentations?'

'Yes.'

'I made them with my thumbnail… Those indentations are equal to the length and width of one of the boxes. I assume they were all the same size?'

'They looked uniform to me,' said Steiger.

'Good. Now, what about the rope handles?'

'Ordinary ten-millimetre hemp rope, passed through pre-drilled holes and knotted on the inside, I'd reckon,' said Steiger. 'There's a whole reel of it at the garage block.'

'And the nails, did you notice the nails?'

'Yes, all bright and shiny.'

'Can we get any?'

'No need; we've enough nails to put ten thousand boxes together, let alone twenty.'

'But they'll be as rusty as hell.'

'They won't be by the time I've finished with them.'

'Okay, I'll leave that to you. Tomorrow, I'm going to pack Schwartz off on a fortnight's leave. The cook and the housekeeper can take a break, too, which leaves Anna, Greta and Katrina. Perhaps I can talk Anna into going up to

Flensburg the day after tomorrow. She'll be only too happy to take Greta and Katrina with her. Now, from the logistics point of view, the really difficult part will call for all your... *resourcefulness*.'

Cocking an ear to the window, Steiger stuffed the piece of notepaper in his pocket. 'The ladies are back – sounds like the BMW.'

'Well, let's leave it for now. There's not much more we can do until Carl gets back this evening.' Eyes fixed on the clock, the General drummed out a slow tempo with his fingers on the highly polished side table.

'Something troubling you, Klaus?'

'It's just that, well, I think it would be best if we spoke to Carl together. If I speak to him myself, he'll probably think I'm off my head. He'll be knocking on your door within seconds.'

Steiger smiled, but said nothing.

'I'll give you a call when he returns. And, Hans?'

'Yes?'

'We'll have to move fast.'

When Frau von Menen entered the drawing room, the General was bent over the fireplace, incinerating the last of his nefarious plan.

'You've just missed Hans, darling,' he said. 'I've been telling him about our proposal to move up to Flensburg.'

'Good, I'm glad. I've been wanting to tell Greta for days.'

He kissed her on the cheek. 'Where's Katrina?'

'She's gone up to her room to rest.'

'Is she all right?'

'I think so, but she found the visit to the hospital quite harrowing. She's finally come to terms with the reality of the situation.' Frau von Menen looked dejectedly into the fire. 'We've listened to some awful stories today. Those poor men, they really do need comforting. Poor girl, she never stopped talking about it all the way home.'

'I can imagine.'

'Of course you can, Klaus. I'm sorry. You and Hans know better than any of us.'

In her innocence, she had given him the excuse he was looking for. 'Nothing to forgive, Anna. Let's just say that Hans and I are the lucky ones and leave it at that. As a matter of fact, it's not far short of something I want to speak to you about.'

'Which is?'

'I think we should start making preparations to move to Flensburg as soon as possible.'

'What, right away?' She reached out and tugged at his sleeve. 'Have you heard something?' she asked nervously.

'No, but December is coming up fast,' said the General, struck by a sudden feeling of guilt. 'And before we know where we are, it'll be 1945. By then, who knows where the Russians will be.'

Frau von Menen pondered the idea. 'I suppose you're right,' she said. 'I hadn't quite thought of it that way.'

'Sorry, Anna, but we *must* start thinking about it. I was wondering if you, Katrina and Greta might go up there the day after tomorrow, start arranging things with Ingrid; you know, accommodation, that sort of thing. We ought not to be leaving it to the last moment. Besides, Greta loves it up there and there's nothing to keep Katrina here. I'll release Ursula and Elizabet for a couple of weeks. Maybe Schwartz, too.'

She stood before him, her face full of a hollow expression, arms tucked tightly against her bosom, her chin resting on her clasped hands. 'The things we've heard today… Klaus, truthfully, how long do you think we've got before the Russians arrive?'

He cupped her face in his hands. 'About four months, I'd say, maybe five, but we'll be up on the Danish border by then. They won't get that far.'

'Dear God.'

'It'll be all right, Anna. We'll be safe in Flensburg. I'm sure of it.'

'In that case, I'll speak to Katrina and Greta this afternoon. You're sure the three of you will be okay?'

'Of course.'

'Should we take the BMW?'

'Yes, and Hans will make sure you have enough petrol to get you there and back. But please stay clear of Kiel. The Allies are keen on destroying the docks.'

Von Menen arrived back shortly after six, looking like the cat who'd caught the pet budgerigar without quite knowing what to do with it.

'Is there something wrong, Carl?' asked his mother.

'Er... no,' von Menen replied hesitantly, glancing at the General, 'but there is something I have to tell you both. There's no point in me beating about the bush. I'm leaving the country again, all very hush-hush. They want me to go back to South America.' He paused again, hoping that the psychic would reach his father. 'They want me to try and re-establish diplomatic relations with Argentina.'

'When is this likely to happen, Carl?' asked the General, fearing that his entire plan was about to collapse.

'Six or seven weeks, maybe, but I've a lot of work to do first.'

Consciously aware that something was still not right, his mother sat down on the edge of von Menen's chair, a strand of hair dropping down over her cheek, her face resembling a piece of choice Dresden china with a fine crack.

'There's something else, too, isn't there?' she said.

'Yes, Mother, there is.'

'I think I know what it is. You're not coming back, are you?'

Von Menen took a deep breath. 'No, I don't think I am.'

She put her arm around his shoulder, then rose to her feet and stepped back.

He feared that she might go on a wild gallop around the garden, but no.

'I'm so happy for you, Carl. You'll be much better off there,' she said. The General nodded in agreement, as Anna continued playfully, 'Maybe you could find a nice little place for us. We could teach the others Spanish.' She headed towards the door, humming a few bars of Ravel's stirring *Bolero*. 'I'm just going to check on Katrina.'

Von Menen gaped in amazement as his mother left the room. 'Goodness, she took that well, Father.'

'She seemed to, but deep inside I suspect she's hurting a lot.'

'Do you think she meant it? About you all going to South America, I mean?'

The General, a picture of bewilderment, stared silently at the door. 'To be honest, Carl, I'm not quite sure, but it sounds like a good idea.'

'You'd consider it?'

For the General, the horns of dilemma had passed into history. 'If, by some fluke, the Russians arrive here before we've had time to get to Flensburg,' he said, 'there are at least two people I know who'll be making a one-way trip to Siberia – Hans and me! Believe me, by the time they've finished with us, we'll be fully conversant with the infinite varieties of human depravity. Does that answer your question?'

Von Menen reached out and grabbed his father's arm. 'Look, I can arrange everything! I've got money out there, quite a lot of it. As for Vidal, well, as you've said, he might not even be around. Trust me,' he pleaded. 'For heaven's sake, the least you can do is try.'

The General walked forlornly over to the window and stared out across the grounds. 'The von Menen family has been here for, God, I don't know how many years. And now it's all coming to an end.' He turned and faced his son. 'What matters now, Carl, is that you are going back to...' He paused, shook himself out of his deep despondency. 'That's a thought... How on earth are you going to *get* back – by submarine?'

'No – by plane and boat, I hope, which is why I went to see Ulricht Hoffman last night.'

'Your mother mentioned you'd be seeing him. How is he?'

'Fine, considering what he's been through. He asked to be remembered to you. He's with Deutsche Lufthansa.'

'Yes, your mother said.'

'The fortunate thing is that his schedule for the next few weeks includes a couple of trips to Madrid; in fact, he's going there the day after tomorrow. It's irregular, I know, but he's delivering a message to Juan for me. You see, Juan knows my situation. He's keeping an eye on sailings from Spain to South America.'

'To an old soldier like me, Carl, it sounds a bit like Mata Hari, relived.'

Von Menen grinned. 'Not quite, Father, I could never dance like Mata Hari!'

'And your... preparations. What did the Little Corporal agree to?'

'Everything; that is, as much as a U-boat can accommodate.'

'A shipment of arms by submarine?'

'Yes... but only after a furious row between von

Ribbentrop and Dönitz. It seems Dönitz tried his damnedest to block it, but conceded in the end... on Hitler's orders!'

'Uncle Manfred will be pleased,' smiled the General. 'Anyway, you've told me *your* interesting news, now it's my turn. Do you recall what I told you, not long after your return, about the rats leaving the sinking ship? Well, they're already storing the cheese, laying the foundations for their exodus, so to speak.'

'You'd best explain, Father.'

'My trip to Berlin yesterday – it was to the Reichsbank. I've been tasked with the safe delivery of 26.5 tonnes of... well, they didn't exactly mention the word *gold*, but that's what it is.'

'Twenty-six-and-a-half *tonnes*? Heavens.'

'It's a lot, isn't it?'

'I'd say it is. When I left Argentina, gold was selling for 136 pesos an ounce. That's about thirty-three, thirty-four US dollars.' Von Menen took out his pen and a scrap of paper, and hurriedly jotted down some figures. 'My God, that's over thirty million US dollars!'

The General was well versed with the weight of twenty boxes. Now he was reckoning their value – over $700,000!

'Let me get this straight,' he said. 'In 1941, one US dollar was worth 2.5 Reichsmarks... but nowadays, I wouldn't have a clue.'

'Simple, Father. One million US dollars will buy you, let me see, one thousand brand new Ford saloon motor cars!'

'As many as that?'

'Yes, as many as that. But where's it all going?'

'Ultimately, I don't know. If I had to hazard a guess, I'd say it's going in the same direction as you – South America – though *my* remit terminates at Priwall.'

'Why?'

'Just look at the location. Priwall's the ideal place. They've got the choice of aeroplanes, float planes and… submarines.'

'But you're an officer of the German *army*, Father. Why you and not—'

'The SS? Because they're just using me, Carl. If anything goes wrong, they'll have someone else to blame!'

The General pressed the bell at the side of the fireplace. Within half a minute, Schwartz appeared.

'Schwartz, please tell Hans "five minutes", there's a good fellow. Oh, and something else – there's a fortnight's leave for you, starting tomorrow.'

'Why, thank you, General.' Schwartz inclined his head and deftly departed.

'Carl, slip on your jacket and come with me.'

When von Menen and the General stepped through the wicket gate into the garage block, Steiger was already there. He had lit an oil lamp, shadows dancing on the whitewashed brickwork.

With encouragement from the General, von Menen turned to Steiger and put to him the salient question.

'Hans, how would you and Greta like to go to Argentina with the rest of the family?'

Steiger gazed insensibly at von Menen. 'Are you serious?' he asked.

'Very serious.'

Steiger looked questioningly at the General. 'Is this true, Klaus?'

'Yes, Hans, it's true.'

Joyous excitement swept across Steiger's face. 'Do you want my answer immediately, or can you wait two seconds?'

'Do I take that as a "yes"?' smiled von Menen.

'*Most* positively,' asserted Steiger.

'And Greta?'

'She'll be ecstatic.'

'Well, Father, that's the four of you sorted out. All we have to do now is convince Katrina and Jürgen.'

'Leave that to me,' said the General.

'That's settled, then.' Von Menen moved as if to depart.

'Not quite,' said the General. 'There's something we need to talk to you about. Hans, will you tell him, or shall I?'

'I think it best if it came from you, Klaus.'

The General fixed his son with a hypnotic look. 'Carl, the gold I was telling you about? We're having some of it.'

Von Menen stood motionless, his brow looking like an old, creased shirt, his eyes settling upon Steiger. *Flipped his lid.*

'This is no collective delusion, Carl. We're serious, deadly serious,' said Steiger.

'He's right, Carl,' said the General. 'We've thought it through, very carefully. We *can* do it and we're going to do it.'

Von Menen threw his hands in the air. 'You're talking like a couple of renegades,' he said, shaking his head. 'You can't be serious. If you're caught, you'll be shot.' His thoughts turned to his mother, Greta, Katrina, Jürgen, even Aunt Ingrid. 'Have you told...?'

'We've told no one, except you,' said the General. 'That's because there's a small problem we need to overcome. You see, we need some help.'

The word "help" hung on the General's lips for some time. It rang in his son's ears for even longer. Von Menen drew his hand across his forehead and snapped his eyes shut, trying to squeeze out the reality. He knew exactly what his father meant, but his mind dismissed it.

'You're both mad,' he breathed, 'absolutely mad.'

'Maybe,' replied the General, 'but right now, the whole damn world is mad.'

Von Menen opened his eyes and studied the calm, tranquil look on his father's face; the face of a loving father, a celebrated battlefront General. 'It's me, isn't it? You want *me* to help you?'

'Yes.' The General's brief reply was filled with all the emotion of a desperate man – love, guilt, hope, loss and fear, all in one word. 'We're not putting any pressure on you. You can refuse. We'd understand.'

Von Menen's stomach was as taut as a coiled spring. 'I can hardly believe what I'm hearing,' he said. 'You two, of all people.'

'Circumstances change, Carl. People change, countries change,' replied the General, his voice sombre and desolate. 'All we're asking is that you think about it.'

21

At first light on Friday morning, Steiger set out for his brother's farm near Neukloster, making a short detour past the entrance to a fine country house.

The next day, Frau von Menen, Katrina and Greta left for Flensburg. With the departure of Schwarzt and the rest of the staff, only von Menen and the General remained at the house.

Von Menen found the General sitting quietly in the library, a brown canvas bag beside his feet, a blank expression on his face.

'Going somewhere?' quizzed von Menen, nodding at the bag.

'Oh, that. No, I'm not going anywhere.'

They sat silently for a while, each seeming as though he had something to tell the other, but didn't know where to begin. Eventually, the General spoke.

'You were right, Carl. It was a foolish idea; a dangerous one, too. If it had just been a question of Hans and me, then maybe, but involving you, well, it wouldn't have been right. You have enough problems to contend with.'

'So, what *is* in the bag?'

'Oh, just a few tools. My idea was to strip some lead off the roof and use it as a decoy for the gold.'

Von Menen smiled and picked up the bag. 'In that case, we'd best roll up our sleeves, hadn't we?'

'You mean…?'

'I mean I've decided to help you.'

The General rose slowly to his feet and placed an arm around his son's shoulders. 'Thank you, Carl,' he said quietly. 'Without you it wouldn't work, but now…'

'So, where do we start?'

'The flat roof, over the east wing, between the central dome and the sloping turret.'

'Haven't been up there in years, but I think I know where you mean.'

'That wing's been closed for years so the weatherproofing doesn't matter. We'll dump the lead over the parapet and into the courtyard. Fifteen to twenty square metres should suffice.'

'Before we start, Father… I've told Hans everything, about Maria, the arms *and* Vidal. I managed to have a word just before he left for Harald's place.'

'Good, he'll appreciate your confiding in him. I'd advise you not to tell anyone else, though. The ladies would worry themselves sick. And Jürgen has enough worries already.'

The entire flat roof was surrounded by a low brick parapet, a freezing cold wind hurtling over the top.

'A present from Stalin,' shouted von Menen, his voice almost lost in the icy blast.

'The dark clouds, too, I shouldn't wonder,' replied the General.

An hour later, the heavens opened, a torrent of rain falling upon them like a vertical sea. Within minutes, they were soaked, hands raw, faces chafed, bodies racked with cold. Yet they pressed on until it was almost too dark to see.

Fighting the fierce, buffeting wind, the General edged nearer the parapet and peered over the top. 'We'll call it a day,' he hollered. 'There's at least a quarter of a tonne down there. The rest can wait until tomorrow.'

The next afternoon, just as the General was dumping the last piece of lead over the parapet, a light appeared on the horizon.

'Lights!' shouted von Menen. 'Father, the field glasses!'

'It's okay,' said the General, peering through his binoculars. 'It's Hans.'

Steiger drove into the courtyard, backed the Steyr up to the workshop and opened the boot. They descended quickly and hurried across the courtyard to meet him.

'Well, Hans?' asked the General.

Smiling broadly, Steiger gestured to the open boot. 'See for yourselves – sides, ends, bases and lids, all cut to the exact measurements. The rest is under the blanket on the back seat.'

'Marvellous. Any strange looks from Harald?'

'No, I had the run of the place. Harald left the farm just after I arrived, didn't get back until nightfall. By then, I'd finished everything... even drilled the holes for the rope handles. Any word from Keppel?'

'Nothing.'

'Good.' Steiger glanced around the courtyard. 'I see you've been busy, then.'

'Damned heavy stuff, but I think we have enough. If not, there's plenty more up there.'

'Which reminds me,' said Steiger, with a studious look. 'The lead... My schoolboy physics tell me that the relative density of gold is greater than lead, which means that a kilo of lead will need more room than a kilo of gold.'

'True,' agreed the General. 'Let's hope there's enough spare capacity inside each box to allow for the difference.'

'You're with us, then, Carl?' whispered Steiger, as they headed towards the garage.

'Well, somebody's got to keep an eye on you two. I just hope that the three of us don't end up debating the merits of it inside Plötzensee Prison.'

'Don't worry, we won't be going to Plötzensee Prison.' Steiger gave him a playful slap on the back. 'Anyway, welcome to Club Daring, it's good to have you with us.'

'I forgot to ask you, Carl,' said the General. 'Your mother mentioned something about you calling at Borsigwalde the other day.'

'That's right.'

'The ordnance factory?'

'Yes, to arrange that ammunition I told you about.'

'Nine-millimetre parabellum?'

'Yes, for the Schmeissers.'

'Crated?'

'Er… yes, wooden boxes… there's a scarcity of pressed steel, so they say.'

Steiger, who'd seen through the General's questioning, smiled and turned on his heels. 'Follow me, gentlemen,' he said, hastening through the garage and into the storeroom at the far end.

Bemused, von Menen and the General followed, the dog bringing up the rear. Yeremenko stopped at the door, perked his nose and backed away, the reek of petrol almost overwhelming. Steiger grabbed a corner of a large canvas sheet and yanked it clear, revealing a veritable Aladdin's cave – sacks, packing crates, cardboard boxes of varying shapes and sizes, and at least two dozen jerry cans full of petrol! At the front, stacked one on top of the other, were four wooden cases, each marked with the same inscription, PK-88.

'Did you see any of these at Borsigwalde, Carl?' asked Steiger, tapping the bottom case with the toe of his boot.

'Thousands.'

'Good God, Hans!' exclaimed the General. 'Where the hell did all this come from?'

'Saved over the years, Klaus,' joked Steiger. 'You know how frugal I can be.' He delved to the back of the cache. 'Saved two of these as well,' he added, removing the hessian wrapping from a pristine Schmeisser. 'Thought they might come in handy someday.'

The General cupped a hand across his mouth, mumbling through his fingers. 'How the hell I've managed to stay out of trouble these last twenty-eight years, I simply do not know.'

Steiger hauled out one of the wooden cases and levered off the lid. 'These are standard field ammunition boxes,' he said, 'originally dimensioned for 7.92 rifle cartridges, but nowadays they're used for all types of small arms ammunition.' He fetched out one of the five cardboard cartons, packed sideways on, and broke it open. 'Inside are another fifty-two smaller packs, arranged four deep, in rows of thirteen.' Steiger opened one of the packs and emptied the contents into von Menen's hand. 'Sixteen rounds of lead point, nine-millimetre parabellum. This is what they'll be sending to Argentina: the same box, but zinc-lined!'

By mid-afternoon, hundreds of bright, shiny nails were piled on top of the workbench and Steiger had fashioned the first of the twenty boxes. It tipped the scales at 6.75 kilograms.

'If Fischer's figures are right,' said the General, 'then whatever's in those boxes back at the Reichsbank must weigh *marginally* below 25.5 kilos, assuming, of course, that our timber is about the same weight as theirs.'

Von Menen and Steiger pressed on while the General

returned to the house, bringing back the next set of useful implements.

'What do you think, Hans? They're the sturdiest I could find... cast iron, I think.'

'They look robust enough to me,' replied Steiger, feeling the weight of the large cooking pan and eyeing the two roasting trays.

Von Menen fetched up one of the finished boxes and placed it on the bench. Steiger plopped one of the roasting trays inside it. 'Just right,' he said. 'There'll be enough space at each end for the rope handle knots, too. As for the weight, well, we won't know until we've cast the first ingot.'

'All that matters is that we get 25.5 kilos in there,' maintained the General.

At the far end of the workshop, von Menen was busy trimming down the lead sheeting, cutting it into small, manageable pieces, weighing it and placing it into separate piles. Using the age-old process of trial and error, he soon worked out the approximate amount needed to tip the scales at the right weight.

Monday 20th November 1944

The boxes were finished; twenty piles of lead, each weighing 25.5 kilos, waiting to be smelted.

At midday, Steiger got through to his contact at Hamburg. He raced across the courtyard with the news.

'It's on, Klaus! Wednesday, nine-thirty; Carl and I will leave for Hamburg at first light. With luck, we'll be back at the house by mid-afternoon. What do you think?'

'If the operation had been scheduled for tomorrow,' replied the General, thinking out loud, 'then Keppler would have informed us by now... but Wednesday, that's different. If we get a message tomorrow from Keppler saying Wednesday, then we'll be too late.'

'But you've always thought Sunday, Klaus.'

'I still do, Hans, I still do… Keppler might be stupid, but he's not *that* stupid. He'll favour a time when the Reichsbank building is practically empty and the streets of Berlin are at their quietest, notwithstanding a visit by a swarm of Mosquitos. It *has* to be Sunday, and Sunday evening at that.' The General inched up his sleeve and checked his watch, an inspiring look in his eyes. 'Right, let's go for it!'

Steiger cleaned out the forge, packed the core with paper and heaped on the kindling. When von Menen arrived with the first barrowload of coke fuel, they were ready to start. The General peered in the direction of the storeroom, an anxious look on his face.

'Don't worry, Klaus,' said Steiger, 'I've moved all the petrol to the old groom's quarters.'

He lit the paper, the kindling wood taking hold, the coke beginning to smoulder. A moment later, a blast of air from the bellows sent a spray of sparks scurrying towards the canopy, chased by bright yellow flames. Soon, the heart of the forge was like a glowing sun.

'Burning at 327.5°C. That's what it takes,' said Steiger.

Von Menen, mesmerised by the glow of the coke, didn't hear a word. The General just smiled.

'What we need now is a load of sand,' said Steiger. 'Don't suppose there is any, Klaus?'

The General shook his head. 'I don't think so. Would dry, fine soil do?'

'Better than nothing,' said Steiger.

'Anna wouldn't like it one bit,' mumbled the General, 'but if there's no alternative… Carl, the orangery… Some dry soil. We'll use that.'

Two excursions with the wheelbarrow and von Menen had dumped a large pile of soil on the workshop floor. Steiger formed it into a neat rectangular mound.

'What's it for, Hans?'

'I'll show you.' Steiger placed one of the cast iron trays on top of the mound. 'If we empty the castings on to the concrete floor, sooner or later there's a chance that one of the trays will crack. This way there's a better chance of them staying in one piece.'

Steiger eased the large, heavy pan towards the side of the heat and dropped in the first piece of lead. A second lump followed. 'I don't think we should risk more than about five kilos at a time,' he explained. 'The handle won't take the weight.'

As soon as the lead had melted, Steiger, his forehead beaded with sweat, slipped on a pair of heavy-duty leather gloves, wrapped his hands in sized offcuts from an asbestos welding blanket and eased the pan away from the heat, the molten lead streaming into the roasting tray. He repeated the process until the first pile of lead was gone.

They waited for the contents of the roasting tin to solidify. Then Steiger turned it over. A shiny ingot dropped out. He took a deep breath, heaved the ingot from the mound of soil and carried it over to the workbench. The moment of truth had arrived, the workshop full of silent trepidation.

'It's now or never,' said Steiger, lowering the ingot into the box.

'Alleluia!' beamed the General. 'It fits.'

'Perfectly,' added von Menen.

At dusk, they blacked out the windows, the work continuing beneath the faint light of a solitary forty-watt bulb. By eight o'clock, nearly half of the boxes were full.

For two hours, von Menen had said nothing, his mind

on other things – Maria, Vidal and the arms shipment. The General had noticed; Steiger, too.

'We'll call it a day,' said the General, tactfully. 'We're tired. If we continue, we're sure to make a mistake. We'll restart at, say, ten in the morning?'

Steiger nodded. Von Menen said nothing.

'Ten suit you, Carl?' asked the General.

'Fine, except that I have some business to attend to late tomorrow afternoon. I'll leave as soon as it gets dark. In the meantime, what do we do about this lot?'

'The same as yesterday,' replied Steiger. 'I'll bunk up in here. There's enough warmth and it'll save us having to clear everything away.'

'Don't forget, Hans... the light switch by the door doesn't work. You'll have to use the secondary switch in the storeroom, just around the corner.'

'I know,' grinned Steiger. 'It took me the best part of fifteen minutes to figure that out last night.'

Tuesday 21st November 1944

Von Menen took the ferry to Travemünde and motored up the coast, arriving at Neustadt just before six o'clock. He left the Delahaye in a side street and walked the rest of the way, the sky inky black, rooftops hardly visible.

The whitewashed end-of-terrace house was in total darkness, the curtains drawn. Von Menen made his way down the passageway towards the only entrance, his footsteps short, his breathing quiet, Vidal's instructions humming in his head: *'Good evening. My name is Javier Gomez. I'm a Spanish ex-patriate collecting on behalf of wounded members of the Spanish Blue Division, serving on the Russian Front.'* Reply: *'My husband was with the same division. He was killed last June.'*

311

He knocked lightly on the door. It moved inwards slightly. Something was wrong. Von Menen checked the street again – still empty, eerily quiet, not a soul around. Nudging the door open with his flashlight, he stepped inside.

The sink-tap, dripping merrily, was playing a thin metallic beat on the base of a pan. Moving silently through the kitchen, von Menen made his way into the hall. A door on the left was slightly ajar. As he neared it, a clock chimed, a cat let out a frightening shrill, shot into the hall and bolted into the kitchen.

Heart racing, the pit of his stomach turning in silent panic, von Menen gathered his thoughts and gingerly pushed open the door, the beam of his flashlight sweeping ahead of him, left, right, over a russet-brown rug and along the skirting, a polished brass coal scuttle glinting back at him. Suddenly, he froze, a cold chill crawling through his veins. A woman, prostate across the hearth, dark hair, slim, skirt high above her knees, eyes wide open in deathly panic, a black stocking around her neck, the loose ends trailing across her chest.

"Grace Martens". Dead.

Von Menen coasted into the courtyard, heart pounding, a dozen more knots in his stomach.

At the edge of the blacked-out workshop window, he saw a faint chink of light. His father and Steiger were still at work.

'It's me,' he called, pushing open the door.

'My God, Carl, you look terrible,' said Steiger.

'I *feel* terrible. I've just got back from Neustadt. I went there to see a contact of Vidal's, thinking that if I got a message to him now, assuring him that everything's proceeding favourably, it might take the heat off Maria.'

'And?' asked the General.

'She was dead – strangled. Only about twenty-five, I reckon.'

'You'd best sit down,' said Steiger. 'I'll go and fetch some brandy.'

'Thanks, Hans, but I'm okay.'

'Any idea who…?' asked the General.

'None at all. But one thing's for sure, from now on I'll be working blind, praying to God that Vidal *thinks* everything's okay.'

The General placed a hand on his son's shoulders. 'Look, we'll figure something out, I'm sure of it.'

Von Menen prisoned his face with his fingers. 'It's Maria I'm worried about,' he said, 'desperately so. Hell, what a frightening mess.' He took a deep breath and shook his head. 'Anyway, what's the progress with you two?'

'One more box left.'

'No news from Keppel, I suppose.'

'Nothing.'

It was nearly eight o'clock. Steiger was just about to nail down the lid on the very last box when Yeremenko jumped to his feet, pricked back his ears and whimpered.

'Quiet, Yeremenko,' whispered the General.

'What is it?' said von Menen.

'The dog's heard something. I did, too. A car, I think, in the distance.'

Steiger tiptoed into the storeroom and switched out the light. The General eased back the blackout curtain and glimpsed through the window.

'It's totally black out there; can't see a thing. Maybe I was hearing things.' He replaced the curtain and patted the dog on the head. 'Switch the lights back on.'

Steiger flicked down the switch and made his way back

to the workshop. Suddenly he stopped. 'You're right, Klaus,' he whispered. 'There's someone out there. I'm sure I heard footsteps.' The dog was back against the door, whining faintly, nose to the floor.

'Hush… Lights,' whispered the General.

Steiger picked up his Schmeisser, glided back into the storeroom and switched out the light again.

'I still can't see anything,' murmured the General.

'I can't see anything from this window, either,' said Steiger, softly. 'Perhaps it's a fox.'

A moment later, Steiger threw on the light as the workshop door burst open, Yeremenko barking loudly. Steiger flattened his body against the storeroom wall, the Schmeisser still in his hands. The General saw the Luger. Von Menen saw the face, gasped and felt the kick of a mule in his stomach.

The spectre from hell gazed into von Menen's eyes like a red-hot poker, almost reaching the back of his skull. 'I don't believe it,' he said, shaking his head. I just don't believe it… It *was* you, at Neustadt, trying to make contact with an Argentine agent.'

Von Menen gathered his senses. '*Dead* Argentine agent,' he said; 'dead after you'd finished with her, anyway.'

'Dead or not, *you* were there.'

The dog barked again. 'Quiet, Yeremenko!' shouted the General, an askance eye on the open door to the storeroom. 'Carl, do you know this man?'

'Yes, his name is Heinz Müller, *used* to be with Schellenberg's outfit, but he's with the Gestapo now. We crossed paths in Buenos Aires. He once *tried* to kill me. He must have—'

'Followed you,' interrupted Müller.

Shaking his head in apology, von Menen looked at the General. 'Sorry, Father; I saw no one, I suspected no one. The street was empty. It was pitch black.'

'So you are the illustrious General von Menen,' Müller said. 'Father and, perhaps, *accomplice* of the traitor Carl von Menen.'

'Traitor?' snapped the General.

Müller sniggered. 'What other motive would your son have for visiting a known agent of a foreign power?'

'Why don't you ask him?'

'Well, von Menen?' asked Müller.

'Your suggestion is quite preposterous. She was an official contact of the German Foreign Office.'

'Rubbish. She is, or rather was, a contact of a known Argentine agent who worked at the Blohm and Voss yard at Hamburg, found in unauthorised possession of detailed drawings of the new electro U-boat. He was arrested two days ago. But that can wait... My immediate concern is *this.*' He motioned his hand, a wide sweep across the workshop, scooping up the puzzling scene. 'All those boxes? Very strange. Very intriguing.' Slowly, his grin transformed into an ugly scowl. 'Both of you move over to the door! Now!' he snapped.

'Why?'

'Because I need a telephone.'

'Ah, you're alone,' said von Menen, straining at the leash, wanting to rush forward and grab the Luger.

'The telephone is out of order,' said the General calmly, tugging at the back of his son's jacket. 'Instead of taking us to Berlin to be shot, why don't you just shoot us NOW!'

At that, the light snapped out.

'DOWN!' bellowed Steiger.

The General crashed to the floor and von Menen fell flat across the dog as the Schmeisser opened up, a hail of nine-millimetre parabellum driving into Müller's chest, shards of brick zipping across the room, ricocheting off the wall and playing a tinny tune on the canopy of the forge.

The noise faded, the workshop silent again, a waft of burned cordite drifting in from the storeroom.

'You okay, Father?' asked von Menen breathlessly.

'Yes, you?'

Von Menen felt hurriedly about his body. 'I think so.'

Yeremenko struggled free and crouched behind the General.

'Good boy, good boy… it's okay,' said the General.

Steiger ambled into the room, ejecting the empty magazine and stuffing it beneath his belt. 'A product of Hitler's Germany,' he said, nodding at the lifeless heap on the floor. 'There are ten good reasons why this country's in such a mess, and he's nine of them!'

'You read the cue brilliantly, Hans,' said the General, bending over Müller to count the bullet wounds. 'Nine out of sixteen. Not bad.'

Von Menen dropped down on the nearest stack of boxes. 'Christ, Hans, between Father's "Now!" and the first round, it seemed like a lifetime. My heart was in my trousers.'

'The first time it happened to me, Carl, something else was very nearly in my trousers,' joked Steiger. 'Anyway, we've got to find Müller's car and get rid of him.'

Von Menen delved into Müller's jacket, fished out an ignition key and made for the door. 'It can't be so far away. I'll take a look.'

'Mind yourself, Carl,' shouted Steiger. Make sure there's no one else around.'

Von Menen reappeared fifteen minutes later. Müller's body was still lying on the floor, stripped clean, his clothes and possessions adding fuel to the dying forge.

'The car's outside,' von Menen said. 'A black Opel. It

was about 100 metres down the drive. I've taken everything from the inside: maintenance books, Gestapo log book, fuel book, etcetera.' He held out a wad of papers.

'Best stick them on the fire,' said the General.

Von Menen did so, then nodded at the body. 'What are we to do with *him*?'

'Hans has an idea. The lake, down by the shooting hide, where the banking is shuttered… the water is at least four metres deep.'

Von Menen made off in the Opel, windows down, Müller propped up in the passenger seat, Steiger following in the Steyr; no masked headlights, no moon, just the fear of pressing darkness and sudden deep water. It was all on instinct. Only by luck did they find the hide.

The Steyr right behind, von Menen inched the Opel gingerly towards the banking, released the handbrake and jumped out. Steiger did the rest. A low gear, a gentle nudge, a groan of reluctance and the Opel tipped over the edge. The sound of bubbles and then silence.

Müller had been unceremoniously laid to rest.

The next morning, von Menen and Steiger left for Hamburg at first light. Two hours later, Steiger telephoned the General.

'We've got it… same colour, same fittings and no divisional markings. There's a new hood, too, just like mine. I've got spare number plates, as well… We'll be back soon.'

At one o'clock, von Menen drew up in the courtyard, Steiger following in the *new* Steyr, parking it in the garage block next to his own. The bodywork looked the same – field grey paint, soft canvas hood, lights, mirrors, tyres and tow-bar.

'Hans, this is going to hurt you a great deal more than me,' the General warned.

Steiger closed his eyes, raised his hands in supplication and grimaced as the blacksmith's hammer crashed down on the boot lid, the front near side door and finally, the front wing.

'That should do it,' said the General, stepping back to admire his handiwork.

Steiger opened his eyes and shuddered. 'Well, Klaus, I know rank has its privileges, but…'

'An absolute necessity, I'm afraid. They've got to look as identical as possible.'

'They will do when I've replicated the old girl's number plate and added a touch of ageing… a few scratches here and there, some mud and a smidgen of axle grease.'

★

Friday 24th November 1944

Von Menen and the General hurried over to the garage block. They found Steiger admiring the finished article, the two Steyrs indistinguishable from each other.

'Did I hear a motorcycle?' asked Steiger.

'You did,' replied the General. 'The courier's been. It's on for Sunday night. They've met our entire logistical requirements: seventy men, a detachment from Field Gendarmerie and one from Coastal Artillery; ten Opel trucks, two Kübelwagons and two motorcycles. They're travelling down from Hamburg on Saturday evening. We've to rendezvous on Sunday at Jägerstrasse, 15h00.'

'Well, we're as ready as we ever will be,' said Steiger. 'Both engines are running as smooth as silk. I've increased the tyre pressures to compensate for the extra weight and worked out the configuration for the boxes. There's just one thing…' Steiger walked over to his own vehicle, pulled out a roll of camouflage netting from the boot and dumped it in the footwell of the second Steyr. 'You'll need this, Carl. After you've parked up, drape it over the vehicle and weigh it down. There's a full-length animal-skin coat in the back, too. It'll be damn cold in that wood.'

After lunch, the three men set out for the woods near Holdorf, the scene of the General's previous early-morning recce and the place where his plan would either triumph or fail.

Steiger took the Mercedes as far as the makeshift hut, turned full circle and pulled up on the Gadebusch side of the clearing.

'This is where I want you to wait with the second Steyr, Carl,' said the General. 'From here, it's about twenty-five metres to the edge of the wood and beyond that, it's open farmland.' He pointed south-east. 'You can see the Gadebusch road quite easily. The horizon is about 1.5 kilometres from here, maybe a bit more, so the lights of the vehicles will come into view two minutes or so before they pass the end of the track. But remember, the lights will be masked.'

'So I wait for two motorcycles, a Kübelwagon, ten trucks, another Kübelwagon and then you?' asked von Menen.

'Yes, two single headlamps, twelve pairs and then us. You can be absolutely certain that we will be the very last vehicle. When we approach the incline, we'll drop back as much as we dare and then, as soon as the last vehicle is over the horizon, we'll be down this track faster than Fritz von Opel.'

'ETA?'

'Assuming we leave Berlin at 18h00, and allowing for a half-hour stop at Perleburg, we should arrive here around

00h30, maybe a bit earlier. So make sure to be here no later than 23h30.'

'I'll arrive before eleven-thirty,' von Menen assured him.

'When you leave the wood, keep well clear of Gadebusch, Rehna and Grevesmühlen, especially Rehna. We don't want some wide-awake individual eyeing the same vehicle twice! I suggest you make a right at Holdorf and make your way back to the house via Grevesmühlen. If you've got time, recce the route tomorrow. Any questions?'

'What time can I expect you back at the house?'

Steiger did a quick mental calculation. 'It's about twenty-seven, twenty-eight kilometres from Holdorf to Dassow and perhaps another ten to Priwall,' he said. 'That'll take about forty-five minutes. Allowing three hours for the unloading and another forty-five minutes for the journey back to the house, I'd say we'll be home sometime after five o'clock.'

'If you're wondering what to do with the gold when you get back, Carl,' said the General, 'lock the Steyr in the garage and stay with it. We'll deal with it when we return. I've something in mind already.'

'When do we load the dummy boxes?' von Menen asked.

'Sunday morning,' replied the General. 'And one last thing. If anything goes wrong here, before we arrive, don't get inventive... just be the diplomat your grandfather was.'

'Don't worry, Father,' replied von Menen, patting the breast of his jacket. 'I've an operations order in here with two signatures on it: one is von Ribbentrop's, the other is Bormann's!'

'Bormann? Interesting... Seems we're all working for the same outfit.'

22

At six o'clock in the morning, Carl and Steiger began loading the boxed lead into the second Steyr, Steiger having configured the loading arrangement already: two forward of the front passenger seat, four across the rear footwell, six on a wide length of timber across the back seat, and eight in the boot.

'Two, four, six, eight,' Steiger said, 'handles in line, front and rear.'

Von Menen drove the loaded Steyr back into the garage, placed an identical piece of wood across the rear seat of its empty "twin", then joined Steiger in the storeroom.

'Found it,' called Steiger, peeping up from behind his hoard. 'I knew it was here somewhere.' Drawing a Walther P38 from its holster, he wiped it clean with a piece of oiled rag, fed eight rounds into the magazine, slammed it into the butt and handed it to von Menen. 'Signatures or no signatures, Carl, you'll be on your own out there. Best take it with you.'

At eight o'clock, the three men met in the Steigers' parlour, soaking up the heat in front of the hearth, enjoying toasted bread, cheese, the rarity of butter and a huge jar of honey.

'Don't forget, Carl,' said the General, 'if we have to

abort, I'll call you from the Hotel Gröbler, asking you to *"Tell mother that I didn't have time to call and see Great-aunt Helga."* If we're not at the woods by 02h00, leave anyway.'

Standing by the kitchen table, his red-piped breeches and black calf-length boots masked beneath a long, grey-green leather greatcoat, General von Menen looked at his watch.

'Right, let's synchronise – eight-fifty.'

Steiger, wearing his favoured field cap, peak pulled square above his eyes, picked up one of the three magazines lying on top of the table and clipped it to the underside of his Schmeisser. Slipping the other two into the pouches attached to his belt, he slung the sub-machine gun over his shoulder. The General reached for his cane and stalled.

'Best take it with you, Klaus,' said Steiger sensitively. 'Stalin's sent another offering from the east – sub-zero temperatures and an icy wind. The courtyard is thick with frost.'

'You're right, Hans; don't want to be seen leaning on your shoulder, now, do I?'

Steiger smiled. 'Right, *General*, ready when you are, *sir*.'

They made their way across the courtyard, von Menen trailing behind. A final confab in the garage and Steiger sparked up the Steyr, the air-cooled V8 engine bursting into life, a muffled scream roaring through the garage block.

Thumbs up from Steiger and they were off.

The house was deathly quiet, the hours ticking by, von Menen's hidden scepticism about the whole plan transforming into a spiked, nagging doubt, the same tormenting questions pecking at his mind. *Will I make it to the woods at Holdorf? What if the Steyr breaks down?*

Even with the signatures of von Ribbentrop and Bormann in his pocket, twenty boxes of lead would take some explaining. The thought of being stopped with twenty boxes of *gold* didn't bear thinking about. *What if Keppler changes the itinerary, the location?* He shook his head despondently, each question leading to the same, frightening conclusion – doom!

Von Menen studied the well-thumbed photograph of Maria, passed around the family a dozen times, and felt the dainty white handkerchief with its faded red kiss, her image branded in his mind, the sound of her voice lingering in his ears. He thought about Lutzi Helldorf, Sigi Bredow and Gustav's mother, too, cursing himself for his hopeless inability to help them.

Walking into the drawing room, he gazed at the paintings of his forefathers hanging from the walls, his mind spinning with the tormenting notion that the von Menens were about to leave Mecklenburg forever. *What a damn mess.*

★

Every road in the vicinity of the Reichsbank was cordoned off, adjacent sidewalks festooned with a tangled mass of barbed wire, field grey uniforms everywhere. The Reichsbank had become a fortress within a fortress.

Steiger brought the Steyr to a halt a metre short of a long red-and-white pole.

'Papers!' demanded a corporal in a brusque tone.

In the damp greyness of evening, the capless General von Menen was just another soldier. The General handed his documents to Steiger, who passed them through the open window.

'You must be as blind as a bat, soldier,' said Steiger. 'This vehicle is flying the pennant of a general and the flag of an army commander.'

The corporal snapped to attention. 'Herr General von Menen,' he said loudly, 'I'm...'

Two privates rushed over to the barrier, raising it at breakneck speed. Another raced around the corner into Kurstrasse, skidding to a halt beside a parked Kübelwagon. Before the second syllable of the name *Menen* had left his lips, the door of the Kübelwagon flew open and a captain leapt out, hastily adjusting his tunic.

Steiger turned into Kurstrasse and halted, the Captain hurriedly opening the door.

'Captain Klessen, Herr General. My apologies, sir, I'd no idea *you* were coming.'

The General stepped out. 'Bit of a surprise, for you, then,' he smiled.

'Er... yes, sir.'

'Army Field Police, I see.'

'Yes, Herr General, Berlin district.'

'And the men over there? Coastal Artillery?'

'Yes, Herr General, part of Lieutenant Steckmann's outfit, sir. His unit came down from Hamburg yesterday.'

'And where might Lieutenant Steckmann be?'

'He's...'

'Not here? Well, he'd best be here pretty damn quick.'

Klessen nodded instantly to his sergeant.

Moments later, Fischer and Voigt came out of the building, trailed by a gang of men in buff three-quarter-length work coats. Meanwhile, the young, gangly Steckmann, in full flight along Jägerstrasse, turned rapidly into Kurstrasse, adjusting his stride as he neared the Steyr.

'Lieutenant Steckmann, Herr General. Sorry I'm late, sir,' he said, still breathless. 'I've been visiting my mother in Dahlem, sir.'

The General raised his head, a heavy fragrance reaching his nostrils. 'Seems your mother has an expensive taste in perfume, Lieutenant.'

Steckmann's cheeks turned bright pink.

The General turned to Klessen. 'How many men do you have, Captain?'

'Seventy, sir, including Lieutenant Steckmann and myself.'

'Vehicles?'

'Ten Opel trucks, two Kübelwagons and two motorcycle combis, General.'

'Right. We move out at 18h00, which gives us' – the General glanced at his watch – 'three hours to complete the loading. Warrant Officer Steiger will explain the details.'

Steiger stepped forward. 'Gentlemen, the operation involves the relocation of a consignment of small boxes; 820 boxes, to be precise. Each truck will carry eighty boxes. Six men will be assigned to each truck – two up front and four in the back.'

'That's only 800 boxes, Sergeant,' noted Steckmann. 'You said 820.'

'The weight factor is critical, Lieutenant,' intervened the General. 'The remaining twenty boxes will be carried in my staff vehicle. Does that answer your question?'

'Yes, *sir*,' replied Steckmann.

'Carry on, Sergeant Steiger.'

'Sir. Each truck will be loaded in Kurstrasse. Your men will be on board before loading starts and they will remain on board until ordered otherwise. As each truck is loaded, it will move along Kurstrasse and make way for the next truck in line. That process will be repeated until all trucks are loaded. The two motorcycle combis, each displaying orange markers, will lead the column; Captain Klessen will come next, then the ten trucks, followed by Lieutenant Steckmann in the second Kübelwagon. General von Menen will follow in his command car. The formation will remain in that order at *all* times. No overtaking, no stopping and no exceeding fifty kilometres an hour.'

The General tugged lightly at Captain Klessen's sleeve, ushering him to one side. 'Where do you come from, Captain?'

'Leipzig, sir.'

'What's your geography like?'

'Pretty good, sir.'

'Ever heard of Priwall?'

'I believe it's near Travemünde, General.'

'You believe right, Captain. That's where we're going, Priwall. Appraise the two outriders, but no one else. Understand?'

'Not even—?'

'*No one!*'

'Yes, sir!'

'And make sure they understand to keep their mouths shut. If I hear the word *Priwall* on anyone's lips…'

'Begging your pardon, sir, they're both Army Field Police; they won't say a word.'

'Good… because right now, Captain, it's very cold back east. Understood?'

'Perfectly, sir.'

'Good. Tell them I want traffic priority all the way. We're not stopping anywhere, except Perleberg.'

'Perleberg, Herr General?'

'Yes, there'll be a field kitchen waiting for us there. When the convoy enters the market square, it's to go straight past the Roland statue and assemble at the far end. Organise the parking so that the trucks are in tight formation, sideways on. Only two men at a time to leave each truck. And something else, Captain…'

'Yes, sir?'

'It's Sunday. Instruct your men that there's to be no skulking around and no loud chatter.'

'Yes, sir.'

'Any questions?'

'No, Herr General.'

'Right, let's get to work.'

By five-thirty, only the Steyr remained unloaded. Four men in brown smocks lumbered up with the last two trolleys, stopping at the rear of the vehicle. Eyeing the twenty boxes, Steiger feigned a look of bewilderment, cursing like a soldier who just wanted to go home. A glance in the boot, a look inside the vehicle and the order was given.

'Two boxes on the floor, forward of the front passenger seat, four across the rear footwell and six across the rear seat. Make sure the handles are facing front and rear.' He moved to the back of the vehicle and opened up the boot. 'The other eight will fit in here,' he said.

Captain Klessen rolled into Perleberg, made his way through the market square and parked just short of the field kitchen. Next came the ten Opel trucks, followed by Lieutenant Steckmann in the second Kübelwagon, and finally the Steyr.

Smiling confidently, the General checked his watch. '21h00, Hans. So far, so good.'

★

Von Menen looked at the figure reflected in the huge mirror hanging in the hall. In Steiger's long animal-skin coat he looked like a Siberian fur trapper from the far side of the Urals.

Outside, a waxing gibbous moon played hide-and-seek behind low scudding clouds, painting a spooky image across the sky. Only Count Dracula was missing.

Von Menen set out in the late evening, the Rehna-Gadebusch road completely empty. South of Holdorf, he doused the lights, coasted down the incline and turned into the woods, the Steyr surging up the track. Reaching the corrugated hut, he swept round in an arc and came to a halt on the Gadebusch side of the clearing.

He switched off the engine, leapt out of the vehicle and arranged the camouflage netting, weighing it down with a few short lengths of wood, and covering it with a liberal scattering of leaves. It merged into the woods like a tangled mass of undergrowth.

It was bitterly cold and deathly quiet, just the sound of the engine cooling and the sporadic hoot of an owl. Von Menen pulled up the deep furry collar of his coat and slumped back into his seat, eyeing the Gadebusch road through a chink in the netting. In the half-hour to eleven o'clock, he counted just one set of lights.

For want of something better to do, he wagered with himself as to when the next vehicle would pass. When it did, it was almost eleven-twenty, the faint glow of its rear light fading towards Gadebusch. But suddenly, it stopped, the rear light becoming slowly more visible as the vehicle reversed up the road and backed onto the track.

The whine of its engine grew louder, the vehicle closing in on the Steyr metre by metre. Heart beating wildly, von Menen hardly dared breath. He took out the Walther, released the safety catch and placed it on the passenger seat, watching anxiously as a large Mercedes came to a halt ten metres short of the clearing.

Offering a silent prayer for the camouflage netting, von Menen slumped deep into his seat, peering watchfully through a narrow slit at the bottom of the windscreen. Engine still running, the driver's door of the Mercedes pushed open. A man stepped out, walked slowly to the back, his uniform as sinister as the night itself.

Gestapo.

Von Menen made ready with the Walther, death just ten strides away. The man drew to a halt, pulled open his topcoat, unbuttoned his trousers and gazed at the heavens, legs akimbo, hands on hips, the ache in his nether region dissipating slowly. A voice rang out from inside the car.

'Don't let him get cold, Ferdinand!'

"Ferdinand" made his way back to the car and all von Menen could hear was a deep voice and girlish laughter, followed by a brief period of quiet and, finally, the creaking of springs.

Wrestling with panic, von Menen peered at the luminous dial of his watch, waiting with calculated optimism for the flame of a cigarette lighter and the inevitable glow of two cigarettes. It was just past midnight.

Glancing to the south, his anxiety almost swamped him: a lone, faint light in the distance, then another and then two more. The first of the column was over the horizon!

And then, as if by some divine intervention, the engine of the Mercedes fired into life. Within seconds it had reached the end of the track and was gone.

Von Menen sparked up the Steyr, leapt out and wrenched off the camouflage netting, just as the two outriders passed the end of the track, followed by the first Kübelwagon. He flung open the two front doors counted off the headlights: one, two, three... nine, ten, eleven, and then the second Kübelwagon, twelve!

Some moments later, Steiger roared down the track like a Tiger tank at full tilt, halting within feet of him. Steiger leapt out and hurriedly transferred the General's pennant and flag, the General just a few strides behind.

'Any problems, Carl?' he whispered, limping across the clearing as fast as his gammy leg would allow.

'Not to speak of... You?'

'So far, so good. See you in the morning.'

'Good luck.'

As soon as the General was aboard, Steiger roared down the track, turned left onto the Rehna road and disappeared. Von Menen gathered up the camouflage netting, transferred it to the other Steyr and followed, but only as far as Holdorf.

At Priwall, the two motorcycle combis made their way along Mecklenburger Landstrasse, turned right into the harbour entrance and pulled up alongside the guardhouse, the convoy following in line. Steiger spurted down the outside and halted before the barrier, the General adamant that the twenty boxes would be unloaded first, the chance being that they would find a cosy place at the bottom of the pile.

Baumer was waiting. 'Morning, General. *Just* on time,' he said, cynically. 'Follow me.' He ordered the barrier raised, then headed towards a black BMW parked just up from the guardhouse.

'I see what you mean, General,' said Steiger. 'An inflated, pretentious little man. Needs a lesson or two in manners, I'd say.'

The column moved slowly along the quay, rounded a large red-brick building and came to a halt beside a huge concrete pillbox set with heavy steel doors.

'The bunker of all bunkers,' quipped Steiger.

'A *staging* bunker, I shouldn't wonder,' replied the General.

Two men in civilian clothes, their overcoat collars turned high to meet the stiff brims of their Homburg hats, stood in front of the doors, a neat line of trolleys beside them.

Baumer made his way back to the Steyr. 'One truck at a time along the apron, General,' he snapped. 'They're to park right by the entrance.'

Steiger inched forward, stopping a few metres short of the steel doors, another posse of men in brown work coats nearby.

Baumer rushed over to the Steyr and banged heavily on the bonnet. 'Are you stupid or something? I said one *truck* at a time, not this heap, you idiot.'

The General stepped from the vehicle, hurried round to meet Baumer and drilled him a piercing look. 'Because of the weight factor,' he said brusquely, 'we could only get eighty boxes in each truck, so we had to put the remaining twenty in my command car.'

Baumer sniggered, turned on his heels and called over his shoulder.

'Follow me.'

The steel doors opened onto a small, unlit chamber, four metres wide and six metres long, with another pair of doors at the far end.

'A blackout chamber,' whispered Steiger. 'When the outer doors are open, the inner doors are closed.'

Beyond the chamber was another anteroom and beyond that a drift tunnel, lit every five metres by a low-powered lamp. Descending steadily at a gradient of one in six, the drift stretched for at least thirty metres, turned sharply right and continued at a similar gradient for a further thirty metres, eventually spewing out into a massive repository, the air full of the smell of newly-rendered concrete. It was comfortably warm, a mass of overhead hot water pipes rumbling in unison with the drone of ventilation fans.

Baumer was standing at the far end, the two men in Homburg hats close by, the floor crammed with irregular shapes, each covered by ghostly white sheets.

The nation's riches. The concrete womb of mother Germany.

'The boxes are to go here,' Baumer said, voice echoing

through the chamber, 'but keep the arrangement tight. Stack them to the ceiling, if need be.'

By four o'clock, just one truck was left; Baumer, much to the curious amusement of a group of young soldiers, painstakingly counted every box.

As the last few boxes were being unloaded, a devilish, fresh-faced young conscript muttered beneath his breath, 'Seven hundred and eighty-four... Three hundred and ninety... Six hundred and...' Baumer walked over to the youngster, withdrew his Luger and pistol-whipped him across the face, a deep, ugly gash opening across his right cheek, blood pouring over his tunic.

Baumer casually re-holstered the weapon. Klessen, snorting like a bull, rushed to confront him, but Steiger cut him short.

'Corporal!' bellowed Steiger. 'Put that man in a truck and get him to Lübeck Hospital – immediately!'

Baumer, fuming at the intervention, felt a sudden, sharp crack on his ankle, as Steiger pushed him unceremoniously to one side and forced his feet apart.

'Listen, Baumer,' he said angrily, 'I don't take kindly to that kind of behaviour. Neither does General von Menen. You'll forgive me for mixing my animal metaphors, but you'd best be aware that I can be as quiet as a field mouse or I can roar like a lion. You'd best work out which one applies to a skunk like you.'

An evil look in his eyes, Baumer's hand glided slowly towards his re-holstered Luger, but Steiger had reached the limits of his patience. He turned calmly to one side, cocked his Schmeisser and stuck the barrel end under Baumer's nose.

'Touch that,' he said in a whisper, 'and your body weight will increase by the value of at least sixteen rounds of lead point, nine-millimetre parabellum.' He glanced quickly at the group of men fussing around the heavily bleeding conscript. 'And no one here will have seen a damn thing.'

Baumer was almost on fire with rage and everyone could see it, including the General, who had just emerged from the bunker.

'One more thing,' continued Steiger. 'Your house – it's on the outskirts of Warin, I believe – a large white place, elevated from the road?' The detail caught Baumer unaware, Steiger sensing his change of mood. 'As for counting the boxes,' he continued, in a low voice, 'there's no need. I can tell you now that twenty are missing…'

The General's ears pricked up.

'They're in a very safe place, though,' continued Steiger, 'buried somewhere on your ninety-acre estate. You won't find them this side of the year 2000. And just in case anything else *untoward* happens, a letter, addressed to your boss, Heinrich Müller, giving the precise location of *where* they're buried, is in very safe hands. Now, do you still want to play Hannibal, or are you going to go home like a good little boy?'

'Sound advice, Baumer,' said the General, buttoning his amusement. 'And if I were you, I'd take it. But before you go home, there is something you have to do – sign this!'

Baumer opened the envelope, pulled out the single sheet of paper and read it:

HANDED INTO THE CUSTODY OF SS HAUPTSTURMFÜHRER BAUMER: EIGHT HUNDRED AND TWENTY WOODEN BOXES, CONTENTS UNKNOWN.

The General held up his pen. Baumer took it, scribbled hurriedly across the bottom and skulked back to the bunker.

Just before five o'clock, the two Steyrs were back in the garage block; the General, already onto the next phase of his plan, headed towards the far end, oil lamp swinging in his hand, Steiger and von Menen bringing up the rear.

The General stopped beside an old gig propped up on its end, its shafts reaching towards the ceiling.

'We need to pull it out, Hans.'

Steiger and von Menen pulled it back and wheeled it clear.

'Of course, the tunnel!' exclaimed von Menen.

'The jemmy, please,' said the General, 'and that length of wood by the wall. As soon as I've got some leverage, jam the wood in the gap and hold the slab steady. Hans will grab the corners and upend it.'

One heave and the slab came up, a deep void below. Steiger eased it back and leaned it against the wall.

'I suspect there'll be some water down there,' said von Menen.

'Doesn't matter,' replied the General. 'There are at least twenty steps and we only need ten, two boxes on each step.' Make sure not to use the first step, though, otherwise we won't get the slab back on.'

Von Menen and Steiger fetched up the twenty boxes from the Steyr and stacked them at the tunnel entrance, lumbering them down the concrete stairwell one by one. It was exhausting work, but the rope handles on the boxes and the heavy handrail at the left of the staircase made the work less arduous.

'That's it!' shouted the General.

'That's nineteen… We're a box missing,' said von Menen.

'I know,' replied the General.

Von Menen and Steiger emerged from the darkness, the General standing expectantly over the last box, eyes riveted to the lid, as if it held the secret of the Holy Grail itself. Soon, four more eyes were upon it, the garage block bursting with a nervous silence.

Steiger picked up the jemmy and offered it to the General as if it were the Olympic torch. 'The honour is yours, Klaus,' he said.

'I hope I've got this right,' said the General with a nervous smile. 'I seem to recall seeing *exactly* the same piece of timber this morning.'

Von Menen and Steiger looked on, mesmerised, the suspense mounting, the cleft widening as the General worked the jemmy in – half a centimetre, a centimetre, then a wide gap until the last stubborn nail gave way and the lid broke free. They gasped in wonderment; the General smiled triumphantly. 'I knew there had to be two bars in there,' he said. 'And they're not even hallmarked... No swastika, nothing.'

Von Menen brushed a finger lightly over one of the two ingots. 'It certainly has a fascination,' he said, 'and yet somehow, it's hard to conceive the relevance of a lump of yellow metal.'

'Know what you mean,' said Steiger, 'but throughout history, men have adventured for it, murdered for it, even gone to war for it.'

'Whatever men may have done in the past, Hans,' said the General, 'it's the future we're interested in, and for us, those two shiny blocks of metal *are* the future.'

'Well, Father,' sighed von Menen, 'we've got this far; what next?'

'A large cognac.'

23

The German Foreign Office had once been the splendid headquarters of von Ribbentrop's empire, but now it was just a wreck with minimal purpose. Picking his way gingerly through the ruins, von Menen followed the makeshift signs, the air heavy with the stench of smoke, dampness and rubble.

Werner's improvised "office" was an abject mess: the door hanging obliquely from its hinges; the windows boarded up; the floor littered with shards of plaster, masonry and splintered wood. Against the wall stood the charred, dank remains of a rolled-up length of carpet – a deep maroon colour, as von Menen recalled it.

Above the fireplace, a huge square of flock wallpaper hung down like a limp flag, teased from the wall by a constant trickle of water leaking from above. A large section of the ceiling was missing, a thin shaft of light spearing through a hole in the roof, dodging the timbers and settling upon the spot where once had stood a handsome mahogany desk. Now, it was just another boarded-up hole in the floor. The glittering chandelier was missing, replaced by another gaping hole from which a jumbled mass of cables emerged, one leading directly to a small lamp on a makeshift desk.

'Recognise the room, Carl?' asked Werner.

'Herr Wehman's office, I think.'

'The *late* Herr Wehmen,' replied Werner. 'Killed in last year's November air raid, I'm afraid.' He glanced down at the boarded floor where Wehmen's desk had once stood. 'The story goes that he was working late and when the alarm sounded he refused to leave – just sat there, defiantly, in full SS regalia, quite drunk, apparently. All his secretary could hear when she closed the door was a loud rendition of 'Deutschland über Alles'...' Werner paused, stared pensively at the massive hole in the ceiling and shook his head. 'Or was it the Horst Wessel song? Can't remember.'

'And his secretary?' asked von Menen, a pained look on his face.

'Oh, *she* made it to the shelter, as did most of them.'

Von Menen closed his eyes in relief. 'But Wehmen was killed?'

'Well, everyone assumed he was. They never did find his body. All they found, two floors down, was his mangled SS dress dagger. Three days later, a workman found a shoe with a foot in it, but... well, who knows.'

I wonder if his Argentine passport went with him.

'And his secretary... Clarita Brecht, I think her name was... Still with the Foreign Office, is she?'

'No, left earlier this year. Married a much older chap, a doctor at the Charité, I believe.'

'A doctor? When I left she was engaged to a soldier, a captain, Otto somebody or other.'

'That's right, she was, but he was killed in 1942. Anyway, enough of that.' Werner dipped into his briefcase, pulled out a dark green dossier and smiled. 'You've won them over, Carl,' he said. 'It's all go. Everything's set. All we need is a date and we'll have that within the next week or so.'

Von Menen hid his relief, but the wave of ecstatic joy sweeping through his body almost overcame him, his mind's eye full of the image of the woman he loved so much. He'd beaten von Ribbentrop and now he'd beaten Hitler.

Folding his arms, Werner lolled back in his chair. 'There's something bothering me, though. It's bothering others, too.'

'And that is, sir?'

'Your resolute conviction that you can get to Argentina under your own steam.'

'I'm sure I can, sir, in fact I *know* I can.'

'You mean you *think* you can... getting to Lisbon and finding a ship is not the real problem. The *real* problem is what comes *after* Lisbon. Maybe you hadn't realised it, but every neutral ship heading for the South Atlantic has to pass through the Gibraltar Control Point, which means an encounter with the Gibraltar Examination Service. They're not exactly the Royal Navy, but they're just as professional. You'll be scrutinised very thoroughly. The fact is,' continued Werner, jabbing his finger at the file, 'I have the authority to put you into Argentina by a second submarine. You can be underway in five weeks.'

'With respect, sir, I know it won't be easy, but I'm convinced I *can* get through and I'll get there much quicker than I would by submarine. And since time *is* a very important factor...'

Werner stood to his feet. 'What you need to appreciate,' he said, looking von Menen straight in the eyes, 'is that this entire operation will be monitored from the very highest level. The truth is,' he said solemnly, 'if things *do* go wrong...'

Von Menen was thinking hard. He'd sold the cake and now he was trying to sell the recipe. The notion of spending week after week beneath the angry waters of the Atlantic sent a cold shiver down his spine. He'd never been in a submarine in his entire life and if he believed half of what Jürgen had told him, he wasn't sure he ever wanted to. Submarines were for men who grew beards, didn't bathe or shower and lived week after week amid the stench of diesel oil, stale air, urine and other bodily odours.

'If you don't mind, sir, I'd prefer to stick to the more conventional means of travel. If ever it starts to look questionable, then, yes, I'll go in by submarine. But I'm sure I can make it.'

'Frankly, I wouldn't relish the idea of a submarine myself,' said Werner. 'Besides, you'd look a bit silly with this...' He reached down and flicked open the lid of a large cardboard box, a tiny red chimney peeping up from a mock terracotta roof. 'It's a doll's house, modelled on a Spanish hacienda. I had it made last week. Rather original, don't you think?'

Von Menen shrugged, the relevance lost on him. 'You mean I'm to take it with me?'

'Yes, there's a vitally important reason for it, too, so keep it safe, very safe. I'll signal you about it in due course. Now, I'd like to move on to the matter of one-time pads... We've a few *home* station sheets left, so it follows that you've enough *out* station pads to see you through the initial stages of the operation.'

'I have, sir,' replied von Menen, sparing a thought for the hidey-hole beneath the floorboards at the safe house.

'Good, because this time, you won't have the luxury of diplomatic immunity. Nonetheless, I'll arrange for new ciphers to be sent out with the U-boat.'

'Will there be a need for me to make direct wireless contact with the submarine, sir?'

'No, all signals concerning your rendezvous with the U-boat must be sent directly to the Foreign Office. From there, they'll be relayed to U-boat Headquarters.

I'll be liaising with U-boat HQ at all times. Any message *from* the U-boat, intended for you, will be sent first to U-boat HQ then relayed to the Foreign Office for onward transmission. As for the rendezvous itself, you'll be advised of the U-boat's ETA approximately five days in advance.'

'Codenames, sir?'

'The U-boat will be referred to as ANDROMEDA, Your codename remains the same – AKROBAT. But you'll have a new radio security code; as will I. As previously, if under duress, leave out the code and remember if you have to abort, your duty is to minimise the risk to the U-boat. Under such circumstances, signal me immediately.' He noticed the unsettled look on von Menen's face. 'Does that pose a problem?'

'Possibly, sir. You see, I'm going to have to find some way of maintaining contact with my source *and* be on station at the same time…'

'I'm sure you'll work something out,' said Werner confidently.

'I'm concerned, also, about the rendezvous position, in terms of distance from the coast, that is.'

Werner massaged his brow and sighed. 'We've had a real problem with that one. U-boat Headquarters has insisted on a depth of at least twenty metres. After some thought they've come up with a position thirty-four nautical miles due east of…' Shaking his head, Werner handed von Menen a typewritten sheet of paper. 'Here, see for yourself.'

Von Menen studied the bearing. '36° 18`S 56° 04`W… thirty-four nautical miles isn't too bad, sir,' he replied, recalling the range of *Margarita*. 'And identification?'

'Three pennants – white, black, white, in that order. Without them, the U-boat will regard you as hostile. If you're under duress, leave out the black pennant. Any questions?'

'No, sir.'

'The consignment will go from Lübeck-Siems. I've arranged storage facilities just back from the quay. It's not exactly a warehouse, but it's adequate.' Werner removed a small envelope from the green folder, pushed it across the desk. 'You'll find the necessary passes in there. The guard commander knows to expect you, but remember, it's a restricted area and heavily patrolled. When you arrive, the guard commander will notify the dockyard manager and he'll escort you to the warehouse. The double doors at the front of the building are fitted with two heavy-duty padlocks. Two keys are inside the envelope. Don't lose them. As for the shipment itself, the Schmeissers and the light machine guns will arrive on 6th December, direct from the Haenel factory at Suhl.'

'Mm, 6th December. That's next Wednesday, isn't it? What time?'

'Sometime "after two o'clock", whatever that means. They'll be in specially built, non-descript packing cases, small enough to facilitate loading through the torpedo-loading hatch.' Werner sheaved through the dossier. 'The prisms you asked about... We've managed to obtain two sets. They'll be sent to Lübeck next Wednesday, same day as the Schmeissers. It'll save you an added journey.'

'I suppose they're the right ones?' said von Menen.

'Well, the experts say so,' asserted Werner, stifling a tired yawn. 'Anyway, I think that just about covers everything, Carl. All that remains now is the ammunition and you've got that in hand yourself, right?'

'Yes, I'm calling at Borsigwalde this afternoon.' Von Menen checked his diary. 'I'll aim for the week beginning 11th December, if that's okay?'

'Fine, but there'll be no movement from U-boat Headquarters until January, at the very earliest, which means you'll be spending Christmas with your family. As for money—'

'I've enough to see me through the next few months at least, sir.'

'Good. I'll arrange for the U-boat to bring out a further supply of US dollars and Swiss francs.'

'Travel documents, sir?'

'You're going back as your old friend, Kurt Lindemann. You'll have a birth certificate in the same name, too. As soon as we know *when* you're leaving, the passport will be *customised* to include all the relevant visas. There'll be other additions, too – Gestapo Border Police stamps, evidence of your return to Geneva, a couple of trips to Stockholm and so on. And I'll have some letters of introduction prepared for you, from banks and other institutions. All I have to do then is feed the relevant information into the system at Tempelhof. As for your flight, I'll take care of the tickets myself.'

Reflecting privately on the passport that he'd left with Juan Cortes in Madrid, von Menen felt a shameful spasm of guilt at Werner's innocent naivety, especially where Kurt Lindemann's onward passage to Argentina was concerned.

'One last thing,' said Werner, a note of caution in his voice. 'When you arrive in Argentina, you'll be on your own. If things go wrong, you'll need to work out your own salvation.'

'I accept that, sir,' replied von Menen, mindful of the fact that he was already working on his own salvation.

'Before you go,' said Werner, 'there's something highly confidential I have to tell you, entirely off the record. You asked me about a lady called Lutzi Helldorf.'

Von Menen's eyes were like two massive searchlights.

'Well, I have some news. She's alive and, just as you thought, she's in Flossenbürg. Sorry, but that's *all* I can tell you.' Werner held out his hand. 'Since this is the last time we'll be seeing each other for some time, Carl, I'd like to wish you good luck. If there's anything you need, then you'd best speak now or get a message to me at Krummhübel.'

'There is one thing, sir,' replied von Menen, mindful of the wider benefits his efforts would bring to certain members of the Nazi hierarchy.

'Yes?'

'I need a favour, sir, a *big* favour…'

★

The gold was hidden safely beneath the garage block and Steiger had returned the "borrowed" Steyr to Hamburg, leaving the next part of the General's plan heavily dependent on the outcome of von Menen's visit to the ordnance factory at Borsigwalde.

Von Menen arrived back at ten o'clock in the evening. As he closed the garage door, Steiger called out from the far side of the courtyard.

'We're over here, Carl!'

He drifted into the Steigers' parlour and sank into an armchair by the side of the fire. 'Berlin is a city of haunting, empty places,' he lamented. 'It's a complete mess. The chaos is unimaginable.'

The General thrust a large brandy into his hand and patted him lightly on the head. 'Here, drink this.'

'Thanks. After nearly 400 miles, I need it. I seem to have been on the road all day.'

'The arms shipment,' enquired the General, with unusual impatience, 'is the news good?'

'Yes. They're still working on a departure date for the U-boat, but I can tell you with confidence that it will leave from Lübeck-Siems.'

'When is the shipment due to arrive?'

'The small arms arrive next Wednesday, direct from the Haenel plant. They'll be stored in the Flender-Werke Shipyard and I have to be there to receive them.'

'And the ammunition?'

'Monday 11th.'

'Remind me,' said the General, in deep thought, 'did you say four tonnes?'

'Yes, why?'

'Hans reckons there'll be at least sixty boxes, about one truckload, maybe two.'

'Sixty-six, to be exact, and yes, just *one* truck, a heavy Büssing-NAG.'

Playing with his thoughts, the General fumbled with a handful of lead point, nine-millimetre ammunition.

'I don't know how we're going to do it,' he said slowly, 'but somehow, we've *got* to get that truck to the house.'

Suddenly, Carl's face was carved with doubt and fear. 'Surely you're not going to hide the gold in the ammunition boxes!'

The General exchanged a knowing look with Steiger. 'It's the only way,' he said.

Carl leapt to his feet. 'What if someone finds it at sea? Hitler would abort the whole operation, order the U-boat back. The Gestapo would be swarming around this place like ants in summer. We might just as well book the undertaker now. It'd be the end for all of us: you, mother, Hans, Greta *and* Maria! Hitler would go mad.'

'Hitler's mad already,' contended the General, 'and he's also dogmatic, very dogmatic. I can count on the fingers of no hands the times he's changed his mind. As for the risk, well, these days everything's a risk, especially life.' Reaching for support, he looked at Steiger.

'Your father's right, Carl. Even if you get back to Argentina and the gold follows you, there's no guarantee that *we* will; when the war's over, there'll be lots of bargaining between the Allies. You know the kind of thing… if we can have *that*, you can have *this*. There's still the risk that your father and I will end up in Siberia, as pawns in exchange for something, or someone, else.'

'But why can't you keep the gold here for a while, hide it, change it in Sweden, Switzerland or wherever?'

'Carl, you're talking like the Saint of Utopia himself,' said his father. 'What use is it here? As for changing it, how do you suggest we do it? Come on, think about it.' The General entrenched his position, like the brilliant soldier he was. 'There's half a tonne beneath the garage block… *half a tonne*! We can hardly put it in the back of the BMW and drive through every roadblock this side of Switzerland! We need it in Argentina, Carl… Argentina!'

Von Menen dropped back into his chair. 'Sorry, Father… you too, Hans. I'm being…'

'Uncommonly selfish, or perhaps naïve?' said the General. 'No, you're thinking about someone you care about, someone special. That's precisely what Hans and I are doing.'

Von Menen picked up his drink. 'Okay, what's the plan?'

A smile rippled across the General's face. Steiger reached for the brandy bottle and recharged the glasses.

'Remember what Hans said about the wooden ammunition cases, the PK-88s?' said the General. 'Inside each one there are five cardboard cartons; inside each of *those* there are fifty-two smaller packs, arranged four deep in rows of thirteen. Fifty-two packs weigh nearly ten kilos, which means the contents of an entire box weighs about fifty kilos. One gold ingot weighs something in the order of 12.5 kilos… so all we've got to do is take twenty ammunition cases and replace half the contents with two ingots. Weight-wise, no one will know the difference.'

'We can compensate for the difference in volume by using one of these,' said Steiger, holding up a small off-cut of timber.

'It seems plausible,' mused von Menen. 'But how on earth are we going to get that truck to the house?'

'I have an idea,' said the General, 'but that's for tomorrow. For the moment, I think you'd best get some sleep. You look absolutely done for. Just one thing... Frau Helldorf sent her driver, Eberhard, with a message this afternoon. She arrived back at Schwerin last night. I'm sure she'd be thrilled to see you. Perhaps you could drive down tomorrow evening.'

'I will. I've got some good news for her, for all of us, in fact – Lutzi's alive.'

★

Von Menen's visit to Schwerin was another hard-bitten reminder of Germany tearing herself apart at the seams: Frau Helldorf, whose husband had been killed in action during the first war, was slowly coming to terms with the loss of another son.

When von Menen gave her the news that Lutzi was still alive, she collapsed into his arms and wept uncontrollably.

'I'm sorry, Carl,' she said, 'but I'm not just crying for Lutzi, I'm crying for the baby, too. You see, Lutzi is six months pregnant!'

Von Menen was almost in tears himself when Frau Helldorf told him what had happened.

'The Gestapo called here two days after Lutzi had received the distressing news about Gustav's death,' she explained. 'They took her into the hall and told me to wait in the drawing room, but I could still hear the ranting and raving. Lutzi was sobbing her heart out. I tried to get into the hall but the door was slammed in my face. I saw the rest from the window in the drawing room. It was terrible. They just threw her into the back of a car.'

'And Sigi?'

'They arrested her for good measure. As you know, she was released when nothing stuck, but I haven't seen or heard of Sigi in months. I wrote to her several times, always sending the letter to the address of one of her mother's friends in Dahlen. Eberhard delivered them personally, but I never did get a reply. Everyone's terrified of the Gestapo.'

It was a very moving and remorseful time for von Menen, though his remorse had little to do with Gustav's solid-gold Patek Philippe wristwatch, which Frau Helldorf insisted he should have as a lasting reminder of Gustav. The halo of guilt above his head was for something else, something he'd taken from a mahogany keep-safe box during Frau Helldorf's absence in the kitchen. He hoped and prayed Gustav would forgive him the reason why.

24

Monday 4th December 1944

Frau von Menen, Katrina and Greta arrived back from Flensburg late in the afternoon. They had not been in the house long when news arrived concerning Schwartz, the General's orderly – he'd been detained by the Army Field Police at his home town of Koblenz on suspicion of being a deserter. General von Menen ordered his immediate release and instructed Schwartz to take a further week's leave.

Later in the week, the cook and the housekeeper telephoned on successive days. Fifteen-stone Ursula had been hospitalised with a broken leg and Elizabet, full of apology, had found so much grief at home that she would not be returning, leaving Frau von Menen, Greta and Katrina to do all the domestic chores.

Frau von Menen viewed the idea of becoming joint cook, cleaner and housekeeper with muted indifference. There were other things on her mind. A gentle reminder from the General that Manfred and Eva were expected on Friday was met with an unusually sharp reply.

'No, I haven't forgotten, Klaus!'

'Heavens, Anna, what's got into you?'

'The conversation we had before I went to Flensburg? Were you *really* serious, about all of us going to Argentina?'

'I love Germany, Anna, you know that. It is my heart

and soul, but our prospects here amount to nothing. Going to Argentina is the best option we…' He paused, looking forlornly at the photograph of his parents standing on a side table, then corrected himself. 'It's the *only* option we have. And the fact that we'll be joining Carl will make things a lot easier for us, so why the sudden doubt?'

'Greta and Katrina *are* quite taken by the idea. We talked about nothing else while we were at Ingrid's.' She noticed the frown on his face. '*Only* between ourselves,' she hastened. 'We were entirely discreet. Katrina is all for it. Her feeling is that no child of hers will stand much of a chance in a Germany administered by the Russians and she's right.'

'Has she told Jürgen?'

'Not yet, but she thinks he'll leap at the chance.'

'And Greta?'

'Oh, Greta's ecstatic about it.'

'Then that leaves just you.' He squeezed her hand a little tighter. 'And if I know you, Anna, I'd say there's something troubling you.'

Frau von Menen, her eyes fixed rigidly on the intricate pattern of the rug in front of the hearth, raised her head slowly. 'Klaus, like you, I've had some long and meaningful conversations with Carl about life in Argentina. Some of it I like; some of it I don't. It sounds like a nice country, yes, but it seems to me that there's an element there that might easily have been cloned from Hitler himself. What I'm trying to say is, I don't relish the idea of stepping out of one nightmare into another!'

'It concerns me, too, Anna. But you're forgetting something.'

'What's that?'

'You're forgetting the horror that's bearing down on us from the east. Fate is closing in on us fast, very fast, and this time it will affect all of us.' He studied her face more closely, running his fingers lightly across her cheeks, brushing back the hair at the side of her face. 'We'll just have to pray that when the rest of the world realises what's been happening here, those countries with similar ideas will come to their senses. And we don't have to stay in Argentina. In time, we might even make it to the United States.'

'Yes, but there are other factors to consider, Klaus.'

'Such as?'

'Money, for one thing. Our savings here are worthless. We've very little in Switzerland, there's nothing left in Spain and we're never likely to see any of our investments in London and Paris ever again. And what about our possessions, our family heirlooms? Apart from what we've taken to Flensburg, everything we have is *here*.' She jabbed her finger meaninglessly towards the floor.

'I realise that, but we can always take a few more things to Flensburg. It's a big house. Ingrid won't mind. As for the rest, we'll just have to be ruthless. And where money's concerned, well…' He paused, minded to tell her about the gold, but thought better of it. 'Well, I'm sure we'll be able to sort something out. Besides, there's enough in the account in Malmö to tide all of us over for some time.' Mention of Malmö spurred him in the direction of another problem. 'Did you speak to… about…?'

'Yes.'

'And?'

'She thought it was rather a lot, but she's convinced he can arrange it.'

Friday 8th December 1944

Von Menen was in a more relaxed frame of mind after Wednesday's visit to Lübeck-Siems, content in the knowledge that the first phase of his plan had concluded on schedule. Lodged at the Flender-Werke Shipyard were the component parts of one hundred Spandau light machine guns, five hundred Schmeisser sub-machine pistols and the entire optical elements for the attack-and-search periscopes of two Santa Fe class submarines.

After dinner, however, when he was alone in the library with Manfred von Leiber, he sensed that an awkward moment was about to unfold. Von Leiber lit up a huge cigar and drew on it with short, quick puffs, the end turning a battleship grey.

'Have you ever met von Ribbentrop, Carl?' he asked, chasing away the smoke with his hand.

'Yes, but only fleetingly and that was over four years ago.'

'What's your opinion of the man? Is he as egotistical as some people make out?'

'More so, I'd say. Beneath the suave manner is uncompromising naivety *and* incompetence. Why do you ask?'

'No particular reason, just curious.'

Von Menen reached for his glass of cognac and caught the guarded expression on the Vice Admiral's face. 'Is there something else?'

Pinching at the loose fold of flesh beneath his chin, von Leiber studied his 'nephew' like a man about to make a telling move in a tight game of chess.

'Tell me, Carl,' he said in a low voice, 'ever come across a man by the name of Günther Werner?'

Von Menen's glass seemed as if it was stuck to his lips. 'Er... yes, as a matter of fact, I have.'

'Me, too. Nice chap. I believe he's connected with some ultra-secret department at the Foreign Office. Came to see me the other day, wanted to smooth out a few ruffled feathers. Seems there's been a furious row between von

Ribbentrop and Dönitz concerning a matter, well, let's just say it's a matter which Dönitz has washed his hands of completely. That's why it's been pushed on to me.' An infectious smile formed in the Admiral's eyes.

'You know, don't you?' said Carl. 'Me, Werner, the secret department at the Foreign Office… and, quite obviously, one of your submarines.'

'I assume you're referring to *Andromeda*?' whispered von Leiber, gazing at his glass. 'You know, I feel a little bit like Stanley, when he came across Livingstone in the darkest depths of Africa – Herr *Akrobat*, I presume?'

Von Menen held up his hands in surrender. 'Okay, Uncle Manfred… So, what led you to suspect me? It couldn't have been Werner, surely?'

'No, Werner was the epitome of discretion. Not once did he mention your name, or any other name, for that matter.' Von Leiber moved forward, the leather chair creaking as he reached for the ashtray. 'No, it was simply a matter of reasoning. You see, some months after Argentina broke off diplomatic relations with Germany, your parents were discreet enough not to mention how it had affected you. Naturally, I inquired about you, but I was circumspect enough not to put them on the spot. It was fairly obvious, however, that you did *not* make for Madrid, like other members of the mission. If that had been the case, you'd have got a message to your parents, but you didn't. Then, when I thought back on your sudden and unexpected appearance in Berlin, I simply put two and two together.'

'Well, it's very hush-hush. In fact, at first, I wasn't entirely frank about it with Mother and Father. As for you… well, I had every intention of telling you later.'

'No need, Carl. The sensitivity of such matters is abundantly clear to me. In any case, I was only teasing. I'm sure you realise that.'

'But there *was* a need for you to know. You mean a great deal to me. I've always looked upon you as a kind of, well… second father, I suppose. It's a relationship I respect and cherish very dearly.'

Von Leiber turned sideways, a sudden lump rising in his throat, his hand moving slowly across his eyes, as much to disguise his pride as to shield his mild embarrassment.

'You see, Uncle Manfred, there's every good reason why you *should* know.' The smile left von Menen's face, his tone earnestly serious. 'Whatever the outcome, I'm not coming back. There's someone over there I'm very fond of.'

'A lady, eh?'

'Yes, we're hoping to get married.'

'Well, Carl, it's a bit of a shocker, but I really can't say that I blame you. I wish you both every happiness.'

'Thank you,' said von Menen earnestly. 'Anyway, on the question of U-boats, I have some interesting and perhaps welcome news for you. Werner wouldn't have known about it when he saw you, but I can tell you now that you only have to facilitate the one incursion.'

'One, two, a dozen, it doesn't make a damn difference to me, Carl. You know my feelings about the war. My only concern is to keep as many men alive as I can and for as long as I can. In that sense I'd feel a lot happier despatching a boat to the relative safety of the South Atlantic than sending it to an almost certain watery grave in the North Atlantic.'

At that moment, the General entered the library. The three men entered into a long discourse about the worsening situation for the German army. Given Hitler's profound obstinacy and the fact that after three long years he had decided finally to vacate his headquarters in East Prussia, the General and Vice Admiral were at one on the opinion that "the Little Corporal" might, perhaps, force a desperate offensive in the west. They did not discount the possibility of some initial success, either, but they were adamant that it would end in disaster.

'In the west, as in the east,' said the General, 'all the signposts for the German army are pointing towards Berlin.' On that despairing note, he switched the conversation to matters of a family nature. 'Any news of your mother, Manfred?'

'Not since her last letter, which I received about four weeks ago.' Von Leiber shook his head, his despondency obvious. 'Why on earth she feels she has to stay there, I'll never know. The smaller house at Wismar never suited her, but it was a damn sight easier for me and much less of a worry.'

'That was ten years ago, Manfred. None of us could have envisaged the mess we'd be in now,' replied the General.

'True, but even then, I still had to cope with the Polish Corridor. I'm thinking seriously about going to Marienburg and bringing her back with me, forcibly if needs be. Eva has offered to look after her.'

'Be very careful, Manfred. When the Russian advance gets going again…'

'Don't worry, Klaus, I'll watch myself.'

'Incidentally, hope you don't mind me asking such a personal question… Talking about Eva…'

But just then, Frau von Menen and Katrina walked into the room, accompanied by Eva, who had been unusually quiet throughout dinner.

'If you'll excuse me,' said von Leiber, sidestepping into the hall. Moments later, he returned with a bottle of chilled champagne.

All were bemused except Eva, who seemed as though she was about to explode.

'Glasses?' asked von Leiber.

Von Menen shot to his feet and rushed to the dining room. The cork was just leaving the bottle when he returned. Von Leiber filled the glasses and Eva handed them out.

'Klaus, Anna, Carl, Katrina,' he announced, nodding to each in turn, 'I have something to tell you.' The General's jaw dropped in anticipation. 'I have asked Eva to be my wife and… she's accepted!'

The General was the first on his feet, shaking von Leiber's hand. Eva, her face aglow with happiness, became the immediate focus of attention, Anna and Katrina showering her with affection.

'When's the big day, then?' asked von Menen.

'Next Monday, 18th December, eleven o'clock.'

The immediate celebrations over, the ladies retraced their steps to the drawing room.

'Where's it to be, then, Manfred? Berlin?' asked the General.

'No, Klaus, the Marriage Registry in Lübeck. Nothing fancy, just a simple ceremony. Naturally, we want you all there, Hans and Greta included – I take it they'll be back by then?'

'Oh, yes, they've only gone over to Bützow for a few days.'

'There's one other thing, Klaus. It'd mean an awful lot to me if you'd do the honours.'

'Best man, you mean? I'd be proud to.'

'And Carl, I know Eva would be very touched if you would give her away, so to speak.'

'I'd consider it a great honour.'

'The wedding breakfast, Manfred; why don't you have it here?' suggested the General.

'Klaus, you've saved me the embarrassment of asking you. With Eva's celebrity it would be far more discreet. Thank you.'

'That settles it, then,' smiled the General. 'We'll all come back here. If I know Hans, he'll have all the ingredients for a veritable feast and we've still got two cases of champagne left in the cellar.'

Eventually, the details following von Leiber's unexpected announcement gave way to the one topic that had rarely been far from their thoughts.

'Have you thought what you might do when the war is over?' asked the General.

'I haven't done much else these last few months, Klaus, but I think I've finally reached a decision.' Von Leiber re-lit his cigar. 'We're both military men, Klaus,' he said. 'If the worst comes to the worst, we'll be judged in the same light as those who got us into this bloody mess in the first place. I'm not waiting around to be placed on trial for the atrocities committed by the SS – I'm going to get the hell out of it.'

'What, leave Germany altogether?'

'That's right. As soon as the end is in sight, I'll have Eva leave for her hideaway at Meersburg, on Lake Konstanz, and the moment the curtain drops, I'll join her. When the time's right, we'll cross into Switzerland, make for Eva's villa at Lausanne.' He moved to the very edge of his chair. 'Klaus, I'm very fond of all of you. Eva is, too. Her place at Lausanne is enormous. It's your decision, of course, but you're more than welcome to join us.'

The General found himself not knowing what to say, the realisation of what lay ahead biting deep into his mind. Finally, he spoke, his face burdened with anxiety.

'Manfred, it's just the sort of thing I'd expect you to say, but as it happens, you've stolen my lines. The truth is, we'll have to decline. You see, we're hoping to join Carl in Argentina.'

The two men shared a private gaze, a collective moment

of nostalgia, the memories rushing back. Von Leiber broke the silence.

'In that case, Klaus,' he said, 'I think you and I had better start enjoying ourselves.'

At that, the General upped and made his way to the cellar to collect another bottle of champagne. In the brief interlude, von Menen stole the opportunity to resolve a question that had been on his mind since his last meeting with Werner. How von Leiber would react, he wasn't sure.

'Father would never have asked you himself, Uncle Manfred, and I sincerely hope that you will forgive *me* for doing so, but...'

'Yes, Carl?'

'Well, it's Jürgen. You see—'

Von Leiber zipped a finger across tightened lips and winked. 'It's all in hand. Not a word to your father, though. I have to speak to Jürgen first.'

'But how on earth...?'

'I told Werner that for a long-range incursion to succeed, we would have to use the very latest technology. With that at the back of Hitler's mind, I knew Dönitz would never argue against it. I was right – Hitler ordered the urgent deployment of a Type XXI submarine. Something tells me that he wasn't guided *solely* by my advice, though. Something else is afoot. I'm sure of it. As for Jürgen, well, in terms of working up, his boat is considerably ahead of the others.'

25

Downstairs in the Steigers' parlour, a drama of unthinkable scale was unfolding.

'My God, Greta!' cried Frau von Menen, collapsing onto the settee, 'I think I need some smelling salts.'

Frau Steiger flopped down beside her, her usually rosy-red cheeks turning a pale shade of grey. Her husband poured them two large glasses of schnapps. Frau von Menen took a gentle sip, then downed the rest in one. Placing her empty glass on the side table, she pressed her hands together, wedging them in the fold of her dress.

'In case I might have misunderstood you, Klaus,' she said, turning slowly to face her husband, 'did you say *"robbed the Reichsbank"*?'

Gathering himself to reply, the General sent Steiger a near-hopeless look. 'Not in the exact sense, Anna,' he replied, his voice labouring; 'it was the SS who *really* stole it. All we did was to take some of it for ourselves.'

'But how do you know that they did, as you say, *steal* it?'

Flexing his nostrils, the General gulped a lungful of air, gave his wife a steadying look and said, 'Anna, the war is lost and the Nazi hierarchy knows that it's lost. Even as we speak, they're trying to save their own necks, queuing up to get out of Germany and making damn fine sure that they don't leave empty-handed. Don't you see, apart from fulfilling their own personal lust, they need the money to finance the rebirth of the Nazi Party?'

'And they're taking more than enough to do that,' added Steiger.

Frau von Menen looked appealingly at Frau Steiger, searching for a ray of reality. 'For God's sake, Greta, tell me I'm dreaming this.'

Frau Steiger fixed her husband with a steely look. 'I wish I could, Anna, I wish I could.'

'You do realise that if you're caught, we'll *all* be shot!'

The General parked himself on the arm of his wife's chair. 'Anna, we won't be caught, I promise.'

'Definitely not,' agreed Steiger, as he encouraged his wife to force down another glass of schnapps. 'We've planned it meticulously. Nothing can go wrong.'

Breathing deeply, Frau von Menen pushed her drained, limp torso into the back of her chair. 'Well, at least Carl's not involved. I suppose that's something,' she said. Seeing the sheepish look on the General's face, she clasped her hands about her head. 'Oh, my God, Klaus, you haven't. You haven't involved Carl, have you?' Reluctantly, she allowed him to take hold of her hand, the General massaging it gently.

'Anna, we couldn't have done it without him.'

'But—'

'It's a question of survival, and the will to survive transcends all else, *you* know that. If you think we've lost our decency, then fine, but we *are* going to survive. Hidden beneath the garage floor, there's a new beginning for all of us: for Hans, Greta, Katrina, Jürgen *and* the baby, especially the baby. It's our future. It's a new start for us.'

Frau von Menen looked pleadingly at Frau Steiger, though her question was aimed for the man she had always regarded as incorruptible. 'And what, exactly, did you steal? Reichsmarks, Swiss francs, American dollars…?'

'Gold bullion.'

'Gold!'

Frau von Menen rolled her eyes in disbelief, Frau Steiger gaping in horror, her half-empty glass of schnapps slipping from her hand and dropping to the floor. They stared at each other, a look of stupefaction on their faces.

'*How much?*' they cried in unison.

'About half a tonne,' said Steiger.

Frau Steiger screwed the gold wedding band from her finger, weighing it in her hand. 'A half-tonne of this!'

'It's not as much as you think, Greta,' said the General. 'It might seem a lot, but it's only forty ingots.'

The look on Frau von Menen's face transformed from shock to suspicion. 'Why are you telling us this, Klaus? There must be a reason?'

The question rolled from her tongue and fell into the General's lap like a four-inch artillery shell. 'Well, er…'

An earnest eye on his wife, Steiger raced to the rescue. 'What Klaus is trying to say, Anna, is that we just want you to be *aware* of what's happening, that's all.'

'In truth, we'd rather you didn't know,' said the General. 'It's just that there's something we have to do, something you'd otherwise find very strange.'

The two men were not quite sure whether it had been the effect of the schnapps, the comfort of the roaring log fire or what, but within twenty minutes, their wives' anxiety had eased. The initial shock had passed and curiosity was burgeoning. Intrigued, they listened carefully as the two men unveiled their plan.

Early on Sunday morning, von Menen and Steiger left for Berlin and checked in at the Savoy Hotel.

At three o'clock, von Menen set out alone for the south-west suburb of Dahlem. A maid, on the downward side of sixty, arms like piano legs and wearing a heavily starched pinafore, answered the door.

'Good afternoon,' said von Menen, hat pressed against his chest. 'My name is Herr von Menen. I'm looking for Herr Hoffman.'

'Just a moment, please.'

Von Menen waited by the door, peering along the tree-lined avenue. A moment later, the maid returned.

'Please come in, Herr von Menen.' She showed him to the drawing room and offered him a chair. 'Herr Hoffman isn't here at the moment, but his mother will be along shortly.'

Moments later, Frau Hoffman appeared, von Menen rising to his feet to meet her. He pressed her hand lightly.

'After all these years, it's very nice to meet you again, Frau Hoffman.'

'Yes, it's been a long time. You were wearing a very elegant uniform, as I recall. Please, do sit down.' Gathering in the sides of her dress, Frau Hoffman sat beside him. 'Ulricht mentioned that he'd seen you... Said something about you being with the Foreign Office, or have I got it wrong?'

'No, it's quite true, I am with the Foreign Office – what's left of it.'

'Quite; a lot has happened these past few years.'

'Yes, I... I was very sad to hear about your daughter-in-law.'

'That's the war for you, Carl. These days, everyone has someone to grieve about.'

'Of course. Anyhow, I just dropped by on the off-chance of seeing Ulricht. Obviously I've picked the wrong day.'

'Yes, he left for Madrid yesterday; should be back sometime next weekend. Is there anything I—?'

'Er… no, thank you. It was a social call, really. He asked me to keep in touch… Since I happened to be in Berlin, I thought I'd call round. I did try phoning, but' – he shrugged – 'well, you know what the phones are like.'

'I believe he wrote to you the other day. In fact…'

She paused, reached for a bell at the side of her chair and jingled it a couple of times. A faint knock on the door and the maid walked in.

'Gertrude, did you post that letter, the one which Ulricht left?'

'No, ma'am, it's still in the hall.'

'Good. Will you fetch it, please?'

The maid returned and handed Frau Hoffman the envelope.

'It's for you, Carl. Since you're here, you might as well take it with you.'

Von Menen slipped the envelope into his pocket. 'Thank you. I'll read it later.'

It was almost seven o'clock when von Menen left the blacked-out suburbs of Dahlem and set out for Kurfürstendamm. As he turned into Hohenzollerndamm, curiosity got the better of him. He pulled up by the side of the road, anxious to read Hoffman's letter.

Dear Carl,

I've tried phoning several times, but without success. What a nightmare the phones are!
Returned from Madrid last night. Had lunch with your friend, Juan, the day before. What a nice fellow. I like him very much. He asked me to pass on his very best wishes.
Roll on Christmas – they're switching me to Route 7 that week – Berlin/Copenhagen/Oslo. It's a bit safer!

Hope you're keeping well.
Best wishes, Ulricht.

P.S. Nearly forgot. Juan insisted I tell you about Carmen Rodrigues (an old flame of yours?). She's getting married on 20th January, spending her honeymoon in Las Palmas! Lucky girl… Lucky man!

Von Menen had never heard of Carmen Rodrigues in his entire life, but the message was as clear as a spring day in the Bavarian Alps. Las Palmas might be the perfect destination for two newlyweds, but it was also a transit port on the Spanish/South Atlantic sea-route. Cortes's message meant only one thing – there was a sailing to South America on 20th January, meaning he would have to leave Berlin by the 15th at the very latest.

Overtaken by a sudden sense of urgency, he headed straight for Wilhelmstrasse.

The duty officer at the Foreign Office was in a lethargic mood.

'Sorry, but calls to Krummhübel at this time of an evening have to be very urgent,' he explained.

'But it *is* urgent,' insisted von Menen. 'I must get a message to Herr Werner immediately.'

'I'm sure,' smiled the duty officer. 'It's always urgent, it's always immediate.'

An SS guard standing five metres away closed in on the conversation. Von Menen reached into his pocket, pulled out the written authority issued by von Ribbentrop and countersigned by Bormann. He held it in front of the man's face.

'How much more urgent could it be?' von Menen said angrily.

The duty officer went into a blind robotic spin. Ushering the SS guard away, he instantly supplied a pen. Von Menen wrote down the message and passed it to him.

URGENT – Documents MUST be available by 14th January at latest.

Von Menen

'I cannot over-emphasise how vitally important it is that this reaches Herr Werner immediately,' he stressed.

Now, it was up to Werner.

Monday 11th December 1944

After a taxing and frustrating hour, the switchboard operator at the Savoy Hotel finally put von Menen through to the plant foreman's office at the ordnance factory at Borsigwalde.

'Herr von Menen speaking.'

'Yes, sir. Are you calling about the delivery you're expecting?'

'As a matter of fact, I am.'

'Well, it's being loaded right now, sir.'

'Good… I'm in Berlin at the moment, but my car has broken down and I'm the only person authorised to accept the consignment at Lübeck-Siems. In fact, I'm the *only* person who has access to the storage facility…'

'Oh, I see.'

'I was wondering if I might hitch a ride on the truck, if that's okay?'

'Just a moment, sir.'

Von Menen waited with bated breath. Steiger, who had remained patiently next to him throughout, crossed his fingers.

'Are you there, sir?' asked the plant foreman.

'Yes.'

'It's okay.'

Von Menen covered the mouthpiece, a smile skimming across his face. 'He's swallowed it,' he whispered.

Steiger punched the air with his fists.

'It's not our usual policy, you understand, but given the circumstances, I think we can make an exception. As it happens, there's only one driver and I imagine he'll be glad of your company. Between you and me, sir...' The foreman's voice was much quieter now. 'It'll be a blessing in disguise, really. Don't get me wrong, Erich's a good man, but he's prone to a drink or two.'

'In that case, I'll see to it that he stays sober,' chuckled von Menen.

'That'll be the day, sir. What time can we expect you? The driver needs to be on his way by ten at the latest.'

Von Menen looked at his watch. 'I'll be with you just after nine-thirty.'

'Ideal, sir.'

Replacing the receiver, von Menen turned to Steiger. 'Let's run through it one last time, Hans. You and Father will be waiting just the other side of Schönberg, right?'

'Yes, just beyond the railway line. I'll start flagging you down the moment I catch sight of the truck. All *you* have to do is keep your eyes peeled for a moving red light.'

'And when we stop, you ask the driver where he's heading?'

'That's right, and when he says Lübeck-Siems, I'll introduce the pretence about the diversion, you know, the road being closed to heavy traffic...'

'*And* that the Travemünde ferry is out of order until four o'clock in the morning?'

'Right. All you'll have to do then is suggest to the driver that, since you've got time to spare, you'd like to make a slight detour – something along the lines of visiting an aunt who you haven't seen for a few years. She's a companion to some spinster who has a big house beyond Dassow.'

'And after we arrive, my "aunt" invites the two of us to stay overnight?'

'That's about it,' affirmed Hans. 'The rest will be down to your father and me.'

Von Menen thought for a moment. 'The driver... his foreman says he's partial to a drink. Perhaps I could get him into a nice mellow state before we reach Schönberg. I've a bottle of Ansbach in my bag.'

'Great idea,' agreed Steiger. 'If he's a drinker, you'll be his best friend by the time you reach Schönberg.'

Erich Krenz was about sixty, short and stocky, with a big, round face, a blushed, veined complexion and a nose like an electric light bulb. Even at nine-thirty in the morning, the odour of alcohol on his breath eclipsed the ever-present smell of cordite, clinging to his thick reefer jacket like soot on a sweep's hat.

It may have been the effect of his early morning "fix", but when the heavy Büssing-NAG truck pulled out of the munitions works at Borsigwalde, it was obvious to von Menen that Erich Krenz was a born talker, third-rate singer, fourth-rate theatrical mimic and fifth-rate military strategist, a man who had all the answers to Hitler's increasing problems. They had just passed Friesack when von Menen pondered his next move.

'Fancy something to eat, Erich?'

'Thank you, sir, but I've got sandwiches. Nothing special, but if you're feeling a bit peckish...' – he glanced at von Menen's pocket, the bottle of Ansbach poking out – 'I'm more than happy to share them with you.'

'Very kind of you, Erich, but I meant something hot, a proper meal.'

'Oh, I see. In that case, sir, I'll say no, if you don't mind. I've other uses for my food and lodging allowance.'

'You don't need any money, Erich, I'll treat you.'

Krenz's eyes lit up like a pre-war Christmas scene along Kurfürstendamm.

When they left the Hotel Gröbler, Perleburg was in complete darkness. Krenz had consumed over two bottles of wine and a good deal of schnapps. He seemed fine until he reached the open door, took a whiff of cold air and almost fell to his knees.

'Are you okay, Erich?' asked von Menen.

Krenz's reply was incoherent.

By the time they had reached the door of the cab, Krenz could hardly walk and von Menen wasn't fooling himself. If the truck was going any further that day, it was he who would be doing the driving.

They were not yet on the far side of Schönberg and the light waving ahead was not red: it was white, and it was growing brighter all the while. Krenz was fast asleep, snoring loudly.

This was not the plan.

Von Menen felt for his Walther, but realised it was hopeless. The road was blocked in both directions; Alsatians barking loudly; uniforms everywhere, the field grey of the Wehrmacht and the awesome colours of the SS and the Gestapo.

A corporal rapped on the door of the cab. 'OUT!'

Von Menen's heart rate quickened. He could see it all: his parents, Hans and Greta, all arrested; Gestapo swarming all over the house. Next stop, Gestapo Headquarters and then... Plötzensee Prison! He stepped down from the cab and stood anxiously by the door.

'Something wrong?' he asked.

The corporal said nothing.

A Gestapo officer crossed the road, spun von Menen round and pushed him up against the door, kicking his legs apart. He found the Walther immediately, tossed it to the corporal and bawled out at the top of his voice.

'Hauptsturmführer!'

An SS officer raced over to the truck, followed by a half dozen soldiers.

'Search the back!'

'Captain!' yelled von Menen. 'You're making a big—' The corporal jabbed the butt of his rifle into von Menen's side, the pain forcing a piercing wince, his knees weakening.

'Name?' screamed the SS officer.

'Carl Franz von Menen.'

'What are you doing? Where are you going?'

'Sorry, but I can't tell you.'

'Corporal!'

Another jab to the kidneys. Von Menen winced again, knees buckling as he dropped to the running board.

'Stand up!' screamed the corporal, hauling him back to his feet.

By now, Krenz was lying in a stupefied heap by the side of the road, oblivious to everything.

'I'll ask you again,' said the officer. 'What are you doing? Where are you going?'

'Sir!' cried one of the men from the back of the truck. 'Ammunition!'

'Before you make any mistakes,' groaned von Menen, 'you'd best look in the top pocket of my jacket.' He felt the muzzle of a Luger grinding into the small of his back as the SS officer pushed his hand across his shoulder, dipped into his pocket and pulled out a folded piece of paper.

Führer Headquarters

To whom it may concern:

BY COMMAND OF THE FÜHRER
You are hereby ordered to comply with any request which the bearer, Herr Carl Franz von Menen, sees fit to…

Signed: Joachim von Ribbentrop, Reich Foreign Minister
Signed: Martin Bormann, Head of the Party Chancellery.

Hands trembling, lips quivering, the SS officer turned a deathly pallor.

'Corporal!' he shouted. 'Get those men out of the truck… NOW!'

Von Menen snatched the Führer Order from him and stuffed it back in his pocket. 'Now, Hauptsturmführer…?'

'Dreesen, sir, SS Hauptsturmführer Dreesen!'

'Hauptsturmführer Dreesen,' said von Menen, clutching his side, 'I'm not much interested in why you are *here*, but I would like to know what the hell you think you're *doing!*'

'My apologies, Herr von Menen. We're looking for the crew of a Mosquito, brought down in neighbouring Grabow. A farmer says he saw two parachutes—'

'Did you find the two parachutists in the back of the truck?'

'No, sir,' replied Dreesen, nervously handing back the Walther.

Von Menen gestured towards Krenz. 'Then kindly put that man back in the cab and order your men to retreat down the road. I want that barrier lifted within thirty seconds. Then…'

'Yes, sir?'

'I want to speak to you at the rear of the truck.'

Boiling with anger, von Menen waited at the back of the large Büssing-NAG, Dreesen's footsteps approaching along the tarmac at a brisk pace. Dreesen stepped round to the back of the truck and walked straight into a wall of knuckle, his nose split, right to left. Von Menen yanked him up against the tailgate and held him rigid.

'Now,' he whispered, 'have you any idea where the Russian front line is?'

Dreesen answered in the negative.

'Strange,' said von Menen, shaking his head, 'neither do I, but if you breathe one word about me, this truck, *or* its contents to anyone, I guarantee that you'll have the answer to that question within twenty-four hours. Understand?'

'Yes, Herr von Menen.'

Just after six o'clock, the truck was on the far side of Schwerin. Krenz stirred, groped for the Ansbach, took a quick swallow and fell into another deep sleep.

Von Menen saw a red light in the distance, moving left to right, two hundred metres ahead. Cutting the engine, he coasted to a halt.

'Evening,' said the "sergeant". 'Where are you heading?'

'Lübeck,' replied von Menen, nodding in the direction of the passenger's seat.

Stirred by the sound of Steiger's voice, Krenz opened an eye, uttered a few garbled words then closed it again.

'Sorry I'm late,' whispered von Menen, clambering down from the cab, 'but I had an altercation with the Gestapo, the other side of Ludwigslust.'

'The Gestapo!'

'Yes, a road block… not to mention a demonstration in the finer uses of a rifle butt and a physical grilling by a young Turk of an SS captain. Seems they were looking for two parachutists, seen bailing out of a Mosquito near Grabow.'

Steiger looked up at the heavens, a near-full moon in the sky. 'But you're okay?'

'Apart from what feels like a couple of bruised ribs, yes.'

'And the driver? He looks completely gaga to me.'

Von Menen closed his eyes and gritted his teeth. 'You wouldn't believe how much it's taken to get him in that state. He's drunk more than two-thirds of a bottle of schnapps and the best part of three bottles of wine.'

The General, waiting patiently to act out his own part, joined them from the far side of the road.

'My God, Carl, what have you done to the man?' He peered through the open door of the cab. 'It smells like a distillery in there.'

'He's completely smashed, Father. Whatever you do, don't throw a match in there.'

'Well, one thing's for certain,' said the General, gesturing at the lifeless shape in the passenger seat. 'The original plan's out of the window.'

'I know,' agreed Carl. 'He doesn't even know which planet he's on, let alone the fact that he's *somewhere* near Lübeck. I might just as well drive up to the house and sit with him in the cab, whilst you two get on quietly with it.'

'But we can't *quietly* hammer down the lids of the boxes,' contended Steiger.

'How long will it take you once the boxes are unloaded?' asked von Menen, checking the contents of the near-empty Ansbach bottle. 'Taking the lids off the cases, removing the ammunition and concealing the…?'

Steiger pondered, looked at the General. 'I reckon about an hour and twenty minutes – four minutes for each box.'

'Certainly no more,' agreed the General. 'We've already fetched it up from the tunnel. It's all waiting.'

The General crossed his fingers as the big Büssing-NAG inched forward, clearing the arched entrance to the courtyard with a couple of centimetres to spare.

The unloading only took twenty minutes. By eight-thirty, von Menen was on a night-time "mystery" tour of Mecklenburg, with what looked like a ventriloquist's dummy as his only passenger. Krenz had sailed into oblivion. Only the in-out movement of his chest belied the fact that he was still alive.

Back at the house, the General and Steiger were working frantically, discarding the right amount of ammunition and replacing it with gold, Frau von Menen and Frau Steiger alongside, emptying the discarded ammunition into the void below the trapdoor, both assured by Hans that it would not explode.

When the truck finally returned to the courtyard, Steiger was just hammering down the lid on the last box, the women disposing of the last of over 40,000 rounds of ammunition. In what seemed no time at all, the twenty boxes were reloaded. Krenz hadn't stirred once.

'Is there any left, Carl?' asked Steiger quietly.

'Any what?' replied von Menen.

'Whatever it is he's been drinking.'

'Just a slight drop, why?'

'Because we could do with some of it ourselves!'

The two women suppressed their tittering. Easing Carl to one side, the General spoke very quietly.

'The boxes we've opened, Carl, can be identified by a small, discreet cross, which I've scratched at both ends of each box. Now, how long will you be at the Flender-Werke Shipyard?'

'About an hour; there's plenty of labour up there.'

'Good, Hans will give you an hour's start. When you leave the dockyard, he'll be waiting a safe distance back from the main entrance.'

'In that case, Hans, take the BMW,' said von Menen. 'Krenz saw the Delahaye race past earlier this afternoon. If he comes round and sees another, well, who knows?'

The unloading at the Flender-Werke Shipyard went like clockwork. When the storehouse door slammed shut, Krenz was still in a deep state of intoxication.

Von Menen stuffed a few Reichsmark in his pocket and headed back towards the guardhouse, leaving the truck twenty metres short of the barrier. A brief word with the guard sergeant, and Krenz was allowed to remain in the cab. The sergeant would ensure his safe departure at first light the next day.

Meanwhile, Erich Krenz slept on.

26

Monday 18th December 1944

The proceedings at Lübeck's Marriage Registry Office were as discreet and as private as Eva and Manfred could have wished for.

Back at the house, a joyous surprise was in store for the newlyweds when Katrina and Jürgen asked them if they would be godparents to the baby Katrina was expecting in March. Eva, full of emotion, tears of joy trickling down her face, replied without giving the question a thought.

'Yes, yes, yes!' she shouted, totally overcome by the surprise.

For Jürgen, the next best thing to euphoria was about to unfold in the relative calm of the library, where Manfred von Leiber was waiting for him.

'I need to speak to you about something, Jürgen, and before I start, you can forget about rank. The conversation we're about to have is between Jürgen Lanze and Manfred von Leiber. Understood?

'Perfectly... Manfred.'

'I take it you know about Carl returning to Argentina?'

'Yes, he told me this morning.'

'Do you know why?'

'Haven't a clue.'

'I'm not familiar with the entire story, myself,'

explained von Leiber. 'It's all very hush-hush, but I do know that he's to rendezvous with a U-boat off the coast of Argentina.' He lit up another cigar, puffed on it vigorously for a few seconds and then, with a distorted smile, said, 'The U-boat will be disembarking some... er... *equipment* for him.'

'He didn't say anything about that.'

'No I don't suppose he did, but it will affect you.'

'How?'

Von Leiber's teasing smile added length to the moment. 'Because it's your boat he'll be meeting! It's why you were ordered back to Lübeck-Siems.'

Jürgen stared silently at the ceiling, his face full of puzzlement, chin in hand. 'First, Katrina asks me if I'd like to start a new life in South America,' he mused, seeming if he were talking to himself, 'then Carl calmly announces he's going back to Argentina sometime after Christmas. Now you come along and tell me that *I'm* to meet him off the coast of Argentina.' He fixed von Leiber with a searching look. 'Am I missing something?'

'No, but the chances are you'll still be alive when the war's over, and if my judgement is right, it *will* be over by the time you get back to Germany. All you'll have to do then is sit tight and wait for the right moment.' A grave look washed over von Leiber's face, a haunting reality trickling into his mind. 'So far this year, Jürgen, we've lost more U-boats than I care to think about... over 600 since the war began. It's hideous, completely hideous. My aim is to keep as many sailors alive as I can, by whatever means it takes. And before you ask me about Dönitz's master plan for a last great offensive, take it from someone who knows – it's all garbage.' Von Leiber stubbed out his cigar and folded his arms across his chest. 'With your skill, Jürgen, and with all the latest technology a Type XXI has to offer,

I'm confident that you *will* make it to the South Atlantic *and* get back.'

'Well, I'll certainly do my best, Manfred.'

'And one last thing, *Lieutenant Commander.*'

'Yes, *Vice Admiral?*'

'Not a word to anyone.'

'Sir.'

Jürgen started towards the door, suddenly checking his stride, a thought zipping through his mind. 'There must be a great deal of sensitivity attached to this operation.'

'Naturally.'

'Then perhaps I should tell you about a certain midshipman—'

'Beiber?'

'You know of him?'

'I know *everything* about him. He's a political appointment, a *very* political appointment. Don't worry, though, he's being replaced by sub-Lieutenant Janssen.'

★

Tuesday 19th December 1944

West of Berlin, the roads were a chaotic mess, the delays unending. It was nearly five o'clock when von Menen arrived at the Foreign Office, a scribbled note waiting for him.

My Dear von Menen,

Seems that we have missed each other again.

My apologies for dragging you down to Berlin at such short notice, but having other matters to attend to in Berlin, I thought we'd meet halfway. Left Krummhübel at five-thirty this

morning. A nightmare of a journey.
Anyway, there's an envelope waiting with the duty officer.

Yours, von Althoff
P.S. The suitcase is a present from Herr Werner.

Von Menen studied the envelope, the gummed flap at the back embossed with the seal of the Foreign Office. The writing was unmistakeably Werner's.

Avoiding the unending delays along Heerstrasse, von Menen headed for Friedrichstrasse, crossed over Unter den Linden and made his way over the Weidendammer Bridge. One hand on the steering wheel, he was about to open the letter when, just south of Elsasser Strasse, his head shot sideways, like a pin drawn to a magnet.

There is only one woman in the whole of Berlin with a carriage like that.

He brought the Delahaye to a screeching halt, leapt out and hastened back along the sidewalk. Glancing over her shoulder, the woman made hurriedly into Oranienburger Strasse, her pace quickening, the image of a grey coat fading in the distance. For a moment, he lost sight of her, and then, in an instant, he saw her again, the same cream beret bobbing up and down in the darkness, weaving left and right, the only cream beret in a sea of people.

Suddenly, she broke into a run, as if being chased by a pack of wolves. Von Menen was running, too, pushing, shoving, rounding piles of rubble as though his life depended on it. Faster, faster.

Breathless, the woman finally drew to a halt, turned and waited for him, her shoulders down, her face pained, a crumpled brown paper bag in her hands. She looked different.

'Sigi,' said von Menen, his voice faltering at the last syllable. 'It *is* you. Why...?'

A sad, ashen-grey face peered back at him, eyes dark and hollow, not a hint of make-up nor a trace of cherry-red lipstick. Sigi Bredow had aged. He reached out for her hands, felt the roughness of her skin, saw the totally worn look on her face and the tears in her eyes.

'I'm so sorry, Carl,' she said, her voice quavering, choking out the words. 'I knew it was you, I recognised the car. It's just that, well, I didn't want you to see me looking like this. You do understand, don't you?'

He placed his arms around her, held her tight. 'Sigi, Sigi, dearest Sigi,' he whispered, 'you've no idea how pleased I am to see you.'

Von Menen took out his handkerchief, dabbed the tears from her eyes and pressed it into her hand. He took hold of the pitiful paper bag she was carrying, placed his arm around her waist and ushered her forward.

'Come on, Sigi, let me walk with you.'

'I hear you've seen Gustav's mother,' she said, still choking out the words. 'Poor Lutzi. I've cried so much for her. She's pregnant, but you know that, don't you?'

'Yes, Sigi, I do. Frau Helldorf told me.'

'Such a nice lady. When she wrote that you were back, I couldn't believe it. I've thought about you a lot, wondering how you are, what you're doing.'

Von Menen gazed thoughtfully into her eyes, brushed away her tears and kissed her gently on the forehead.

'Sigi, darling,' he said, 'forget about me, I'm fine. It's you I'm worried about. I went to Lützowstrasse and saw the remains of the villa. I've been frantic with worry.'

'The villa,' lamented Sigi. 'Gone, over a year ago. Mummy and I were out at the time, but...'

'Your father?'

'Yes, Daddy was killed.'

He squeezed her hand. 'I'm so sorry, Sigi.'

'Save your pity for the others, Carl, there are many far worse off than us.'

'But where are you living?'

'Mummy and I have a room off Alexanderplatz. Nothing special, but it's adequate. We can't afford anything better. They've frozen all our money.'

'Are you working?'

'Yes, at Borsigwalde. I've just finished my shift. A bus picks me up along Chausseestrasse at six in the morning and brings me back in the early evening, usually between six-thirty and seven. I just happened to get away a bit early today.'

'Which factory?' asked von Menen hurriedly.

'Munitions. I pack boxes of ammunition, twelve hours a day, six days a week.'

'Hell, Sigi, how do you cope?'

'With great difficulty. The Allies try repeatedly to bomb us out of existence, but our Nazi masters somehow manage to get the place up and running again – unfortunately.'

They had passed Artillerie Strasse and were approaching the burnt-out remains of the Mitte District Synagogue when von Menen suddenly remembered his car.

'Sigi!' he said, giving her a gentle tug, 'my car! Come on, I'll give you a lift home. You can get changed and we'll go out to dinner.'

She looked at him as if he were an alien from a far-distant planet. 'This is Berlin, Carl, 1944. You do not just walk into a restaurant.'

'We'll go to the Savoy. They know me there. I've got spare clothes in the back of the car. They're sure to have a room and I'm certain they'll be able to find *something* for us to eat... Pavlova, perhaps?' he teased.

Sigi's face gave way to her first real smile. 'You know, I never did go back to the Eden.'

They both laughed.

Suddenly, von Menen was gripped by a surge of uncertainty. 'Er, it's okay, is it?' he asked. 'Going to the Savoy? Only, it's just occurred to me that you might...'

'Have a man friend? Carl, in the old days I was a bit feisty, yes. I frightened men to death, including you. But now...' She looked down at her drab grey coat. 'Who would have me looking like this?'

In the one-bedroom apartment in Alexanderplatz, von Menen chatted freely with Frau Bredow whilst Sigi brought forward her one great treat of the week – her Saturday evening bath. She fetched out her best dark-blue suit and her last pair of silk stockings, before treating herself sparingly to a few treasured drops of fragrance from her last bottle of perfume.

An hour later, bedecked in her mother's only fur coat and trailing the distinctive fragrance of Chanel No 5, Sigi Bredow glided into the lobby of the Savoy Hotel and, for the first time in months, turned a dozen heads.

'So, when did you get back?' she asked, once they were seated.

'About a couple of months ago. Before then, I'd been in Madrid.' His lying didn't seem to matter anymore.

'And what do you think of the improvements to this *wonderful* country of ours?' she asked cynically.

'Horrific, Sigi, absolutely horrific.'

'It's worse than horrific, Carl. Unless you've seen it for yourself, you wouldn't believe the degree of brutality and cruelty that exists in this *magnificent* Third Reich.'

Through the sleeve of her dress, she began rubbing the inside of her left forearm, just as she had in the car, as if something was hurting her. Glimpsing a bright pink mark, von Menen slipped his hand across the table, placed it gently on her wrist and eased up the hem of her sleeve, nausea stirring in his stomach, his eyes settling on a series of small round scars. He drew the sleeve back and hid the disfigurement, a mixture of puzzlement and sorrow spilling from his eyes.

Sigi's eyes were welling with tears again, her bottom lip quivering, like a child who wanted to cry but knew that she had to be brave.

'Is there more?' he asked gently.

'Don't, Carl, please.'

'Sigi…'

She turned away, and for what seemed like an eternity, she said nothing, until finally she began to speak.

'Not in my entire life will I ever forget that day, Friday 28th July, a week after the attempt on Hitler's life. They came to take Lutzi… They'd already killed her brother by then.'

'The Gestapo?'

'Yes, and because I was at the apartment when they arrived, they took me as well. But Lutzi fared much worse than I did.' Sigi shook her head. 'A night doesn't go by when I don't hear her cries,' she said, fiddling nervously with the garnet dress ring on her left hand. 'The insufferable screams, the insane agony. I only saw her once. She looked awful, her face bruised, her eyes black and blue, a deep cut across her forehead. Two days later, they took her away. I could hear her sobbing in the corridor outside my cell. It wasn't until I received the letter from Gustav's mother that I knew she was in Flossenbürg.'

He reached across the table and squeezed her hands. 'And you, Sigi?'

'I spent another five days at Gestapo Headquarters and then they released me. After that, I found myself working forcibly at Borsigwalde.'

Von Menen gritted his teeth, gestured towards her left arm. 'It's unimaginable, Sigi. Who on God's earth would want to do anything like that?'

'Believe me, Carl, there are plenty of depraved people on Prinz Albrecht Strasse. One of them was an outright savage, as evil as the Devil himself.' She tossed back her head. 'My God, the pain... Each time he lit up a cigarette, he would stare at me, a frightening, malevolent look in his eyes... I fainted several times.'

'His name, Sigi? Do you know his name?' Von Menen was almost exploding with anger.

Sigi shook her head. 'I can't rightly remember. It's pointless, anyway. There's nothing anyone can do about it. It's not worth the risk. It's best to... well, to try and forget it.'

'Sigi, please, try and remember.'

She thought for a moment. 'Braun... Baum... Baumer, something like that. What they call a Hauptsturmführer, a captain. He had an ugly, long scar across his left cheek.'

Von Menen purposefully steered the conversation towards the memory of a much happier Germany – the recollection of the gaiety and liveliness of pre-war Berlin and the thought of dear, departed friends.

But time was short. At five-thirty the next morning, Sigi and tens of thousands like her would be trudging the cold, dark streets of Berlin on a constrained vocation of false salvation. Von Menen saw her safely to her apartment, a longing smile on her face as she listened to his parting words.

'I'll be back, Sigi, I promise. A happy Christmas to you and your mother, and...'

'Yes?'

'Don't give up.'

The evening's unexpected turn of events had eclipsed the one, all-important reason why von Menen had gone to

Berlin in the first place – the envelope which he'd collected from the Foreign Office.

When he opened it in his room at the Savoy, he found a second envelope inside, marked TOP SECRET. It contained the passport of his old "friend", Kurt Lindemann, several visas and a birth certificate in the same name. Flicking through the pages, he noted it had been franked with German and Swiss Border Police stamps, showing that "Lindemann" had left Berlin for Geneva on 28.10.1944 and had arrived back on 11.1.1945. A tingling sensation raced up his spine when he read the date of departure on the Deutsche Lufthansa airline ticket: 15.1.1945.

The next day, after calling briefly at the Borsigwalde munitions complex, von Menen left the northern suburbs of Berlin and headed for the peace and tranquillity of Mecklenburg.

27

Wednesday 20th December 1944

While von Menen had been in Berlin collecting the documents that would deliver him from the misery of war-torn Germany, Jürgen Lanze had been wrestling with the thorny problem of how to get a 1600-tonne submarine to the South Atlantic – and back!

With a round trip of over 15,000 nautical miles in prospect, and little hope of refuelling at sea, the boat's endurance would be stretched to its limits.

'I can see by the look on your face, Jürgen, that you're still concerned about the lack of refuelling facilities,' said von Leiber, mindful of the distance involved.

'Using the Regelbunker we can squeeze in an extra twenty-six plus metres of fuel,' commented Jürgen, 'which will give us an extra, say, 1,500 miles, so we might *just* make it there and back... but only at a desperately low speed.'

I know, Jürgen, I know,' replied von Leiber, 'and I'm still working on it. Believe me, if it's at all possible you'll be refuelled at sea... Anyway, let's turn to the cruise itself,' he continued, unrolling a large chart.

Lanze studied the detail with mounting disquiet. 'A bold, dangerous and risky voyage,' he said solemnly.

'Can't disagree with that, but if you stick to the prescribed course, you'll reach the rendezvous point in forty days *and* have enough fuel left to get you back home. South of the Equator, your penultimate position lies 112 nautical miles due east of the rendezvous point... About eleven hours sailing at ten knots—'

'There's not much depth off the Plate estuary, Manfred, and I'll need all of eleven fathoms to "hide" the boat.'

'I know, it's notoriously shallow... Five miles east of the Cabo San Antonio Lighthouse, it's shallower still; little more than six and a half fathoms.' Lanze winced at the thought of it. 'Your final position will be just short of eleven fathoms, but reaching it will be very challenging – the run-up from the twenty-metre contour is only just over eight fathoms!'

'Mm... tricky, indeed. Whatever, I'll start my final run when the sun goes down and when I arrive, I'll wait on the bottom.'

'That's what I would do. As to your concerns about fuel, just pray that we can get another U-boat to you. Failing that, you're on your own. And finally, some personal advice: do not engage the enemy and make Bergen your return destination... irrespective!'

Von Leiber took his leave. No sooner had he left the room when von Menen walked through the door.

'This matter of Argentina, Carl... What's all this about equipment?' asked Jürgen.

'Didn't Manfred tell you?'

'No. Neither did your father. In fairness, though, I suspect he thought it best if it came from you.'

'Well, to put it simply, Jürgen, there's a faction inside Argentina that would like to see a change of leadership. They'd like to replace the present dictatorship with a dictatorship of their own, one that would embrace Germany and restore diplomatic relations between our two countries, but they need some help.'

'A shipment of arms?'

'Yes, Schmeisser machine pistols, among other things.'

'And you're the middle man?'

'In the material sense, yes.'

'And the *material* is where I come in.'

'Yes, it's already waiting at the Flender-Werke Shipyard, in a storage building back from the quay.'

'That much I do know,' said Lanze. 'Manfred told me that the key to the building would be delivered to me personally, by someone called... von Althoff?'

'Highly likely,' confirmed von Menen. 'Von Althoff is a kind of general factotum for the man I report to.'

'And the gold... That's at the Flender-Werke Shipyard, too?'

Von Menen smiled. 'Father's told you about the gold, then?'

'Yes, last night.'

'You're not shocked?'

'I've been at the front for over five years. *Nothing* shocks me anymore.' Lanze looked von Menen in the eyes. 'When I'm at sea, my immediate concern is for the welfare and protection of fifty-six officers and men, *and* the safety of the boat. Yet always on my mind is the most important part of my life – Katrina. I think about her constantly. It helps me keep my sanity. So, if Katrina wants to start a new life in Argentina, then Argentina is where we're going.'

Von Menen flicked a glance at the door. 'Manfred doesn't know about the gold... Mother does, but I'm not so sure about Katrina. I certainly haven't told her.'

'I've already spoken to your mother about that and we've agreed not to say anything. Katrina's got enough to worry about, what with the baby and all.'

A smile washed across von Menen's face. 'Well, sailor

boy, looks like we'll be meeting up at... well, 36° 18`S 56° 04`W, to be precise.'

'For you, Carl, perhaps, but not for me; we *sailor boys* don't use geographical co-ordinates... we use grid references, superimposed on standard naval charts, which show the ocean divided into quadrants, each identified by two letters of the alphabet. Every lettered quadrant is divided into nine squares and each of those nine squares is sub-divided into nine smaller squares. In turn, the smaller squares are sub-divided until what we're left with is an ocean covered by a multiplicity of minute squares, each one representing an area no larger than a few nautical square miles. In our case, we'll be meeting at the intersection of GK9198 and GK9432.'

'More importantly, Jürgen, when do you expect to sail?'

'Around the end of January, I believe.'

'Duration?'

'About forty days, so Manfred reckons.'

'Which leaves me a month or so to finalise the operation at the other end, assuming, of course, that you'll reach your final position around 14th March.'

'And the vessel I'm to rendezvous with?'

'Some kind of large, fast patrol boat, I imagine. The question is what to do about the gold. I'll have to come back for it.'

'Come back? How?'

'A fishing boat. I bought it some time ago. She's small, but very robust. She'll take half a tonne easily. Can you remain on station until I get back?'

'Two days, that's all I'll have.'

'Understood... You know the recognition signs?'

'Yes, three pennants – white, black, white, in that order. You'd best make sure they're flying, too, otherwise your fast patrol boat could easily end up with an unsolicited gift of

200 kilos of Hexanate high explosive in its lap.'

Just then, Steiger phoned from downstairs, a note of urgency in his voice. Von Menen excused himself, found his father, and together they hurried to the Steigers' parlour.

'What's the problem, Hans?' asked the General.

'Greta and I have just got back from Lübeck, and…'

'Go on.'

'Providence, call it what you like, but I missed the turning into the drive. When I pulled into Westphal's farm entrance to turn around, a BMW was parked twenty metres down the track, a man sitting behind the wheel. It was Baumer's car. I recognised the number.'

'Baumer! You're sure?'

'Definitely. No doubt at all.'

'Was he alone?'

'Seemed to be.'

'Did he see you?'

'I wouldn't think so. I was wearing my hat and my collar was turned right up.'

'Baumer,' muttered von Menen. 'I wonder…'

'Wonder what?' asked the General.

'Sigi Bredow. She said the Gestapo officer responsible for those horrible cigarette burns was called Baumer, but surely it can't be the *same* Baumer, because Sigi was held at Prinz Albrecht Strasse in Berlin.'

'Oh yes it could,' said the General, exchanging a knowing glance with Steiger. 'Keppler, the SS Standartenführer we dealt with at the Reichsbank, admitted as much. To quote: *"posted there to help with the interrogation of some of the suspects involved in the plot to murder our glorious Führer. His success rate was very high".*'

Anger boiled in von Menen's eyes.

'Klaus, I wouldn't normally sanction a *personal* motive for killing anyone,' said Steiger, 'but…'

'I know, I know,' said the General, shaking his head. 'We've got to get rid of *him*, before he gets rid of *us*.'

'It's me he's after, Klaus,' said Steiger. 'I was the one who shamed him. He's not the type who'd share that kind of humiliation with his friends. That's why he was on his own. It's a personal thing. He's spoiling for revenge, waiting for the right moment. Leave him to me.'

Thursday 21ˢᵗ December 1944

Von Menen returned from Lübeck at eight o'clock in the evening.

'Which one did you use?' asked Steiger.

'The one inside the railway station.'

'And?'

'I called the Schwerin Gestapo Office, said I had some information for Hauptsturmführer Baumer. The operator said he wasn't there, that he'd left at four o'clock and wouldn't be back until seven tomorrow morning.'

'Which means he'll be leaving home around five-thirty,' reckoned Steiger. 'Right, let's run through the rehearsal we did on your mother's car.'

The temperature was well below zero, the cold piercing through every layer of their thick clothing. Steiger turned off the main road and on to a narrow woodland track, bringing the Steyr to a halt fifty metres in from the road. He looked heavenwards and thanked God for the clear, star-studded night and a first-quarter moon. *Perfect.*

'The entrance to Baumer's place is a few hundred metres up the road on the left,' said Steiger. 'It's a big house, with an entrance on the outside of a hairpin bend. When you turn into the drive, the first thing you encounter is an unfenced wooden bridge about forty metres long. It straddles a wide section of the…' Steiger paused, stroked his chin. 'God, I can't remember the name of the river. Anyway, the river enters the grounds from the west, follows the course of the hairpin bend and flows out of the estate a kilometre or so to the east. Its widest part is just inside the entrance. There's a steep gravel drive on the far side of the bridge, about 200 metres long and straight as an arrow. It leads all the way up to the house.'

'Is the river deep?'

'At this time of the year, yes. I've known it to flood over the bridge and out onto the main road.'

'How do you know all this, Hans?'

'The bridge was built by my great-grandfather. My family's had a connection with the estate for a long time; I used to go there with my father. Either side of the entrance there's a high stone wall, giving way to a row of high pines. The whole place is very secluded.'

'So, when Baumer leaves the house, there's only one way he can go when he reaches the bridge,' noted von Menen.

'Through the main entrance, unless he fancies a swim,' chortled Steiger.

'And on the other side of the road?'

'Another high stone wall, marking the boundary of the Langer estate. There's a couple of convex mirrors affixed to it, so anyone leaving Baumer's place can check for vehicles approaching along the main road.'

'And behind the wall?'

'Dense woodland.'

'How do we get into the estate?'

'Another bridge, about half a kilometre down the road. From there we can approach the house from the west. It's all woodland, so there's plenty of cover. You've got the tools?'

Von Menen felt the pincers and the short length of

softwood dowelling inside his breast pocket and nodded.

'Just in case the clevis-pin's been replaced by a nut and bolt,' said Steiger, 'you'd best take this.'

Von Menen slipped the small adjustable spanner into his pocket.

'And remember,' added Steiger, 'whether it's a clevis-pin or a nut and bolt, don't leave it on the ground – bring it back with you.'

Steiger checked his watch. Half past midnight. He reached into the back of the Steyr and grabbed his Schmeisser.

'I'll wait for you at the fringe of the wood,' he said. 'If there's the slightest hint of trouble, stay on the ground until you hear the first burst of fire from this, then run like hell.'

Steiger lay hidden beneath a large laurel bush, the house enveloped in darkness.

Pincers in one hand, the adjustable spanner in the other, and a short length of dowelling wedged under the strap of his wristwatch, von Menen wormed his way within a foot of the BMW. He inched gingerly beneath the running board, rehearsing in his mind's eye the process he'd practised a dozen times on his mother's car. Just as he felt for the clevis-pin, the front door to the house opened wide, a faint glow of light spreading out.

No blackout rules for the Gestapo.

Prostate beneath the car, von Menen was stiff with cold, his heart racing wildly. First he heard the footsteps and then he saw the Jackboots, nearing the BMW step by crunching step. He reasoned that it had to be Baumer. Thirty metres away, Steiger listened vigilantly for the first sign of trouble, the Schmeisser cocked, ready to go.

The car door pulled open; von Menen heard it, Steiger saw it; a man in grey breeches leaning inside, a voice cursing the cold. The door slammed shut again, the man made his way back to the house and the porch light went out.

Numbed with cold, his concentration waning, von Menen could barely move, yet somehow, the clevis-pin came out and the thin, short length of dowelling went in.

Steiger beamed a smile of relief as he watched von Menen struggling awkwardly over the last four metres to the laurel bush, his vaporised breath trailing behind him. 'Now it's my turn,' he whispered. 'The clevis pin, Carl.'

Von Menen could barely move his fingers. He dipped into his pocket, pulled out the pin and handed it to Steiger.

'Make your way back through the trees and wait for me on the far side of the road,' said Steiger.

Von Menen fetched Steiger a baffled look. 'Where are you going, Hans?'

Steiger nodded in the direction of the house. 'He's an important man. When the police arrive in the morning, they'll be looking for evidence, and we don't want to disappoint them, do we?'

It was two o'clock when they reached the Steyr, the flask of hot coffee laced with schnapps a welcome relief. They rested, then padded their way along the inside of the high stone wall, stopping fifty metres short of the hairpin bend.

'Right,' said Steiger, switching the screw cap on the jerry can for the one he'd wired with the detonator, 'you wait here. I'm going on alone.' Steiger delved into his canvas bag, pulled out a reel of cable and slipped a short length of wood through the hole in the middle. 'Grab hold of this, Carl, and keep a tight grip on it. I'll pull the cable out as I go along. Okay?'

Von Menen nodded.

'When the drum stops spinning, don't yank back on the cable. And whatever you do, don't let the cable get anywhere near the generator terminals.' He looked down at the jerry can, checked the wires of the detonator peeking through the small hole in the top of the screw cap and thumbed the blob of plasticine, firming the wires in place. 'It breaks my heart to waste twelve litres of petrol,' he said, 'but if that's what it takes... Anyhow, I'll see you shortly.'

Steiger hastened along the inside of the wall, making towards the apex of the hairpin bend, drawing out the cable with one hand and carrying the jerry can in the other.

Fifteen minutes later, he was back. The long, cold wait began.

Steiger stood stiffly upright, cupped his hand around his ear and caught the faint sound of the BMW. It was five-twenty.

'He's on his way,' he murmured.

Von Menen strained his ears. Steiger, his fingers so numb he could hardly move them, fumbled frantically with the terminals on the hand-held generator.

'That short length of dowel should be snapping right about... now! Bet he's pumping that foot brake like mad, wondering what the hell's gone wrong, thinking about the high stone wall and the deep water left and right.'

A few seconds later, the road noise from the BMW changed as it rumbled across the narrow wooden bridge. 'Obviously he didn't fancy the water,' quipped von Menen. 'He'll be breaking the land speed record by now.'

Counting off the seconds, Steiger glanced at von Menen and flicked the key on the generator. A noise like the rush of thunder broke the silence, a mushroom of brilliant orange spearing the sky.

One tonne of Germany's finest engineering lay in a mangled heap at the foot of the wall, engulfed by a sheet of flaming petrol. Moments later, there was a second violent explosion. 'The fuel tank's gone,' said Steiger. Two doors, the boot lid and a wheel went hurtling down the road. 'These heavy smokers,' joked Steiger, 'they'll never learn.'

Gathering in the cable, they raced back along the wall towards the Steyr, the glow from the burning BMW still visible in the distance. Von Menen stopped and took one last look.

'Don't dwell on it, Carl,' said Steiger. 'Believe me, what we've just done will appeal to the collective consciences of all decent-minded Germans.' He tugged at von Menen's sleeve. 'Come on. Let's get the hell out of here.'

The next day, with the Mecklenburg countryside blanketed in six inches of snow, the accident was reported in the late edition of the local press.

FREAK CAR ACCIDENT CLAIMS ONE DEATH
Detectives find vital clue... The victim has not yet been identified.

Saturday 23rd December 1944

Von Menen raced back from Lübeck like a man possessed, the Delahaye hurtling through the archway and coming to a screeching halt in the courtyard. Stumbling into the Steigers' parlour, he dropped the day's edition of the Nazi news-sheet *Völkischer Beobachter* on the table and crashed into an armchair.

'Page three, Hans,' von Menen said, almost breathless. 'Read page three,' he repeated, shaking his head in despair.

Steiger picked up the paper and turned to page three, his face contorting with every word.

The body of the victim found in the burned-out wreckage of a BMW near Bützow early on Friday morning has been identified as...

He looked incredulously at von Menen. 'Standartenführer—'

'Friedrich Keppler,' interrupted Carl. 'Read on, Hans.'

At first, local police thought the body might have been that of Hauptsturmführer Felix Baumer, but in a dramatic telephone call to the Gestapo Office at Schwerin, it was revealed that Hauptsturmführer Baumer had been summoned urgently and unexpectedly to a new appointment at Gestapo Headquarters in Berlin early on Thursday evening. Friedrich Keppler, a former colleague of the Hauptsturmführer, had been staying at the address since leaving Führer Headquarters at Rastenburg. He was believed to have been on his way to Hamburg. Police are not treating the incident as suspicious.'

'Hans, Baumer is still alive!'

'Maybe, but he's in Berlin.'

'All the same, he's still a threat.'

'Yes, but in Berlin he won't have time for personal diversions – not yet, anyway. But you're right, he will be back.'

28

On Christmas evening, Jürgen and Katrina Lanze, armed with two bottles of schnapps and a basket of Stollen cakes, made a surprise visit to the naval barracks at Priwall.

They were expecting to see only a handful of men, but when they arrived they were astonished to find that almost two-thirds of the crew were there, one of them Joachim Krauz, the chief helmsman, his face a picture of grief. Krauz had arrived at Hamburg in a joyous mood only to be greeted with the anguishing news that his wife and daughter had been killed in an air raid. The family home had been completely destroyed.

The Lanzes listened aghast to the stories of men who had abandoned all efforts to reach relatives in the east, forced back by columns of fleeing refugees, frantic to escape the tidal wave of Russian retribution that was sweeping through East Prussia.

'The Russians are storming west, Captain,' a young torpedo mechanic told Lanze, almost in tears, 'and no one can stop them.'

They returned to the von Menen estate forlorn, alarmed and resolute in one purpose – to put Germany behind them.

In most German households, the spirit of Christmas prevailed, but a constant deluge of grim news overshadowed the traditional festive mood. As the year petered to an end, the final chapter of Nazi Germany was already being written.

Eva von Leiber set out for Lake Konstanz. She had been gone a mere four hours when Manfred, against all advice, headed east in a desperate attempt to coax his mother into joining Eva at Meersburg.

The next day, Klaus and Anna von Menen left for Flensburg, taking with them the key elements of six vitally important documents, locked safely in the General's attaché case.

Von Menen, meanwhile, busied himself with the preparations for his departure to Madrid, checking every item of his possessions for any tell-tale sign that would link him to the country he was about to leave forever.

Three days later, the General and his wife arrived back at the house. At their behest, the entire family, including the Steigers, gathered around the large walnut table in the library.

'Before I start,' said the General, 'there is something I want you to know. I have it on unquestionable authority that certain elements within the Nazi hierarchy, perhaps acting arbitrarily, are putting out peace feelers in Sweden. Whilst I do not share their optimism, I thought it only fair to tell you, should any of you wish to change your minds.'

Heads shook vigorously.

The General squeezed his wife's hand and smiled. 'Good, that's the way Anna and I feel. Now, I believe Jürgen has something to say.'

Jürgen remained seated, a profound expression on his face. 'An electro-type submarine, similar to my own,' he said, 'arrived at Lübeck-Siems three days ago and no one is allowed within 100 metres of it. The crew, billeted in special quarters at Travemünde, are forbidden to associate with, or speak to, any other naval personnel. Yesterday, however, one of the yard engineers told me that the boat is fitted out like no other submarine he's ever seen – polished hardwoods, specially adapted sleeping quarters, luxurious bathrooms, day quarters and… a private dining room.'

Von Menen exchanged a meaningful look with the General. 'Looks as if you were right, Father. Seems we're not alone in this enterprising venture of ours after all.'

'Which is precisely the point I'm making,' said Jürgen. 'Peace feelers or no peace feelers, the Devil's circus is already looking for a new show ground.'

'In that case,' said the General, 'we need to press on.'

Jürgen, Steiger and von Menen moved to the back of the General's chair, all eyes on the open pages of a German Road Atlas.

'I estimate that in five to six weeks the main thrust of the Russian armoured advance will be here,' said the General, pointing to a spot west of the River Oder, 'about sixty kilometres east of Berlin.'

The women gasped in alarm.

'In the Baltic,' he continued, 'it's not so easy to forecast, but my guess is that by the end of January they'll be hammering on the door to West Pomerania. By then, of course, Carl will be in Buenos Aires, Jürgen will be somewhere in the South Atlantic and, hopefully, the rest of us will be up in Flensburg, awaiting Jürgen's return.'

'If I may, General,' said Jürgen, noting the look of alarm on Katrina's face, 'I have a voyage of eleven to twelve weeks ahead of me. Even if I leave home waters at the end of January, which I hope to do, I won't be back until about 20th April, by which time – if Manfred's predictions are right – most U-boats will have retreated to Norway, meaning I'll have to get from Norway to Flensburg.'

'Where do we go from Flensburg?' inquired Steiger.

'Odense, Copenhagen and then Malmö,' replied

the General. 'From Malmö, we'll head directly for Gothenburg.'

'Do you know *when*?' asked Greta anxiously.

'Afraid not, Greta. We could find ourselves in Gothenburg for quite some time, but we'll have decent accommodation and enough money to last several months *and* buy our passage to South America.'

'What do we do for papers?' asked Jürgen.

'That was the reason for our visit to Flensburg,' explained the General. 'Remember the photographs I took, on the day of Manfred and Eva's wedding? Well, there was a hidden reason for that – we each now have a Swedish *laissez-passer*.' He turned and smiled at Steiger. 'Hans, you and I will have to hope and pray that our fame doesn't extend beyond the borders of Germany, because from now on, we're all Lithuanian refugees.' The General feigned a slight cough. 'We have Aunt Ingrid to thank for that.'

'And Ingrid?' asked Greta. 'Has she decided what she's going to do when the war ends?'

'She's leaving for Sweden next week,' explained Anna, 'so we'll have the whole house to ourselves.'

'Where are the documents now, Klaus?' asked Steiger.

'In a very safe place – beneath the scullery floorboards at the house in Flensburg.'

'Where do we go to from Gothenburg, Daddy?' asked Katrina excitedly.

'Bilbao, then on to Madrid. And talking about Madrid, I think Carl has something to say... Carl?'

'Whilst I've no wish to alarm any of you,' stressed von Menen, 'you ought to be aware that my assignment is not without risk. Frankly, I've no idea how it will end. But I do know that this plan of ours will not succeed without some form of communication, and since direct communication is not an option, we'll have to use the next best thing –

an intermediary. The person I have in mind is my friend in Madrid, Juan Cortes, who I trust completely. Mother, Father and Katrina know him from the past; in fact, Mother has known his family for years.'

'Did Greta and I ever meet him?' queried Steiger.

'No, Hans, you didn't. He's not known to Jürgen, either, but that's not relevant.'

'It's years since Juan was here,' said Katrina. 'If he walked in here now, I doubt I'd recognise him.'

'I don't suppose you would, Katrina, but I'll come to that later. For the moment, I want to deal with the situation as I see it: when the war comes to an end, Germany will be plunged into mayhem. The whole of Europe will be in a state of turmoil. Even if hostilities were to end in March, I don't see you striking out for Argentina until late summer or early autumn. Whenever you leave, though, you can be assured that I will have updated Juan with my post box number, contact telephone number and rendezvous address.'

'Any idea where the rendezvous address might be?' asked the General.

'I'll come to that in moment, Father, but first, I'll deal with Katrina's point... Quite possibly, you won't recognise Juan, but more importantly, he might not recognise you, either. Moreover, the identities waiting for you at Flensburg could easily change, so there's little point in me furnishing Juan with names that might not even exist in, say, six months' time. But I do have a plan...'

Von Menen spent the next half-hour explaining the means by which each would identify themselves to Cortes. 'When satisfied as to your bona fides, Juan will then – and only then – provide you with the means by which to contact me in Argentina,' he explained. 'Lose any of the items I'm about to give you and you won't get further than Madrid.'

'And in the meantime, if something happens to Juan?' inquired Jürgen.

'Likewise, Jürgen, your journey will end in Madrid. Now, Father, to answer your question… when you arrive in Argentina, go straight to the Hotel Toscano, at Dolores. From there, you can contact me in Buenos Aires using the telephone number or post box number that Juan gives you. But be sure to use the code word, *Frederick*. When I hear *Frederick*, I'll join you immediately.'

After dinner, Carl adjourned to his bedroom, whiling away the next hour with Katrina's calligraphy set and several bottles of ink. A steady hand, four pens and six shades of ink later, he'd perfected the vital amendments to his Spanish birth certificate.

The next day, as a pale winter sun faded in the west, a despondent Eva von Leiber returned unexpectedly from Lake Konstanz. After her joyous time in Mecklenburg, she had found it impossible to come to terms with the loneliness of Meersburg and was desperately worried about Manfred.

The harrowing ordeal of her exhausting two-day journey was written all over her drawn and tired face. If the von Menens, the Steigers or the Lanzes had any doubt about their vision of a new future in Argentina, Eva's vivid exposé of the state of the cities she'd passed through on her long, wearisome journey from Meersburg dispelled it for good.

In the evening, von Menen packed his few belongings in the suitcase he'd collected from the Foreign Office in Berlin, the origin of the seemingly well-travelled piece of luggage prominently labelled on the inside of the lid with the inscription *Made in Switzerland*.

Steiger, meanwhile, using all the skill of a surgeon, delicately cleaved apart the double-flap lid on the cardboard box containing the doll's house. He slipped the three envelopes intended for Cortes inside one flap, and a fourth, which von Menen fetched hurriedly from his bedroom, inside the other. A flat iron and a concoction of homemade gum did the rest. His wife tied up the box with a mile of string and braided a neat carrying handle at the top.

Everything was in place.

29

The Ardennes offensive was over. Hitler's reckless plan to halt the advance of the Allies in the west had failed, and it was failing in the east, too. The Russians were closing in fast.

With no news of Manfred von Leiber, Eva was convinced that she would never see her husband again. Secretly, the von Menens thought likewise.

Finding the temptation to bring forward his departure almost irresistible, von Menen went off in search of Steiger. He found him in the garage block, assembling a comprehensive "tool" kit for Flensburg, including two Walthers, two MP-40 machine pistols, a box of stick grenades and a case of nine-millimetre ammunition.

'Hans, about the Delahaye…'

'You're not going to ask me to ship it over to South America for you, are you?' jested Steiger.

Von Menen smiled. 'No, just making sure that you've no use for it, that's all.'

Steiger flicked a glance at the Steyr. 'Thanks, Carl, but I'll be using *Helga* here to take a few things up to Flensburg. Then, when Greta and I finally leave, we'll take the BMW. Your parents and Katrina will follow a few days later in the Mercedes.' He cast another glance at the Steyr. 'Sadly, I'll have to torch this old girl before we leave.'

'And petrol? I've got plenty of coupons left.'

'Thanks again, Carl, but we've got more than enough.'

Steiger could see the deeply worried look on von Menen's face. 'There's something else, isn't there?'

'Actually, Hans, there is. It's the matter we discussed the other evening; you know, your offer to take me to Berlin on Sunday?'

'Go on.'

'Well, I'm thinking of slipping away on Saturday morning, alone, very quietly, taking the Delahaye with me. Since you've no use for it, I'll give it to Sigi Bredow.'

Steiger smiled sympathetically. 'By all means take the Delahaye... though it wouldn't be wise for you to leave on Saturday morning. Your mother and Greta are arranging a farewell dinner for you.'

Saturday 13th January 1945

The occasion was no more joyous than a poignant entry in an obituary column, the strain growing in Anna von Menen's eyes.

In less than nine hours, von Menen would be on his way to Berlin, the Delahaye fuelled up, his suitcase and the doll's house loaded in the back. Laden with anxiety, his mother stuck to him like a barnacle on a ship's hull and Katrina was rarely less than an arm's length away. Frau Steiger hid the real extent of her emotions behind a dainty pink handkerchief, while Frau von Leiber, feeling totally inadequate, looked like the lost and forlorn soul she was. Jürgen, who had slipped away from Priwall, tried his best to lighten the tone, but failed miserably.

Von Menen chose his moment carefully. 'Mother,' he said, noting the time, 'there are a couple of things I need to discuss with Father, Jürgen and Hans. If you'll just give me a few minutes...?'

Reluctantly, she let go of his arm.

The four men stood by the fireside in the library, the very same room where their hopes and dreams had been schemed.

'I need this moment to get rid of my own emotions before I say my goodbye to the ladies,' said von Menen, feeling the pangs of unease in his stomach. 'But there's another reason. I'm mindful how much this whole thing depends on me and I know that it could easily go wrong. If it does, I want you to know that it won't be for the want of trying.'

'We realise that, Carl,' said the General. 'A few weeks ago, it was just a dream. Then it became a hope. What we're trying to do now is turn hope into reality. Our expectations of you are no more than they are of ourselves.'

Jürgen and Hans nodded in agreement.

'Thank you.' Von Menen stepped forward and placed his hands on Jürgen's shoulders. 'God speed, Jürgen. Your charge is, perhaps, greater than mine... I'll be praying for you.'

'Don't worry, Carl, just make sure to have a drink and some fresh food waiting.'

'You've got it.'

Steiger smiled, stuck out his hand and von Menen took hold of it, tugging the big man forward, whispering in his ear.

'I know you can look after yourself, Hans, even where Baumer's concerned, but please, watch out for *them*... and every night, give Greta a kiss for me.'

'Everything will be all right, Carl,' said Steiger. 'I promise you.'

As Steiger and Lanze headed downstairs to the Steigers' parlour, von Menen flung his arms around the General's shoulders.

'This isn't like us, is it Father?' he muttered, feeling the emotion rising between them. 'But this time, at least I have the chance to say goodbye. Whatever happens, I want you to know just how much I love and respect you and I want to thank you for everything you've ever done for me. Like you, I've always been an optimist and I'll try my damnedest not to let you down. Somehow, though…'

He paused and they drew apart.

'If it doesn't work out, Carl,' said the General, 'it won't be for the want of us trying. We might think we can forge our destiny, but fate always has the last word. *We've* placed ourselves in this danger. It's *us* who are living on the edge. I know you'll make it, Jürgen too, but if *we* don't,' he said, with a smile of resignation, 'well…'

He placed his arm around his son's shoulder. They made to join the others. Stopping just short of the door to the drawing room, the General turned and smiled; a fatherly smile, a loving smile, born from childhood days, the long summer grass down by the lake, sandcastles on the beach at Graal-Müritz and the gaiety of Lübeck at Christmas time.

'Like you, Carl, I'm not normally given to sentimentality, but when you leave this house tomorrow morning, do so knowing that *I* love you very much, too. I couldn't have wished for a better son.' He grabbed von Menen's hand and held it tight, as if it were for the last time. 'That's it, son. I'm off to join Hans and Jürgen.'

The women were waiting by the fireside. Eva von Leiber, all of a fluster, rushed to kiss him on the cheek, and then hurried from the room. Frau Steiger was less hasty.

'If I'd been fifteen years older,' he whispered in her ear, 'Hans wouldn't have stood a chance.' He could sense her chortling through the tears. 'That's better,' he said. 'Don't cry, we'll all be together again soon. Now, just one last favour…' She nodded on his shoulders. 'When I walk through the door, try and keep Mother here, will you?'

She nodded again, then finally let go, allowing him to dab the tears from her eyes. Von Menen turned to his sister.

'Well, Sis,' he said, spawning a feigned a look of joviality as he glanced down at Katrina's swollen tummy, 'seems I'm saying goodbye to two of you. If it's a boy, he'll be just like Jürgen, if it's a girl, she'll be just like you. Either way, we'll all be winners.'

She flung her arms around him and held him tight. 'I love you, Carl. Promise me you'll take care of yourself.'

'I will, and you must do the same for me, okay?'

'Yes, I promise.'

He turned and moved straight into the outstretched arms of his mother, neither saying anything. She held him close, then slowly drew her head away, her eyes welling with tears. Finally, she reached up and searched his face with her fingers, like a young mother exploring the face of her new-born child for the very first time.

'It'll be all right, Mother,' he assured her.

She held him tight again, just one last embrace, until something deep inside her told her to let go, her arms falling limp by her side.

Cupping her face in his hands, he kissed her on the forehead and made for the door, leaving her staring at the smouldering embers in the hearth. She heard the click of the latch, turned on her heels and hastened towards the door.

'Anna!' called Frau Steiger, hurrying after her. 'Let him go.'

Frau von Menen stopped, turned and walked back towards the fireplace, the worry of the last few months showing in her drawn and weary face. Fighting back the tears, she looked into Frau Steiger's eyes.

'I'm never going to see him again. I just know it.'

Von Menen tiptoed down the staircase. He left the house by the side entrance and made his way quietly across the courtyard, no time for reminiscing, no curdling thoughts of nostalgia, no fleeting last look at the house.

Outside, it was still pitch black. As he made to slide back the garage door, someone inside did it for him. Steiger and Lanze were there. A moment later, so was Frau Steiger, hurrying across the courtyard with two cardboard boxes, one on top of the other.

'Forgive the presumption, Carl,' she said, 'but we've put a few things together for Sigi.'

Now it was von Menen's turn to feel emotional. 'Thanks, Greta, it's very thoughtful of you. And thank Mother, too, will you, please?'

She reached up, flung her arms around his neck and squeezed him tight. 'Take care, now. We'll be thinking about you.'

'I'll be thinking about you, too, Greta.'

With that, she kissed him on the forehead and disappeared into the darkness, taking her tears with her.

Von Menen turned to face Steiger. No playful punches, no jokes, no words of advice, just a solid, warm embrace.

'Don't concern yourself about things at this end,' Steiger assured him. 'Everyone will be fine.'

'Thanks, Hans, thanks for everything.'

'Here,' said Steiger, delving into his pocket, 'I'd like you to have this.' He handed von Menen a small, jagged piece of metal, about an inch square, worn and shiny from its lasting home in his jacket pocket. 'It's one of two pieces a surgeon took from your father's leg in 1916,' he explained. 'Your father gave them to me as a keep-sake. I've kept them ever since. They've brought us a great deal of luck. Maybe this one will do the same for you.'

'Thanks, Hans, I'll take great care of it.'

Von Menen turned to Lanze, placed his hands on his shoulders and gave him a slight tug.

'Jürgen, I didn't say so last night, because I didn't want to alarm Katrina, but the fact is, I know you have the most dangerous task of all. While I have only myself to worry about, you have the burden of looking after over fifty men. Take care. I'll be praying for you.'

They hugged, parted and von Menen made for the door.

'One last thing,' said Steiger, his voice signalling a playful tone. 'When you get to Berlin, just remember… there's *another* lady waiting for you in Buenos Aires!'

Von Menen smiled, climbed into the Delahaye and drove through the archway, conscious of the waves from the upstairs windows of the house.

★

Von Menen was out of luck. Johann Ritter, face etched with exhaustion and apology, had no room available at the Savoy. Instead, von Menen accepted a cup of coffee, then headed off in the direction of Alexander Platz.

It had just turned noon when he passed by the burned-out hulk of the Kaiser Wilhelm Memorial Church on Kurfürstendamm, a symbol of the perpetual nightmare facing the city's hard-pressed emergency relief services. Berlin was still 'breathing', but only just.

In Germany, Sunday was no longer a day of rest and Sigi was still at work, but Frau Bredow was graciously welcoming, if not slightly flummoxed.

Placing the two boxes on the floor by the sideboard, von Menen noted the small suitcase standing by the door.

'My apologies, Frau Bredow,' he said, glancing at the brown leather case, 'perhaps I've called at an inconvenient time?'

'Not at all, Carl, do sit down. I'm only going to Potsdam for the night. It's my sister's sixtieth birthday.'

'Then maybe I could give you a lift,' replied von Menen, already halfway to his feet.

'That's awfully kind of you, Carl, but my brother-in-law is collecting me at three-thirty.' She picked up her handbag from the sideboard and fastened the clasp. 'Staying in Berlin long?' she asked.

'Just briefly. I thought I'd call in and see Sigi. I promised her I would when I saw her before Christmas.'

'Yes, she told me. I was sorry to have missed you when you called, but I was still at the Charité Hospital at the time. I do voluntary work there, sometimes until the early hours.'

'So Sigi mentioned.'

She glided into the bedroom, the conversation continuing through the open door. 'She was very excited to see you... Didn't stop talking about it for days. You cheered her up no end.'

Frau Bredow returned to the drawing room, closing the bedroom door behind her.

'That damned wretched Gestapo... call themselves *men.* They're nothing but a bunch of cowards. Sigi's got a much better job at Borsigwalde now, in the office, better hours and more money. She's much happier; well, as happy as one can be in these awful times.'

The news brought an innocent smile to von Menen's face.

'Ordinarily, she wouldn't have been working today, but

she offered to do some paperwork. Her reward is a little extra money and a day off tomorrow.'

'I'm happy for her,' said Carl. 'I don't suppose she's had any news of...'

'Lutzi?'

He nodded.

'Afraid not. As far as we know, she's still at Flossenbürg, waiting to go before that appalling People's Court.'

Picturing the consequences, von Menen tried to shake the thought from his mind. Glancing at the two boxes he'd brought down from Mecklenburg, he drew himself to his feet.

'Nearly forgot,' he said. 'My family would hate you to think they were being patronising, but they asked me to bring down a few things for you and Sigi. They're mainly homemade,' he added: 'preserves, cakes; some cheese and butter, that kind of thing. There are a few cans of meat in there, too.'

Frau Bredow moved over to the sideboard and peered inside one of the boxes. Three years ago, it would hardly have been big enough to accommodate her jewellery, most of which had pedalled its way through the greasy hands of Berlin's black-market racketeers in exchange for warmth, food and the occasional luxury of perfumed soap.

'How very kind of your mother,' she said, clearly overwhelmed. 'Do give her our sincere thanks, Carl. Perhaps when this damn awful war is over, I'll be able to repay her in some way; that is, if we ever get our money back.'

'She wouldn't hear of it. She knows how difficult life is for those living in the cities.' He glanced nervously at his watch, sighed and said, 'Well, I suppose I'd better be on my way.'

'Where are you staying?'

'Er…'

'You haven't got a room, have you?' she said perceptively.

'Well, not yet, but I'm sure I'll find somewhere.'

'Not yet, not ever, I think,' she said convincingly. 'You can stay here, if you like. It's not much, but you're more than welcome. I'll leave a note for Sigi. She can make up a bed for you on the settee.'

Frau Bredow went off in search of a pencil and paper.

'There's a small piece of ham and a few potatoes in the larder,' she called out from the hall. 'Sigi's quite adept at making things go a long way these days.'

Steiger's decorous advice went flashing through his mind.

'Now, where was I?' she said, reappearing. 'Oh, yes… Sigi finishes much earlier these days. The bus drops her at Oranienburger Strasse at five o'clock. Why don't you surprise her? She's still very fond of you, you know… Thinks you're such a *gentleman*.' There was a certain look in her eyes; the word "gentleman" and her subtle glance at the settee a trifle off-putting. 'If you leave here at, say, four-forty, you'll be there in plenty of time.'

Von Menen pulled up as the bus came to a halt, tooted on the horn and leapt out to open the door. A gleeful Sigi, bubbling with delight, climbed in.

'This is a surprise,' she said, undoing her headscarf. She shook her head, running her fingers aimlessly through her hair.

'A nice one, I hope,' he smiled.

'Of course, but how did you know—?'

'I just guessed you'd be here around this time,' he said, cutting her short.

She chatted incessantly and when the car came to a

halt outside her apartment, she asked, 'How long are you staying in Berlin?'

'Just the one night.'

'The Savoy?'

He conveniently escaped the question, climbed out of the car and opened the passenger door.

'Mummy's not at home at the moment, but you're welcome to come in for a while, stay to dinner, if you like,' her tone implying nothing more than politeness and civility.

'I'd love to.'

They went inside, Sigi returning quickly to her earlier question. 'So, where *are* you staying, at the Savoy?'

'Sigi, I have a confession to make,' he said sheepishly. He pointed towards the boxes lying beside the sideboard then gestured to her mother's note waiting on the table. 'I was here earlier,' he revealed.

She read the note, a surprised look on her face. 'Oh,' she said.

Von Menen felt the awkwardness of the moment. 'If it's not convenient, Sigi, I'm sure I could find a hotel *somewhere*. I only came here expecting to stay for a few hours. It was your mother who suggested that…'

She caught the flustered look on his face, walked over to him and kissed him on the forehead. 'Of course you can stay. If it's okay with Mummy, then it's okay with me. Now, about dinner, just give me a moment and I'll get things started.'

Von Menen moved over to the cardboard boxes. 'Will this help?' he asked, pulling out a bottle of champagne.

She smiled, the memories racing back. 'Mm, wonderful, haven't had champagne in ages.'

Von Menen opened the window and placed the bottle on the stone ledge. 'There are a few other things in there, too,' he called, as she busied herself in the kitchen.

'Such as?'

'Come and see for yourself.'

Sigi returned to the drawing room, dipped into the open box and pulled out a small bottle of Je Reviens Worth perfume.

'Sorry, I couldn't get you any Chanel No 5,' he said.

'Ah, but this is wonderful, Carl. Soap as well, toothpaste and *three* pairs of stockings – my colour, too.' She held them up to the lightshade, her sudden, half-bewildered look taking him by surprise. 'You're not dabbling in the black market, are you?'

'Me! Goodness, no. They're just a few presents from my family in Mecklenburg. They sent down some food, too. It's in the other box.'

'Well, it's very sweet of them and it's very sweet of you, too, Carl.' She leaned forward and kissed him on the cheek. Then, as if overwhelmed by her good fortune, she whispered in his ear, 'And thank you for everything else. I know it was you who fixed the job for me at Borsigwalde. I'll never forget it. I was very down and you gave me a reason to go on.'

He squeezed her hand reassuringly. 'It was nothing, Sigi, just a word in the right ear.'

Sigi busied herself in the kitchen, the conversation flowing through the open door. Eventually, she came out, peeked excitedly into the second cardboard box and kissed him again, warm and gentle, not lingering, but long enough for him to sense the softness of her lips, taste her warmth and capture the smell of her femininity.

The roughness of her hands had gone, the sheen was back in her long hair and her eyes were full of liveliness. Her vitality was back, too, not the playful vitality that had been there over three and a half years ago, but something else, an imaginative energy that he had never seen before.

Sigi was different. She was not *just* a beautiful lady, but a complete and dignified woman, a woman who had been languishing beneath a veneer of immaturity for too long.

Von Menen was confused, mystified and enamoured, too. This was not the Sigi Bredow of yesteryear; not the same Sigi who had once bared her bosom at the late-night Königin Café, poured champagne down the cleavage of a minx at Sapini's and howled with laughter from a box at the Berlin Opera when the rest of the house might otherwise have heard a pin drop. This was a different Sigi, a Sigi with a new depth of awareness, a far-reaching intellect, a Sigi who, after the war was over, was determined to go into politics and '*rid Germany of this evil element once and for all*'.

Fate had delivered von Menen the thinking man's Aphrodite. Something was happening, an agonising temptation bearing down on him like a steam press, veiling the memory of someone else. He knew it was wrong and he tried to shake it off, but the desire came rushing back, again, again and again, each time more tormenting than the last.

The talking stopped and the kissing started, long, deep and desirous; arms, hands and legs everywhere, the pent-up feelings of yesteryear about to explode.

'Oh, Carl, dear Carl, we shouldn't...'

But the hours were ebbing away. He wanted her desperately and she wanted him, the same desire, strong, deep and powerful, the kind of love, affection and closeness they'd never shared before.

He woke at four the next morning, wrestling with an inner conflict that was tearing at his heart, the mellowing effect of the champagne gone, reality back, vivid and sharp, banging at his conscience like a blacksmith's hammer. He'd betrayed Maria and dishonoured himself. Now, as he made ready to leave, he faced the same shameful burden of betraying Sigi. He agonised over trying to forget her,

415

leaving her there, going to Tempelhof alone and washing his mind clear, but Sigi insisted. And when he recalled the plan he had in mind, he knew he had to agree with her.

At Tempelhof Airport, von Menen was completely lost, his mood reflecting a depth of torment that had taken just thirteen hours to evolve, the flames of anxiety licking at his heart.

Sigi stood silently by the side of the car, watching as he took out his suitcase and the large cardboard box containing the doll's house. She was shivering, partly through cold and partly through nerves – the venue, the time, the suitcase, the man.

Von Menen threw his topcoat around her shoulders and they walked silently towards the terminal. He stopped at the door, placed the box and his suitcase on the floor and turned to face her.

'Well…'

Her bottom lip trembling, she reached up and pressed a finger to his lips.

'Please, don't say anything,' she said, tears coursing down her cheeks. 'In all these years, you never took me seriously and I wanted you so much. It was always you. It still is.' She tried to be brave but her voice faltered. 'Yes, it was my own fault,' she confessed, sobbing uncontrollably, 'I know that now… The immature, reckless Sigi Bredow, good for a bit of fun, but nothing else. Now look at me. I've suddenly grown up.'

Frozen by the events of just one night, von Menen stood silent and expressionless. She fixed him with a spearing look, her eyes more beseeching than ever.

'I *still* want you,' she urged, 'and after all these years, I think, perhaps, you want me.'

Von Menen was speechless, emotion choking back his

words, his shallow nod barely perceptible, his eyes doing all the talking. He knew he was in a mess.

'But if the truth's known,' she went on, 'for some reason, you can't have me, can you?'

He placed a hand across his forehead, drew it down over his face, as if trying to wash away the anxiety. But the anxiety was still there. He moved towards her and held her tight.

'I'm sorry, Carl,' she said, 'I'm making a complete fool of myself.'

'No you're not,' he whispered. 'You're right, Sigi, I did see something in you last night, something which...' He paused, shaking his head in despair. 'But there's nothing I can do about it.' His eyes filmed with water.

'I think I know,' she said in a faint voice. 'You're not coming back, are you?'

He drew away from her, fumbled in his jacket pocket and pulled out the keys to the Delahaye, pressing them into her hand. 'Listen carefully, Sigi... I want you to take my car. In one of the boxes I brought for you, there's a wad of petrol coupons. Do you have any relatives in the west?'

She nodded 'Yes, my aunt... my father's sister. She lives in Cologne.'

'Sigi, it's no secret that the attacks on Berlin will intensify, and for sure, the Russians will get here first.'

'I know, Mummy and I worry about it all the time. We've heard some awful stories.'

'I don't want to alarm you, Sigi, but they're not stories. It's why I want you and your mother to get out of Berlin as soon as possible. Your best bet is with the Americans or the British. Go as far west as you can. You're sure to be okay in Cologne. With the coupons, you'll find some money, including American dollars. There's enough to last you for five or six months. If you need anything else, try and get in

417

touch with my parents. They'll be moving to Flensburg. Their new address is in an envelope inside one of the boxes.'

At that, a man in a Lufthansa uniform poked his head through the terminal door.

'Are you going to Munich, sir?' he called.

'Yes,' replied von Menen.

'Then you'd best hurry, the flight's closing.'

They embraced one last time. She gave him back his coat and he picked up his two pieces of luggage. She allowed him a few yards and then sprinted after him, grabbing him by the sleeve.

'Carl, listen! Please listen! I love you! I'll wait for you! My aunt, in Cologne… Her name is Ursula Bredow. She lives at…'

A passing truck drowned out her voice, and with that, von Menen was gone.

The DC3 climbed heavenwards and through the darkness. "Kurt Lindemann" took his final glimpse of smouldering, war-torn Berlin.

It was seven-ten and at that very moment, some 320 kilometres to the south, a cell door clanged shut behind one of Flossenbürg's many inmates.

Werner had done his job. Lutzi Helldorf was free.

30

'Thank God, Carl,' said Cortes, looking at his watch. 'I'd just about given up on you. I was beginning to think you weren't coming.'

'I came as quickly as I could,' said von Menen, somewhat puzzled. 'From Ulricht's message I assumed the ship would be sailing on 20th January. What's the problem?'

'Ulricht got it wrong; she's scheduled to sail on Thursday! You'll need to be there when she arrives in Lisbon. If you're not, someone will grab your place!'

Von Menen looked heavenwards and sighed dejectedly. 'Maybe there's a train?'

'There is; it leaves Madrid at nine o'clock tonight, arrives Lisbon at around ten-thirty tomorrow morning. I've booked you a first-class sleeper.'

Von Menen's eyes brightened.

'The ticket's with all your other documents. You've got just two and a half hours,' said Cortes, checking his watch. 'No time for dinner, I'm afraid. You'll have to eat on the train.' Cortes was halfway to the hall. 'I must phone the shipping agency,' he shouted. 'They've given me until eight o'clock this evening to confirm the booking.'

Von Menen was in the process of extracting the three envelopes from the lid of the cardboard box when a gleeful

Cortes returned to the room, waving a small reddish-brown document and a coffee-stained piece of paper.

'Your passport, Carl, *and* the telegram about your "grandfather". They've been under lock and key since last October.'

Von Menen tucked them inside his jacket pocket and handed Cortes the three envelopes. Over a glass of wine, he explained the finer details of his family's proposed escape to Argentina, but said nothing about the gold and made no reference to the arms shipment. Cortes listened vigilantly and questioned nothing.

Von Menen mused about the fate of the Swiss passport and its matching birth certificate; it was too useful to discard, yet too bulky to conceal in the neat little hidey-hole vacated by the three envelopes. Cortes disappeared from the room, returning with a silver-framed photograph of his own grandfather, along with a length of black ribbon.

'Where we Latins are concerned,' he said, 'observing the conventional symbols of grief is a sacred process. It's up to you, of course, but I doubt anyone would wish to disturb a photograph like this, not with all the accompanying evidence, anyway.'

He levered back the grippers at the rear, withdrew the wooden backing and slipped the passport and the birth certificate beneath the photograph.

'You'd best make a note of the name, Juan; I might be using it in a couple of months!'

'Don't worry, it's in my head: Kurt Lindemann.'

Cortes wrapped the black ribbon around the edge of the frame and tied it off with a bow on one of the corners.

'There you are, your dearly departed Spanish grandfather.'

Von Menen emptied his suitcase, soaked away the *Made*

in Switzerland label and repacked the contents, ensuring to leave the photograph conspicuously on top. He looked at his watch for the third time in under a minute. Beneath the veneer of calm, a sense of urgency was building.

'We have a bit of time, Carl,' Cortes assured him. 'Enough for me to tell you about your shipping passage. You're booked on *Monte Amboto*, a small cargo ship, about 3,000 tonnes. She's expected at Buenos Aires around 13th February, so you'll have plenty of time to relax, if that's the right word. To alleviate the boredom, I've put together a few books for you. I've also got you this.'

'*La Vanguardia?*' asked von Menen, looking at the name of the newspaper. 'Friday 22nd December? I don't understand.'

'You will when you study the obituary column. Your dearly departed grandfather is in there, died 18th December. I went for the most impressive entry. As you can see, I took the family name from your Argentine passport – Menendez. Quite impressive, don't you think, that thick, black border?'

Von Menen laughed. 'You're in the wrong job, Juan – you ought to be with the Spanish Secret Service.'

'I thought it would add a little flavour.'

Von Menen pulled a wad of notes from his wallet. 'The ticket, Juan... pesos or Swiss francs?'

'Neither,' Cortes shrugged. 'Consider it your wedding present.'

His words sent a spasm of guilt through von Menen's mind, the glaring image of a distressed Sigi Bredow, abandoned outside the terminal at Tempelhof Airport, gripping his conscience.

'This is government business, Juan,' he said, shaking himself free of the memory. 'I can't have you paying for that. Anyway, you'd best take it. I've no need of it.'

'Goodness, Carl, it wasn't *that* much. I didn't *buy* the ship!'

'Keep the balance on deposit for when my family arrives.'

In Madrid, the lights were burning brightly, a cosy unhurriedness reflecting inside the cafeteria at Delicias Station.

After her own tormenting ordeal, Spain remained remote and detached from the conflict raging elsewhere in Europe. No fires. No sirens. No bells. No crump of ordnance.

Von Menen climbed aboard the train and waited in the corridor, head through the window.

'Bon suerte, Carl,' shouted Cortes.

The train pulled out beneath a thick cloud of steam, the engine hissing and screeching, the carriages jerking and shuddering. Von Menen stuck out his arm and waved one last time. 'Adios, mi amigo! Muchas gracias.'

At the frontier town of Valencia de Alcántara, nobody seemed in a hurry. While one locomotive was swapped for another, Portuguese customs officials and agents of Franco's Political Social Brigade asked the same questions.

'Your passport, please. Name?'

'Carlos Menendez.'

'Where have you been?'

'El Casar de Talamanca, north-east of Madrid.'

And so it went on, foreseen and predictable, for what felt like hours. Finally, with the day still sleeping in the east, the newly changed locomotive belched out a huge cloud of black smoke, the wheels spun furiously and the train moved out.

Von Menen flopped back on his bunk and smiled. He had been awake all night, but now he was free. He was only five hours from Lisbon.

Accompanied by a station porter, von Menen walked the short distance from Rossio Station and checked in at the Hotel Avenida Palace.

Anxious for news on the arrival of *Monte Amboto*, he slipped a very handsome tip to the concierge, set the man to work and adjourned to his room. He did not have to wait long.

'She arrives tonight, señor, ten o'clock... Sails for Gibraltar tomorrow.'

Von Menen breathed a huge sigh of relief.

Saturday 20th January 1945

Monte Amboto passed through the straights of Gibraltar at first light, stopped engines and dropped anchor one mile west of Europa Point.

The war in Europe may have been raging for over five years, but von Menen had played no real part in it. Now, for the first time ever, he was about to meet the enemy face-to-face, the advice given by Werner about the British Examination Service ringing in his mind – *'They're not exactly the Royal Navy, but they're just as professional. You'll be scrutinised very thoroughly.'*

A knock on his cabin door signalled the arrival of the Captain, a charming, affable figure, full of apology for the *slight detour,* as he humorously put it.

'Sorry about the inconvenience, Señor Menendez, but it's a matter of routine. The British, you see, insist on clearing all merchant ships bound for the Americas, which means that we can't proceed any further without the requisite Navigation Certificate.' The Captain shrugged in resignation. 'If we don't comply here, we'll have to put in at Freetown. Personally, I think it's best done here.'

'Does it take long?'

'No more than a couple of hours. They'll seal the radio room and then, if they're terribly keen, they'll send down a couple of divers.'

'Divers? What on earth for?'

'Mines... Sometimes they check that we're not in cahoots with the Germans. You know, towing a couple of those big prickly things to release on our way out.'

'Surely they wouldn't suspect you of that, would they?'

'I don't imagine so, señor,' grinned the Captain, 'but they check all the same. Then they rummage through the holds, check the ship's manifest, cargo, crew, passengers and the rest, which is really why I came to see you.'

Von Menen's face showed contrived indifference, though inwardly he was thinking about Werner's offer of a submarine and wishing to hell he'd taken it. He was, after all, a German, on a neutral ship, in British territorial waters, wearing civilian clothes – a spy! The realisation of it sent a pang of fear racing through his body that nigh on screwed his feet to the floor. *If they find out, will I be shot or hanged? Will they do it in Gibraltar or take me to London?*

'How can I help you?' he asked the Captain.

'Your passport, Señor Menendez, I'll need your passport.'

Von Menen fished out the document from his suitcase and handed it over. 'Will they need to see anything else?'

'I don't think so, señor. They're usually very prompt. If they need to speak to you, I'll show them to your cabin.'

Quickening footsteps approached along the narrow corridor, accompanied by the sound of voices, English voices. Von Menen stood by the edge of his bunk, heart beating wildly, waiting for the expectant knock on his cabin door.

'Señor Menendez… His Majesty's Examination Service, Port of Gibraltar, sir,' called a voice in broken Spanish.

Two knocks in quick succession.

'A moment, please,' replied von Menen. He took a long, deep breath and pulled open the door.

Two officers in dark blue uniforms stood there; one holding a clipboard, the other, von Menen's passport. The officer with the passport spoke first.

'May we come in, señor?' he asked in Spanish.

'Of course.'

'Do you, by chance, speak English, señor?'

Von Menen shook his head.

'Your name is Menendez?'

'That's right, Carlos Menendez.'

'From Argentina?'

'Yes.'

'Born?'

'7th December 1915, Córdoba.'

'Your father – is he Argentinian?'

'He *was*, yes, but he was born in Spain.'

The officer looked again at the passport. 'It says here that you arrived at Lisbon on 6th October last year.'

'That's right.'

'And the purpose of your visit?'

'To see my grandfather. My mother received a message from my great-aunt, saying that he was dying. She thought it right that I, being the eldest grandson, should go and pay my respects. My father is dead, you understand. Apart from my great-aunt, who's a spinster, he has no other living relatives in Spain. They're all in Argentina.'

Von Menen pulled out the crumbled telegram from his suitcase and handed it over.

'Mm, I see. Do you have any other evidence of this?'

Acting the role of the doleful grandson, von Menen

ambled over to his bunk, picked up the copy of *La Vanguardia* along with the solemnly-framed photograph of his "grandfather", and showed them to the officer. 'I'm afraid that's all I have,' he said. 'The death certificate and will are still with the notary.'

Handing the newspaper to his colleague, the officer studied the photograph like an art expert examining an old master. He turned the frame over, his eyes on the four metal clips holding in the backing. Behind von Menen's appearance of balanced calm, his heart was thumping madly.

'The obituary entry seems genuine enough to me, sir,' confirmed the younger officer. 'Ernesto Carlos Menendez, died 18th December 1944.'

The older officer puckered his lips, took one last look at the photograph and handed it back to von Menen.

'Our condolences, señor. You'll appreciate that we still need to search your cabin.'

'Of course.'

The younger officer rummaged through his suitcase while the other flicked open the lid of the cardboard box. 'A doll's house?'

'Yes, a belated Christmas present for my daughter. One of my grandfather's friends made it for her.'

'Very nice.' The officer picked up his clipboard and handed von Menen his passport. 'Everything seems to be in order. Have a good trip, and our apologies for the inconvenience.'

Von Menen closed the door, gasped a huge sigh of relief and fell down on his bunk.

At two o'clock, *Monte Amboto* weighed anchor and set course for her long, slow voyage to the South Atlantic.

31

In the Baltic, the unstoppable Soviet Army surged on towards Danzig, spreading fear, desperation and panic throughout the German community. Through freezing cold winds and driving snow, columns of war-weary refugees trudged west, exhausted, hungry and terrified, running a gauntlet of rape, pillage, torture and death. Vengeance was the order of the day. Only the barbarity of Himmler's brutal SS killer squads equalled the widespread wickedness.

Further south, elements of the Red Army's Byelorussian Front had reached the River Oder, leaving Stalin poised to take the biggest prize of all – Berlin! For the Third Reich, the end was looming up fast.

★

Saturday 3rd February 1945

There was still no news of Manfred von Leiber and the von Menens were convinced there never would be.

For Eva, the strain was unbearable. Mindful that the von Menens were in the final stages of preparing to leave for Flensburg, she thought it best if she returned to Konstanz immediately. The von Menens having failed to coax her into staying another week, she set off on what would be a four-day nightmare journey to Meersburg.

At seven o'clock the in the morning, the courtyard covered with a glistening layer of frost, Katrina, heavily pregnant and teeming with emotion, said a private farewell to Jürgen.

At the Flender-Werke shipyard *Andromeda* was ready to sail, armed and fully loaded with over 252 metric tonnes of fuel and enough provisions for a twelve-week patrol, a secret consignment of arms, 500 kilograms of gold and the best bunch of officers and NCOs a captain could ever wish for:

Lieutenant Horst Reidel, First Watch Officer;
Sub-Lieutenant Wilhelm Meyer, Second Watch Officer;
Sub-Lieutenant Reinhard Mohle, Chief Engineering Officer;
Wilhelm Janssen, Midshipman;
Joachim Krauz, Chief Helmsman;
Manfred Schulz, Leading Telegraphist;
Bruno Krupp, Chief Diesel Mechanic;
Willi Frenz, Chief Electro Mechanic; and
Helmut Becker, Chief Torpedo Mechanic.

Jürgen Lanze waited patiently at the foot of the gangway, face turned against the freezing wind. Lieutenant Horst Reidel, the flaps of his special fur hat pulled down over his ears, remained alone on the open bridge, eyes for'ard, scanning the quay, no fluttering pennant for company. Meanwhile, below deck, conjecture was rife, the crew waiting anxiously.

Shortly after three o'clock, Reidel leaned over the bridge.

'It's here, Captain,' he bellowed.

A black Mercedes crawled slowly along the quay,

halting at the head of the gangway. The rear nearside door swung open and out stepped a man in a heavy dark coat and black Homburg hat.

Lanze saluted him. They shook hands and exchanged a few words, before the dour, unsmiling man pulled a large dark-blue envelope from his attaché case and handed it over. Lanze saluted a second time. The anonymous man climbed back into the Mercedes and the vehicle pulled away.

Retreating to his cabin, Lanze locked the envelope in his safe, then scrambled up the tower to join Reidel on the bridge.

'Initial course setting as discussed, Horst,' Lanze said. 'Orders to be opened at fifty degrees latitude.'

'So, it's Bergen, the Iceland-Faroes gap and...'

'Who knows?' said Lanze, with a tinge of conscience.

The sky darkening, the wind growing ever more biting, Lanze peered over the bridge, a mere handful of workmen on the quay below. In the distance, a dockside crane trundled back and forth like a giant giraffe on wheels.

'Okay, Horst. Let's go. Manoeuvring stations. Muster deck crew.'

Reidel bellowed down the pipe and the two massive MAN diesels thundered into life, a tremor rushing through the superstructure, NCOs and ratings bubbling up through the galley hatch, the quay deserted – no jubilant crowds, no "at ease" line-up on the for'ard or aft' deck, no Siegfried-Line chorus, no symbols, trumpets or drums, no band at all. Even the Flotilla Commander was conspicuous by his absence.

'All set, Captain.'

Lanze glanced for'ard and aft'. 'Let go the lines!'

The gangway pulled clear and the lines snaked in. A tug, fussing on the starboard side, teased the grey hulk clear of the quay, then slinked away.

Diesels humming a steady rhythm, *Andromeda* moved slowly out of the Untertrave and began her short journey downriver. She cleared the southern mole, took up her position astern of the escort minesweeper and followed her into the Bay of Lübeck.

South of Gedser, Lanze detached the escort vessel and blurred down the pipe.

'Full speed!'

Gambling with his own reckoning, the chief helmsman, Joachim Krauz, who could read Lanze's mind like a book, sensed that they were heading for seas that would be bristling with mines beneath skies full of enemy aircraft.

Some hours later, Lanze confirmed his instincts.

'Helmsman!'

'Captain?'

'New course – two, eight, zero.'

Krauz rolled his eyes and took a deep breath. 'New course, Captain; two, eight, zero.' *The Skagerrak. Mines every metre. So cheap, the RAF's giving them away.*

Fourteen miles east of Grenen Point, *Andromeda* surfaced and charged for the Norwegian coast, the night black, a last quarter moon hidden by low clouds.

'We'll reach deeper water in about four and a half hours, Captain,' Reidel calculated.

'Good,' said Lanze. 'But don't spare the fuel. We'll run at high speed all night.' ·

A warming mug of coffee in his hands, Lanze checked his watch – 06h30.

'Where are we, Horst?' he asked.

'Somewhere off Stavanger, I reckon, passing the mouth of Bockna Fiord.'

'We'll give it another half hour, trim for snorkel and resurface at 17h00.'

Lanze had barely closed his lips when a call blared up through the pipe.

'ALARM!!! CONTACT! AIRCRAFT! Bearing one, seven, zero; range: 4,000 metres, closing.'

Lanze and Reidel turned, caught the first drone of the Sunderland's engines, tumbled through the hatch and almost flew down the tower.

'DIVE, DIVE, DIVE! THIRTY METRES!'

The first stick of bombs fell as *Andromeda* dipped into the sea, waves washing over the for'ard casing, four thunderous detonations battering the port side, the submarine shuddering violently.

'My God, he's close!' shouted Lanze. 'Hold on!'

Perspiration was suddenly the common bodily function, anxiety the shared emotion. A minute later, four more deafening detonations came in quick succession – *BOOM! BOOM! BOOM! BOOM!*

The boat lifted violently, valves hissing, a tympanic racket from the galley, Janssen wishing he'd joined the army. The lights flickered, went out, then came on again. Damage crews darted from compartment to compartment, tools in hand, respirators at the ready.

'Number One!' cried Lanze.

'Captain?'

'Distance to Kors Fiord?'

'About eighty-five miles, Captain.'

'Helmsman!' called Lanze. 'Hold your course!'

He turned to Reidel.

'He'll suspect we're running to Bergen, so he'll think we'll change course and try to fool him, but we won't... Tell Mohle I want seventeen knots.'

Reidel looked astonished.

'We've never done it before, I know, but it's what this lady's all about. Seventeen knots!'

The floor plating seemed to go ahead of them as Mohle turned up the screws, the boat responding positively, the control room steady at last. Four more detonations sounded way to port, and a minute later, four more, fainter still. Janssen smiled and finally let go of the large brass valve he was clinging to, his face awash with relief.

An hour later the submarine rose again to snorkel level, the sky clearing as the two big diesels yawned back to life.

The elements of mother nature were at their most unforgiving, but Lanze pressed on.

Andromeda was mid-way between the Iceland-Faroes gap, ploughing through mountainous seas enraged by freezing, hurricane winds, the boat reacting violently, icicles hanging like trinkets from the barrels of the two twin anti-aircraft guns, the for'ard and aft' casings encrusted with ice.

The thought of deeper water was tempting enough, but in spite of the cruel conditions, Lanze was determined to push on, snorkelling by day, surface running by night. Eventually the storm abated, the boat making passage through calmer waters. Fifteen days after setting off, fortune smiled. *Andromeda* had broken out into the North Atlantic.

Wednesday 21st February 1945

All officers and senior NCOs had gathered in Lanze's quarters, anxious to learn the secrets of the dark-blue envelope.

'Gentlemen, for your ears only. We are heading for the South Atlantic, thirty-four nautical miles east of the coast of Argentina, borderline between naval quadrants GK9198 and GK9432,' revealed Lanze.

A unified sigh of relief filled the small, cramped room.

'We're not going...?'

'Hunting, Janssen? No,' reassured Lanze. 'We're delivering some groceries.'

'Groceries, Captain?' the midshipman replied. 'You mean, the boxes we loaded at—?'

'I mean *groceries*, Janssen. That's all I can tell you.'

'It's a hell of a long way, Captain,' observed Mohle. 'Even with the Regelbunker full, we'll need to be very frugal with fuel... I mean, do you think we'll make it there *and* back?'

Reflecting inwardly on the one part of the orders that had come as a complete shock, even to himself – *'then recce the north coast of the Gulf of San Matias'* – Lanze shrugged.

'Quite possibly not,' he admitted, 'but once we get back into the North Atlantic, there's a chance we can rendezvous with another U-boat. Hopefully they'll have enough fuel for us to see us safely back to Norway.'

He turned to the leading telegraphist. 'Schulz, this is a particularly sensitive mission. As we approach our final position, messages on the special key Enigma will be in triple code. Secondary one-time pads are in my safe. I'll speak to you about that later.'

Lanze switched his gaze to Reidel. 'Number One, this is going to be a long patrol, and by normal standards, perhaps a fairly dull one. Nevertheless, regardless of the inactivity, we need to keep the crew energetic. Everyone must be kept physically fit and mentally alert. There'll be lots of drill.'

He flicked his attention to the midshipman. 'Janssen, I think I can say with some certainty that this will be a wearisome and boring passage. Apart from keeping the men sharp, we need to keep their vitality and interest at peak levels, so I want you to organise a routine of interesting recreational events, competitions, that sort of thing. Start with a general knowledge contest, arrange a chess tournament, cards, anything. Appoint one of the junior NCOs to lend a hand. And I'd like you to start a weekly news bulletin. Invite the men to make contributions, announce birthdays and anniversaries; you know the kind of thing. There's a lot of talent on this boat, so use it.'

The men nodded their agreement. The long troop south had begun.

32

The horizon was all the proof he needed and yet von Menen could scarcely believe his eyes – Montevideo was in sight. After twenty-six days at sea, all that stood between him and Maria now was a ten-hour ferry crossing, a warm evening breeze and... Colonel Filipe Vidal!

He disembarked at Montevideo, spent a restless night at the Hotel Pyramides followed by an even more restless day of waiting, before taking the overnight steamer to Buenos Aires.

Wednesday 14th February 1945

The ferry docked at Buenos Aires two hours after dawn. It was Valentine's Day and wonderfully warm, the sky a clear pastel blue, the air fresh and clean.

The smell of charred wood, damp rubble, gas and the nauseating stench of decaying flesh was back in Berlin. Buenos was bright, clean and alive; the buildings had walls, doors, windows and roofs; the streets and sidewalks were free of craters and debris, surrounded by a kaleidoscope of colours: purple jacarandas, tall and stately, lush green grass and the brilliance of summer flowers – petunias, snap dragons and marigolds.

Von Menen walked the entire distance to the Hotel Phoenix, carrying the doll's house by its braided handle in one hand and suitcase in the other, the encumbrance outshone by the excitement of seeing Maria.

He checked in, placed a hurried call to Maria's apartment and then, remembering that her phone would be tapped, hung up at the first ring. Instead, he rang the Clínicas, which patched him through to Maria's ward.

'Ward six, Sister speaking.'

'Doctor Maria Gomez, please?'

'You've just missed her. She's doing her rounds. Can I take a message?'

'No, thank you, but perhaps you can tell me what time she finishes duty.'

'Six o'clock this evening. Shall I say who called?'

'Er, no, thank you.'

He hung up and scribbled a brief message:

Dearest Maria,
Happy Valentine's Day.
Please meet me at Plaza Congreso, seven o'clock tonight.
Love, C.

He slipped the note inside the handkerchief he'd been carrying for over a year, placed the handkerchief inside an envelope, took it to a florist's shop on Santa Fe and asked for it to be delivered to the Clínicas with fifty red roses.

The sun was arching over the rooftops, a crimson glow fading in the west. Even the birds had retreated to the trees.

Von Menen checked his watch. It was nine o'clock and he was beginning to think that Maria would never appear. The notion of two people hurrying to meet in a wild embrace was waning.

Just then, a taxi nudged out of Avenida Montevideo and halted by the corner. A woman in a plain pink dress stepped out. A joyless look on her face, she seemed strangely lethargic, even hesitant, but it was definitely Maria.

He leapt up from the bench and waved, but her reaction was negative. No smile, no haste. Thinking that he might have been led into a Vidal-inspired trap, von Menen looked around, but could see no cause for concern.

She inched across the plaza, footsteps unwilling, face strangely severe. They were just four metres apart, von Menen sensing a dense barrier between them. He could almost feel it.

When they finally met, his affection was promptly rebuffed. Maria was cold, austere and distant, like a stranger he had never met before. When he tried to get close to her, she began to weep loudly, snatching the odd gasp of air, like a child throwing a tantrum. He moved to console her, but she pushed him away. Von Menen was awash with doubt, confusion, shock and disbelief.

'What's wrong, Maria?' he asked, wondering if he'd met the right woman.

Her hands folded into dainty fists, drumming relentlessly against his chest. 'Why? Why? Why?' she cried. 'Why did you leave me?'

Confused, he reached out for her wrists. She tried to wrestle free but he held her tight, her forehead falling upon his chest.

'Because I had to, Maria, I had to. You know that. We talked about it, remember?'

Her sobbing stopped, her face a pitiful portrait of agony, sorrow and grief. He looked at her, a deep, penetrating look, thought of Templehof Airport, saw the same tears that Sigi Bredow had shed and felt the pangs of his conscience.

'I had no idea where you were!' she shouted. 'No idea how to contact you! No inkling of when you'd come back! Nothing! And I *needed* you!'

Humiliated, he looked beyond her. When he finally had the nerve to face her again, she set him another rock-hard gaze, bristling with scorn and indictment, a look that reawakened his own anxiety. Gritting his teeth, he grabbed her by the shoulders and held her rigid.

'Don't, Maria! Don't! I don't need this anxiety! I'm sick of it!'

'*You're* sick of it? How callous, how insensitive can you be? What do you think *I've* been doing these past twelve months? I'm wasted to the core with emotion. I've cried myself dry.' Her fists were pounding his chest again, tears streaming down her cheeks. 'You – left – me – *pregnant!* Pregnant, do you hear?'

His heart froze, an anaemic shade stretching across his face. He lowered himself to the bench and buried his head in his hands. She sat down beside him, listening to him mumbling through his fingers, his voice full of guilt and remorse.

'I… God, I'm so sorry, Maria, I'm so very, very sorry. If I'd have known, I would never…' He paused and faced her, searching for something other than forgiveness. 'What…?' he paused again, the question too painful.

'I miscarried last May,' she said, 'two months after you left.'

Von Menen sat in shame and guilt, staring at the green dome atop the Congress Building.

'And your parents…?' he asked quietly.

She stole another quick breath, the tears welling up in her eyes again. 'I never told them. I didn't tell *anyone*. By then, Daddy was too ill. I just couldn't burden him further. He died last October… Another heart attack.'

Von Menen's chin dropped to his chest. 'I'm very, very sorry, Maria, truly I am.'

He moved a little closer. Grudgingly, she allowed

him to place his hand on top of hers and they sat quietly, neither saying anything, until eventually he placed his arm around her shoulder and pulled her close.

'Whatever you think, I *do* love you,' he said softly.

She regarded him with some suspicion. '*Really* love me?'

'Of course I do. I've just travelled halfway around the world to be with you,' he said, silently begging her to believe him.

'And you're back for good?'

'Yes. I won't be returning to Germany, ever!'

As they walked along Avenida de Mayo, an air of calm settled over Maria.

'Have you a hotel?' she asked.

'Yes, the Phoenix, on San Martin,' he replied weakly.

The silence lengthened again. Then, just as they crossed Talcahuano, Maria said nonchalantly, 'Remember Uncle Filipe?'

Von Menen's throat went dry. He swallowed repeatedly. 'Er, yes, of course I do.'

'He was killed in a road accident two months ago.'

She announced the news almost as indifferently as she'd mentioned the name. Von Menen's heart skipped a beat, his pace slackened, his mind spinning into overdrive. Perhaps he'd misheard.

'Sorry... what was that?' he asked timidly.

'Uncle Filipe – he was killed in a road accident, just before Christmas. His car crashed into a ravine... burst into flames.'

'A... road accident?' asked von Menen gingerly, not daring to believe his ears.

'Yes, a senior naval officer was killed with him... Ortiz, I think Mummy said his name was. The funeral was a grand affair. Everyone was there... Perón *and* his girlfriend. The army arranged everything. Aunt Isobella didn't have to do a thing.'

A ten-tonne weight of suspicion landed inside von Menen's head. *I bet the army arranged everything... the brakes, the ravine and the fire. Bet they supplied the mortician, issued the death certificate and got rid of the car, too.* It was murder; murder by car accident.

Von Menen's mind was split down the middle – an excess of remission on one side, a surfeit of doubt on the other. The question gnawed at him: *How much do the Federal Police know about me?* He needed answers and he needed them fast.

They walked in silence as far as Avenida 9 de Julio, von Menen thinking all the while. He chose his moment as they crossed the wide boulevard.

'A year ago last January, Maria, when Argentina broke off diplomatic relations with Germany, did... well, did anyone speak to you about me?'

'No. Should they have done?'

'Well, I *was* a German diplomat and I *was* ordered out of the country.'

'So?'

'Well, it's only natural to assume that the authorities would want to be sure that I'd left. I mean, somebody must have told them about *us* – Uncle Filipe, perhaps?'

'Apart from the very immediate members of my family,' she said, noting the anxious look on his face, 'hardly anyone knew who you were. None of my colleagues at the Clínicas knew much about you, and certainly none of my neighbours did. You told me not to say anything. Remember?' Her last word was seared with cynicism. 'That leaves Mummy, Aunt Isobella, my cousin Eduardo and me. Certainly no one spoke to *me* about you and no one spoke to Mummy about you, either. As for Aunt Isobella and Eduardo, if anyone had mentioned your name to them, they would have told me about it.'

They reached the Hotel Phoenix, von Menen feeling like a condemned man waiting to be sentenced; Maria seemed friendlier, though less than happy.

'So, what now?' he asked.

'I don't know,' she said. 'You've been away for over a year and suddenly, out of the blue, you turn up again, thinking nothing has changed. But it *has* changed... I've changed.' She fixed him with a searching look. 'Believe me, I very nearly didn't come this evening.'

'Is there someone else?' he asked, fearful of the answer.

'No, there isn't,' she replied, shaking her head. 'It's just that, well, a lot has happened to me this last year and I'm still trying to come to terms with it.'

'I realise that. I'm not looking for clemency.'

'I need time,' she stressed, walking away towards the taxi rank. 'I'll be in touch.'

He made his way with her along the sidewalk. 'If you do call,' he whispered, '*please* don't ask for me by name... ask for room twelve.'

She inclined her head, then got into the taxi without a backwards glance.

It was von Menen's turn to feel abandoned, like the unlucky child at the party – the music had stopped and there he was, in Buenos Aires, with no chair to sit on.

His mind spinning like a gyroscope, he reached for his suitcase, poured a large measure of cognac, sat on the edge of the bed and tried to analyse the whole damn mess.

Maria had every cause to be angry, but he felt sure he could win her over. The real test of nerve lay in the demise of Vidal and his co-conspirator, Ortiz.

If what Maria had told him was true, his name had never entered the equation; not where the Federal Police were concerned, anyway. Maybe Vidal had said nothing. Perhaps he'd never been questioned. Given the politics of Argentina, it wasn't unreasonable to suppose that he and Ortiz had been murdered on the whim of Buenos Aires intrigue.

Quite possibly, nobody knew anything about the arms shipment. Nobody in Germany knew anything about Vidal because von Menen had never revealed his name, his Nazi masters acknowledging that his secret source had never once failed to provide accurate, high-calibre information.

But his thoughts soon moved back to Maria and the question of how much he should tell her. Enlightening her with the fact that he had been in Argentina throughout her traumatic experience last May *and* when her father had been seriously ill would be like throwing petrol on a dying fire. No matter how he looked at it, he was destined for a life of invention: whatever he told Maria now would be a falsehood. The existence of Carlos Menendez was different: that much, he would have to reveal.

Von Menen's assessment of his situation was not based on the alignment of the stars or fingers-crossed hope, but on cautious reasoning – so much so that he was determined to proceed with the operation as planned, as if Vidal were still alive, as if, in fact, the coup was still in the making. What mattered now was Maria, his family, the Steigers and the half-tonne of gold. The German Foreign Office would soon be out of the equation forever.

The next day, von Menen strolled the streets of Buenos Aires looking and feeling like a free man. No one seemed to care who he was or what he was doing. No one followed him. No one watched him.

He used the opportunity to catch up on current affairs, initiating casual chats in cafés and purchasing a stack of newspapers. It seemed that during his lengthy absence, there had been a slight shift in the political mood in Argentina, with the hard-bitten Farrell-Perón regime showing some sign of softening, albeit only a flicker.

While some elements of the military still hankered for a regime of extreme National Socialism, Perón had wised up to the stark reality that he had backed a losing double – Italian fascism was dead and German Nazism was heading in the same direction. But Perón was still the undisputed champion of the national labour movement, with an ardent following of several million die-hard Peronists.

With one eye on the ballot box and the other on international opinion, the guileful Perón, ably assisted by the glamorous Eva Duarte, was *hinting* at the advancement of a democratic Argentina. At least, that's what some people thought.

Languishing on a bench in Plaza San Martin, von Menen checked the date on his copy of *La Nación* – Thursday 15th February – and calculated that Jürgen would be on his way.

With that thought, images of his parents, Katrina, Hans and Greta Steiger crept into his mind, followed by that of Sigi Bredow. And with the beseeching memory of Sigi haunting him, his fretting about Maria drifted into a haze, though only briefly. *'I need some time… I'll be in touch.'*

How much time? A day? A week? A month?

Two days later, there was a light knock on von Menen's door. It was nine o'clock and he was about to go out for dinner.

'There's a call for you in the lobby, señor,' said the bellboy. 'A lady.'

Von Menen hastened downstairs and picked up the receiver.

'Hello!'

'It's me. I'd like you to come over... that is, if you want to.'

'Of course I do, Maria. But are you...?'

'Sure? I'm as sure as I'll ever be.'

Supper was already prepared and the table laid, an air of welcome calmness over the room, Maria noticeably warmer.

When they sat down, she spoke endlessly about her late father, the general state of the country, Perón and 'that woman Eva', but after a while, she realised his thoughts were a million miles away, his face blank and expressionless.

'You're not listening, are you?'

'I'm sorry, Maria... it's just that, well, there's something on my mind, something I need to speak to you about. The reason...' he hesitated, not knowing where to begin.

'Go on,' she prompted.

'The reason why I left in such haste last year was to try and salvage something from the worsening diplomatic situation between Germany and Argentina. As it happened, I failed.'

Lie number one. He stared momentarily at the large juicy steak on his plate.

'As soon as I arrived home, I realised that Germany was facing certain defeat. From that moment, I contrived to get back to Argentina... back to you.'

Seeing the intense quandary on his face, she reached across the table and took hold of his hand. 'There's something else, isn't there?' she asked fearfully.

'Maria, Germany is one big mess. If I sat at this table for a whole month I couldn't explain the true depth of the situation. It's catastrophic. Germany is finished. The whole country's in ruins. Everywhere, people are just waiting for the Allies to pick over the bones.'

'Surely, it can't be that bad,' said Maria. 'I've read that the Russians are close to Berlin, but—'

'It's bad, Maria,' he said, cutting her short, 'desperately bad. It's an absolute nightmare.'

'And Berlin itself?'

'Berlin?' He shook his head despondently. 'What do you remember about Berlin?' His voice was quiet and solemn.

She shrugged. 'Unter den Linden, Kurfürstendamm, the Tiergarten, I suppose.'

'And what do you remember best about Kurfürstendamm?' he asked, anticipating her reply.

'Kaufhaus des Westens?'

He strained across the table, appealing for some real understanding. 'If you went to KaDeWe right now, Maria, all you'd be able to buy is rubble. It's gone... the same as thousands of other buildings in Berlin. You cannot believe the level of destruction. Practically the whole of Wilhelmstrasse is in ruins. Unter den Linden is much the same. Remember the Hotel Kaiserhof?'

'Yes.'

'Wrecked... The whole city's a huge pile of rubble. There's hardly any form of communication. Trains and buses, what's left of them, operate when they can.' He looked again at his plate. 'This kind of meal is unheard of; food is getting scarcer by the day. The country is disintegrating.'

She sat in silent trepidation, her face stricken by the news. It was not the Germany she remembered.

'That's not the all of it,' he cautioned. 'The worst is yet to come.'

'What do you mean?'

'The Russians... I read in the newspapers that they're within a short train ride of Berlin.' His mind flashed back to Mecklenburg. 'Hopefully, my family will be leaving for Flensburg soon. And then… they're hoping to come here, to Argentina.'

'But that's wonderful! When?'

'As soon as they can; like me, they've got false papers.'

She looked at him, a half-curious, half-puzzled look in her eyes. 'False papers, *like you*? Does that mean… you're no longer Carl von Menen?'

'Yes. I've got a passport in the name of Carlos Menendez… but that's not to say I intend to remain Carlos Menendez. Does it make a difference?'

'Personally, no,' she replied, her surprised look turning to one of amusement. 'But what will I tell Mummy?'

'That's where I have to ask you to be patient, Maria. Frankly, I don't think we should enlighten your mother, not for a while, anyway. I need to lay low for at least a couple of months, until I've sorted things out.' He reached out for her hand. 'I need to be very cautious,' he said. 'All I'm asking is that you be patient a while longer. Perhaps it would be best if I took an apartment a little further out of town, maybe somewhere the other side of the Congress Building. I'm not asking you to leave this place – not permanently, anyway – but I would like you to come and join me, at some stage.'

She pursed her lips and thought for a moment. 'Am I to understand from all this that your return to Argentina is to remain a secret, that you don't want me to tell anyone, including Mummy?'

'Yes, that's precisely what I'm asking you.'

'Well, as far as Mummy's concerned, it's not a problem. She and Aunt Isobella left for the United States last week and they're likely to be away for at least eight, maybe nine, months.' She noted the look of apprehension on his face. 'There's something else?'

'Yes. I need you to appreciate that there are certain things I have to do.'

'Such as?'

'Well, occasionally, I'll have to go away for a while, disappear for the odd few days. I need your understanding on that.'

'I've put up with you being away for the past year, Carl, remember? So I don't suppose the odd day here and there will be that difficult.'

The following week, when the evening traffic had subsided, von Menen took a taxi to a street north of the Congress Building, between Rivadavia and Corrientes, and agreed a six-month lease on a two-bedroom furnished apartment. He moved in the very next day. Maria joined him a few days later.

A deluge of love and affection, aided by warm balmy nights and the soft silk sheets von Menen had often dreamed about, helped turn the clock back. Soon, their relationship was on an even keel. But von Menen was still plagued by the tormenting image of Sigi Bredow at Tempelhof. It wouldn't go away and he wasn't sure that he wanted it to.

Something was lingering in Maria's mind, too – a shade of doubt, a hint of suspicion. The name had changed, but so had the man. Carlos Menendez was not the man she had met in 1941. But for some strange, peculiar reason, which she couldn't explain, even to herself, she willingly accepted the bizarre and intriguing existence he had fostered upon her.

In a perverse kind of way, she even acquired a buzz of excitement from it – watching his sudden moves whenever a letter fell through the mail box, the telephone rang or a car pulled up outside. She especially liked it when he asked her to arrange a post box number and send a tele-type message to Juan Cortes.

Von Menen had been back in Argentina for over a fortnight and the need to signal Germany was weighing heavily on him, which meant, as warned, he would need to disappear for a few days. Maria took the announcement calmly. Smiling, she kissed him on the cheek and reminded him that when he returned, she would doubtless be on duty at the hospital.

He took the morning train to Dolores, continued by coach to the coast and made the last twelve miles by taxi.

Jorge Rosas spotted the taxi as it turned in front of the cottage. He tied up his horse and hurried to meet his friend and mentor.

'Hello, Jorge. Good to see you again.'

A coy smile rippled across Rosas' face, a garbled greeting sounding from his lips, hands and eyes doing all the "talking".

'Are you well?' asked von Menen.

Rosas reached into his pocket, pulled out the moth-eaten exercise book which von Menen had given him some six months earlier, and studied it closely.

'Yaahh, dan-ka, Herrrr Men-en-dez.'

'Excellent, Jorge. Well done.'

Rosas held out his hands, a sad look in his eyes.

'My grandfather?'

Rosas nodded.

'He died, last December.' The sombre note in his voice added substance to the lie, the deceit coming naturally, as if, in fact, his grandfather really had died.

Respectfully, Rosas dipped his head. Then, with a gesture of helpfulness, he looked up and pointed to the shed.

'My car?' asked von Menen. 'It's okay? Every Sunday, you drove it to the end of the track and back, as I asked you to?'

Rosas nodded.

'You've kept the battery charged? And the battery on the boat?'

More nods.

'Good man, Jorge, thank you.'

With a fistful of pesos in his hand, Rosas happily set off.

The evening was warm, still and quiet, with only the hissing sound of the radio and the velvety *tap, tap* of the silent Morse key for company.

At eleven-forty, von Menen's signal was picked up by his old "friend", Albert Falk. A moment later, off went the short message:

HELLO. AKROBAT ON STATION.

Von Menen switched to the "Receive" section. The acknowledgement, brief and joyous, came within seconds:

THANK YOU. ANDROMEDA ETA 10 MARCH.

Jürgen was expected in less than two weeks!

Repeated knocking on the door to Enrique Rivera's house failed to draw any attention. Eventually, a neighbour came out and explained. Bowing to family pressure, Enrique had moved out just before Christmas and was now living with his eldest daughter at Dolores.

Von Menen continued along to the quay, the ordinarily brown waters of the River Ajo glistening beneath a clear blue sky.

Hibernating beneath a swathe of grey tarpaulin, *Margarita* was as still as the day itself. He removed the coverings, fitted the battery and filled the fuel tank. At the third crank, the engine fired into life.

After six months of idleness, *Margarita* was "breathing" again.

33

In Mecklenburg, snow had been falling steadily for three days, leaving the burned-out hulk of the Steyr looking like a misshapen igloo.

Hans and Greta Steiger had already left for Flensburg in the BMW, leaving the General, Anna and Katrina to join them on Wednesday.

With only four cards standing on the lid of the Steinway, Katrina's birthday had passed almost unnoticed, but it mattered little to her. The Russians were less than forty miles from Berlin, and the only thought on her mind was that of escape.

Some 800 kilometres to the west, where the southern reaches of the Lincolnshire Wolds met the vast open landscape that had become the main springboard of the Allies' bomber offensive, the weather was less gloomy. Spring was just a few weeks away, snowdrops were out and crocuses were beginning to break bud.

In the cosiness of her farmhouse kitchen, homely Jenny Chatsworth busied herself around a blackened stove, stealing an occasional glimpse through the window, one eye on the weather, the other on the five-bar gate at the end of the yard. Her baking done, a tray of cakes lay cooling on the table, the kettle whistling merrily on the hob. Soon, her husband Wilf would be in from the fields.

Upstairs, their son John, twenty-five, full-time bomber pilot and would-be farmer, had washed, shaved and slipped into his uniform. The choice had been his: four shires, a Fordson tractor, a pitchfork and the "reserve" occupation of farmer, or something else. He'd chosen the "something else" – the blue serge battle dress of the Royal Air Force, now embroidered with the insignia of a flight lieutenant and the blue-and-white ribbon of the Distinguished Flying Cross. A warrior of the skies.

Hands the size of the unabridged version of the Oxford dictionary and shoulders to match, John Chatsworth was about to embark on the routine he disliked so much, wondering if his parting words to his parents would be the same as they'd been the last time. *'Well, Mum, I'll be off, then. Don't worry about me... promise?'* His mother would smile, or try to. *'Cheerio, Dad. See you later.'* – fingers crossed in the knowledge that "later" might easily be 'never'.

And the "never" list was growing: his brother George, lost at El Alamein in 1942; cousin Harry, fallen on the beaches at Normandy; Uncle Les, swallowed up by the jungles of Burma; and his old school pal Henry "Harold" Larwood, killed in action during the ill-fated raid on Nuremberg. Chatsworth sat on the edge of his bed, staring at the photograph of George, a lump rising in his throat.

There was also, however, one particular photograph that brightened his eyes and lifted his spirits. He picked up the letter lying beside it and slipped it in his tunic pocket, the contents still fresh in his mind.

I'll be home Monday evening... arriving on the last bus from Lincoln... a candle in my window by the time the church clock chimes ten...

Please, take care. See you tomorrow.
Love you lots, Jean.

He adored her, loved her deeply, her green eyes, long blonde hair and a girlish face that could turn the heads of a whole squadron. Jean was the *real* wind beneath his wings. With luck, they'd be married at the end of May.

By then, God willing, the war would be over; peace, a new future, a home of their own, lush green meadows and sandcastles on the beach at Mablethorpe. It was tantalisingly close. Yet though his tour was almost finished – twenty-nine down, one to go – the haunting fear was still there: a burst of cannon fire, flak, a ball of fire and then... gone.

Chatsworth sighed, picked up his bag and headed downstairs. His parents, smiling uncomfortably, were waiting by the kitchen table; the same old act of bravado, a mixture of angst and love. He dealt with it in his usual inimitable fashion.

'How's the weather, Dad?'

'Oh, still unsettled, son, but it's improving. Sky's beginning to...' He halted, aware that clear skies and a full moon were the dread of every night-time bomber pilot.

Chatsworth rolled off the familiar words, the ritual following its usual pattern. 'Right, then, I'll be off. See you both later.'

His mother stood before him, reached up on her toes, cupped his face in her hands and kissed him on the cheek. 'Take care, now,' she whispered.

'I'll be fine, Mum. Don't worry. And don't come out, it's too cold.'

From the door, they watched him cross the yard to the open barn and toss the bag of cakes his mother had baked onto the back seat of his car. One last wave, a honk on the horn and he was gone, looking like a cuckoo in a blue tit's nest behind the wheel of his tiny Austin 7.

Chatsworth took the long, circuitous route to the aerodrome, the car flat-out by the time he'd reached High Barn, spluttering and wheezing on a mixture of tractor paraffin and one-hundred octane aircraft fuel. Thanks to a deserted road and a moderate tail wind, he made East Kirkby bomber base in a record twelve minutes.

The base was alive with activity: noisy tractors hauling bomb-laden trailers; bowsers feeding fuel-hungry Lancasters; colonies of engineers, technicians and armourers; blue and khaki everywhere. Inside the officers' mess, the atmosphere was buzzing. A group of men stood huddled beside the notice board, eyes glued to the newly posted battle order. Chatsworth's navigator, Eddie Sutherland, was at the head of the throng.

'Well, Eddie?'

'Affirmative! It's bacon and eggs for us, Johnny boy. We're on! *Yorker*'s going tonight; our last sortie.'

'What time's the briefing?'

Sutherland scythed his way through the horde of blue. 'Two o'clock... If you don't mind, I'll grab a couple of hours' kip. Had a late one last night, young beaut' from Skeggy... I think she loves me. You okay?'

'Ask me tomorrow.'

'Know what you mean. Anyway, how's that beautiful green-eyed WREN of yours?'

'Still beautiful, still green-eyed.'

'Lucky devil. And to think, you'll have all those haystacks to romp on in the summer.'

'Away with you... see you at two. And don't be late.'

The curtains were drawn, the lights on, a dense milky-white smoke hovering above the heads of 150 airmen, short-cropped hair glistening with Brilliantine, battle-hardened heroes alongside "second dickey" novices. Some were laughing, some were talking, while some were given to quiet reflection.

'Attention, gentlemen, please!' called the Squadron Adjutant.

The chattering stopped, the room fell silent, a mass of blue serge rising to its feet. In walked the Station Commander, followed by a string of officers, from Squadron Commander to Gunnery Leader.

'Enter the board of management,' whispered Ken Betts, Chatsworth's flight engineer.

Wing Commander Danny Beaumont scythed his way through the fug and climbed on to the stage.

'Gentlemen, please sit down,' he said, drawing back a pair of faded green curtains to reveal the night's target. 'For those of you hiding lighted cigarettes and perhaps burning your fingers, or, more importantly, the uniform of His Majesty's Royal Air Force, you may *continue* to smoke,' he added dryly. A barrage of lighters and the smell of high octane fuel filled the room – the tobacco barons of West Virginia were back in business.

The tapes on the chart led directly to the city of Kiel, but with one curious addition. At the end of the well-worn path to the East Coast of Schleswig Holstein, the tape dipped south, terminating at a point between Lübeck and Travemünde.

'Gentlemen,' said Beaumont in a loud voice, 'tonight, Group is putting up 220 aircraft, including twenty Lancs from our own squadron. The main target is Kiel.'

A voice rang out from the middle of the hall. 'Not Kiel again, sir! Can't we go somewhere nice and warm for a change?'

'Afraid not, Mr Braithwaite,' replied Beaumont, homing

in on the source of the facetious comment. 'Adolf has run out of warm places... besides, since your flight will be the last to leave, it ought to be nice and warm by the time you get there.' A rustle of laughter spread through the hall. 'Now, some of you are quite familiar with the Kiel run, but this time it's different, so try and keep awake.' He drew his pointer along the length of the narrow tape. 'While your route will be at the usual 20,000 feet, your bombing level will be *8,000* feet.'

The hall filled with sharp intakes of breath. A battle-worn flight lieutenant, wearing the DFC and bar, sprang to his feet. 'That's a bit low, isn't it, sir? I mean, we'll be going in courtesy of the Lincolnshire Road Car Company next.'

More laughter.

'Point taken, Mr Saville, but this job has got to be done accurately.' Beaumont turned to a young, seemingly diffident officer standing by his side, a roll of charts tucked under his arm. 'Gentlemen, allow me to introduce our new Met man, Flight Lieutenant Crawford. He joined us only a few days ago.'

Crawford cleared his throat. 'Gentlemen,' he said, a hint of nerves in his voice, 'the weather has remained unsettled for the past few days.' A chorus of cheers rang up from all quarters. 'But I anticipate some changes later this afternoon, perhaps even clear skies by eight o'clock tonight.' The cheers gave way to groans. 'Winds are easterly, light to moderate, and by late evening they should have eased further still. And...' – Crawford stalled, conscious of the recoil his next announcement would bring – 'the moon is almost full.'

Amid widespread groans of discontent, Dixie Deans, Chatsworth's tail gunner, a pugnacious cockney who had seen more action in the skies above Germany than he had in all of his bare-knuckle days along London's Mile End Road, leaned forward and tapped his mate, Tommy Reynolds, on the shoulder.

'There you go, Tommy,' he whispered. 'You know what you're always saying about your mother-in-law. Well, tonight's your chance... you'll be able to see her jumping over it!'

'And finally,' Crawford continued, 'when you reach the German coast, you can expect medium scattered cloud, becoming a continuous sheet, especially on your approach to target.' He turned to Beaumont. 'I think that's it, sir,' he said, with some relief.

'Thank you, Flight Lieutenant Crawford.'

Crawford was followed by the intelligence officer, the navigation leader and the bombing leader, all with their own words of "advice", before Beaumont took up the reins again.

'Gentlemen,' Beaumont said, 'you will be pleased to know that you will not be alone in the skies over the Reich tonight. Numbers four, six and eight groups are going to Essen with 400 aircraft. A further 250 aircraft from one and three groups will be visiting Gelsenkirchen, while another forty-eight aircraft will be involved on radio counter-measure sorties. In addition, some seventy Mosquitos will be on Siren tours across Germany, and you'll be heartened to learn that our glorious allies have been bombing synthetic oil plants all day long. So, while you can anticipate the usual anti-aircraft fire as you cross the coast and approach target, I doubt you'll see many fighters. They're as rare as rocking horse dung these days.'

A wag of a flight sergeant sitting at the back of the room stood to his feet and raised his hand. 'Excuse me, sir,' he said, 'what was that you said... rocking horse...?'

'*Dung*, Jackson, but for you, I'll rephrase it to rocking

horse *shit*; you know, the stuff you've been up to your neck in ever since you arrived here.'

The room erupted with laughter; even Jackson saw the funny side of it.

Beaumont returned to the wall chart. 'There is a secondary target tonight,' he said, 'which calls for a slightly different task by six of our own aircraft.'

He announced the six call signs. *Yorker* was one of them. When the room had cleared of all but those concerned, Beaumont tapped the aerial photograph with his pointer.

'This was taken three days ago,' he said. 'The location is Priwall, south side of the River Trave and opposite Travemünde.' The pointer indicated as he talked. 'The intelligence boys reckon that the jetty, which runs north to south, is about 150 yards long. These four objects either side of it are your targets.'

'Can't quite see from here, sir, but are they submarines?'

'Yes, Cosworth, they're submarines, though not *ordinary* submarines. They're the new, ocean-going electro type. Your task is to destroy them...' – he paused and fixed each of the six pilots a look – 'from 5,000 feet.'

There was a unified sigh of disbelief.

'Hush, gentlemen,' said Beaumont, searching for the dapper Flight Lieutenant Saville. 'Sorry, Sammy, but the six of you will be on your own – there'll be no help from the Lincolnshire Road Car Company!'

Chatsworth spoke over the mutterings. 'What about fighters and anti-aircraft batteries, sir?'

'I'm coming to that now, John,' replied Beaumont, drawing a reassuring look from the briefing intelligence officer. 'Perhaps you'll encounter the odd fighter, but even that's very doubtful...'

'One is one too many,' muttered Ken Betts.

'On the minus side,' continued Beaumont, 'the odds

are you'll encounter more than the usual amount of anti-aircraft fire.' He flicked another quick glance at the intelligence officer. 'The number of anti-aircraft gun emplacements in the neighbourhood is uncommonly high,' he said sombrely. 'Other than that, intelligence has nothing to add.'

A voice piped up from the second row. 'Markers, sir? What colour?'

'Yellow. But remember, Kiel is red. Any other questions? No? Then good luck.'

Chatsworth grabbed a quick cup of tea, then went off in search of his navigator.

Eddie Sutherland was surrounded by maps, weather reports and astrology charts; sharpened pencils, slide rules and calculator at the ready.

'Well, Eddie, it's a bit different. Never been to this Priwall place before; can't say I'm looking forward to it, either, not from 5,000 feet with all that flak around.'

'Yeah, looks as though we might be in for a fair old ride over target... not to mention the bloody welcome we'll get over Jerry's coast,' agreed Sutherland.

Chatsworth peered at the paperwork. 'So, what do you reckon?'

'Getting there won't be a problem,' replied Sutherland. 'True course is 076. For Kiel, you'll need to steer magnetic 081 and follow the main stream in from Helgoland. We'll skirt Kiel to the south, make over Preetz and turn on to 183 magnetic, just short of Lensahn. That'll place us virtually due north of target, with just twenty nautical to go. It means we'll be running the entire length of the target. After the release, you can do a one-eighty port, come north over the Mecklenburger Bucht and Fehmarn

Island, and pick up the wake of the main force east of Flensburg.'

'Time to target?'

Sutherland studied his calculations. 'Headwind fifteen... groundspeed 185... assuming seven minutes to the Lincolnshire Riviera, we ought to pass over the German coast in just under an hour and fifty-seven. As for target, I'd say two hours forty-three.'

'Sounds good to me, Eddie. Now, let's get some grub before the vultures scoff the lot.'

The warm-up drills complete, the time for pre-flight rituals had arrived.

Dixie Deans relieved himself over the tail wheel, the wireless operator obsessively kissed the same fifteen rivets on the starboard side and last, but not least, the bomb aimer "Chalkie" White picked ten blades of grass from beside the apron and pushed each one inside his left boot.

Back on board, Chatsworth called up the crew.

'Okay, Skipper!' crackled through his headset half a dozen times.

Yorker was ready to go, ground crew waiting for the word to 'prime'. Signalling the forward ground mechanic, Chatsworth took the throttles.

'Right, Ken, we have it.'

Betts rolled his head, selected the magneto switch, pressed the starter button and the starboard inner fired up, smoke belching from the twelve exhausts, the prop stammering. Then, with a deafening roar, the mighty Rolls Royce Merlin thundered into life.

'Brake pressure two-thirty, Skipper,' said Betts, glancing at the brake pressure dial.

The port inner fired up, the port outer and, finally, the starboard outer.

'Port generator okay, Skipper,' called the wireless operator.

The four Merlins howled a thunderous roar, *Yorker* vibrating like a giant tuning fork, the noise deafening. Chocks clear, brakes off. Seven men and thirty tonnes began to roll. Like a leashed greyhound straining for the "off", the bomber stood waiting at the end of the runway.

'Come on. Aerodrome Control Pilot,' muttered Betts impatiently. 'Give us the light… GREEN! All clear, Skipper.'

Chatsworth glanced at his watch – one minute past eight. His powerful hand encased the four throttles, easing them forward gently, the port outer marginally in advance of the others, countering the bomber's habit of swinging to port. The speed picked up, fifty… seventy… ninety knots, the tail lifting, the ground rushing by, the whole crew feeling the ride.

The heavy bomber clawed itself into the cold, dark skies above Lincolnshire and set course for Germany, seven men harbouring the same haunting thought: *Will we be back?*

At 21h04, *Yorker* crossed the German coast, the skies a patchwork of low scattered clouds and sporadic bursts of flak.

Welcome to the Third Reich.

Some minutes later, "Chalkie" White reported red markers ten miles ahead, the pathfinders already over Kiel.

Suddenly, the heavens erupted. Bursts of anti-aircraft fire peppered the night sky, the probing, menacing beams of high-powered lights sweeping through the darkness. A voice crackled over the intercom.

'Mid upper to Skipper.'

'Go ahead, Tommy.'

'One of our lot's been "coned", Skipper, just above us,

rear of the starboard wing... a half-dozen lights on him. Looks as though he's sitting on top of the Koh-i-Noor diamond.'

Seconds later, Reynolds came back, his voice more hurried.

'He's been hit, Skipper, port wing's blazing like a furnace!'

'Keep your eyes peeled for chutes, Tommy.'

'Shouldn't be too difficult, Skipper... talk about Blackpool illuminations! Wait. One's out... two... three... four... five... six... seven. They're all clear, Skipper.'

'Well done, Tommy.'

South-east of Kiel, "Chalkie" White eased himself gingerly into a prostrate position above the emergency floor hatch below the forward turret. Suddenly, Dixie Deans came on the air, a real sense of urgency in his voice.

'Skipper! Fighter! Starboard quarter... a 110, I think... he's turning on to us! Corkscrew starboard, Skipper! GO! GO! GO!'

Chatsworth flung the bomber into a steep, diving turn. 'Diving starboard!' he called, as a short burst of cannon fire swished over the tail plane. 'Rolling! Diving port!'

Deans, flying by the seat of his pants, opened up with a halo of fire from his quartet of Brownings.

'Climbing port!' shouted Chatsworth. 'Rolling... climbing starboard... levelling out... 10,000. You okay, Dixie?'

The gutsy Deans replied in typical cockney humour.

'Affirmative, Skipper, you've lost him. Blimey, he weren't half shiftin'; must be trying to make the last show at the Windmill Theatre.'

Never lost for the odd spot of banter himself, Tommy Reynolds piped up in his broad Lancashire accent – 'Or the last bleedin' waltz at the Blackpool Tower Ballroom!'

'Okay, okay, quiet now,' interrupted Chatsworth. 'Well done, everyone. The fun's over. Keep your eyes peeled. We still have a job to do.'

They flew on in silence, until Eddie Sutherland piped up.

'Navigator to Skipper... six minutes to target. Turn starboard, one-eight-three... get down to bombing height.'

Chatsworth brought the Lancaster around and began the final approach. "Chalkie" White, not to be outdone by the meticulous calculations of Eddie Sutherland, had spotted the handiwork of two Mosquitos.

'Yellow markers ahead, Skipper,' he called.

White waited for his cue, a curtain of pom-pom fire racing up from below, chased by streams of tracer arcing lazily and gracefully through the night sky past the Lancaster like a trail of shooting stars.

'Bomb aimer, it's all yours,' called Chatsworth.

'Gotcha, Skip. Steady, now. Five degrees starboard... coming on nicely... another two degrees starboard... stead-eee... stead-eee. Left, left. Bomb doors open. Stead-eee, Skip, stead-eee. Hold it there, Skipper!'

There was a pregnant pause.

'Bombs gone, Skipper. Hold her steady a tick, I need a photograph.'

White eased himself round in the tight confines of the bomb aimer's compartment, opened the small aperture at the rear, shone his flashlight into the bomb bay and rubbed his eyes.

'Skipper!' he shouted. 'We have a hang-up.'

'Hang-up?'

'Affirmative, Skipper, just one.'

White worked his fingers hurriedly along a panel of switches.

'Any luck, Chalkie?'

'Sorry, Skip, I've tried every switch and she's still there. Only one thing left for it...'

White scrambled out of his cramped compartment, squeezed past the engineer, the navigator and finally the wireless operator. Easing himself across the main spar, he prized up one of the floor plates, the bomb hanging directly below. Prostrate across the floor, White got to work, first with a long screwdriver and then with a tool that looked something like a fisherman's gaff.

'She's free, Skipper, gone! Bomb doors closing.'

'Well done, Chalkie. Okay, everyone, we're going home.'

Seconds later, there was a vivid flash in the blacked-out countryside below.

'Bet that caused a flutter in some poor old farmer's chicken run,' said Dixie Deans.

Chatsworth made a 180-degree turn and gunned the Lancaster over the Mecklenburger Bucht. Beyond Kiel, he swung west, placed the bomber on a course for the North Sea and the pacifying shores of England. Dancing in his mind was the joyous sight of a candle, flickering in the bedroom window of a green-eyed WREN at Little Steeping.

Welcome home, sweet Johnny, welcome home.

34

Andromeda was 550 nautical miles south of the Equator, the sea as calm as a city canal, the night sky peppered with shimmering stars.

In the confines of his cramped quarters, Jürgen Lanze was in a buoyant mood, confident that he would reach his penultimate position by 9ᵗʰ March. Stripped of fatigues, the crew worked and relaxed in the comfort of shorts. Spirits were high and the mood was jovial. Those not sleeping took turns on deck, smoking, talking or simply gazing in awe at the heavenly spectacle.

The welcome change in the weather brought further conjecture. Some thought they were making for South Africa; others, Chile; while the jokers insisted that they were heading for a remote island in the South Pacific, a palm-clad hut and a hula-hula girl for each man.

Down in the galley, the cook's excitement was mounting. If the doctor's predictions were right, the very next day, Franz Rouff would be a father for the third time. A young torpedo mechanic from Dresden did a hurried mock calculation on his fingers, devilishly inquiring how on earth it could be, when, for the whole of last June and July, the crew had been at the Blom and Voss yard at Hamburg, while Frau Rouff had been at Stuttgart.

The stocky Rouff, weighing half the size of a Friesian bull, picked up a frying pan and held it close to the young man's nose. 'You might have been at Hamburg, sonny, but I was at Stuttgart,' he growled.

In the wardroom, Janssen was laying the foundations for the next weekly news-sheet as Mohle and Krauz, the giants of the chessboard, prepared to do battle in the first semi-final of the chess championship.

When Lanze appeared on the bridge, Reidel, smitten by the eminence of Sirius, was singing to himself.

'What was that, Horst?' asked Lanze, a puzzled look on his face.

'Oh, just doing my Richard Tauber bit...'

Lanze raised an eyebrow.

'You know, "A tropical moon, a sleepy lagoon"?'

'Sorry, Horst, you know me, couldn't tell the difference between Strauss and a set of church bells. My wife would gladly confirm that.'

At that, Schulz poked his head and shoulders above the hatch, stretched out his arm and tugged at the hem of Reidel's trousers. Reidel turned and Schulz, his face full of silent futility, flicked his head, beckoning the officer below.

Looking like the grim reaper himself, Schulz handed Reidel a half-flimsy, Reidel's eyes falling on the short, heart-wrenching message.

PERSONAL: FOR KORVETTENKAPITÄN LANZE. REGRETS. WIFE AND PARENTS-IN-LAW KILLED IN AIR RAID, MONDAY 26TH*. DEEPEST CONDOLENCES. DÖNITZ.*

Reidel propped himself up against the periscope housing and read the message again.

'*Dear God.*'

'I thought it only right to inform you first, sir.'

Reidel took a long, deep breath and sighed heavily. 'You were right to do that, Manfred. Thank you.'

As soon as Schulz had gone, Reidel ushered a short message to the bridge.

'Number One, sir.'

'Go ahead, Horst.'

'Sir, Captain Only message, in your quarters.'

'I'm on my way.'

Lanze pulled back the long green curtain and found Reidel standing beside the bunk, a silent, heart-aching look of grief on his face. The words 'I'm deeply sorry, Jürgen,' had scarcely left his lips when Lanze raised his hand, waved away the awkward agony and sat down. Staring longingly at the smiling photograph of Katrina sitting on his desk, he drew his hand across his face and, with a twisted look, he spoke.

'How strange, Horst. For some inexplicable reason, I always knew there'd be a problem. It must have been, well, premature, I suppose.'

Reidel looked again at the message, then sat down on the edge of the bunk. 'Jürgen,' he said quietly, his voice labouring, 'I'm... I'm afraid it's not *just* the baby.'

A parched, arid feeling settled in Lanze's throat. He tried to swallow, but he couldn't. His body was limp and cold, a prickly, nauseating sensation in his stomach.

'No, Horst, it can't be,' he croaked. 'Not Katrina. I don't...' He shook his head. 'It's a mistake, it *must* be a mistake.'

Reidel put an arm around Lanze's shoulders. 'I'm sorry, Jürgen, I'm deeply, deeply sorry, but I'm afraid it's true. Your parents-in-law, General von Menen and his wife... they were killed, too. It was an air raid,' he said softly.

Eyes misting with tears, Lanze picked up the photograph of his wife and pressed it to his chest, gripping it so tight that his knuckles turned white.

'If you don't mind, Horst,' he said, looking completely dazed, 'I'd like to be left alone for a while.'

'Of course, Jürgen. I understand.'

Reidel placed the message reverently on the desk and left the cabin.

Friday 2nd March 1945

Von Menen returned to the cottage, taking with him twelve cases of wine, half a dozen bottles of cognac, several cartons of cigarettes and four boxes of cigars, which he stored at the hut alongside *Margarita*.

A little after midnight, he began decoding the latest signal from Berlin. At first, it seemed routinely concise – OK POLARIS ETA 10 MARCH – but the dots and the dashes kept coming.

Unlike Jürgen, there was no one to soften the impact, understand the emotions or extend the much-needed comfort of sympathy. Instead, von Menen was about to become his own private messenger, the unwitting self-harbinger of grief and horror.

He had already deciphered the words "Mother", "Father" and "Sister", but not until he'd reached the first syllable of the word "killed" did the ice-cold feeling of fear and panic race down his spine. The morbid horror of war had finally reached its way into Carl von Menen's life. In one harsh, cruel moment, the spectre of Germany had come back to haunt him. The von Menen dream was in ruins.

Devastated, confused and lonely, he sat down on his bed and cried unashamedly.

At first light, totally dispirited, von Menen boarded *Margarita* and headed for the tranquillity of the open sea.

That evening, he called Maria from the local hotel and told her he would not be back for at least ten days. Hiding the existence of the transceiver, he said nothing about the disastrous news from Germany. She sensed that something was wrong, but she did not ask what.

Von Menen sank beneath a blanket of deep depression, Maria a hazy image. All he could see now was a recurrent vision of the three people who had meant so much in his life, surpassed occasionally by the consoling notion of Jürgen's imminent arrival, the hope of mutual solace and the answer to a question that was piling agonising uncertainty upon crushing grief – had Hans and Greta Steiger survived?

As the days passed, von Menen emerged slowly from his shell of sorrow and heartache, and began focusing on the matter of his rendezvous with *Andromeda*.

He drove into town and refilled *Margarita*'s three spare fuel cans. If Rivera's advice was right, it would, he hoped, be enough to cover the round trip to the rendezvous point.

★

Friday 9th March 1945

Jürgen Lanze was slowly coming to terms with the reality of what had been the most devastating news he had received in his entire life. Though it was heartrendingly difficult, he was beginning to think like a commanding officer again.

Reidel, who had shouldered much of the responsibility for the running of the boat, had shown unswerving loyalty and support, as had the rest of the crew.

Thanks to Krauz's reckoning, *Andromeda* was bang on schedule. At seven o'clock on Friday evening, Lanze sent another signal to U-boat headquarters – ANDROMEDA ETA AKROBAT 21h00 LOCAL 10 MARCH.

Following a westerly course, with just 112 nautical miles to go, Lanze trimmed the boat for snorkel depth and began the final run to the rendezvous point. Von Menen received the relayed signal from the Foreign Office a little after midnight.

Saturday 10th March 1945

At three o'clock in the morning, *Andromeda*, now running on her electric motors, crossed the 100-metre contour. Seven hours later, the first note of warning echoed through the control room.

'Less than thirty metres beneath the keel, Captain.'

Lanze flicked a glance at his Number One. 'In a few hours, Horst,' he said calmly, 'there'll be a lot less than thirty metres under the keel.'

To the west, *Margarita* was clear of the coast and less than three hours from the rendezvous point, intermittent flashes from the Cabo San Antonio Lighthouse growing steadily dimmer.

On board the submarine, the depth of water was decreasing rapidly.

'You have fifteen metres beneath the keel, Captain!' called Janssen.

Moments later, the readings came thick and fast.

'Twelve metres, Captain… ten… eight metres, Captain.'

Unconcerned by Janssen's uneasy expression, Reidel shrugged as the boat maintained a cautious six knots, a constant eight metres beneath the keel. Lanze was savouring the thought of the last twenty miles when Janssen yelled out.

'Five metres beneath the keel, Captain!'

Reidel moved across the control room, stood behind the operator, eyes glued to the needle on the fathometer.

'Four metres, Captain... three... two...!'

Janssen looked anxiously at Mohle, then glanced quickly at Reidel, a mild tremor passing through the deck plating. *Andromeda* had "kissed" the bottom and was skimming along the ocean floor.

A minute later, a note of optimism from Janssen.

'Two metres beneath the keel, Captain.'

Lanze turned to Meyer and caught the look of relief on his face, both smiling as the next two readings were shouted out.

'Four metres, Captain... five metres. You still have five metres, Captain.'

Lanze checked his watch. Nine o'clock. A smile rippled across his face.

'Both engines, stop! Up periscope!' he shouted.

The hydraulics whined. Lanze stood back, removed his cap and wiped the perspiration from his brow and neck. Replacing his cap, the peak hanging over his collar, he peered through the scope, the horizon empty. Then, as he swept over the starboard bow a second time, he froze, a small vessel less than a thousand metres ahead.

'New course: two-nine-zero... slow ahead!' he called.

Soon, the vessel was less than 500 metres away, sitting in mirror-smooth seas beneath a sickle moon, pennants of white, black and white limp on the masthead.

It has to be Carl.

Through the darkness, von Menen couldn't see the gentle wake from *Andromeda's* periscope, nor could he hear her silent electric motors as she moved closer to his position.

A smile fed into Lanze's eyes. 'Gentlemen,' he said, 'we have reached our final position.' He stepped back from the scope. 'Stop motors!' he shouted. 'SURFACE!'

Manfred Schulz winked at the chief diesel mechanic and held out his hand. 'Bruno, you owe me fifty Reichsmarks.'

'Boat is rising, Captain... bridge is clear... hatch is free, sir.'

'Take charge, Number One,' said Lanze, before turning to Schulz. 'Telegraphist!'

'Captain?'

'With me... and bring the Aldis.'

Lanze, with Schulz close behind, scurried up the ladder and rushed through the conning tower, water spilling off his shirt as he scrambled onto the bridge.

Aboard *Margarita*, von Menen could scarcely believe his eyes. After cruising over 7,800 nautical miles, *Andromeda* was just a whisker away.

'Signal that vessel, Schulz:"*IDENTIFY YOURSELF*".'

Schulz flashed off the message, the Aldis lamp blinking merrily. Von Menen responded. Perplexed, Schulz handing the reply to Lanze.

'Can't make any sense of it, Captain... Must be ciphered.'

Lanze hastened to his cabin and decoded the message: *AKROBAT*. Immediately, he called the control room.

'Number One?'

'Captain?'

'The vessel is friendly, I repeat, the vessel is friendly... Muster gun crews! Six men and two light machine guns on the aft' casing. Number Two...' – Meyer's ears pricked in a flash – 'prepare to launch the inflatable. Have six men stand by on the for'ard casing, six below the torpedo loading hatch.'

A moment later: 'Captain!' cried Meyer. 'A man has just

left the wheelhouse… he's on deck… I see him through the glasses… He looks bewildered.'

'He's alone?'

'Seems so, Captain. Can't see anyone else.'

Lanze hurried back to the tower, brought up the heavy 12x50 Zeiss binoculars and noted the stunned look on von Menen's face.

'Schulz,' he chuckled, 'send the message, *"THIS IS ANDROMEDA"*.'

Von Menen flashed back: *ALLELUIA.*

Aboard *Margarita*, von Menen was engulfed by a huge dilemma: the sudden realisation that Jürgen might, perchance, be unaware of the catastrophic news from Germany. He watched apprehensively as the small inflatable drew nearer and bumped alongside *Margarita*. Von Menen caught the line, Lanze scrambling aboard without a word.

The two men stood and looked at each other, their faces telling the same, worn picture of grief and pain. Von Menen's dilemma lifted. Jürgen knew, all right.

'God, it's good to see you, Jürgen. I'd like to give you a big hug, but I suspect that at least two 12x50s are pointing in this direction, right?'

'Right. The important thing is, Carl, we know how each of us feels.'

They shook hands and sat down on a wooden case, just forward of the wheelhouse.

'When did you find out?' asked von Menen.

'A week ago, last Wednesday. You?'

'Two days later… I still can't believe it.'

'Neither can I.'

'Apart from everything else, I can't stop thinking about the Steigers… I mean, were they all together or not?'

'When I left the house, Hans told me that he and Greta would be leaving for Flensburg on the last Sunday in February.'

'Meaning that Katrina would be following later, with Mother and Father?'

'Yes,' replied Lanze, with a pained expression, 'after Katrina's birthday.'

'Damn, Jürgen, it's so hard to accept.'

Lanze looked up at the night sky. 'It's the war, Carl, the lousy, stinking war,' he said in a melancholy voice. 'In every home, in every town in Germany, there's sadness of one form or another.'

'And for what?' said von Menen.

'For nothing,' replied Lanze contemptuously. 'It's all been for nothing.'

Haunted by the same agonising thoughts, they sat in quiet contemplation until von Menen asked, 'Any news of Manfred?'

'Nothing. The news from the Baltic is dreadful. Before I left, your father, well, he didn't think Manfred would ever be seen again.'

'God, what a damn mess.'

'Have you said anything to Maria?'

'No… If I did, she'd know about the radio and I've no intention of compromising her. Besides, there'd be a lot of awkward questions and right now I could well do without that.'

'Yes, I suppose you're right. How did she take to your sudden reappearance?'

'With great difficulty at first, but she's okay now.' Von Menen buried his head in his hands, rubbed his eyes and then looked up at the sky. 'I have another big problem,' he said. 'Insignificant compared to all else, but a problem, nevertheless.'

'What's that?'

'My contact is dead. *Allegedly* killed in a car accident, but if you ask me, he's more likely to have been murdered.'

The revelation seemed lost on Lanze, who had another wave rolling through his mind: the carefree, girlish image of Katrina, running across the courtyard to welcome him home.

'Jürgen?' prompted von Menen, craning his neck. 'Did you catch what I said?'

'Oh, yes, Carl, I caught it, all right, but it no longer has any relevance to me. I couldn't care less if your contact was standing on the moon with Mussolini, the Emperor of Japan and Hitler himself. I knew something was wrong when I saw this.' He gestured around the deck. 'It's about the slowest-looking patrol boat I've ever seen.'

'Yes, but somehow I've got to get rid of a few tonnes of arms and ammunition. We can't just dump it over the side in front of the whole crew. That would pose all sorts of questions, especially when you're...' von Menen halted. 'You *are* going back, aren't you?'

Lanze nodded towards *Andromeda*. 'I have a full complement of officers and crew over there, Carl, and like me many of them have lost virtually everything. Doubtless some would jump at the chance of internment in Argentina, but there are others with wives and children, sweethearts and relatives in Germany. It's my responsibility to see that they get back there.'

'I thought so, which is why I think you'll agree to my idea.'

'I'm listening.'

'The signals I send to Germany... they contain a duress code, meaning that if my circumstances change...'

'You mean, if you get caught and you're *forced* into sending a signal...?'

'I simply leave out the code. That way, the home station will know immediately that something is wrong. At my last briefing, my boss stressed that the safety of the U-boat was

474

paramount... so when I leave here, ostensibly with *some* of the consignment, anything could happen. I could send a duress signal tomorrow night.'

'In which case, they'd withdraw me immediately, with most of the munitions still on board,' figured Lanze.

'Exactly. That would relieve you of any awkward questions when you get back.'

'*If* we get back. Our fuel situation is critical. My original calculations were based on a return cruise to *this* position only, but when I eventually opened my orders, my calculations went straight out of the window.'

'How do you mean?'

'Remember the meeting we had in the library, just before you left? I mentioned that another electro boat was being fitted out at Lübeck-Siems... polished oak and all that?'

'Yes.'

'Well, surprise, surprise... I've been ordered to reconnoitre the north coast of the Gulf of San Matias, just west of the River Negro, which means I won't have enough fuel to get back to Bergen. It's a foregone conclusion that I'll have to take fuel from another U-boat in the North Atlantic.'

'Seems you have a problem.'

'Indeed... but our immediate task is to get those ammunition cases off my boat and on to this old girl, which begs the question, how much weight will she take?'

'A tonne, maximum, but by the time I get back, I'll have dumped everything over the side... everything except the gold, that is. If I'm to clear the sandbanks at the mouth of the River Ajo, I must leave here by one o'clock at the latest.'

Lanze looked around the deck. 'Talking of cargo, what's all this we're sitting on?'

'A little something for you and the crew – wine,

cigarettes, tobacco, fresh meat, fruit, vegetables, chocolate and bread. Some of it I brought down from Buenos Aires, some of it I picked up at Dolores yesterday.'

'In that case, my dear thoughtful brother-in-law, let's get to work. Got that torch handy?'

'Yes, right here.'

'Well, since you know how to use it, you'd best signal the boat and tell them we're coming alongside. And remember, Carl, when we get there, no familiarity – I call you "señor", you call me "Captain". Understood?'

'Understood, *Captain*... Just as well I've never met any of your crew before, isn't it?'

When *Margarita* tied up forward of *Andromeda's* tower, men were already feverishly at work on the for'ard deck. Stripped to their waists, two ratings dropped down from a rope ladder, and with wide smiles began passing up cases of wine, fresh fruit and vegetables.

A while later, the flow of cargo reversed, as cases of "ammunition" were hauled up on rope harnesses through the torpedo hatch and lowered cautiously on to the deck of *Margarita*, von Menen checking each case carefully, ensuring that the twenty with his father's special identity mark were kept separate from the rest.

Thirty minutes after midnight, the transfer was complete.

Lanze glanced up at the bridge, turned to von Menen and said quietly, 'With luck, you'll see me before the year is out, hopefully with Hans and Greta.'

'I sincerely hope so, Jürgen.'

As they were about to part, Lanze dipped hurriedly into his jacket pocket and pulled out a very thick package. 'Nearly forgot,' he smiled. 'For you. Your salary, I imagine.'

'Make sure the three of you get here, Jürgen,' said von Menen. 'I'm relying on it.'

From the bridge of *Andromeda*, Lanze watched wistfully as *Margarita* pulled away. At 200 metres, *Andromeda's* Aldis lamp began to blink: FROM THE CREW. WHOEVER YOU ARE, THANKS.

Von Menen smiled, picked up his torch and flashed back. A PLEASURE. GOD SPEED.

By the time *Margarita* had reached the sandbanks, the seabed had played host to half a tonne of nine-millimetre ammunition. All that remained on deck now, hidden beneath a pile of ropes and canvas sheets, was forty bars of gold bullion.

Sunday 11th March 1945

At 03h00 local time, an erroneous message of duress was received at the German Foreign Office's wireless headquarters.

INITIAL STAGE COMPLETE.

NEXT RENDEZVOUS 21:00 LOCAL 11 MARCH.

The security code was missing!

Tuesday 13th March 1945

Von Menen took *Margarita* to a position just beyond the mouth of the Ria Ajo and dumped the radio and the rest of the paraphernalia over the side. The unceremonious act of defiance marked the end of his association with the German Foreign Office for good.

The radio and its accoutrements had gone, the spare battery was in the back of the car and the one-time pads had been burned. At the cottage, the floorboards in the "study" had been screwed down for the last time. All that was left of von Menen's clandestine life now was the money and the blank identity cards.

Thursday 15th March 1945

Von Menen returned to Buenos Aires, taking with him the cash Lanze had delivered and the money he'd retrieved from beneath the floor of the cottage. It amounted to the equivalent of over $40,000 USD, enough to provide for a comfortable long-term existence, even without the gold.

Maria responded to his long-term absence with the same degree of tolerance and indifference as she had done previously. Outside the bounds of contented domesticity, their relationship continued under a cloak of intrigue and expedient silence – he said nothing and she asked no awkward questions.

Meanwhile, his visits to the cottage continued. He checked regularly on *Margarita* and continued his tuition with Rosas, relishing the few days of freedom from the confines of his apartment in Buenos Aires, where he remained hostage to his own circumstances.

On the political front, the Farrell-Perón administration was still clinging to its mollifying *promise* of renewed democratisation. As the gap between Argentina and the Axis partnership widened further, they began currying favour with the near-victorious Allies. For von Menen, their wooing of Roosevelt proved too untimely by far, when, on 27th March, Argentina declared war against Germany!

Defunct spy or otherwise, von Menen now saw his life in Argentina in an entirely different perspective. Using one of the blank identity documents Vidal had given him, he concocted another pseudonym, drove down to the cottage, replenished the tanks of *Margarita* and stored several cans of gasoline in the hut alongside the quay.

For the moment, he would take his chances in Argentina,

but if things went horribly wrong, he would strike out across the River Plate and head for Uruguay.

In Europe, Germany's demise was approaching fast. The Red Army was about to kick down the door to Berlin, and the US and British armies were advancing rapidly towards the River Elbe, the line which would form the boundary between the Western and Russian zones of occupation.

On 16th April, seven days after the execution by the SS of Canaris, Oster and Dietrich Bonhoeffer at Flossenbürg, the Red Army began its final assault on the capital. Completely surrounded, Berlin was all but dead, her life-blood ebbing away beneath a relentless barrage of Russian artillery, the streets full of the killed and injured. At one o'clock on the afternoon of Monday 30th April, Soviet troops sprang from their positions around the Kroll Opera House and stormed the Reichstag. It was the moment the Russians had been waiting for.

Deep in his bunker below the Reich Chancellery, Adolf Hitler, a physical and mental wreck, retired to his private quarters and shot himself. Two days later, the German garrison in Berlin surrendered. On 7th May, Germany capitulated.

The futility of Hitler's war had left millions dead, maimed and missing, the survivors struggling beyond the margins of existence. Germany's cities were buried beneath enough rubble to fill a hole 1.5 kilometres square, deeper than the height of the Eiffel Tower. Much of it was in Berlin, a city of unparalleled destruction, the toil of centuries laid to waste.

The world had responded to Hitler's crackpot vision of a totalitarian 1,000-year Reich with a resounding 'No!' The fearsome and fiery zeal of Nazi ideology had been beaten and the most evil and wicked form of social engineering had been brought to an end. Those who had refused to believe it, shunned it, or denied it, now saw the truth for themselves, as a ghostly procession of emaciated humans, men, women and children, emerged from the liberated Nazi death camps, eyes sunk deep into their skulls, free to begin a lifetime of mental trauma.

Something else was beginning, too. On the east side of the River Elbe, millions of Germans were faced with the daunting realisation of life under a new totalitarian regime.

General von Menen had been right. The Russians had gobbled up half of Germany, and with it, the whole of Mecklenburg, including the von Menen estate. East of the Elbe, one tyrant had been exchanged for another. His name was Josef Stalin. In his Wagnerian exit from the world, Hitler had left the German nation a legacy of abhorrence and division.

For Maria, the end of the war in Europe brought a renewed, albeit cautious, approach to her future. She wanted to get married. She wanted children. But von Menen did not quite see it that way. *Another few months won't make that much difference,'* he kept telling her.

He revealed nothing about his parents and nothing about his sister; in fact, he said nothing about anything or anybody. She knew something was wrong, yet she stayed silent.

In a way, von Menen wanted to rid himself of the lies, tell her everything, but he lacked the courage. *Where will I start?* he kept asking himself – Vidal and his quest to overthrow Perón, Information Department Three, the cottage, the boat, the car, a half-tonne of gold, or the fact that when she had so desperately needed him, he had been in Argentina all along?

In the end, he convinced himself that it wasn't worth the trouble.

On 6th and 9th August, the Americans dropped nuclear devices on the Japanese cities of Hiroshima and Nagasaki, forcing the Japanese into unconditional surrender. After nearly six years, the greatest military conflict in the history of mankind had finally come to an end.

In Argentina, it seemed that Perón's hollow, lifeless gesture of democracy had come to an end, too. In Perón's eyes, Argentina wasn't quite worthy of democracy yet.

The moderates took to the streets again. Student unrest and public disorder was widespread. Mass demonstrations and protests turned into ugly, violent scenes and street battles were commonplace. Amid signs that the country was slipping into chaos, factions of the ruling military began to falter. Perón tightened his grip on the capital and filled the streets of Buenos Aires with soldiers, Federal Police and shady characters with unrestricted "stop and search" powers.

For von Menen, venturing out became an even riskier business. Whenever he visited the cottage, he invariably set out before dawn and returned late at night. As his shadowy existence continued, his relationship with Maria weakened. They were drifting apart and von Menen knew it.

The war in Europe had been over for almost five months, but still there was no news of Lanze or the Steigers. In a curious kind of way, von Menen thought there never would be. As the reality closed in on him, his gloom deepened, fuelled by another pain that would not let him go – the haunting memory of Sigi Bredow.

With the advent of autumn, Perón seemed at last to be losing his grip on power. Everyone wanted his head. In the weeks that followed, Buenos Aires bore witness to a spate of fast-moving events that left most newspaper editors feeling like children in a toy shop, bank-rolled by

Rockefeller himself. Gilbert and Sullivan could not have scripted it better.

The commonly held view was that Perón had resigned and gone undercover. But those with scores to settle were determined to find him and eventually they did, snug with his partner at a hideaway down by the Tigre. Perón was arrested, but not so the attractive Eva. While the pretenders jousted for the presidency, she set to work.

Within days, Argentina saw its first *real* glimpse of the charismatic and glamorous Eva Duarte in all her powerful glory. Tens of thousands of Perón's "shirtless" supporters, summoned by the zestful Eva, swarmed across the Riachuelo River and headed en masse to the Casa Rosada. If the wind had been blowing in the right direction, the deafening, frenzied chant for Perón's immediate release might easily have been heard in Uruguay.

In no time at all, Perón was free, standing victorious on the balcony of the Presidential Palace, lauding the cheering multitudes.

Von Menen played with the notion that the dapper Filipe Vidal would *never* have realised his dream, and perhaps Juan Domingo Perón would never have realised his, either, without the help of the scheming, charismatic and go-getting Eva.

The next day, at a private civil ceremony in Buenos Aires, the glamorous Eva Duarte became the dazzling phenomenon that was Eva Perón.

A new chapter in Argentina's history was just beginning.

Wednesday 24th October 1945

Von Menen was quite unwell. He had a headache, a temperature, a painfully sore throat and eyes that felt as though they were being pulled into the back of his skull.

When he returned to the apartment with his daily copy of *La Prensa*, Maria was in a contemplative mood, her thoughts buried in a pile of medical papers. Several times, she had advised him to go to bed and rest, but in his misery, he chose to ignore her. Eventually, she gave up, leaving him to a carton of tablets and a bottle of medicine.

He walked into the lounge and kissed her on the forehead. Unmoved by the gesture, she said nothing, but moments later, her silence cracked.

'Someone called while you were out, a woman,' she said, nodding, almost imperceptibly, towards the telephone.

He threw the newspaper to the floor and hastened across the room as fast as his aching legs would carry him. 'Who... When?' His throat was so painful he could scarcely talk.

'I told you, a woman... She didn't give her name.' Again, Maria nodded towards the telephone. 'I wrote down the message, if you can call it a message.'

Von Menen hurried to the sideboard, picked up the piece of paper, his heavy, aching eyes falling upon the scribbled note.

'Tell Carl, Dolores.'

'Did she say anything else?' he croaked.

'No!' Maria looked at his grey, pained face. 'You should be in bed. You should never have gone out.'

'There was no mention of the name "Frederick"?' he asked, wracked by the pain in his throat.

'No, there was no mention of "Frederick". I've told you all I know. For heaven's sake, Carl, why don't you go to bed? You look awful. You can hardly talk! My God, I give up.'

She picked up a folder and he followed her into the dining room.

'Her accent, then?' he asked painfully.

'I couldn't say. She spoke in Spanish, but the line was so

bad it kept breaking up. I could hardly hear her.'

Von Menen was mystified. If it *was* Greta, then why didn't she say so? For that matter, why didn't she mention Hans? Possibly it wasn't the Steigers at all. Perhaps it was Sigi Bredow. Maybe Sigi had gone to Flensburg, met with the Steigers and somehow found her way to Argentina. But why no mention of *Frederick*? And, most baffling of all, why no message from Cortes? He was thinking wildly now.

'You're sure she didn't have an accent?' he persisted, holding his throat.

Maria shook her head, disinterested. 'I've told you, the line was very bad.'

'Maria, it's important,' he said, barely able to get the words out.

'*Carl*, if you're asking me if she was *German*, the answer is, I don't know, the line was very bad. I've told you a dozen times, I could hardly hear a thing.'

'Maria,' he pleaded, his throat burning wildly, 'are you *sure* you haven't forgotten something?'

She scowled at him, said nothing, but beneath her veil of silence, she was fuming. Finally, she snapped.

'Frankly, Carl, I'm fed up with all of this secrecy!' She threw her pen on the floor, jumped to her feet and made towards the door, collecting her coat in the process.

'Maria, please! Where...?' His throat was so bad he could scarcely get the words out.

'I'm going out!' she cried, tossing her head in the air. 'And I don't know when I'll be back.' She closed the door sharply behind her.

Maria found the note when she returned an hour later.

Dearest Maria,
It isn't what you think.
Love, Carl.

POSTSCRIPT

Helmuth-James Graf von Moltke, arguably the leading figure behind the formation of the anti-Nazi group, the Kreisau Circle, was executed at Berlin's Plötzensee Prison on 23rd January 1945. Admiral Wilhelm Canaris met a similar fate at Flossenbürg Concentration Camp on 9th April 1945, as did Dietrich Bonhoeffer and many others.

With Germany close to defeat, Joachim von Ribbentrop fled to Hamburg, Himmler took flight to Flensburg, Kaltenbrunner headed for Austria and Schellenberg ensconced himself in Denmark. All four were subsequently arrested by the Allies: Himmler committed suicide in captivity before he could be indicted, while Ribbentrop and Kaltenbrunner were tried for war crimes, found guilty, sentenced to death and hanged on 16th October 1946.

In 1949, Schellenberg was sentenced to a token six years in prison. He was released in 1951 on grounds of ill health and died in Italy shortly afterwards. He was still only forty-one years of age.

ACKNOWLEDGEMENTS

When I decided to write this book I had no idea how many people and organisations would become involved. For their generous and unstinting help, I am truly grateful to the following:

Rudi Gross, for the many translations he did for me; Bodo Wulfert, a legend at Berlin's Hotel Savoy, and his lovely wife, Eva-Maria. They showed me much kindness during my many visits to Berlin – and still do! – and opened my eyes to the wonderful Hotel Savoy; Peter Geissler, for his help on German historical matters, and Henning Redlich and the late Barbara Redlich for their invaluable information on all matters relating to Mecklenburg.

For information concerning Germany's WWII Type XXI submarine, I owe thanks to Walter Cloots, and similarly to Gus Britton and Christopher Lowe for their enlightening information on Germany's U-boat service. My thanks, also, to Anthony Ward, who guided *Andromeda* safely from Lübeck-Siems to the mouth of the River Plate. Without his help I would have been totally lost.

For his graphic account of WWII night-time sorties over Germany, I owe much to the late John Chatterton, DFC, a former RAF Lancaster bomber pilot, who, while reliving the frightening reality of war, showed me the true meaning of "gentle giant".

David White, an instinctive technical wizard, afforded me much-needed information on WWII radio communications.

My research in Argentina was an incredible experience, due largely to the help of two wonderful people: John Boote, a true gentleman and legendary *estanciero*, and his wife, the congenial, charming and indefatigable Eleanor (Minnie) Boote. Sadly, John is no longer with us, but Minnie remains a true and loyal friend.

I am also deeply indebted to Caroline Hynds, a hawk-eyed genius of an editor, to whom I owe much more than words could ever describe. Thank you, Caroline.

And finally I owe an incalculable debt of gratitude to my adorable and truly wonderful wife, Joan, who was with me on this venture from start to finish, affording me help and encouragement from Berlin to Buenos Aires, always with love, a warm smile and tireless devotion. Thank you, sweetheart.

There are many others who deserve my warmest thanks.

The following sources were, also, especially helpful:

German Foreign Office Archives
Zentrale Stelle der Landesjustizverwaltungen, Ludwigsburg
Institut für Zeitgeschichte, Munich
Jane Baker
Samuel Rachdi, Fahrplancenter
Werner Bittner, Lufthansa Archives, Cologne
Guildhall Library – marine sources
James Ferro, Port Office, Gibraltar
Derek Sansom, Public Affairs, Ford Motor Company, Dagenham
Buenos Aires Herald
Thomas Cook Archives
ADAC – Allgemeiner Deutsche Automobil-Club
David Penn & Paul Cornish, Imperial War Museum
Redoubt Fortress & Military Museum, Eastbourne
Dr Wirtgen, Bundesamt für Wehrtechnik und Beschaffung

Royal Greenwich Observatory
Nigel N C Thorley (Jaguar)
Mike Dutton (BMW 326)
Peter Wurcbacher and Wilf Riding, 1941-44 German railway
    services
Deutsche Bundesbank
National Maritime Museum, Greenwich

Although *Out of Mecklenburg* is a work of fiction, I confess
my thanks to David Khan, whose book *Hitler's Spies*, perhaps
the optimum account of WWII German espionage, gave
me the inspiration to create a "different" kind of foreign
agent. Anyone with an interest in German espionage during
the Nazi era will find *Hitler's Spies* an invaluable source. I
certainly did.

My thanks, also, to Ruth and Leonard Greenup, whose
book *Revolution Before Breakfast* provided me with a graphic
insight into life in Argentina during the turbulent years of
1941-45. It really is an edifying source of information.

The following sources proved similarly helpful in my
research:

Darwin Porter and Danforth Prince, *Frommer's 96 Germany*
Uki Goñi, *The Real Odessa*
Ian Kershaw, *Hitler 1936-1945: Nemesis*
Marie Vassiltchikov, *The Berlin Diaries*
David Miller, *Submarines of the World*
Herbert A Werner, *Iron Coffins*
Correlli Barnett et al., *Hitler's Generals*
Alexandra Richie, *Faust's Metropolis – A History of Berlin*
Louis Hagen (editor and translator), *The Labyrinth: Memoirs
    of Walter Schellenberg*
Walter Warlimont, *Inside Hitler's Headquarters 1939-45*
John Weitz, *Hitler's Diplomat*

V E Tarrant, *The Last Year of the Kriegsmarine: May 1944-May 1945*

Rupert Butler, *An Illustrated History of the Gestapo*

Wolfgang Hirschfeld, *The Story of a U-Boat NCO 1940-1946*

G N Georgano, *World War Two Military Vehicles*

Brian L Davies, *German Army Uniforms and Insignia 1933-1945*

R E G Davies, *Lufthansa*

US Naval Intelligence (compiler), *Uniforms and Insignia of the Navies of World War II*

Tony Le Tissier, *Berlin Then and Now*

John Barnes, *Evita, First Lady*

Bill Gunston, *Jane's Fighting Aircraft of World War II*

N R P Bonsor, *South Atlantic Seaway*

John Keegan (editor), *Atlas of The Second World War*

André Brissaud, *The Nazi Secret Service*

My apologies if I have missed anyone out.

While *Out of Mecklenburg* features a number of real characters, events and Nazi institutions of WWII, it is, in the main, the product of my own imagination. Any inaccuracies, therefore, are mine and mine alone.

Carl von Menen's disappearance remains consigned to the ranks of WWII mysteries until 1985, when a friend from the distant past has the inspired notion that the missing diplomat-cum-spy might still be alive. A dangerous, exciting and breath-taking adventure begins. You can read about it in James Remmer's next novel:

By Samborombon Bay

The hunt for Carl von Menen